EGRETS TO THE FLAMES

EGRETS TO THE FLAMES

A Novel

Barbara Anton

Oceanview Publishing

IPSWICH, MASSACHUSETTS

ISBN-13: 978-1-933515-11-3
ISBN-10: 1-933515-11-2

Published in the United States by Oceanview Publishing,
Ipswich, Massachusetts
www.oceanviewpub.com

2 4 6 8 10 9 7 5 3 1

PRINTED IN THE UNITED STATES OF AMERICA

Dedicated to my cousin, the late Dorothy Matis Hoyman,
a devoted librarian in the Temple University system,
who encouraged my early attempt at writing.

ACKNOWLEDGMENTS

I thank all of those who supported me through the writing of *Egrets to the Flames*. To all the members of writing groups with whom I enjoyed working over the years, especially Donna Singer, Nadja Bernitt, Louie Dillon, J. B. Hamilton Queen, Peg Russell, Joanne Meyers, Madonna Christensen, and McClaren Malcolm. I am most grateful.

A special nod to Iris Forrest, who brought my work to the attention of Oceanview Publishing, and to Donna Singer, who edited my work.

I am especially grateful to authors Patricia and Robert Gussin for their contributions and to Susan Greger, president of Oceanview Publishing, for bringing *Egrets to the Flames* to publication.

EGRETS TO THE FLAMES

CHAPTER 1

Flames lashed the South Florida sky and thundered like an out-of-control freight train, as leaves and tops of sugar cane burned before the January harvest. Crazed egrets soared above the flames on wings stretched wide, circling and dipping, before diving into the conflagration.

In a nearby field, Jamaican cane cutters swung cutlasses in rhythmic, backbreaking strokes, slashing through charred ten-foot stands of cane that towered like sentinels on both sides of Sugarland Highway.

Grower, James Henry Hampton, switched on the headlights as the shiny surface of the road disappeared into churning smoke. He pressed the toe of his boot on the accelerator and the big green Lincoln shot forward, responding to his anger.

When he yanked a cigar from between clenched teeth, a gray wad of ash dropped onto his crisp khaki shirt and rolled onto his jodhpurs. He slapped it away with long, tanned fingers. Without looking at his son Henny in the seat beside him, he spoke in a deceptively even voice. "I'm tired of discussing this. You're not going to marry that cracker and that's the end of it."

"The hell I'm not," Henny shot back. "I'll marry who I damn well please. Beth and I are going to get married right after I graduate from high school, and there's nothing you can do about it."

"We'll see about that. Damn it, boy, have a little consideration. With the environmentalists closing in on me, trying to shut me down, I can't take time out for this marriage nonsense. They're all over TV spouting off about chemicals from the cane fields polluting the Okee. They won't be happy until they take away everything I've worked for my whole life. Don't distract me with this foolishness."

James Henry jammed the cigar back into his mouth. The muscle in his cheek twitched; the cords in his neck tightened. "Don't you understand? I've got to deal with the environmentalists. If I don't win this fight, it could mean the end of cane in Florida."

"So do what you gotta do, who's stoppin' you?" When the car swerved to avoid a wild hog that ran across the road, Henny dug slender fingers into the upholstery; his scuffed sneakers pushed the mat. "I didn't ask you to interfere with me and Beth."

James Henry gripped the wheel, struggling to hold the road. "Damn it, boy, you've got to take control of your life. You can't let some little lowlife decide your future for you."

Henny brushed blonde hair, moist with perspiration, back from his forehead and looked sideways toward his father. "I'm going to marry Beth, so you better get used to the idea."

Behind dark aviator glasses James Henry's eyes hardened to cold steel. "I only want what's best for you, son. I'll see you in hell before I let you throw your life away on that scheming little tramp."

He glanced at Henny, the twitching lip, tears gathering in troubled eyes, and thought: he looks younger than his eighteen years, and he acts a damned sight more stupid. "Damn it, boy," he thundered, "you're still wearing that earring. Didn't I tell you to get rid of that? You look like a friggin' girl. Isn't it bad enough you've got hair as long as a woman's?"

"Not that again?" Henny sneered. "Get with it. You're still back in the dark ages."

"You'll find out which one of us is in the dark if you get yourself saddled with that riffraff." James Henry surveyed Henny's ponytail and his slight frame with annoyance. He prided himself on his muscular body, as lean and hard as that of a mustang, and he wondered why Henny hadn't inherited his traits.

Henny was no James Henry the First, the Second, or the Third, even though he had given him the family name. His ancestors had carved an empire from the black waters of this dismal swamp, but Henny had no such inclination.

"Mama always tells me to do what I think is right, and I'm going to marry Beth whether you like it or not," Henny grumbled.

"Don't you understand, son? You're in position to be top man around here. Why the hell throw that away?" James Henry thrust his cigar to the side of his mouth and bit down hard. He glanced at Henny. "She's pregnant, isn't she?"

He'd seen the answer on Henny's face, but he demanded to hear it. "Isn't she, son?"

"What's that got to do with it? I love her and I want to marry her." Henny swiped at perspiration gathering on his forehead.

"She is pregnant, isn't she?"

"Yes! Yes, all right? Beth is pregnant. So what?"

James Henry drove in smoldering silence, thinking of the struggles, the hardships, the endless hours he and his father and grandfather had spent building the empire he would pass on to his children. He cleared his throat and spoke in a controlled tone. "You don't have to marry her. She can get an abort—"

"She wants the baby."

James Henry snorted. "I'll just bet she does."

"What does that mean? She loves me; she wants to have my baby. Is that so hard to understand?"

"I understand. The question is, do you?"

"What's there to understand?"

James Henry's lips disappeared into a hard line. "You're a grower's son. I set you up to be the most important man in Belle Glade. Don't blow it; she's not worth it. You'll regret it for the rest of your life." He glanced at Henny to see if his words had the desired effect, but he saw only a defiant squint and a set jaw.

"Your granddaddy and I fought crop failures, hurricanes, floods, labor unions, freezes, environmentalists, and God knows what else so you could be in this position. Now this little tramp thinks all she has to do to wind up in the grower's mansion is to get knocked up. Please, son, don't do this. Don't throw it all away."

Ash from burning cane found its way into the closed car through the vents, and Henny flicked away a flake that settled on his arm. "I hate sugar money. If I was poor I could marry Beth and we could have our baby and you wouldn't give a damn about it. You don't care nothin' about me, all you're worried about is the damn sugar money."

"Doesn't it occur to you that it's sugar money that cracker tramp is after?"

Tears formed in Henny's pale eyes. "Don't call Beth a tramp, she's a good girl."

"They're all good girls when you're between their legs."

Henny stiffened. "That does it. Stop! Stop this damn car. Let me out!"

James Henry jammed the accelerator to the floor and the Lincoln shot forward.

Henny screamed, "You son of a bitch!" He yanked the door handle, pushed against the slipstream, and leaped from the speeding car.

James Henry braked and struggled to keep control when the

brakes locked. In the rearview mirror he saw Henny bounce on the macadam, then roll to the side of the road, where he lay, crumpled and still, in front of endless rows of cane.

James Henry jumped from the car and ran back along the highway through a curtain of smoke.

"Henny! Henny! Are you all right?" He dropped to his knees beside his son and felt for a pulse, a heartbeat. There didn't seem to be any. Blood trickled from Henny's nose and mouth. James Henry prayed fervently, "Oh, God, let him be alive! Please, please let him be all right."

He gathered his son in his arms, ran to the Lincoln, and placed him on the back seat. He slid behind the wheel and sped toward home.

When he approached the house, he choked on his breath, thinking, *Grace will never get over it if I've killed him. She'll never forgive me.* As he veered into the driveway, he leaned on the horn.

Grace emerged from the house, her hand shielding pale eyes, as she strained to see why he had summoned her.

The Lincoln swerved and skidded to a stop. "Call an ambulance," he yelled, as he slid from behind the wheel and bolted up the steps.

Paralyzed by confusion and fear, Grace remained motionless.

James Henry ran past her, grabbed the phone, dialed 911, and ordered an ambulance. He hung up and spun toward Grace. "Henny's hurt."

"Hurt? No! What happened Where is —?"

"In the car."

Grace stumbled down the portico steps, following James Henry to the Lincoln. At the sight of Henny's blood-smeared face, the swelling and bruising, she began to cry hysterically. She wiped away the blood and gathered Henny in her arms, whimpering, "My baby, my poor baby, what happened?"

CHAPTER 2

Several days later, Grace paced the portico waiting for James Henry to take her to the hospital to see Henny. When the big green Lincoln appeared at the end of the long driveway, she hurried down the steps.

James Henry braked and stepped out of the car. Tall and lean, with the easy grace of an athlete, he presented an imposing sight in pith helmet and jodhpurs as he strode around to the passenger side to open the door for her.

Grace hesitated at the car and raised a small hand to smooth short blonde hair that lifted on the afternoon breeze. Her eyes met his. "Do you think they might let Henny come home today? He's only been there three days, and his injuries seemed so severe. I hope —"

"Doc Johnson says it's only sprains, cuts and bruises, a slight concussion, nothing serious."

Grace glowered at him. "Nothing serious? He could have been killed."

"But he wasn't. Dumb kid. I guess it's true, God protects drunks and fools." James Henry urged her in and slammed the car door. He jogged around to the driver's side and slid behind the wheel.

Grace glanced at him. "You still haven't told me what made Henny jump out of the car."

"Just trying to talk some sense into him. He'd rather kill himself than listen to his father. He's still hell bent on marrying that field hand's daughter."

"So, it was about Beth. I knew it. You've got to be more diplomatic. The boy's in love, he's vulnerable. You must be gentle with him."

James Henry snorted. "I don't have the time or patience to treat that spoiled brat with kid gloves. The environmentalists are closing in on me. I can't waste time on this nonsense. If he had the sense of a coot, he'd know I can't let him ruin his life. I've got to stop him from doing something stupid."

"Maybe it would work out for them. He loves Beth so much."

"Today. Today he loves her, tomorrow he'll love somebody else."

Grace thought of James Henry's mistress, Vonda, and her pale eyes grew cold. Better Henny should marry his first love, she thought, than keep her as his mistress all his life. As they sped past rows of burning cane, Grace thought of the depth of feeling she still harbored for John — perhaps it's life's irony that first love goes unrequited. She roused from her reverie and turned to James Henry. "You must treat our son more gently — try to be more understanding."

James Henry bit down hard and declared through clenched teeth, "Henny is not going to marry that scheming little cracker, and that's final."

Grace chewed her lower lip; her brows furrowed. She'd say no more now, but her resolve to protect Henny deepened.

James Henry pulled into the hospital parking lot and veered into a space near the entrance. They walked toward the door through smoke that lingered from an early morning burn. When they reached Henny's room, they found him and Beth clamped in a passionate embrace.

James Henry froze. His face distorted, reddened, and

seemed to swell, before freezing into a mask of undisguised hatred. "You little tramp!" he bellowed. "What are you doing here?"

Beth gasped, dropped her arms, and pulled away. Fear darkened her eyes and her lips jerked uncontrollably.

Henny grabbed her, attempting to pull her back. "Wait a minute!"

James Henry yanked her off the bed, knocking a metal basin off the nightstand. It clattered across the floor and skittered to a stop against the baseboard. "Get the hell out of here and don't come back! If you ever come near my son again, you'll be one sorry baggage." He dragged Beth, struggling and whimpering, toward the door.

Henny leaped from bed and grabbed James Henry's arm. "Let go of her!" he screamed.

Grace flung herself between Beth and James Henry, pleading, "James Henry — please. Stop!"

Beth wrenched free and scurried out, the sound of her hastily retreating footsteps echoing down the long corridor.

Henny tried to run after her, but James Henry grabbed his sprained arm and yanked him around so they were face-to-face. "You snot nose," he thundered, "didn't you learn anything by damn near killing yourself? If cracking your skull doesn't do it, what will? What the hell will it take to bring you to your senses?"

"But Beth wasn't —"

"You stay the hell away from that tramp! Don't ever let me find you with her again. Do you hear me?"

Grace forced her way between her husband and her son, trying to shove James Henry back. He set her aside, clamped his jaw, and stormed out of the room just as two nurses ran in to investigate the commotion.

"I'm sorry for the disturbance," Grace said. "Everything is all right now."

The nurses glanced around the room suspiciously and urged

Henny back into bed. One rearranged the bedding while the other returned the basin to the nightstand before leaving.

Henny glanced at his mother apologetically and brushed tears off his cheeks.

Grace gathered him into her arms in an effort to comfort him, but when she brushed his bruised cheek he pulled away.

"I'm sorry, son," she said. "Give it time; it will all work out." Grace waved fingers delicately in front of her face and motioned to the switch on the wall. "I'd better turn that fan on. Perhaps it will diffuse the smell of medication."

Henny grumbled, "Yeah, it stinks. The nurse rubs that stuff on my arm every couple of hours."

"Is it doing any good? Your arm is still so swollen."

"I guess it helps; feels better after she rubs it anyway."

Grace stroked his sun-bleached hair. "Do you need anything?"

James Henry appeared in the doorway. "He needs to get his butt out of here and get back to school." He looked up and down the hall. "Where the hell is Doc?"

"He said I can go home today after he sees me." Henny touched his mother's hand and smiled reassuringly, trying to allay the concern that etched a line above her short, straight nose.

Doc Johnson stepped into the room, removed rimless Ben Franklin glasses, and slid them into the pocket of his white tunic. "Grace!" He put an arm around her shoulders and hugged her gently. "Nice to see you." He grasped James Henry's hand. "Come to pick up your bouncing baby boy?" He turned to Henny and studied the bruises. "So, how are you feeling today, young man? Still stiff and sore?"

Henny nodded sheepishly. "I'm okay. Can I get dressed now?"

Doc patted his shoulder affectionately. "Keep him quiet for another day or two, then bring him in to the office to see me. He'll be fine."

James Henry shook Doc's hand. "Thanks, Doc."

Doc kissed Grace lightly on the cheek, nodded to Henny, and walked out.

A week later, Henny returned to the field office after school, maintaining a sullen silence. He arrived late, and when there, he spent more time studying the racing form than the time sheets. An uneasy, unspoken truce divided father and son.

That evening, as Grace stitched a needlepoint canvas, she glanced at the gilt clock on the mantle, wondering when Henny would come home. Perhaps Beth is caring for him, she thought.

Her Shih Tzu, Jade, got up and scratched, circled, then settled back at her feet.

James Henry put the newspaper aside, righted his recliner, and reached for his drink. He swirled amber B&B in the crystal snifter. "Rain again tomorrow," he mumbled. "We haven't had a good burn in a week."

Grace smiled. It had been years since he'd started a conversation about anything other than the cane. "It will clear over the weekend. I heard it on the six o'clock news." She reached down to pat Jade, who wriggled contentedly.

"Hope so. Sure slows things down when we don't get a good burn." James Henry puffed on his Hoya de Monterrey Double Corona cigar, then rolled it between long fingers.

Grace's eyes returned to the clock; the indentation above her nose deepened. "I wonder why Henny doesn't come home for dinner anymore."

"Who knows why that damn fool does anything."

Grace pushed hair back behind her ear, smoothed the fabric of her softly draped skirt, and crossed slender ankles. "Our daughter called today."

"Yeah? What did Mel want?"

"She's concerned about Henny — wanted to know how he's

doing. Oh, and she said to tell you that she bought something for you."

"They don't have anything in Palm Beach that I want. She should save her money." He drew smoke through the Cuban cigar and savored it before tilting his head back and allowing the smoke to escape.

Grace inhaled, enjoying the familiarity of the nutmeg-cinnamon fragrance. "James Henry, you old fraud, you know you're glad that your daughter is thinking of you."

James Henry shifted in his chair, cleared his throat, and sipped liqueur from the snifter. "The paper says that environmentalists are coming down here to organize picketing. That means trouble."

"Maybe not. You can handle them." Grace picked up a strand of amethyst wool and squinted as she threaded the needle.

"I don't know; they get more support all the time. Use every opportunity to tell their side of the story. Don't mind ignoring the facts, either. Keep harping on the chemical spill, dragging out all kinds of theories to support their contention that the runoff is killing the 'glades." James Henry laid his cigar in the ashtray and swirled the B&B in the snifter.

"Why don't you write a letter to the editor and tell the grower's side. Tom would print it."

"I don't have time for such nonsense. I've got a grove to run — cane to get to the mill."

Grace glanced at the clock again, and laid the needlepoint aside. "James Henry —"

"Yes?"

"I'm worried about Henny. We have to help him before something awful happens to him. I'm afraid he'll have an accident. He drives so recklessly, and he drives when he's been drinking."

James Henry snorted. "Drinking! That's putting it mildly. Drunk is more like it."

"Maybe you should let him marry Beth. She's —"

James Henry shot out of his chair. "Over my dead body. No way will I allow it, no sir, by God I won't. He'll go to Florida State next fall, just like I did. Then he'll marry a good woman and he'll take over here like I did. He'll have children capable of taking over when he's gone."

Grace froze. She was accustomed to his outbursts, but the intensity of this tirade shocked her. "Well, I guess you have his life all planned for him."

"You're damn right I do, and I don't want to hear any more about it."

"But —"

"I said I don't want to hear any more about it." James Henry slammed the brandy glass down and stormed out.

Grace looked after him in stunned silence. Henny would get no help from him. She heard the groan of the garage door going up, and she knew he was going to La Vonda Wood. Even after all these years his infidelity still rankled. Why, if he still desires his first love, can't he understand that Henny should have his Beth?

She sat silently for a moment before going to the phone on the desk to call Melisandra. Perhaps she could help her brother.

CHAPTER 3

Melisandra lay on the cushioned wrought iron chaise beside the pool of her Palm Beach estate. The last rays of sun sketched palm leaf patterns on the patio, and gulls screeched over the nearby shore.

Mel slapped away a tear. *I don't care if I do still love Jason, she thought, I've got to get on with my life; I've been hurting long enough. I cannot, I will not, go on grieving.*

She flopped over onto her stomach and punched the cushion with her fist. "Damn it," she muttered. "We're divorced; Jason is gone; I have to accept it!"

The ring of the phone on the table beside her jolted her from her thoughts.

"Yes? Oh, Mama! It's so good to hear your voice. You sound so much better than you did last night. How is Henny today?"

"Doc saw him this morning and said he's doing fine."

"Oh, thank God! That's great news. Give him my love."

"I will."

"I hope you're calling to say you're coming to spend a few days with me. You deserve a change of scene after that ordeal."

"No, honey. I can't leave now. Henny is improving, but he needs me to protect him from his father. James Henry is still adamant that he not marry Beth, and it's destroying Henny. I don't know what to do."

Mel's lip twitched. "I'll come home and talk to Daddy. In the meantime, tell Henny to ignore him. It's none of Daddy's business whom Henny marries."

"James Henry only wants what's best for him. He —"

"Daddy just might forget about Henny and Beth when he hears my news."

"What news?"

Mel smiled, picturing the crease forming over her mother's patrician nose.

"Mama, I've decided to propose to Gatti."

"Propo . . . Gatti? Who's Gatti?"

"You remember. The prince I told you about."

"Oh, I thought you were kidding about —" Grace's voice trailed off uncertainly.

"No, I'm not kidding. I'm going to propose to him tonight. I just made up my mind. All the women in Palm Beach are vying for his title, and it will be a kick to be Princess Melisandra for a while, even if it does mean I have to kiss a frog."

"Darling! Don't talk like that." Grace hesitated, then continued warily. "What about Jason? I was so sure you two would reconcile."

Mel felt a sudden tightness in her chest at the mention of his name. "Jason's gone, and I need an escort. I'll let you know if Gatti accepts my proposal. If he does, I'll come home and we'll plan the wedding. Call me as soon as you tell Daddy. I can't wait to hear what he has to say."

Mel pictured her mother's pale blue eyes clouding and her delicate hand shielding the mouthpiece of the phone. "Bye, Mama. I love you."

Mel hung up quickly, before her mother could dissuade her.

Babette, the maid, came across the patio carrying the newspaper. "Is there anything else you wish, madam?" she asked in heavily accented French.

"No, merci," Mel replied absentmindedly as she glanced at the front page.

Babette nodded respectfully and walked back to the house.

Mel scanned the headlines. "Oh, no, not again," she murmured, before throwing the newspaper aside. *I wish they would stop reporting about those damned environmentalists picketing the cane fields; it only inspires the protesters to continue. Daddy will be furious, and he'll make life hell for Henny — and for me, when he hears my news.*

Princess Melisandra. She allowed it to form on her lips then she said it out loud, giving it just the hint of an accent. Marrying a prince might be fun. She laughed — even a half-assed prince without a country. "Princess Melisandra." *Daddy will have a roaring fit. I love it.*

She stroked remnants of lotion that clung to her arms, thinking, *Gatti seems to be attracted to me, or maybe he's attracted to my money, my lifestyle. I wonder how he really feels about me.*

"Does it matter?" she wondered aloud. "If all I want is an acceptable escort, who cares if all he wants is a bottomless purse?" She shrugged elegant shoulders. A fair exchange, she decided.

Mel glanced at clouds outlined in copper and noted the amber hue overtaking the sky. She swung long legs down from the chaise, groped for her slippers, pushed dark hair back from her face, and sauntered toward the cabana.

As she entered the curtained room, she lifted her sunglasses to the top of her head, stepped out of her bikini, and pulled on a yellow silk robe.

She went to her bedroom, sank onto the chaise in front of the huge window overlooking the Atlantic Ocean, and contemplated her long nails. She picked at the edges of the enamel, sighed, and reached for her telephone directory. *The princess needs a manicure. If I'm going to bag a prince, I'd better call the salon and have my nails done.*

Then a wry smile lifted the corners of her lips. *Painted nails are the wrong bait,* she thought, remembering that all the beauties in Palm Beach were eager to support Gatti as he wished to live. *I can. I will — for a while. It will be amusing.* She picked up the phone and dialed the jeweler instead.

Mel instructed the jeweler to send a courier with cuff links for her selection. Gatti would be surprised. She had hardly acknowledged his flirting with her at the club when she was married to Jason. But she was divorced now, and she would take control. Gatti would dance to any tune she hummed, if money were to be his reward. *That's the only thing I like about the damned sugar cane,* she thought — *the money.*

Later that evening, Mel stood at the library window thinking of Jason and watching waves crash against the seawall, when Babette ushered the jeweler's courier into the room. She allowed the curtain to fall over the window and motioned the impeccably dressed courier to her desk.

Appearing obsequious and intimidated by the luxurious surroundings, the courier spread a velvet cloth over the desktop and nervously displayed a selection of cuff links.

Mel dismissed the diamond-studded links as too garish, and the black onyx as too large. "These," she said, as she examined etched platinum links under the desk lamp.

"A perfect choice, madam." The courier bowed, vigorously polished the links, and placed them in an ebony-colored suede box. He handed them to her with a flourish.

Mel smiled at the theatrics, took the box from him, and snapped the lid closed. "Thank you," she said. "You may bill me."

The courier nodded deferentially and was gone.

Mel reached for the phone, looked up Gatti's number in the Palm Beach register, and dialed. "Hello, Gatti? This is Melisandra Hampton Coles. I was just thinking about you."

After a slight pause, he muttered, "You were?"

Mel smiled at his confusion. She had never given him more than a cursory nod when they met at parties or at the club, and there had never been occasion for her to call him. "Would you join me for cocktails this evening?" she asked.

"Cocktails? Uh, *si*. Yes, of course."

"Let's say in an hour. About sevenish."

"Seven? At your home? *Si*." Then Gatti found his charm. "Yes, of course, Melisandra. I am delighted that you call. I have been thinking of you. You looked ravishing last Saturday evening at the club. Your gown, it was exquisite, an Oscar de la Renta, no?"

Mel suppressed a giggle. "See you at seven." She placed the phone in the cradle. *Come into my parlor, Mr. Fly*, the spider thought as she walked to her dressing room.

Promptly at seven p.m. the doorbell rang simultaneously with the first of seven chimes from the ornate sculpted clock on the mantle.

Mel smiled and leaned back against down-filled cushions on one of two facing sofas in front of the fireplace.

When Babette ushered Gatti into the great room and announced him, Mel noted the body-hugging Italian tailoring and the clearly custom-made shirt.

"Melisandra! *Buona sera*." Gatti glided across the room toward her, lifted her hand and kissed it. "A delightful surprise, I hear from you."

He's better looking than I remembered, Mel thought, as she motioned toward a chair. "Please, sit down. What would you like to drink?"

He sat where she'd indicated. "Cassis Royale."

Mel motioned to Babette, who stood off to the side waiting to take their drink orders. "Cassis Royale for the prince; the usual for me."

Babette nodded and withdrew.

Gatti's dark eyes sparkled as he appraised the antique-filled room: the Degas, the Matisse, and the thick, lustrous Oriental rug. He caressed the knot of his mauve silk tie, glanced at his watch, and returned his gaze to Melisandra. "Eez almost dinnertime. Perhaps you will join me for dinner at the club — after we have had cocktails."

"Perhaps." Mel toyed with him, enjoying his discomfort. She had dipped into the gene pool to acquire the subtlety and finesse of her mother and a measure of James Henry's directness and arrogance — an interesting mix.

Appearing nervous and uncomfortable, Gatti ran a hand over meticulously styled dark hair and asked, "You weel be attending the polo matches tomorrow, no?"

Mel shrugged and glanced toward Babette, who entered with their drinks on a small silver tray. She set Mel's drink on the carved table in front of the sofa and Gatti's on the table by his chair. She nodded slightly and withdrew.

Mel removed a slice of lime and ran it around the rim of the glass before squeezing juice into the gin and tonic and dropping the lime into the drink.

Gatti sipped from his Cassis Royale, set it aside, and said, "Prince Charles, he plays polo at the club tomorrow. His party — they will be seated in my box. It would pleasure me to have you join his guests while we play."

"Thank you," she said, not committing.

Mel sipped her gin and tonic, scrutinizing Gatti over the rim of the glass, while simultaneously hating Jason for bringing her to this. Finally, she set the drink on the cocktail table, relaxed into the soft cushions, and stretched her tan arm over the back of the sofa. She ran a jeweled hand over the antique satin and waited for Gatti to speak.

Gatti tugged at his jacket. "What ees new? What things of excitement have been happening to you?" He probed, trying to discover why he had been summoned. He ran manicured fingers along the lapel of his gray silk suit. He straightened the tie that had been so carefully chosen and passed his hand over the back of his hair, sensing that a trap was about to be sprung and feeling helpless against it.

He's a handsome bastard, Mel thought, but right now he looks like a hungry mouse. Mel sat up and stretched without diverting her steady gaze. "Something will be happening to me in the near future," she said. "You, too."

"Me? *Quando?* What?" A nervous smile played with his moustache.

Mel reached between the sofa cushions, withdrew the black suede box, and tossed it to him.

It was unexpected, and his reflexes were just quick enough for him to deflect the box rather than to catch it. He bent to pick it up from the Oriental rug.

"Open it," Mel said.

Gatti lifted the lid and his eyes devoured the costly links. She watched him subtly note the jeweler's logo and the imprint in the metal: Platinum. "*Non capisco.* I do not understand. What ees thees?"

"A little bauble for you." Mel appraised his reaction through lowered lids.

Gatti glanced from the links to Mel, then back to the links, wondering why she was doing this.

"I thought we'd celebrate our engagement tonight and marry next month," she said.

The suede box slipped from Gatti's hand and he quickly retrieved it. "Marry?" he asked dumbly.

"Yes. I'd like to contract for a few years of your time."

Gatti silently mouthed words, then abandoned them before they were spoken. He looked from the platinum links to Mel, and she smiled at the fantasies she perceived forming behind his eyes. When he regained his royal composure, he said, "Melisandra, my darling." He pocketed the links and came to her, taking her hands in his. He lifted them to his lips and kissed them excessively.

Mel smiled. "I'll have my attorney draw up a prenuptial agreement."

CHAPTER 4

After they finished dinner, Grace and James Henry walked out onto the portico. They sat side by side in wicker armchairs, enjoying the cool breeze of the January evening. Spanish moss quivered in gnarled oak trees that rimmed the lawn, and evening doves cooed contentedly on the red tile roof. Jade followed them out and jumped up onto Grace's lap.

"Melisandra called today," Grace said, petting Jade and looking out across the lawn and gardens to the pond.

"Oh? What did she want?" James Henry's cigar glowed brightly as he inhaled nutmeg-cinnamon flavored smoke.

"She's getting married again."

"Married?" He snatched the cigar from his mouth and swung toward her. "I just paid for a divorce. What the hell do you mean, she's getting married?"

"Just that, dear, she's getting married."

"Who to?"

"We don't know him." Grace shifted slightly in the wicker chair, reaching around to rearrange the pillows. "His name is Gatti. A prince, I think."

"A prince! Some damned impoverished prince? Now there's a recipe for disaster. Has she lost her mind? I'm not paying for another wedding and divorce. What the hell is the matter with that girl?"

Grace watched as great blue herons flew to their nests in the mangroves, allowing James Henry's tirade to run its course. "She's coming home for a few days so we can plan the wedding. Isn't it nice of her to include her mother in the preparations?"

"I'm not paying for another big wedding and that's final. The unions will be pulling the cutters out of the fields any day now. There will be no money for this foolishness — these phony marriages and quick divorces. Didn't we teach her that marriage is a lifetime commitment?"

Grace winced and remained silent for a few moments before rallying. "I don't think she wants another big wedding — just a few friends." She stroked Jade and watched the sun sink behind the pond, the alizarin-colored rays enhanced by smoke that lingered from the day's burn.

"Humph. To her, a few friends means half of Palm Beach. Damn freeloaders. What does she think I am, the Bank of England?"

"She'll have Yvonne as her maid of honor, no other attendants. Yvonne looked so beautiful at Melisandra's first wedding, so blonde and delicate, so tiny and fragile standing next to Melisandra. Oh, the wedding will be lovely! Masses of white orchids around the chapel, tapered candles in —"

"That's enough!" James Henry bellowed. He ground out his cigar in the ashtray, slammed his hands on the arms of his chair, and stood abruptly. "I think I'll drive around for a while."

Grace stiffened. "Sit with me a little while longer, please." She regretted the catch in her voice, fearing it revealed she knew where he was going.

"I've got to go see what the damned environmentalists are up to."

She watched James Henry jog to his car and pull away. *It's my fault*, she thought. *Everything changed after Henny was born.*

She looked out at stars glittering in the pale night sky, and her thoughts turned to Melisandra and her prince. Will she be happy with him? *She was so in love with Jason when they married; I thought it would last forever. What went wrong?*

She sighed, disturbed by thoughts of her children: Melisandra marrying a man they didn't know, Henny on a path to self-destruction, and Jeffrey living in far-off Japan with a bride they had never met.

She dabbed a soft linen handkerchief at the moisture forming in the corners of her eyes and drew back into the cushions, envisioning her husband lying with his mistress. This was not the life she had planned. She thought her marriage would go on happily forever, but she had reckoned without the fatal attraction of La Vonda Wood.

She glanced toward the door thinking of the day James Henry had carried her over that threshold. He was so happy then, so in love. Why did things go wrong? Had James Henry discovered her secret? Was it possible that he knew but hadn't mentioned it?

When a ragged wisp of cloud eclipsed the moon, Grace set Jade down and walked into the house across that same threshold, but this time with a heavy heart, knowing that her husband lay with his mistress.

James Henry's tires sprayed crushed shells as he pulled into the parking lot at La Vonda's Café. He parked beside a red Chevy pickup, walked across the lot, and stepped into a haze of smoke, stale beer, and blaring music.

He made his way to where Vonda leaned over the bar between two large glass jars that held pickled pigs feet and hard-boiled eggs. She had positioned herself so her fleshy breasts were on conspicuous display in the low neckline of a clinging turquoise dress.

Damn her, James Henry thought, *she displays those breasts like two grapefruit on a tray.*

Vonda was talking to three men James Henry didn't recognize. They leered, transfixed, as the globes rose and fell. When Vonda saw him, she yelled, "Jim! Speak of the devil." She tossed her thick mane of red hair like a matador challenging a bull with a cape, leaned over the bar, and took James Henry's face in her hands. She kissed him open-mouthed and gestured toward the men.

"These guys are down here to save the earth. I tried to bribe 'em, offered 'em a freebie if they'd back off, but they're hell bent on picketin' you." She threw her head back and laughed raucously.

It was hard to tell who was more embarrassed, James Henry or the environmentalists. He'd left home to get away from problems, and here they were, waiting for him. *Can't escape*, he thought.

He accepted the beer Vonda handed him, turned to the environmentalists, and raised his glass in a toast. "Here's to the good earth."

The men lifted their glasses solemnly in a return salute. One of them said, "Right." They drank in silence.

Vonda came around the bar, took James Henry's hand, and led him to her booth, where her poodle Mam'selle waited. James Henry pushed Mam'selle aside and slid in.

Indignant at being disturbed, Mam'selle glowered at him and shook her beribboned topknot in annoyance.

Vonda slid in next to James Henry and consoled Mam'selle, then she laid one hand on James Henry's. With the other she brushed an imaginary piece of lint from his shoulder. "What is it, baby? What's wrong?"

"Henny's got some cracker knocked up — wants to marry her."

"Well, ain't that a hog hoot! And what has little Henny's daddy all in a snit? That she's knocked up or that he wants to marry her?"

"Damn it, Vonda, what the hell kind of a wife would she make for him?

"Yeah, right. Why don't you just give her a few hundred bucks for an abortion and get rid of the little inconvenience?" The edge on Vonda's voice went unnoticed.

"She wants the baby."

"Oh, well, that proves that she's not good enough for the Hamptons."

James Henry slammed the glass to the table. "Are you being sarcastic or what?"

"Sarcastic? Me?" Vonda batted heavily mascaraed lashes.

"I just can't let her tie Henny down. Hell, he's registered at Florida State next fall. What kind of a way is that to start college — with a wife and a kid?"

"Yeah. I hate to admit it, but you're right. A guy shouldn't tie up too soon; he always regrets it; makes it hard for the woman and the kid later on. He'll leave her anyway, might as well be sooner as later."

Vonda pulled a compact from her pocket, opened it, and studied her face. She wiped an imaginary lipstick smear from her teeth and snapped the compact shut. "So, what else is new?"

"I just can't get through to Henny; he won't listen to reason. Damn fool jumped out of the car the other day when we were arguing about it — going sixty miles an hour."

"Yeah, I heard. Lucky he wasn't hurt bad. He wasn't, was he?"

"Nah. A sprained wrist, cuts and bruises, slight concussion. I was scared as hell. I thought he'd killed himself. Should have knocked some sense into him, but it didn't."

Vonda waved her empty glass toward her husband, Chip, at the bar.

Chip nodded, drew two beers, and brought them over. He exchanged a few words of small talk with Vonda and James Henry, his friend, before a patron called him back to the bar.

James Henry took a long draught of the fresh beer. "Henny's carrying on like a damn fool. Out drunk every night, then he sleeps half the day, cuts school, comes in late for work"

"He drives that Jag like he's at the Indy 500. He's gonna kill somebody one of these days." Vonda's bangles clanked as she stroked James Henry's hair.

"I don't know what to do. I can't talk to him. He was such a good kid. I don't know what's gotten into him."

"Ah, they're all alike, kids today — wild, crazy."

"Not your Steve. He married a good woman — Etta gave him two fine sons — twins."

"Yeah, I lucked out there — didn't we?" Vonda punched his arm, threw her head back, and laughed. The environmentalists glanced over at them.

James Henry lowered his voice. "I've got to do something, Vonda, before Henny screws up too bad."

"Yeah, I suppose so."

"Trouble is I don't know what to do."

"Why don't you ground him?"

"Now how the hell am I going to ground a grown man? Tie him up?"

"Why not? You tie me up." Vonda giggled and tickled his ribs.

"Cut it out, Vonda, this is serious. I'm really worried about that kid."

Vonda laid her hand on his. "I know, baby, but it will all work out, one way or the other. It always does."

The warmth of her hand comforted him. "Yeah, you're right, one way or the other." He swallowed the last of the beer and grabbed her arm. "Come on. Let's go upstairs."

"I thought you'd never ask." The turquoise dress worked up her thighs as she slid out of the booth.

James Henry looked over at the environmentalists. "You go on," he said to her, "I'll be up after I have another beer."

"Oh, right. You'll come up five minutes later and no one will figure it out."

"Go ahead," he growled.

Vonda's laugh, a mixture of hurt and defiance, caused Chip to glance up. She tossed her red mane, positioned her hand on her hip, and announced loudly, "Good night, all. I'm going to go upstairs now and go to bed. Good night, Jim."

Chip lowered his head and began washing glasses.

Vonda swaggered up the stairs, aware of the effect her ascent was having on the men at the bar.

Damn her, James Henry thought, she's only happy when she's making a spectacle of herself. He finished his beer and started to leave, but the urgency in his groin stopped him. To hell with all of them, he decided. He crossed the bar and climbed the stairs with as much dignity as he could muster.

He turned the knob and stepped into the dark room. He was just about to tell Vonda to turn on a light, when he tripped over her, sprawled naked on a bearskin rug. "What the hell?" he said as he backed away.

"Ain't this a hog hoot? I bought it at a garage sale. Ever do it on a bearskin rug?"

She smiled at his open-mouthed stare and shifted to an even more seductive pose that she had seen in the latest *Playboy*. She ran her hand over the fur provocatively, purred, and bared glistening teeth.

James Henry stood transfixed as she ran her tongue slowly across her lips. Every sinew alert, he salivated like a hungry rat smelling cheese. Damn her, he thought, every time with her is like the first.

When James Henry came back down the stairs, satisfied and relaxed, he was glad to see that the environmentalists had left. He drove home and called his field boss, Vonda's son Steve, from a phone in the library. "What did you find out?"

"Not much. Only that the 'vironmentalists have been talking to TV reporters again, trying to stir things up."

"Did you talk to Vic over at the TV station?"

"Yeah."

"What did he say?"

"Said there wasn't much he could do about it. It's news."

"It's news, all right. It's all over the papers and TV. Well, I guess we've done all we can do tonight."

"Guess so."

James Henry hung up and went to the kitchen. He took a beer from the refrigerator and was about to pull the tab when Grace opened the door and came in. The line above her nose quivered with concern, and tears puddled in lackluster eyes.

"I've been waiting up for you," she said. "We have to talk about Henny."

"Not now. I'm tired."

"Please, we must talk. He's so —"

"Not now, Grace." James Henry shoved past her and bolted up the stairs two at a time to his room across the hall from hers. He showered and flopped on the bed, but he was unable to sleep. He wrestled with visions of Henny ruining his life by marrying Beth, living with her and her field hand father and her drunken mother. For damn sure she'll never move in here, he vowed.

He forced his thoughts away from Henny and concentrated on the cane. With the environmentalists bearing down, he knew there would be some changes, and he feared for life as he knew it.

CHAPTER 5

James Henry checked the clock in the field office: ten a.m. He was due to meet with Jamison and the environmentalists in an hour. He shoved on his aviator glasses, grabbed up his pith helmet, and went to pick up Steve. He found him leaning against a moss-draped banyan tree in the south field.

Steve swung into the Lincoln, slammed the door, and mopped his brow. He lifted his peaked cap and ran fingers through thick dark hair. "Sure is hot for January, hotter than the innards of a goose."

James Henry pulled onto Sugarland Highway and headed for the meeting in Clewiston. "How you doing?"

"Okay."

"Etta and the twins?"

"Etta said to say thanks for those remote-controlled cars you sent over for the boys' birthday. Can't drag them away from them long enough to eat. But that's five-year-olds, all it takes is a new toy."

"I thought they'd like them."

"Yeah. You hear any more from the 'vironmentalists? I wonder what they'll come up with today."

"Who knows? When we get in there, I'll do the talking. You keep your mouth shut. I just want you there for back up. A second pair of ears, in case I miss something."

"Okay, Jim. I sure hope you can work things out. We got to get that cane to the mill."

"It's hard to work things out with men that don't know a damn thing about cane. They have no idea that nothing would grow in that muck until my granddaddy added chemicals back in the thirties. Fertilizer didn't help, but when they used chemicals — bingo — that worthless muck turned into fertile soil. Black gold they call it now. There's just no way to grow cane without using chemicals."

"All they're saying is you got to stop polluting the Okee. You know the chemical runoff causes problems all the way to Key West. You gotta stop that somehow. Maybe if you'd chip in the penny a pound for the cleanup, that would —"

"See? That's why I don't want you talking in there. I'm not going to let Jamison shake me down. If he wants the Okee cleaned up, let him and those damned environmentalists come up with the money."

"I don't know. It might be cheaper in the long run to pay for the cleanup than to pay off all those senators and lobbyists you got working for you." Steve swiped cane ash from his cheek. "I'd rethink that one if I was you."

"Well, you're not me. The union will soon be down here again jacking up the row price, Senator Rechett wants a contribution for his re-election campaign, and the lobbyists raise their fees every year — I tell you, Steve, I've got to draw the line somewhere."

"Yeah, Jim, they all got their hands in your pocket."

"One pocket I don't mind, but I'd like to keep the other one for myself."

The two men rode in silence through dark green cane that formed walls on both sides of Sugarland Highway from the road to the horizon. James Henry parked at the Clewiston Inn, and Steve matched his long, purposeful strides as they made their way toward the meeting room.

"Remember to keep your mouth shut," James Henry said as he opened the door to the meeting room.

When they entered the barren conference room, they found several men already there standing around drinking coffee. James Henry hadn't expected anyone but Jamison and his assistant, but there were four other younger men. They exchanged greetings, and Jamison introduced the kids as environmentalists. They took seats at a long folding metal table.

"Thank you for coming, Mr. Hampton." Jamison said. "We look forward to working with you on these issues, since they concern all of us."

James Henry waved his cigar, indicating that Jamison should get on with it.

"Well, Mr. Hampton, your meeting with us is a step in the right direction. We have to work together to save the ecological system for future generations."

"Yes, yes, but it will be a bitter future without sugar to sweeten it up a little."

"We're not advocating doing away with sugar, although that might not be a bad idea." Jamison glanced around the table. "Refined sugar, anyway."

"Sugar never hurt anybody." James Henry scraped his chair back and folded his arms over his chest.

Jamison shifted uneasily and continued. "We're worried about the amount of chemicals used in the cane fields. Since you have to increase chemical nutrients and fertilizers every year to replace those lost by planting the same crop year after year, the—"

James Henry interrupted by bouncing his aviator glasses on the table impatiently and remarking, "Not that again."

Although Jamison had witnessed James Henry's obstinacy at meetings with the American Sugar Alliance, he had hoped he might have better luck talking to him man-to-man. He ignored the comment and continued. "Since single crops are more susceptible to pests, and because insects become genetically resistant to certain pesticides, you're using more chemicals every year, and —"

"You know that to be a fact?" James Henry made no secret of his contempt for what he perceived to be Jamison's ignorance of cane farming.

Jamison continued. "The Everglades National Park and thousands of acres outside the official boundaries have been contaminated. The runoff from cane fields drags the chemicals into the canals and sloughs and wetlands. Eventually the chemicals drain into Florida Bay where fish and plant life are affected."

James Henry puffed on his cigar; smoke crawled along the conference table. The kid wearing chinos coughed.

Jamison continued. "There's almost no sign of life in Florida Bay, and that was once a valuable marine ecosystem. It's as valuable in its own right as the Everglades. We must protect it."

Steve shifted uneasily and glanced at James Henry, but said nothing.

"Sixty percent of all herbicides, ninety percent of all fungicides, and thirty percent of all insecticides are carcinogenic, and —"

James Henry pantomimed playing a violin and hummed derisively, "It seems to me I've heard that song before."

Jamison continued undaunted. "And these chemicals are all responsible to some degree for cancer, birth defects, nerve damage, and genetic mutations. You just cannot continue to release harmful chemicals into the environment."

"You're just an encyclopedia of knowledge, aren't you?" James Henry intoned, looking down at the long cigar he held between tanned fingers. "I suppose you also know that I have the added expense of irrigating the muck to stop shrinkage. Shrank three feet a year for lack of water before my granddaddy began irrigating. What didn't shrink oxidized until he planted a cover crop to keep the soil from blowing away. There are only a few feet of muck over solid limestone around here. Once that muck is gone it's gone for good. You can't grow cane or anything else in solid rock."

"Nevertheless, Mr. Hampton, we must work together to clean up the environment before it's too late."

The young environmentalists nodded and murmured agreement.

"Just what do you propose I do about it?" James Henry drew on his cigar, exhaled, and watched a long stream of smoke drift toward the ceiling where the slowly circulating fan dispersed it.

"You and the other growers in the alliance must get involved in cleanup efforts. You must pay your fair share."

"The Environmental Protection Agency just fined us $85,000. Let them use that for starters."

"That was for violating federal air pollution standards," Jamison said, "but that's another matter. Let's not get into that."

"Cut to the bottom line," James Henry said. "What is it you want from me — specifically?"

"The tax payers give you three billion a year to —"

"Hold it! The taxpayers don't give a penny to the cane growers."

"Are you saying that sugar consumers aren't taxpayers? The subsidy system makes sure that sugar sells for twice what it would sell for on the world market. That means every family of four contributes about $20 a year to the pot."

"I'm saying that not one cent of tax money is paid to the cane industry."

"You're technically correct, but we can't overlook the three billion dollars growers get in bonuses from government policies that drive U.S. sugar prices higher than the world price of sugar."

"Where did you get the idea that it's three billion?"

"That three billion figure comes from a study by the Commerce Department. If it's not exactly correct, it's close."

James Henry laid his cigar in the ashtray, drummed his fingers on the table, and looked up into Jamison's eyes, contempt and impatience drawing his lips taut. "It doesn't all go to Florida growers. The government subsidizes cane growers in Texas and Louisiana, too, and the beet sugar industry — that's spread over thirteen states. The corn syrup industry gets its share, and corn is grown in twenty-four states. Beet and corn growers take a bigger bite of sugar subsidies than the cane growers, so why don't you go hassle them?"

"We're talking about the sugar cane industry today. You should put some of that government bonus money into cleaning up the mess the cane growers have created. You growers should all contribute a penny a pound to —"

"A penny a pound this year, two pennies a pound next year, and pretty soon we're priced right out of the market. You tell me, is a housewife in Wyoming going to go into a grocery store where offshore sugar is five cents a pound cheaper and pay extra for Florida sugar to save the Okee? Hell, she never even heard of the Okeechobee."

"Nevertheless, you must cooperate by —"

"We do what we can." James Henry retrieved his cigar, propped his elbow on the table, and contemplated the tip of the cigar.

The men around the table looked at Jamison apprehensively. The dark-haired skinny kid with the backpack on the table in front of him said, "No, you don't do everything you can; in fact, you don't do anything to resolve the problem. But you may be forced to before long. A few years ago, nearly 600,000 Florida voters signed the petition to put a state constitutional amendment on the ballot that would add one cent a pound to the price of raw sugar, with that money mandated for cleaning up the Everglades."

"Yeah, and it got knocked down," James Henry replied gruffly. He bounced his sunglasses on the table and chewed the end of his cigar.

"Through the efforts of your lobbyists." Jamison pushed unruly hair back from his eyes and stared directly into the eyes of his adversary.

James Henry threw the cigar down. "By a decision of the state Supreme Court, by damn; a technicality. It contained more than one subject, the language on the ballot was misleading, and it was unconstitutional."

"The legal fees resulting in that decision would have gone a long way toward the cleanup," the kid in the chinos said.

"You've got a helluva lot to say, young fella, but where are you when the muck fires start? In the '40s the smoke from a muck fire went all the way into Miami. It got so bad they had to drive with headlights on at noon; couldn't see to work in the offices in Miami without having the lights on. Those muck fires are no picnic, let me tell you, but my daddy and the others, they fought them as long as it took. They earned me the right to grow cane and I'm going to grow it, by God. You won't shut me down; I'll do whatever it takes to make it pay."

Jamison cleared his throat. "Back to the subject at hand. You still have to overcome the Everglades Forever Act. Cleanup costs will be split between the industry and the taxpayers."

James Henry snorted.

"You're thinking your lawyers and lobbyists will overcome that. Well, perhaps they will — you've got the best lawyers and lobbyists money can buy."

"Every industry has lobbyists. That's the American way. An industry can't operate in this country without lobbyists."

"Very few industries can afford the talent that represents the cane industry," Jamison retorted.

"You can't fault the industry for hiring the best." James Henry pulled a fresh cigar from his shirt pocket and lit it, allowing the smoke to drift into Jamison's face as he puffed.

Jamison waved his hand to clear the smoke. "I'm going to level with you, Mr. Hampton. We need your help. We have to have someone to present our case to the alliance."

"Me? You've got to be kidding. Why me?" James Henry asked incredulously.

"We were told that you are a fair man, that you love the industry and want it to survive. You're a man who fishes and hunts. We thought you would want to preserve this land for your children and grandchildren."

James Henry sat silently, digesting what Jamison had said. He shifted uneasily and glanced at Steve before speaking. "You're right. I do love the Everglades. But I love the cane fields too. I won't do or say anything to endanger the cane."

"We're not asking you to. All we want is your support for the penny a pound supplement."

"I'll think about it."

"Will you talk to the alliance?"

"Maybe, after I think about it."

Jamison looked around the table. The other environmentalists shifted uneasily.

"What about golf?" James Henry asked.

Jamison's eyebrows lifted in surprise. "You want to get together for a game? I'd, uh, like that."

"No, I mean what about the golf courses?"

"What about them?"

"They use as many chemicals on golf courses, maybe more than we use on the cane."

"Golf courses may be a small part of it, but —"

"Small part, hell! There's a new golf course built in the United States every day — every single damn day. Three hundred sixty-five new golf courses a year. That's a lot of golf courses, and a big part of the chemical runoff problem, especially here in Florida."

Caught off guard, Jamison looked around the table, hoping someone would intervene, but the young men dropped their eyes and remained silent.

"You can't blame golf courses, though, can you?" James Henry surveyed the tip of his cigar, enjoying having cornered Jamison. "Hell no. Now you're hitting where it hurts. They'd ram your speech up your ass if you tried to take away their golf courses."

Steve smiled broadly, thinking, *Damn, the old buzzard's got them now.*

"Sugar, now that's a different matter. You strut out your figures to the newspapers and TV broadcasters, and they eat them up. Hit the golf courses, and see how they react. Maybe bury the story on a back page, and you along with it." James Henry glanced at Steve triumphantly, then returned his gaze to Jamison, enjoying his reaction to the surprise tactic.

Jamison took some papers from his briefcase, shuffled them, and stammered. "Let's talk about the Everglades Forever Act." He placed a copy in front of James Henry, who pushed the papers back toward Jamison.

"The law's too complicated. They'll never get funding for it."

Jamison reluctantly gathered the papers and put them back in his briefcase. "The sugar subsidy penalizes every American taxpayer. Maybe the taxpayers will speak at the polls. Maybe they'll vote out the U.S. senators and representatives that take three billion a year from the poor and give it to millionaire sugar growers."

James Henry could barely keep from smiling. If they got voted out of office, he'd just buy them as lobbyists.

"Maybe that penny a pound we want you to contribute to the cleanup will look cheap before it's over." Jamison snapped the locks on his briefcase.

James Henry doubted it. That idea would go into the

Dumpster along with the bright idea to exchange cane fields for other state-owned lands, so the cane fields could be converted back to sawgrass to be preserved and restored.

Jamison leveled his gaze. "You'd better consult with the alliance before you make any decision on this, maybe they'll tell you —"

James Henry jumped up, knocking his chair over. "Maybe I'll just tell you to go to hell," he thundered, resenting the implication that the alliance wouldn't see things his way. He grabbed his pith helmet and glasses, and glowering at Jamison, he stormed out.

Steve got to his feet, nodded to the stunned environmentalists, and followed James Henry.

Jamison turned his hands palms up, raised his eyebrows, and shrugged. Silently the other members of the delegation gathered their papers, stuffed them into briefcases and backpacks, and filed out, frustrated and discouraged.

Steve had barely lowered himself into the car's seat when James Henry revved the motor and screeched out of the parking lot, slamming Steve's door shut.

"So," Steve asked, "what's the answer?"

"There is no answer, you know that. There are pros and cons, but there's no answer. Want a beer?"

"Nah," Steve said. "Drop me by the field. Tell Mom and Dad I said hi." Steve lowered his eyes, thinking about James Henry going up the stairs to his mother. He knew that's where he went whenever he was in trouble.

CHAPTER 6

Later that week when Mel and Yvonne drove to Belle Glade, smoke from burning cane crept through oaks hung thick with Spanish moss. It churned in the heavy midday air, blocking out light, and casting an eerie pall over the highway. The odor, like burning corn, seeped through car windows closed against the noise, the heat, and the ash.

Melisandra drove her Ferrari up the long driveway lined with stately royal palms to the front of Hampton House. She parked under a canopy that extended from the portico and waved away ash that had found its way into the closed car.

She turned to Yvonne and said, "I hate this place. Thanks for coming with me. I just couldn't face three days here in these damn cane fields without you. If it weren't for Mama and Henny, I never would come back. Jeff was right to make a life for himself in Japan."

"It won't be so bad. Three days will pass quickly. You have to help Henny, and you know how your mother enjoys planning a wedding. It will be all right, you'll see." Yvonne, her blonde hair caught in a ribbon at the neck of her Chloé jacket, picked up her purse and reached into the back seat for the lavender chrysanthemums she brought for Grace.

Mel stepped out of the car, smoothed wrinkles from her

blue linen skirt, and reached for her jacket. She draped it over her arm and glanced up at small clouds that spattered across the sky as if thrown from a paint-laden brush. Surveying the lush green lawn that swept to the trees in the distance, she murmured, "It's been too long since I came home to visit Mama. Those jacaranda trees were in bloom the last time I was here."

"Come on, let's go in and see your mama." Yvonne nudged her toward the house.

"What would I do without you?" Mel hugged Yvonne lightly, and they walked up the wide steps of the portico.

Mel pushed open the heavy, hand-carved mahogany door and they stepped into the huge foyer. Their footsteps echoed on the marble tile before being cushioned by the dark Tabriz rug. Mel inhaled the familiar scent of sandalwood that emanated from the carved chest that had belonged to her grandmother and admired the arrangement on the temple table. She stepped up to the gilt-framed mirror that hung over the table and smoothed her long dark hair. "Mama, we're here," she called.

Grace's hurried footsteps drew near. "Oh, Melisandra, Yvonne, I'm so sorry, I didn't hear you pull up. How are you, my baby?" Grace embraced Mel, then turned to Yvonne, who presented the flowers.

"Chrysanthemums! Thank you. What huge blooms, and what a lovely color. I'll have Berlinda put them in water, then I'll arrange them after lunch."

Grace stepped back to admire the women. "You girls look so trim and fit. How do you manage it with all your parties and lunches? But come, let's sit down." She glanced toward the kitchen door and called, "Berlinda, the girls are here. Set lunch on the table, please."

Berlinda came in, wiping her hands on a crisp white apron, her full lips hanging in a pout, her voice a reproving rumble. "Lo, Miss Mel. You late." The old razor scar on her cheek twitched with annoyance and she tossed hennaed hair in disapproval.

Mel smiled and winked at her mother. "Hello, Berlinda. How are you?"

"I jes now clear off the table."

"Well, set it again. Hurry." Grace handed the chrysanthemums to her. "Put these in water, please." She turned back to Mel and Yvonne. "You must be starved."

"We are a little hungry, Mama. We were running late, so we didn't have breakfast. Anyway, we wanted to enjoy the delicious lunch we knew you'd have for us."

"Berlinda prepared all of your favorite foods: stone crabs with mustard sauce, Carrie mango chutney." She called after Berlinda, "Hurry, the girls are starved."

"Hurry 'n' take it off, hurry 'n' put it back on, you'd think the Queen of Sheba be takin' lunch here." Berlinda's mutterings were just barely audible, as she intended. She announced over her shoulder, "Lunch'll be on the table directly. I had to put it all away, now I have to get it all out again. Lucky it's you, Miss Mel. I wouldn't do this for nobody else."

"Sorry, Berlinda," Mel called. She turned to her mother and giggled. "Some things never change, do they Mama?"

Yvonne was right. It wasn't so bad. It was good to see Mama and to be scolded again by Berlinda. She turned to her mother, "What's happening with Henny?"

"I'm terribly worried about him, but we'll talk about that after lunch."

Grace moved a chair out of bright light filtering through the silk Roman shade and motioned for Yvonne to be seated. She went to another window that towered to the fourteen-foot ceiling and closed the drape. "Now that spring is approaching, there is such a glare. But tell me about your prince. Your decision to marry seems so sudden. We haven't even met him, uh, Gatti, the prince. Do you love him very much?"

"Oh, Mama, you're so old-fashioned. Love went out with high-buttoned shoes. It's more like barter now. I get his title; he gets my money, until I tire of him."

"Oh, darling, don't talk like that!" Embarrassed, she glanced at Yvonne.

Yvonne turned away to hide a smile.

"You'll like Gatti, Mama. He's dark and handsome, just like Daddy. Well, no, he's not like Daddy at all, actually, but he is dark and handsome."

"Oh." Grace sighed uncertainly.

Berlinda appeared at the door. "Lunch is served," she said. "I put everything back on the table." She shot Mel a disapproving glance before retreating to the kitchen.

"Come, girls," Grace said, as she shepherded them into the dining room and motioned them to their places.

Yvonne gasped. "Oh, how lovely. So imaginative!"

"Mama, you are so artistic — tucking those strawberry plants with big red berries into the centerpiece. It's just perfect with the strawberry pattern on your china."

"Thank you, my darlings. Come, come, be seated. How long can you stay? I hope you don't get called away as you were last time."

"Three days, Mama." Mel sipped ice water from a pale green goblet. "Then we have to get back to Palm Beach for a party Yvonne has planned. It will be the event of the season."

"Oh, no, we're saving that distinction for your wedding." Yvonne's azure eyes flashed mischievously.

Grace laid her hand on Melisandra's. "I'm so excited about your wedding, dear. Tell me more about your prince. Is he good to you? Will he like us? Oh, I hope Daddy doesn't say something awful."

Mel laughed and patted her mother's arm. "Don't worry about it, Mama. Gatti's a big boy. He can take Daddy's flack."

Grace nodded uncertainly. "What have you planned? Will you get married here or in Palm Beach?"

"Palm Beach, since that's where most of our friends are. Gatti's brother will serve as his best man. It will be a small wedding, but I want it to be very special, so you must help me plan it."

"I will. I will."

When they finished lunch, Yvonne went up to her room while Mel and Grace went to the library to discuss ways they might help Henny.

"You wouldn't know him." Grace sighed. "He's been drinking and he's so pale and nervous; he sniffles and fidgets. I don't know how to help him. What can we do?" Grace twisted a linen handkerchief and looked plaintively to Mel for an answer.

"I'll talk to Henny, and I'll try to get Daddy to lay off."

"I hope Daddy will listen to you. Nothing Henny says makes any difference to him. Henny is so deeply in love with Beth, but Daddy won't hear of his marrying the child of a field boss. He wants him to marry a grower's daughter. You know how he is."

They discussed ways they might heal the rift between Henny and his father, knowing in their hearts that nothing they said would change the mind of either. When they had exhausted all discussion, Mel went upstairs to freshen up.

Berlinda had already unpacked the overnight bags and put things away in drawers and closets, so Yvonne joined Mel in her room.

"What do you want to do now?" Yvonne asked, as she walked to the huge canopied bed and fingered the hand-crocheted spread that matched the canopy. Yvonne had coveted that bed since they were children, and Mel hated it. She smiled when she remembered Grace's horror, when, in her teens, Mel had asked for a waterbed instead.

Mel walked to the window, drew back the curtain, and

looked out over the cane fields. "Oh, these infernal cane fires, I hate them. It's like living in the bowels of hell."

Mel watched egrets rise and fall on currents of air above the flames. "Why do those stupid birds fly into that fire? They get themselves all scorched, and burned, and blackened. They aren't going in for food or sex, so what drives them to do it?"

Yvonne shrugged. "Who knows?" She went to the window and the two friends watched together as egrets soared and dipped above the flames, the feathers on their long bodies singed and rumpled.

Mel said, "Maybe they upset me because they remind me of myself. Why am I getting married? I don't need Gatti for sex. Truth is, he isn't that good. God knows I don't need him for money. He'll cost me plenty before we're through, so why am I flying into the fire again? Why?"

Yvonne shook her head thoughtfully, but didn't answer.

"Look how those vultures circle, waiting for the egrets to make a mistake, a miscalculation. Then," Mel sighed, "they're fodder for the vultures."

The women watched a moment longer before Mel said, "I wonder if Gatti is the egret or the vulture, and which am I?"

Yvonne lifted Mel's hand from the curtain and allowed the curtain to drop across the window. "Stop this nonsense. You've just got prewedding jitters. You're buying a suitable escort, nothing more. You know what you're doing; you've said it many times. Stop fussing and get on with it."

"You're right, of course. It was love that burned me, not a financial arrangement."

"I'd think that after the torture you went through with Jason, you'd never want to fall in love again. An arrangement will be much less traumatic."

"I don't want the grief, God knows, but, oh, the love. When it was good, it was wonderful. I hate to admit it, but I'd fly into those flames again, just like one of those crazed egrets, for just one night when Jason truly loved me."

Yvonne reached out and touched her friend's shoulder gently. "You're a damn fool, you know that?"

"I am being foolish. Well, if I'm going through with this fiasco, we'd better get on with planning a wedding. Daddy doesn't approve of my marrying Gatti one little bit. I hope that's not why I'm doing it. He's still angry because I wouldn't let him marry me off to one of the Lawton boys, consolidate their fields with his by selling his only daughter. Even if I did love one of those cretins, I wouldn't give Daddy the satisfaction."

"You and your daddy don't agree on anything, do you?"

"Oh, there's one thing we agree on. We both think I spend too much money. Wait till he hears that I'm not only going to buy a prince, but I'm buying a place on the French Riviera where I'll summer with him."

"Don't forget, you promised me you'd join us on our boat on the Aegean. Don't disappoint me. I can't be cooped up with Randolph and his cronies without having you there. I'd go mad."

"Don't worry, I'll be there. I'm looking forward to it. Even with that squirrelly countess and her bisexual lover, yachting on the Aegean will be a delight. An ocean away from this cane is almost far enough for me."

Mel picked up the notebook and listlessly thumbed through pages of wedding notations. She didn't really want to marry Gatti, but perhaps it would lift the depression she'd suffered since her divorce from Jason. Perhaps any companion was better than none. Suddenly Mel threw the notebook aside. "I think I hear Daddy. Come on, I've got to talk to him about Henny."

Mel ran down the stairs and into James Henry's arms. She kissed him and felt the security of his tall, muscular frame. Mel loved him in spite of their differences. He had always been there for her when she needed him.

James Henry set her aside and moved toward his leather recliner. "What's this about your marrying some damn prince?"

"You used to call me your little princess. Now it will be official."

"Hello, Yvonne." James Henry pulled her toward him and kissed her lightly on the cheek. "I thought you'd have more sense than to let my girl get tangled up with some phony prince."

Yvonne laughed. "Who am I to question about-to-be-royalty?"

Mel dropped into the chair next to James Henry's. He looked over at her and asked, "Do I have to curtsy to you now?"

"Just bow respectfully, and don't speak unless you're spoken to." Mel glanced at him sideways and snickered.

James Henry growled. "You'll be just plain old Mel around here, missy."

Mel and Yvonne's laughter greeted Grace when she entered the library. "Henny isn't home yet. I wonder where he is." She rubbed her forehead absentmindedly.

James Henry grunted, and poured Dewars from the decanter on the table beside his chair.

Grace started to speak, but stiffened at the sound of a car door slamming. She spun around and looked toward the library door.

Henny slunk into the room, glancing at James Henry from under lowered lids. "Hi, Mama," he said, grazing her cheek with a kiss.

"Oh, Henny, I'm so glad you're here. Melisandra and Yvonne came over all the way from Palm Beach to see you."

"Hello, little brother. Good of you to show up. After all, we drove sixty miles just to see your pretty face. Give your big sister a hug." Mel wrapped her arms around him and kissed his forehead. "Say hello to Yvonne."

Henny nodded to Yvonne and shifted uneasily.

Grace's pale blue eyes sparkled with pleasure. "We were

afraid you wouldn't be home in time for dinner. Oh, son, I'm so glad you're here."

Henny pulled away from Mel and backed toward the door. "I can't stay. Beth's in the car."

"Ask her to come in," Grace said. "She can —"

"No way!" James Henry slammed his glass on the table. "Don't you dare bring that tramp into this house!"

Yvonne rose discreetly and attempted to leave.

"Sit down, Yvonne," James Henry ordered. He turned to Henny. "You go right back out to that car and get that woman off this property. Now!"

Henny turned and bounded out of the room.

"Henny!" Tears welled in Grace's eyes, making them almost transparent. She begged, "James Henry, please, stop him!" Her glance implored Mel to say something in Henny's defense.

"Daddy, wait," Mel jumped up and went to her father's side.

"You keep out of this, young lady."

"You don't know Beth, Daddy. Henny could do a lot worse. Why don't you give them your blessing and let them be happy before Henny self-destructs?"

James Henry wheeled around, splashing Scotch from his glass. "Is that why you're here? Is that what all this kissing is about?"

"Why are you getting so excited? All I said was —"

"I heard what you said. It's none of your damn business. This is between Henny and me."

"I'd say it was between Henny and Beth."

"I'll be damned if it is. He's my son and I know what's best for him." He slammed the glass down on the table and stormed out of the room.

Grace looked after him with stricken eyes.

"Just another one of Daddy's tantrums," Mel said. "Don't worry, Mama, I'll go talk to him." She hugged her mother and went after James Henry.

CHAPTER 7

The next morning Mel and Yvonne slept while stars dissolved in early morning bands of gold, and cane cutters rode to the fields. When the rickety bus stopped, the cutters disembarked into the mist, each holding his cutlass in front of him, his eyes on the lethally sharp blade. The melody of clattering cane accompanied the metallic clicking of the cutter's shin guards, as they rushed to the nearest rows to begin cutting cane.

By the time the field walker reached the fading beam of bus headlights, where he read the price for that day's cutting of a half-mile, double row of cane, Jazzman had already commandeered the Charlie Frank row and begun slashing cane. Lean and muscular, Jazzman specialized in cutting the Charlie Frank rows — the rows on the edge of the field or by a canal or road. Those rows received more light, bore more cane, and were harder to cut, but Jazzman enjoyed the challenge. Whether he chose the hardest rows because they paid more or because of the respect other cutters felt for his prowess, was hard to say.

Jazzman also liked the premium throw-over rows, since they paid the same as the Charlie Frank rows, and with his rhythm and speed they didn't require much additional time. Since he was right-handed, and his partner, Sugar Baby, was left-handed, they could work side by side without getting in each other's way as they felled the cane and threw it across the row.

Jazzman paused momentarily at the end of the row to look back over the stubble. He thought, *that damn coochie row next to the Charlie Frank have a lotta cane, too, but it pay no more.* Jazzman knew with his skill he would easily cut his ton of cane an hour. *I make my rows,* he thought, *damned if I be sent home to Jamaica broke.*

The cutters didn't notice as slashes of orange and gold painted the predawn horizon. Their concentration was absolute. The slightest deviation of a stroke of the cutlass could send them home injured and unemployed.

The pusher's voice rose above the thud of cane cutlasses. "Closer! Cut that stubble closer. You're leaving too much stubble. Watch that pile, man. Neat! Pile it neat. Move, man, move!"

The tall, lean Jamaicans bent to the task, disappearing down the rows into the haze.

At the end of the punishing day, Jazzman stood up slowly, his hand pressed against the small of his back, sweat glistening on ebony skin. He wiped the mixture of sweat and sticky cane juice from his face, glad that another day of cutting cane in the heat of Belle Glade was finished.

Feeling a flush of triumph for having completed his rows ahead of his partner, Sugar Baby, he called, "Hey, mon, do be hurry up. You be too far behind, mon."

Sugar Baby, a squat Jamaican, waved a weary arm and muttered, "Damn hard keep up wid you. Tomorrow Sugar Baby find new partner."

But he wouldn't. It was fatigue talking. Jazzman's laid-back style, his handsome physique, his prowess with the women of Belle Glade's Harlem section were legendary, and the strain of keeping pace with him in the cane field was a small price to pay for the exalted position of companion to Jazzman.

Jazzman reached down and removed his shin guards, then picked up his cutlass and walked gracefully toward the bus for his ride back to the barracks. A few minutes later, Sugar Baby climbed aboard the rickety field bus and they began the ten-minute ride back to camp.

As Jazzman entered the barracks, he snatched a sweat-stained shirt hanging from a top bunk and threw it across the chest of a cutter resting there. "Wash de damn ting, dis place stink like hell." He tried not to breathe in the fumes of sweaty bodies, decaying food, and unwashed clothes as he made his way to his bunk.

He dropped onto the hard slab and put his arm over his eyes to shade them from the setting sun that pierced the uncovered window. *You tink dirt on dat window do be block some light,* he thought, as he rolled over, away from the glare. In a few minutes he had drifted into an exhausted sleep.

"Wake up! Come on, mon, you get up." Sugar Baby's voice seemed far away as Jazzman regained consciousness. "Two hot mamas be waitin' for us down to JACK'S. You get dressed now. Ranilla and Mona waitin' on us."

Jazzman rolled over and looked toward the window. The grimy panes reflected moonlight now. He dropped one foot to the floor, yawned, then got up and staggered toward the shower at the back of the room.

"You do be hurry up," Sugar Baby called after him.

Jazzman tried not to breathe in the stench of the shower as he walked on his heels over the slimy, mold-covered floor. He turned the shower knob and was startled awake by an intermittent flow of cold water.

He washed quickly, eager to leave the barracks. Back at his bunk, he pulled on a clean pair of jeans and his only other T-shirt. The bright red polyester stretched taut across his muscular chest. "Ready, mon," he called to Sugar Baby, who waited by the door. The two cutters walked off into the moonlit night toward Belle Glade and their date with two women from town.

Sugar Baby swiped at his wide, flat nose with a stubby finger. "Cane smell like shit tonight."

"Sure do stink," Jazzman said, looking across the moonlit lake toward the sugarhouse, where cane was processed twenty-four hours a day.

The men left the highway and made their way through rubble on the dark, littered streets of Harlem.

The neon sign announcing JACK'S flashed seductively over the peeling paint of the entrance, seeming to keep time with the raucous music that reached out to them. They followed the sound of Beres Hammond singing "Respect to You" into the dank interior of the club, pungent with the smell of barbecue, cheap perfume, and unwashed bodies. They scanned the crowd at the scarred bar to the right of the door, looking for the two women they had promised to meet.

"Guess they not come in yet," Jazzman said, as they inched their way through the crowd of cutters, whores, and local women out for a good time.

A woman in a tight, short skirt pressed against Jazzman, her cheap gardenia perfume enveloping him. He stepped back, away from the overpowering scent, but she gripped his arm and pulled him closer, rubbing bulging breasts across his hard chest.

"Hey, you big stud, you want Cornilda tonight?" Her voice barely audible over the din of steel drums, she scanned his muscular body, desire and promise in her large eyes.

Jazzman pulled away from her. "No, we got women we meet up wid tonight."

"Okay, next time." She stepped away, her eyes roaming the crowd for another cutter who might be in the market for her wares.

Jazzman and Sugar Baby ordered beers, then leaned against the pockmarked oak bar and drank.

"We get somethin' to eat, mon?" Jazzman asked.

"Yeah, my belly growl."

The men hadn't eaten since breakfast. They didn't like the bland food the growers served from the rice wagon in the field, and stopping to eat cost them time — time that they could use to finish cutting their rows.

The cutters survived in the heat and relentless sun by drinking "petrol," a mixture they concocted from ingredients purchased at the store in town. They usually combined Nutrament with Guinness Stout, carrot juice, evaporated milk, V-8 juice, and eggnog. Now, hungry for substantial food, they went to a table and ordered ribs and rice, then turned their attention to the music while waiting to be served.

Jazzman tapped the table in time to the reggae beat of "Cane Cutter's Lady," while Sugar Baby scanned the crowd looking for the women. "Maybe they not come," he said.

"Oh, they come." Jazzman knew the women in the Harlem section liked the handsome Jamaicans, and his track record indicated that he would score tonight as usual. "Anyway, one woman be good as the next, and plenty here to pick from."

"Yeah, two nice honey babes by d' bar." Sugar Baby gestured with his thumb. "If Ranilla an' Mona don't come, we go pick up dose two babes."

Jazzman turned back to concentrate on the music. He dreamed of having his own group, like Terror Fabulous. He and Terror — Terror was Cecil Campbell then — used to sing together on the streets of Kingston.

Music reverberated at Jazzman's core. He knew it to be his destiny; he could feel it in his soul. Having the dream made the hours in the cane fields bearable. By the end of the season he would have the bankroll he needed to get his group started.

He'd go to old Jessie in town, get his hair jheri curled, and as soon as he got back to Jamaica, he'd get the musicians together. They'd play in hotels where the tourists came, and maybe they would be discovered and brought to the States to record like Beres Hammond or Maxi Priest. It would be a long shot, but he'd go at it like he cut cane — be the best and the rest would follow.

Jazzman thought, no woman be more than a one-night stand to me. No woman be comin' between me and my dream.

The waitress emerged from pink lights that danced around the room to serve their food. When she bent over the table Sugar baby tweaked one of the breasts that bulged above her low cut blouse.

"On, mon, don't be doin' that," Jazzman admonished.

Sugar Baby threw his head back, laughed raucously, and directed his attention to the ribs swimming in hot sauce on the plate in front of him.

The men were devouring ribs, sauce dripping between their fingers, when Mona and Ranilla made their way to the table. Jazzman licked his fingers and motioned for them to get some chairs.

When they were settled, Ranilla reached over and picked up a rib from Sugar Baby's plate. She stripped the juicy meat from the bone. "Um, good."

Sugar Baby circled the plate with his arms and gave her a withering glance.

When the men finished the food, they pushed their plates back, and Jazzman ordered beers all around.

Mona, a light-skinned native of Belle Glade's Harlem section, moved closer to Jazzman and began stroking his muscular arm.

Jazzman smiled, then turned and concentrated on the music.

"You wanna dance?" Mona asked, eager to be in his arms.

Wordlessly, Jazzman rose, and without looking at her, he swept her onto the dance floor, maneuvering gracefully to the reggae beat.

Sugar Baby watched as Jazzman moved adroitly across the crowded dance floor. "Coolest cat in Belle Glade," he muttered with undisguised admiration.

"Forget him, Baby, you look at Ranilla." She grasped his chin and swiveled his head back to her.

Sugar Baby winked and sipped beer from her glass.

"Hey! You get your own damn beer." Ranilla snatched the glass and drained it.

When Jazzman and Mona returned to the table, the kidding and banter led to talk of the upcoming strike.

"You men talking to the union boss?" Mona asked.

"Damn union." Jazzman used a toothpick to dislodge a bit of rib struck between glistening white teeth. "They pull us out; the growers send us back to Jamaica. No work, no pay."

Mona's smile faded. If the union pulled the men out of the fields and the growers sent them home, there would be no more good times with Jazzman until next season.

"The union's right," Ranilla stated. "Growers are all rich old bastards; they should pay more." She wasn't adverse to the Jamaicans having more to spend in the bars of Belle Glade.

"Should pay more, but they won't." Jazzman slapped the table. "Push come to shove, they send us home and use machines to harvest the cane. That's what come of it."

"Oh, geez, I hope not," Ranilla exclaimed, envisioning a long, dry winter without the handsome Jamaicans to buy her drinks and romance her.

As midnight neared, Jazzman suggested they take the girls home. He led the way, and Mona matched his long graceful stride.

Sugar Baby and Ranilla followed along the dark, littered street, alternately kissing and playfully slapping each other. Sugar Baby reached under Ranilla's tight pink sweater and unhooked her bra. She screamed and smacked him with her shiny, red plastic purse.

When they entered the girls' shack, Jazzman and Mona went to her room and he walked to the cot where Mona's children slept. He looked down at them, remembering his own childhood and the late-night visits of strangers. He reached into his pocket and took out some short lengths of sugarcane that he'd wrapped in a plastic bag and laid the sweet treat on the cot beside the sleeping children. Then he took off his clothes and made love to Mona.

CHAPTER 8

James Henry strode into the huge old kitchen at five a.m. He pulled out the captain's chair at the head of the table, took his place under the lighted pewter chandelier, and glanced at Berlinda. "Did you call Henny to come to breakfast?"

"Yes sir, Mister Jim." Berlinda added buttermilk to a bowl of pancake batter and stirred gently. "I called him three times already. He's hungover good. I cain't wake him up."

James Henry scowled. "Call him again, Berlinda."

Berlinda flipped the last of the griddlecakes and wiped her hands on her apron. "I'll call him, but it won't do no good. He's dead to the world." Berlinda shuffled off, the years of serving others showing in her gait. "Won't do no good a'tall."

Berlinda returned muttering. "Used to be such a good chile. I swear I don't know what's got into that boy." She gathered griddlecakes and sausage, put it on a warmed plate, and set it in front of James Henry.

He drained the last of the freshly squeezed orange juice, and generously buttered and syruped the griddlecakes. He said, "No one makes griddlecakes like you do, Berlinda. Damn, I wish you'd make them more than twice a week.

"You'll get 'em Mondays and Thursdays like always."

James Henry shook his head, chuckled, and ate with gusto.

Henny still hadn't appeared when James Henry picked up his pith helmet. "Call Henny again in an hour, Berlinda, and see that he gets to school." He went out and drove to the field office.

It was almost two o'clock when Henny stumbled into the kitchen, bruises from his leap from the car still evident on his face.

Berlinda jammed fists into her waist and surveyed him with distain. "I don't understand you, boy. Your daddy and the cutters been workin' since before sun up, an' here you come stumbling outta bed at this hour. Your mama an' your daddy give you everything a chile could want. Always did. Now look at you, actin' like a spoiled brat. You gotta pull you'self together, boy, stop skippin' school an' git you a education."

"That's easy for you to say. You never —"

"I never, huh? The man I marry run off one night with some little floozy he picked up in a bar. I never seen him again. Left me with five chillun to raise up all by myself. Didn't hear no snivelin' from me. I raised them chillun up, all five of 'em, no help from nobody, 'cept your mama." Seeing that Henny was about to bolt, she said, "You set yourself down. I be puttin' your griddlecakes on right now." Berlinda poured neat rounds of batter onto the griddle, still complaining loudly about serving breakfast in the afternoon.

"Just coffee, black." Henny touched the bruise on his face and winced.

"I swear I don't know what's got into you, out carousin' all night like common trash. You never usta behave like that. I was your daddy, I'd whup you good. Your mama never raise you to act like trash."

Berlinda poured coffee and watched as Henny gulped it, all the while clucking her tongue.

Henny slammed the mug on the table and bolted for the door.

Berlinda called to his back, "You better straighten yourself up. Stop drinkin' an' takin' them drugs, or you wind up dead. You mark my word, you will."

The screen door slammed and Berlinda watched Henny amble to his car and get in. "That boy be headed for trouble," she mused, as she absentmindedly rubbed the scar on her cheek.

She turned abruptly when Grace pushed open the kitchen door and peered in. She thought, *Look at that poor woman, she been cryin' all night again.*

"I thought I heard Henny."

"He gone, Miss Grace. Didn't eat no breakfast, neither. Jes had him some coffee."

"Dear me, I hope he's not ill."

"Oh, he be sick all right. Out drinkin' again all night."

Grace closed the door quickly and went back to the morning room. Light streaming through tall windows flooded the interior. She picked up the latest *Vogue* magazine from the coffee table and sank into down-filled sofa cushions. She turned the pages listlessly, not seeing the fashions.

Henny is drinking to forget, she thought, and his father is being unreasonable. I, too, had hoped Henny would marry one of the grower's daughters, but there's no telling where the heart will lead. Grace laid the *Vogue* aside. *Oh, God,* she prayed, *please alleviate Henny's pain. I can't bear to see him in torment.*

Henny parked his car on the crushed stone driveway at the field office and walked slowly up the steps, coughing when ash from the burn settled in his throat. He glowered at the rough-hewn boards, resenting time he had to spend in the old shanty. He wondered why his father regarded it as some sort of shrine and spent all his time here when he could be in the new air-conditioned main office. The stench of burning cane permeated smoke that swirled around him as he yanked open the door and went in. He passed his father without acknowledgment.

James Henry looked up from his desk, disgust distorting his chiseled features. He laid the tonnage sheets he had been studying aside. "And a cheery good afternoon to you too," he said sarcastically. He glanced at the clock. "It's only two o'clock. Why aren't you in school?"

Henny shrugged. "Got off early today, thought I might as well come on in. I can use the extra bread."

James Henry scowled at Henny's disheveled appearance, his torn jeans and baggy T-shirt with a marijuana leaf stenciled on the front. He's a sorry sight, he thought. He's getting so thin his shoulders are drooping. "What the hell is the matter with you, boy? Stop slouching like an old geezer and stand up like a man. Prepare to take over here someday."

Henny slipped off scruffy sneakers and stuck bare feet under his desk.

"Just make yourself comfortable," James Henry sneered, not trying to mask his disgust.

Henny didn't respond. He pulled the racing form out of his back pocket and began to study it.

Just as James Henry was about to go over and confront him, the door opened and Steve Wood ducked under the door frame. Steve's freshly laundered shirt and jeans hugged muscular arms and thighs. "Afternoon, Steve, what's up?"

"I thought you should know. Those 'vironmentalists are out on the road picketing again." Steve took off his dark blue peaked cap and wiped his forehead with a white handkerchief.

"Damn! What do you think we should do?"

"Maybe if we call the sheriff, he will get rid of them," Steve stuffed the handkerchief into the back pocket of his jeans.

"Yeah, maybe. Try that and keep me posted on what happens."

Steve nodded and was gone.

"You hear that, son?"

"Yeah," Henny replied, his voice flat, disinterested.

"I don't know what to do about those damned picketers. They're not much older than you, so how do you think we should handle them?"

Without looking up from the racing form, Henny mumbled, "Call out the sheriff and his deputies, they're all on your payroll. Maybe set the dogs on the kids. Go on using tons of chemicals, and when the runoff kills the lake and poisons the wells, just pretend you didn't know what you were doing. Oh, and you can get some of the senators you have in your pocket to absolve you of any of the cleanup costs."

"You watch your smart mouth, boy; this is your father you're talking to." James Henry's face reddened. He walked back to his desk and sorted through the tonnage sheets.

Henny got up and went into the bathroom.

Cane ash swirled in the sun's rays that fell across the small room. James Henry cleared some ash from his throat, glanced at his watch, and decided to take a beer break at La Vonda's Café. He called toward the bathroom door, "I'll be back in an hour."

Henny gave no response.

James Henry swerved into a parking space at Vonda's and made his way across the crushed shell lot.

Chip greeted James Henry from behind the bar. "Hey, Jim, ole buddy!" They had been friends since playing football together in high school, and they still shared the favors of their high school sweetheart, Vonda, even though Chip had married her. No one dared mention the gossip this provoked to James Henry, but they teased Chip about it.

Chip drew a cold beer and slid the glass toward his friend. "How's it goin' today, Jim?"

James Henry rolled beer around his mouth before swallowing, dislodging ash from burning cane that stuck in his mouth and throat. "Too damn much wind for a burn today." He set the beer down and wiped cane ash from his face. "Vonda here?"

"Nah, she went out to do some shoppin'." Chip leaned against the back bar and lit a Camel. A light on the ceiling fan threw flickering shadows over sandy hair, muscular shoulders, and a slim waist that belied his years. He jerked a thumb toward some men sitting at the end of the bar. "We're gonna play a little poker tonight. Wanna try your luck?"

"Not tonight. The damned environmentalists are swarming all over the place. I got to take care of business." James Henry lit a cigar. "Who are those guys? They aren't locals, are they?"

"Nah, they're down here fishin'."

"Where they from?"

"Charlotte. Come down every year to fish. Do more drinkin' than fishin' though, and that's a fact."

"Why don't we go fishing anymore? We used to go all the time — and crabbing."

"You know the answer to that better 'n I do. You're always too busy." Chip drew on his cigarette, then laid it in the ashtray and picked up Jim's empty glass. He tilted it and let beer run down the side to prevent frothing as it filled. He set the beer in front of James Henry and picked up his cigarette.

"We ought to make time," James Henry said. "Maybe after the harvest. Yeah, we should get in some fishing next summer." James Henry tapped his cigar on the ashtray and downed a long draft.

"Ought to do a little wild hog huntin', too. That was a blast." Chip glanced to the end of the bar, checking the fishermen's glasses.

"Yeah. Remember when we got tangled up in those moon-vines and damned near drowned in that swamp up around the Econlockhatchee? We came back with the hogs, though."

"Barbecue lasted three days, if I remember right. Vonda called it the Hog & Grog Festival." Chip chuckled and shook his head. "Came in from all over the county for that one. Guess our hog huntin' days are a thing of the past. The state's gonna wipe the hogs out up there or so they say."

"Lots of luck. Those hogs have been there since the Spanish landed."

"Yeah? That a fact?" The men from Charlotte motioned to Chip for a refill. After refreshing their glasses and exchanging pleasantries he returned to James Henry. "The Spanish brought them hogs over? I never heard that."

"Damn hogs wandered off into the swamp and went wild. Before long the whole state was overrun with hogs. Seems the more they try to wipe them out, the faster they breed. Have to kill three-quarters of them, they say, to make any long-term difference.

"I give the environmentalists a week after they hear about killing off the hogs before they're on a 'Save the Hogs' kick," James Henry said.

Chip laughed. "Maybe take some of the heat off you, huh, Jim?"

"I wish."

As if on cue, the flickering TV screen over the bar flashed pictures of picketers lying in the road blocking one of James Henry's trucks.

"Well, back to the real world." James Henry gulped the last of his beer and stood to go. "Now we know why we don't have time for hog hunting. I've got to get out there and try to calm things down." He donned his aviator glasses and headed for the door.

Chip picked up James Henry's glass and wiped the bar. "Take care, Jim."

"Yeah, see you." James Henry threw on his pith helmet and went out into the late afternoon sun, longing for the old days when he and Chip were free to hunt and fish the Enconloc-katchee.

CHAPTER 9

James Henry returned to the café after midnight to see Vonda.

Chip glanced up and greeted his friend. "Hey, Jim, what's new?" He reached for a glass.

"Where is everybody?"

"Slow for this time of night, but we had a crowd earlier."

When his eyes became accustomed to the gloom, James Henry saw Vonda sitting in her booth, turning the pages of a book. He took the beer from Chip, walked over, slid in across from her, and stretched to kiss her cheek.

Vonda brushed the kiss away without looking at him, the air around her heavy with Tabu cologne.

"Are you pouting?"

"I stopped pouting when I was in high school."

What is it then?" James Henry reached for her hand, but she pulled it away. Bangles clanked as she turned the pages of the horoscope book.

"Come on, Vonda, what's the problem?"

"Where the hell you been? You didn't come around for my birthday." Her blouse shifted provocatively as she turned away.

"I sent you roses—two dozen." James Henry glanced around the café. "Where the hell are they?"

"Upstairs."

"Let's go up and you can show them to me."

"I got this great surprise for you, an' you ain't been around in a week," Vonda said, pouting, despite her disclaimer.

"I been in, but you weren't here. What surprise?"

Vonda inserted a long red nail under a page and flipped it. "Never mind."

James Henry reached across the table, closed the book, and pushed it aside. "Now, Vonda, you know those damned environmentalists have me tied up. I have to take care of business. They're trying to close me down; I can't let that happen. I've got to get the cane to the mill."

"Yeah, I seen it on TV. Quite a ruckus. But you coulda stopped by for a few minutes on my birthday."

"I stopped by earlier, but you had Mam'selle to the vet to get her wormed."

"Not wormed, permed! I took her to the groomer to get her tuft permed so it would stand up when I put her hair ribbon on. You never get anything right. You don't listen." She picked up the horoscope book and turned to her lucky numbers.

"Come on, Vonda, let's go upstairs. I'll make it up to you."

Vonda studied James Henry for a moment, then closed the book and set Mamse'lle aside. Mamse'lle shook her permed topknot in annoyance, almost dislodging the pink ribbon. Vonda grabbed James Henry's hand. "Come on, you big bull, I've got a surprise for you."

James Henry slid out of the booth and followed Vonda to the stairs.

Chip lowered his gaze and began whistling softly.

When James Henry and Vonda burst into her room, he pulled her onto the bed, but she jumped up and ran to the closet.

"Hey, where are you going?" He pulled off his boots and dropped his jodhpurs.

"Surprise!" Vonda sprang out of the closet waving a long bullwhip.

"What the hell?"

"Ain't this a hog hoot? I got it from one of them cowboys that rodeoed here last week."

James Henry watched Vonda warily, backing away. "What do you intend to do with that?"

"The cowboy taught me to crack it. Says that's how we come to be called crackers. Old timers cracked these whips to herd the cattle, even to talk. Sent messages by crackin' the whip. So he says, anyway."

James Henry circled her warily. "Put it down."

"No. I'll crack the whip and you jump. The cowboy said if you crack it right you can slice the head off of a snake." Vonda lowered her head and approached. "Why didn't you come to see me on my birthday?" She cracked the whip, striking the bare floor near his feet.

James Henry jumped back. "Damn it, Vonda, that's enough. Put that thing away."

"Come on, play." Vonda wiggled her wrist and the whip zigzagged across the floor. She laughed uproariously and struck the head of the bearskin rug. She dragged the whip across the rug slowly, tauntingly. "Lie down and I'll whip you, you old cuckoo bird."

James Henry grabbed the whip and tried to wrest it from her, but Vonda held on. She grabbed a rose from the vase on the dresser, stuck it between her teeth, and flipped on the CD player. "La Toreador" blasted from the speaker. Vonda danced wildly through the small room, cracking the whip in James Henry's direction and bumping into the bed and dresser. She snatched the rose from her mouth and threw it at James Henry.

He stuck a leg into his jodhpurs.

"Don't do that!" Vonda lashed out at him, and the tip of the whip struck his wrist. Blood poured from a vein, spilling onto the white satin bedspread.

"Oh, shit!" Vonda dropped the whip, grabbed a towel from

the nightstand, and pressed it to the wound, trying to stop the flow of blood.

"Now see what you've done? You cut me." James Henry glowered at Vonda and pushed the towel away. Blood flowed out.

Vonda clamped the towel back over the cut. "Oh, geez, what'll we do?"

"Make a tourniquet," James Henry said.

Vonda grabbed a lacy Victoria's Secret garter belt that lay draped over the foot of the bed, and bound it tightly around his wrist. She picked up the pencil that lay beside the phone, stuck it under the garter belt, and twisted.

Cautiously, James Henry lifted the towel. Bleeding had been reduced to a trickle.

Vonda wiped blood away from the wound and inspected the cut. "That needs stitches," she said. "Put your pants on and I'll take you over to Doc Johnson." She helped him into his blood-spattered jodhpurs and boots.

"Get a clean towel," James Henry said. "I've got to loosen the tourniquet. It's cutting off the circulation."

Vonda ran into the adjoining bathroom, came back with a large fleecy towel, and held it over his wrist. When he loosened the garter belt, blood poured out.

"Put it back. Hurry up. Come on, I'm taking you to Doc's." Vonda grabbed his elbow and steered him toward the door.

"Holy crap," James Henry said, as he redid the tourniquet. "What next?"

When they clambered down the stairs, Chip stopped in mid-drag on his cigarette and gaped at the blood-spattered pair. "What the hell —?"

"We'll be right back," Vonda called as they rushed toward the door.

CHAPTER 10

Damn, James Henry thought as he pulled into the driveway at two a.m. and saw the light on in the library. Why is Grace up at this hour? Something must be wrong. He waited for the garage door to rise, then pulled the car in and set the brake. He rolled his sleeve down to hide the bandage and got out. "Six stitches because of Vonda and that damn bullwhip," he muttered as he walked toward the steps.

Grace met him in the doorway waving a telegram. "It's from Jeffrey!" she cried, her voice breaking with excitement. When she reached to hand the telegram to him, she noticed the dried blood on his pants and shirt. "What happened?" she asked. "Are you all right?"

"Yes, fine. It's nothing — a little cut." James Henry brushed past her and went down the hall toward the library.

"Our son is coming home! Jeffrey is coming home for Melisandra's wedding."

"That right?" James Henry picked up the crystal decanter on the side table and poured two fingers of Dewar's neat. He dropped into his recliner, sighed, and sipped the liquor.

"There's more. Guess what?"

He hated this. Why didn't she just tell him? He reached for the telegram, but Grace drew it away. He rose from his chair and started to leave.

"Wait! Jeffery's bringing Samiko." She held the telegram out to him.

He read it, crumpled it, and tossed it in the wastepaper basket beside the desk. "He's not bringing her here."

Grace drew her breath in sharply. "What do you mean?"

"He wants to marry a Jap, fine. Let him live in Japan with her. She's not welcome in my home."

"Our home."

"What?"

"Our home," Grace stated. "It's my home, too, in case you've forgotten. Jeffrey is my son, and all of my children are welcome in my home — always. Don't you even think of causing trouble with Jeffery and his bride."

"You don't care that he married some Jap?"

"Please! We went through all of this when he told us he married Samiko. I want him to be happy. If Samiko makes him happy, I'm delighted that he married her. And please don't call Samiko a Jap — she is Japanese. Give your son some credit. If he married her, she must be a fine woman."

"Fine woman, humph. Fine Jap women don't mess with foreigners." He turned his back to Grace, took a cigar from the humidor on the table beside his recliner, and lit it.

Grace circled to face him. "Give the boy a chance. Look at what you've done to Henny with your meddling. You're destroying his life. Al least meet Samiko before you make a judgment."

"I know all I need to know."

"Oh, stop. You know nothing about her. Why would you think Samiko is not nice just because she's Japanese? Japanese women are some of the most refined women on earth."

"The ones that bed down with foreigners are whores." James Henry set his glass down and left the library.

Exhausted, Grace slumped into a wing chair. She had no intention of losing her oldest son.

She thought of Henny, off who knew where, doing who knew what, and of Melisandra, heartbroken over her divorce from a man she still loved. She would not allow Jeffrey to suffer that fate. But how would she convince James Henry to accept Samiko?

Mindlessly, Grace reached for the needlepoint in the basket beside her chair. She drew navy blue Belgian wool through a needle, stuck it into the canvas, then dropped the canvas back into the basket. She laid her head against the rich tapestry of the wing chair and closed her eyes. The smell of cigar smoke brought her up abruptly. Her eyes flew open to see James Henry standing over her.

"What's the matter?" he asked. "You got a headache?"

"No," Grace stammered. "I'm just resting my eyes. I was going to work on this needlepoint that I'm giving to Henny and Beth. It will be something I did with my own hands — a gift to remember me by."

"Oh, he'll remember you all right. You've been catering to that kid since the day he was born."

"Are you complaining because I'm good to your son?"

"I'm not happy to claim him as my son. Why the hell does he want to marry some damn cracker? Jeez, a cracker, a Jap, and a gigolo."

Grace winced. "I don't understand you. Your children have always adored you, but you can't forgive them for not allowing you to run their lives. You'll lose all of them if you're not careful. You're always finding fault with Melisandra, you're angry with Jeffrey because he doesn't want to spend his life in the cane fields, and you're unreasonable with Henny. He's so loving, so sensitive —"

"Sensitive. That's the key word, isn't it? The only other person that was sensitive enough for you was that poet you had a crush on."

"What poet? What are you talking about?"

"That creep in high school that you were mooning over when I met you."

"Oh, John. He's not a poet, he's a journalist."

"Yeah, I remember now. He went overseas for some newspaper or something. By the time he came back we were married and had two kids."

"What made you think he was a poet?"

"You have a bunch of poems he wrote to you. I saw them when I was looking in your desk drawer for the scissors."

Grace stiffened; her eyes widened. "You didn't read them?"

"Who wants to read that drivel?"

Grace sank back into the chair; color draining from her face. "You have no right to go into my desk."

"You still mooning over him after all these years?" When Grace didn't answer, James Henry sneered. "You are! By God you are. Well, I'll be damned. You haven't seen him in twenty years."

"Eighteen years," Grace mused absentmindedly.

"Yeah, I remember now. The last time we saw him was when Henny was born. He came back and went to the hospital to see you a few times. He — no!" James Henry's face distorted as realization struck. He ground his teeth and glared at her. "No, don't tell me. No, that's impossible. You couldn't have; you didn't —? No. Did you? Is he —?"

Grace caught her breath, then let it out in a rush. "I'm sorry. I am so sorry, James Henry, I am. I hoped you would never find out — never know. Oh, poor Henny. What are you going to do?"

James Henry turned on her, his jaw tightening. His lips moved, but no sound emerged. Color spread across his face as his eyes locked with hers. He stopped breathing, the realization of her infidelity strangling him. He raised his hand to strike her, held it suspended for a moment, then dropping it before crashing out of the room.

Swamped by a mixture of emotions — fear, panic, terror — Grace thought, *What will James Henry do? Oh, poor Henny! How will James Henny treat him now that he knows? What will he say to him?* Her hand flew to her forehead as she remembered Jeffrey's telegram. *What a time for this to happen, with Jeffrey and Samiko due to arrive in a few days. What should I do? What can I do?*

She thought of the poems and letters in her desk drawer. She knew James Henry would come for them as soon as his thinking cleared. She got up and hurried to the desk.

The door burst open; James Henry burst in and pushed her aside. He seized the desk drawer and pulled it open with such force that the backstop shattered. The drawer crashed to the floor; papers scattered across the rug.

Grace lunged for the ribbon-wrapped poems and letters, but James Henry grabbed them and stormed out of the room.

Grace stood, frozen with fear, clutching the desk for support. She tried to think. Would James Henry tell Henny. Should she? She had to find Henny and explain everything to him before his father got to him. Should she contact Jeffrey and postpone their visit? But Jeffrey was coming for Melisandra's wedding; his visit couldn't be postponed. She began to sob in fear and frustration. When she wheeled around, she bumped into James Henry.

He shoved the packet of poems and letters at her, unopened. Without a word, he turned and strode out of the room.

This was not what Grace expected. More fearful of this reaction than she would have been of a tirade, she stuck the packet in her sewing basket, wondering what this meant. In a trancelike fog, she picked up the drawer, put it back in her desk, then gathered the scattered contents and returned them to the drawer.

Retrieving the ribbon-wrapped packet from the sewing basket, she glanced around in confusion, then took it to the fireplace. She knelt, opened the flue, drew a long match from

the holder on the hearth, and struck it. One by one she burned
the poems and letters. *It doesn't matter*, she thought, *I know
them all by heart — and I'll always have Henny.*

As the papers turned to ash, Grace felt her life ebb. The
secret had been her strength, and now it lay exposed. As flames
leaped and sparked she finally admitted to herself that John
Phillips would never be hers.

There were no tears; there was no grief. Devoid of feeling,
drained of life, she returned to the wing chair and picked up the
canvas. With trembling fingers she began stitching wool into
the emerging motto: FOR LOVE I GIVE ALL.

After she completed only one letter, Grace laid the needlepoint aside, got up, and went to the wastepaper basket to
retrieve the telegram. She laid it on the shiny surface of the
desk and ran her hand over it, smoothing it. Then she read it
again, slowly, savoring it, eager to meet Jeffrey's bride.

She knew she would love Samiko. It was worth chancing
what might come as a result of tonight's revelation. She picked
up the silver frame that held a photo Jeffrey had sent when he
married Samiko, and smiled at the likeness of the lovely young
girl who stood so proudly beside her son. She set the photo back
on her desk, folded the telegram carefully, and placed it in her
Bible.

Grace walked to the window and closed it. Ash from cane
burned that morning littered the windowsill. She brushed it
away absentmindedly. Thoughts of Jeffrey and his bride mingled with her fear of James Henry's retaliation. She wanted to
give Samiko a warm welcome, to make her comfortable in this
strange land and not involve her in family upheaval. What
would James Henry do about what he'd learned tonight? How
would he treat Henny now? Poor Henny.

The sound of the garage door opening startled her. She
heard the squeal of tires as James Henry pulled out of the driveway. "He's going to La Vonda Wood," she mumbled to the

empty room. "Oh, dear God, please don't let him tell her about my infidelity."

As James Henry sped along Sugarland Highway, he realized he couldn't tell Chip and Vonda about what he had learned tonight — he couldn't tell anybody. No one must ever know that Henny was not his son.

He pulled to the side of the road and sat there, beating the steering wheel with clenched fists and yelling, "No! No! No!" He wrenched the car door open and stumbled out.

He was drawn, as if by a force outside himself, into the cane field, where he fell to his knees in the black muck and cried. "It can't be true, it can't. Oh, dear God, I love that boy. Henny is my son, he is. Henny has to be my son!" He staggered to his feet and embraced the cane, clinging to the stalks as he would cling to a lover.

Car headlights flashed by unnoticed, until the flashing red light of the sheriff's car caught his attention.

Sheriff Ratch pulled onto the shoulder of the road and got out. He circled James Henry's car, scanning it with his flashlight. "James Henry!" he yelled. "Where you at?"

James Henry pulled a handkerchief from his pocket, rubbed tears off his face and wiped muck from his hands.

"James Henry! Where you at?" Ratch flashed light into the cane field.

"Right here, Otis. I'm right here."

"You all right?" Otis stepped off the shoulder and came toward him through the cane, directing the beam of the flashlight toward the sound of his voice.

"Yeah, Otis, I'm okay."

"Jeez, James Henry, you give me a scare. Wondered what the hell your car was doin' along the road, the motor runnin', the door hangin' open and all." Otis stared at the black muck stain on his pant legs.

"Just stopped to relieve myself," James Henry said, wiping his pants with the handkerchief. "Stumbled over my own feet and fell flat on my face in the muck."

Otis laughed. "Yeah. Well, okay, as long as you're all right."

"Yeah, I'm fine. Thanks, Otis. Good night."

James Henry watched Otis return to his patrol car and pull away. Alone in the cane, he vowed, "I've got to put what Grace did out of my mind. To hell with what I learned tonight. Henny is my son. I raised him. I love him. Nothing can change that."

He returned to the road, slid into the Lincoln, and pulled out onto Sugarland Highway. *Maybe it will be easier, he rationalized, now that I know why Henny isn't more like me or his brother. I'll never let myself think of this again. What's done is done. It ends here tonight. I won't let this tear my family apart, by God, I won't. Henny is my son and that's the end of it. I married Grace for better or for worse, and we've both had some of each. I'm no saint, and I'm not much of a man if I can't take what I dish out. This ends here, tonight.*

He veered into the crushed shell lot of La Vonda's Café, parked, and went into the smoke-filled bar. Vonda had cranked the jukebox up to a deafening level, and all conversation was drowned out by the cacophony. He slid into Vonda's booth and motioned to Chip to bring a beer.

Vonda sauntered out from behind the bar, smiling as she approached. The bright-yellow sweater dramatized her flaming red hair and strained to reveal her best features. Bangles jangled, orchestrating her sultry walk. Men at the bar followed her with eyes mirroring desire.

She slid into the booth beside James Henry and bestowed a kiss. A mist of Tabu cologne enveloped him. "So, big man, what you doin' back here? Decide you want to get whipped after all? And what's with your pants? Looks like you been wallowin' in the muck."

"My son who married the Jap is coming home."

"Jeff?"

James Henry nodded.

Vonda raised meticulously plucked eyebrows. "Well, ain't that a hog hoot?"

"Grace is acting like it's the second coming of Christ."

"Well hell, your son's comin' home with his bride. You gotta celebrate. Chip!" she yelled, "Bring some champagne over here."

"No!" James Henry called to him, "Don't!" He mumbled, "I'm not celebrating."

"Why the hell not?" Vonda rearranged her bangles.

"She's a Jap, for Chrissake."

She smacked him on the shoulder. "Come on, you old cuckoo bird, loosen up. He's your kid."

James Henry slumped and tapped his fingers on the table.

Vonda stroked his hair. "Jeff's a helluva nice kid. Cut him a break."

"You sound like Grace."

"Couldn't sound like a better woman. Bet she's dyin' to meet the bride. What's the Jap's name?"

"Samiko. Samiko Haikawa Hampton." James Henry snorted.

Chip stepped up to the booth and set two beers on the table. "What's happenin', Jim?"

Vonda snickered. "Jeff's comin' home — bringin' the new bride. Naturally that has Jim in a snit."

"Why?" Chip asked, lighting a Camel.

"Because she's a Jap." Vonda swept flaming red hair back off her shoulder.

James Henry picked up the beer and took a long swallow. "My children! One marries a Jap, one marries a gigolo, and the other one wants to marry a cracker. A hell of a note."

Chip pointed to the picture over the bar of him and Jim standing barefoot with their catch of largemouth bass. "Come on, Jim, you ain't nuthin' but a cracker yourself. You're all dressed up nowadays in jodhpurs and a pith helmet, but you're still a cracker at heart, and we both know it. Hell, they can't even get you outa that shanty you call a field office. You're sure as hell a cracker, and that's a fact."

Vonda glanced sideways at James Henry and snickered.

He grinned self-consciously.

"Chip's right," Vonda said, admiring her long, red nails. "Anyway, what the hell difference does it make to you who Jeff marries? He's the one has to live with her."

James Henry sipped his beer silently.

"Right?" Vonda poked his arm.

"Yeah, I guess." He swung out of the booth and threw a twenty on the table.

"Where you goin'? Ain't you got time for a quickie?"

Chip turned away and walked toward the bar.

"Not tonight, Vonda. So long, Chip." James Henry went out into the night thinking about what they had said. Talking to Vonda and Chip always made him feel better, but the news about Henny was one bitter pill to swallow.

CHAPTER 11

James Henry came home mid-morning on the day of Jeff's arrival. When he didn't find Grace in the library, he poured a drink and went through the rooms looking for her. He pushed open the kitchen door and found her placing yellow roses in a centerpiece.

"Did your son get here with his Jap whore yet?" James Henry sipped his drink, anticipating her reaction.

Grace turned and faced him. "James Henry Hampton, listen to me. I'm going to say this once, and only once — any talk of whores around here will involve La Vonda Wood and no one else."

His mouth went slack; the muscle in his face twitched. Grace had never spoken La Vonda's name before.

He lowered his eyes and cleared his throat. "Did Henny pick up the stone crabs and champagne before he went to the airport?"

"Yes."

"Did he ice them down?"

"Yes, he did."

"Well then, I'll go change." James Henry mounted the stairs two at a time, unbuttoning his khaki shirt as he went toward the shower. *Just how much does Grace know about my visits to Vonda? She's never spoken to me like that before.* He remembered the confrontation a few nights before and thought, *Oh, yeah, tit for tat.*

He had tried to put that night's revelation out of his mind, but it had been gnawing at him all morning. *How could she? It was so unlike Grace. Did she still love that guy after all these years? Why didn't I suspect anything? I should have put it together sooner, but I've got too much on my mind.* He leaned into the spacious marble shower, turned the water on full force, and stepped into the hot pulsating blast. Refreshed, he reached to the warming rack for a towel.

Grace had laid out his new boots and the silk shirt Mel gave him last Christmas. He was pulling the boots on when Grace called, "They're here! They're here!"

He slipped into the shirt and started down the stairs two at a time, buttoning it as he went. When he reached the foyer, Grace was already out on the portico welcoming Jeff and Samiko.

"Pleased to meet you, Mama Grace," Samiko said, bowing and extending a tentative hand. Grace gathered her into her arms, finding her soft accent delightful.

James Henry stepped out onto the portico and stopped short. *The Jap's a pretty little thing,* he thought; *no wonder Jeff married her.*

Samiko's long black hair flowed graceful as a raven's wing, when she turned to focus eyes with seamless lids on James Henry. She smiled shyly and averted her gaze.

Jeff, taller and more muscular than James Henry remembered, said, "Dad, this is my Samiko. She prefers to be called Sami."

"Hello." What the hell did Jeff expect him to do, welcome the Jap with open arms?

Grace frowned at James Henry and moved to hug both Jeff and Sami at the same time. Stepping back, she said to Sami, "Let me look at you. Oh, aren't you pretty! You look just like your picture." She drew her close and hugged her again.

Jeff lookeded into the foyer and said, "Where did Henny go?"

Grace glanced around. "He was here a few moments ago. I'm sure he'll be back soon." Grace took their hands. "Come let's go inside out of the heat and cane ash." She turned to Sami. "Would you like to freshen up after your long trip?" She opened the door to the powder room in the foyer and Sami backed into the room, bowing and thanking her.

"What a charming child," she cooed as she went to Jeff and took his hands in hers. "I love her. I just love her."

"I knew you would, Mama. She'll love you, too. How could she help it?"

James Henry came in and glanced around. "Where's the Jap?"

"Dad! Please don't use that word. My wife is Japanese. It would be more respectful if you ask for Sami by name."

"Respectful," James Henry snorted. "Do you expect —?"

"Shhh." Grace went to meet Sami as she came from the powder room. She put an arm around her shoulders. "All fresh now? Good. Come." She led her to the morning room where muted light streaming through arched windows cast soft shadows across the silky Sarouk rug that almost covered the polished parquet floor. Grace motioned her to the sofa so Jeff could sit next to her and lend moral support.

"Did you have a good trip?" Grace asked. "Your plane seems to have been on time." She picked up a small silver tray that held puff pastry shells filled with creamed stone crab and passed them to Sami. James Henry stirred a pitcher of vodka martinis.

"Smooth flight, no delays. Henny was waiting when we got off the plane." Jeff reached for the martini James Henry held out to him.

"Yes, nice trip," Sami agreed, nodding respectfully to Grace.

"I guess Belle Glade is very different from your home in

Japan." Grace offered another crab puff, but Sami demurred.

"Yes, very different. We live in a big city in Japan — Tokyo."

Sami's pleasant accent induced a smile. "I do hope you like it here, dear," Grace said, glancing out the window at the swirling cane ash. "We want you to visit us often." Suddenly Grace realized that the hot, humid air blowing across the cane fields carried stench from burning cane into the room. She wondered how this lovely child could possibly enjoy her stay in Belle Glade. *Perhaps if I take her to the club and introduce her to my friends' daughters she will feel more a part of us.* "Do tell us about yourself. We're eager to learn all about you."

"Nothing much to tell," Sami responded, straining to speak without an accent.

Jeff jumped in. "Sami's dad is a diplomat, so she has lived in many countries."

"A diplomat, how interesting." Grace glanced at James Henry triumphantly.

Jeff continued, "I can't understand how she could have kept her naïveté and stayed so close to her native customs with all that moving about, but I'm glad she did." Jeff glanced lovingly at Sami and squeezed her slender hand.

Sami's large dark eyes glowed. "Being in a strange land made the bond with my parents much stronger. My mother taught me Japanese customs so I wouldn't forget my heritage. We always speak Japanese in our home."

"I understand." Grace gazed lovingly at Sami, then at Jeff.

James Henry, who had been observing them closely, stepped up with the pitcher of martinis about to refill their glasses, but they all declined.

Jeff said, "So, Dad, how are things here? Good crop this year?"

"Pretty good. How did you two meet?"

Grace leaped to her feet. "You must be starved," she said. "Shall we go in to lunch?"

James Henry set the pitcher on the bar, sipped from his glass, and repeated, "How did you two meet?"

"I'm afraid it wasn't a very dramatic meeting," Jeff said. "When I went to the Haikawa home to take photos for a story I was doing for *Time* magazine, I discovered that Mr. Haikawa was interested in photography. He showed me his darkroom and said I could use it any time. It had fantastic equipment, much better than I had access to, so I took him up on the offer. Sometimes we worked there together. I spent quite a bit of time at his home, and one day I met Sami when she was home on vacation from the university."

"Oh, you attended the university, dear? Jeff told us a lot about you, but he failed to mention that you attended a university." Grace glanced at James Henry and sat back down.

"I graduated last spring, before we got married."

"Was it love at first sight?" Grace asked, her voice soft and expectant.

James Henry hooted.

Sami glanced at him, puzzled.

Jeff said, "We talked over tea, and I discovered that we had similar interests. I liked Sami right away and the love grew." Jeff reached for Sami's hand, but she blushed and withdrew it, unaccustomed to American displays of affection.

Jeff continued, "I enjoyed her company, so I made it a point to get tickets for something I knew she'd want to see."

"American Ballet Company," Sami said, almost succeeding in pronouncing her Ls.

"We went to the ballet, and I knew I'd found the girl I'd been searching for." Jeff glanced at his father. "You thought I had no interest in girls, but that wasn't it. I just didn't want to waste my time with someone with whom I had nothing in common."

"Uh-huh." James Henry turned to Grace. "How about that lunch?" He got up and started for the dining room.

"Shouldn't we wait for Henny?" Jeff asked.

"No telling when he'll show up," James Henry growled. He stood aside and motioned for the women to precede him. Sami bowed slightly as she passed, and James Henry returned a self-conscious nod.

Berlinda stood just inside the dining room door, waiting to greet Jeff and his bride. "Mr. Jeff! I'm so glad to see y'all. My, my, don't you look fine?"

"Berlinda!" Jeff hugged her tightly. "Wait till you see what I brought from Japan for you. You'll look just like a geisha girl."

"Go on with you, Mr. Jeff." Berlinda pushed him playfully.

Jeff reached for Sami's hand and pulled her forward. "This is Berlinda, your competition," he joked. "She was my first love and she's still my best girl. She lets me, and no one but me, lick the batter from the bowl when she bakes a cake."

Berlinda chortled and hugged him.

"This is Sami," he said. "You always told me that one day I'd find the perfect woman and I have."

Sami cupped her hand over her mouth to hide her smile.

Berlinda leaned back on worn heels and studied Sami, top to bottom. "You certainly has found one beautiful woman, Mr. Jeff, you certainly has."

Sami bowed slightly. "Hello, Berlinda."

Berlinda started to return the bow, then changed midway into a curtsy, then abandoned it altogether. "Welcome, Miss Sami," she said. She returned her gaze to Jeff. "I make all of your favorite foods for your home comin', Mr. Jeff. I make everything jes the way you likes it."

"You're a sweetheart." Jeff brushed her cheek with a kiss, then pulled out a chair for Sami.

Berlinda began heaping portions of fried chicken and okra on Jeff's plate.

"Berlinda," Grace admonished, "ladies first. And we haven't said grace."

"Oh, sorry, I jes forget. I'm so happy to have Mr. Jeff back home again." She stepped back and assumed a pious stance.

The family joined hands around the table as had been their custom, but when James Henry attempted to hold Sami's hand she pulled away before realizing what was happening.

James Henry led them in a short prayer, and before they'd had time to release their hands, Berlinda was back to dishing up fried chicken for Jeff. She stopped short. "Oh, I'm sorry," she said, stabbing the pieces she'd placed on his plate with the tines of the serving fork and heaping them back onto the platter. "Ladies first." She held the platter for Sami to select a piece of chicken.

When Berlinda attempted to serve Grace, she said, "No thank you, I'm dieting until Melisandra's wedding."

"When will I meet Melisandra?" Sami asked, her slight accent enhancing Mel's name.

"The wedding will be on Saturday, so we'll drive to Palm Beach tomorrow afternoon," Grace said. "You'll meet her then."

"Oh — it's so exciting! I can't wait to meet her," Sami's dark eyes shone, "and to get to know Henny better."

"I'm sorry Henny couldn't join us for lunch. He had an urgent meeting at school."

James Henry snorted.

Grace glowered at him and tapped the corners of her mouth with her napkin. She turned a gracious smile toward Sami and Jeff and steered the conversation away from talk of Henny.

When Berlinda made another trip around the table with the platter of fried chicken, Jeff threw up his hands. "Mercy! Show me mercy!"

"Plenty here," Berlinda said. "You kin have all you wants."

Sami giggled behind her hand, then turned to Grace and asked, "Will Melisandra wear a beautiful white wedding gown?"

"No, I think not. It's her second marriage. This will be a simple ceremony."

"Oh." Sami looked away, disappointment erasing her smile.

"You should have been here for her first wedding," Jeff said. "We pulled out all the stops for that one, eh, Dad?"

James Henry frowned and did not respond.

"You'll enjoy this wedding," Grace enthused. "It will be simple, but very elegant. We've planned a small reception at The Breakers after the ceremony."

"That sounds nice," Sami said, as she declined another piece of chicken.

"Miss Mel invite me to the weddin' too," Berlinda said. "Lashonda make me a new dress jes for the occasion."

"You're going to have competition, Mama," Jeff said.

James Henry leaned back from the table. "Enough of this chatter, Berlinda. Some of us are still working men. Bring in the dessert."

Berlinda said, "Yes, sir, Mr. Jim," and she hurried toward the kitchen.

"Are you happy the way things are going here in Belle Glade, Dad?" Jeff asked.

"I would be if the damned environmentalists would stop trying to close me down."

"Can you handle them?"

"If I can't, it will be a first."

"Right, Dad, how could I have doubted you?"

"You wouldn't be the first to make that mistake."

Jeff glanced at Sami, bemused by her reaction to his father.

She gazed at James Henry uncertainly before averting her eyes.

"You two plan on staying around here for a while?" James Henry asked.

"Just two weeks. We have our return tickets."

"Hardly worth the trip."

"We would like you to stay longer," Grace said, trying to

smooth the edges of the conversation. "I'd like all of our friends to meet Sami."

"I'm going to show her off every chance I get." Jeff looked lovingly at his bride. "The wedding will be my first opportunity." He turned to Sami. "You'll meet the 'A' crowd. Boy will they be jealous of me!"

Sami blushed and raised a hand to cover the smile on her lips.

James Henry checked his watch. "Where is Berlinda with that dessert?"

Berlinda burst through the dining room door carrying a cake flaming with candles.

"What the hell?" James Henry pulled back, perplexed.

"Happy Birthday, Mr. Jeff," Berlinda sang.

A frown creased James Henry's forehead. "It's not his birthday."

"It is if I say it is." Berlinda set the cake in front of Jeff and handed him a knife. "Make a wish, Mr. Jeff, and blow out them candles." Berlinda rolled back on her heels and watched him with satisfaction. "Fresh coconut cake, your favorite, jes like when you was a little boy."

Jeff sat transfixed for a moment before saying, "Thank you Berlinda. You baked twenty-one of these cakes for me before I left Belle Glade, and you can be sure I thought about them on my last three birthdays."

James Henry shifted uneasily. "Come on, cut the cake. We won't be going to any wedding if I don't get things cleaned up over at the office.

Grace began humming softly, "Happy birthday to you —"

CHAPTER 12

After lunch the next day, the family drove to Palm Beach for Melisandra's rehearsal dinner at The Breakers. The aura was so unlike Mel's first wedding, when she glowed with the hope of first love. Now she sat, pale and listless, distant, showing no emotion. She walked through the rehearsal at the chapel, and sat through dinner with shuttered eyes.

Grace fought misgivings, remembering Mel's wedding to Jason and thinking, *She doesn't look like a woman in love and about to be married.*

The next evening, organ music reverberated through the small chapel, where elegant sprays of fragrant white maritime orchids overflowed marble urns, and nodded gracefully above pale green satin ribbons at the end of each pew. Subdued lighting, provided by hundreds of tapered ivory candles, flickered across family and a few friends.

As organ music swelled, Jeff ushered Grace to the front pew on the right, where she sat beside Sami. As she waited quietly for the ceremony to begin, her thoughts wandered to her own first love.

Despite everything, she was glad she had chosen to stay in Belle Glade and marry James Henry. She couldn't have been happy traipsing all over the world, not even with John beside her. Grace recognized her need for the security of familiar things: Grandma Jefferson's silver, Mama's linens, and the treasures she had accumulated over the years. She had made the right choice, but still —

The muted glow of candlelight, the fragrance of orchids, the gentle touch of the organist, all combined to allay her misgivings about Mel's marriage. Perhaps Gatti would bring her child happiness.

As Grace reached for Sami's hand, she silently thanked God again for uniting her with Jeff. Then her eyes clouded as she thought of James Henry's attitude toward Sami. *I will change that*, she vowed.

A glance around the chapel confirmed Henny's absence. She felt a mixture of sadness and relief when she didn't see him. This wedding would only intensify his frustration at James Henry's not allowing him to marry Beth.

Organ music swelled as Jeff slid into the pew beside Sami. He took her hand in his, their love as palpable as Melisandra's had been when she married Jason.

Mel paused when she and James Henry stepped through the chapel doors. A beam of sunlight coming through a high clerestory window enhanced the pale green silk of her Galanos sheath. It strengthened her prominent cheekbones and reflected blue-black from her hair. But her mouth remained in shadow, unspoken forebodings captured behind expressionless lips. Mel looked up at her father, sapphire eyes mirroring a mixture of indecision and doubt.

Grace thought, *She's beseeching him to stop her.*

Then suddenly Mel stepped forward. With the strains of the "Bridal Chorus" from Lohengrin filling the chapel, father and daughter walked toward the altar.

Grace watched with admiration as Melisandra approached, delighting in the beauty of her only daughter, as slim as the stem of a rose in the elegant designer gown.

James Henry and Melisandra reached the altar. Yvonne took Mel's bouquet of calla lilies softened by sprays of tiny white oncidium orchids, and stepped aside.

Grace brushed away a tear, and glanced self-consciously at Sami.

Sami smiled and whispered, "Merisandra so beautiful."

The music faded.

"Who gives this woman?"

"I do." James Henry placed Mel's hand on Gatti's and stepped away. Grace felt that somehow they had failed their daughter. Why was James Henry giving his only daughter to this stranger? Uneasily, Grace slid over to make room for James Henry to sit beside her.

Mel turned toward Gatti.

He smiled at her eagerly, if not tenderly.

Grace thought, they have a lot in common: friends, lifestyle, maybe —

Gatti slipped the emerald and diamond band on Mel's finger.

The organ came alive with the recessional. The Prince and Princess Anthony Salvatore Davido del Gatti turned, walked down the aisle, and out into the world together under a snow of fresh white rose petals.

At the reception, when Gatti swept Mel onto the dance floor, Sami squeezed Jeff's hand and gazed up at him. Her dark eyes enveloped him with love. He winked at her and led her to the dance floor as the family joined the bride and groom in the first dance.

Sami felt the beat of his heart, the touch of his chin on her forehead. She closed her eyes, savoring the moment.

A few days later, still under the spell of Mel's wedding, Sami lay on the bed in their room waiting for Jeff to come home. She had placed a bottle of plum wine and two cut crystal wine glasses on the rim of the whirlpool tub. When she heard Jeff greet his mother, she slipped his favorite Luther Vandross recording into the CD player. Quickly, she lighted perfumed candles placed around the tub, as Vandross sang, "Forever, For Always, For Love." She ran to the door, flung it wide, and leaped into Jeff's arms with such force that it propelled him backward.

Jeff picked her up and carried her into the room, kissing her as he cradled her in his arms. When he set her down, Sami took his hand and led him to the bath. She turned the winged faucet handle and water shot from the mouth of the golden swan spigot. Bubbles multiplied and rose in mounds as water surged over crystals in the tub. The fragrance of bath oil mingled with the scent of perfumed candles.

Sami slippedout of her slippers and let them drop onto the thick rug. She unbuttoned her dress and shrugged out of it. She smiled when Jeff's breathing quickened as he watched her push the straps of the teddy off her shoulders. When the filmy chemise dropped to her ankles, she stepped out of it and slid her firm young body into the bubbles. "Now you," she said.

She watched intently as Jeff unbuttoned his shirt and his hard chest emerged. The ridges of muscle that spanned his stomach rippled as he moved. When he stepped into the tub, Sami put her arms around his buttocks and held him close. She brushed him with eager lips and smiled up at him.

He lowered himself into the tub beside her and gathered her into his arms. He kissed her hair, moist with steam, and brushed wayward bubbles from her cheek. He kissed her parted lips gently and she responded hungrily. They lay entwined in the warm, sudsy water, their passion magnifying as they kissed.

Jeff whispered into the cleft between small, hard breasts, "I love you, Sami, more than life itself."

Sami replied breathlessly, "I love you too, oh, so much."

She felt the warmth of Jeff's breath on her shoulder as he moved onto her. She rose to meet him, becoming whole, fulfilled. Their heartbeats synchronized as they rose and fell together in the warm water beneath the sheltering canopy of bubbles.

Sami closed her eyes, retaining the image of Jeff's chiseled features, his intense blue eyes, the lock of moist dark hair on his forehead. She resonated to Jeff's strong, sure movement, and surrendered to their pleasure as music washed over them.

When the warm nectar of their passion mingled, they lay together quietly in the perfumed water, satisfied, content, reluctant to break the bond.

Flickering candlelight danced over them; Vandross sang on.

CHAPTER 13

A few days later, James Henry returned to the field office shortly before three. He slapped his helmet on the rack, threw his sunglasses on the desk, and wiped perspiration from his face. He glanced at Henny who was at his desk studying the racing form. "Did that guy who brought those environmentalists to the office call back?"

"No. Dad, listen —" Moisture clouded Henny's eyes; his skin appeared pale and translucent. "We've got to talk. Beth said —"

"Not now, son." James Henry grabbed the phone and dialed. "Busy!" He slammed the receiver back in the cradle.

"Dad, I have to talk to you. Beth —"

"Not now, I said. The damn environmentalists are stopping our trucks and my drivers can't get the sugar to the mill. TV reporters are swarming all over the place."

Henny jumped up and grabbed his father's arm. "Will you forget the damned environmentalists for five minutes and talk to me? This is more important."

James Henry jerked his arm free. "More important? That little cracker is more important than the future of the cane industry? That's a laugh."

"This is my life we're talking about. Don't you understand? I love Beth."

"Love. You don't know what love is." He swung around, picked up the phone, and hit redial. The busy signal sounded and he slammed it down.

Henny faced him over the desk. "What the hell do you mean I don't know what love is? I'm telling you that I love Beth and I'm going to marry her."

James Henry sneered and dropped into the chair behind his desk. "You sure are a one-note band. Don't you understand, boy? That's not what I want for you."

"Who the hell cares what you want?" Henny sniffled and swiped at his nose with a bony finger.

"You had better care or you and somebody else will be eating sand."

"You bastard!"

"You watch your mouth."

"You never loved anybody. You're the one that doesn't know what love is. You didn't love Vonda enough to marry her when you knocked her up, and you don't love Mama enough to stay away from Vonda now."

James Henry sucked in his breath. He felt his face redden and the muscle in his cheek spasm. He had deluded himself that Henny didn't know about Vonda.

"That's enough, boy."

"There's no use talking to you, you cold bastard. You could never understand how I feel." Henny knocked James Henry's phone off the desk, fled to his Jag, and sped away.

James Henry stared after him for a moment, then picked up the phone, and replaced the receiver. He swiveled away from the desk and looked out the small dust-encrusted windowpanes toward the cane. He remembered his crush on Vonda, back when he was Henny's age, before she married Chip. He hadn't even met Grace when he'd gotten Vonda pregnant, but still he wasn't dumb enough to marry her. *Oh, well*, he thought, *Henny will get over it like I did.*

*　　*　　*

Henny, empowered by cocaine, felt an uncontrollable urge to confront his father — to defy him. Less than a mile down the road he braked the speeding Jaguar, pulled off into the cane, turned around in a spray of black dust, and sped back to the office. He vaulted up the steps, threw open the door, and stood there, feet apart, fists clenched, facing a startled James Henry. "I'm going to marry Beth now," he said, "and there's not a damn thing you can do about it." He stared at his father defiantly, before spinning around and running out.

He jumped in his Jag and headed for Beth's trailer on the outskirts of town. He pulled in, pushed through the sagging gate, and went up the uneven dirt path.

Before he reached the door, Beth ran out and threw herself into his arms. The sun bounced off her auburn hair; the gentle summer breeze wafted the sweet scent of her cologne. "Henny! Oh, it's so good to see you. I was afraid that James Henry would keep you away from me."

He nuzzled her neck. "You don't have to worry about that ever again. We're going to get married — right now — today."

"Today, but —"

"We're driving to Georgia."

"Georgia? Why Georgia?"

"There's no waiting there."

"Oh, Henny, we can't. Mama and me got the wedding all planned."

"It's now or never. If we don't get married right away my dad will do something to stop us; I know he will. He'll never understand. We've got to get married before he has a chance to pull something devious."

"But what can he do? We don't need his permission."

"You don't know him like I do. He'll come up with some-thing."

"No. Your father loves you. He wouldn't do anything to hurt

you." She tried to back away, but he pulled her closer, frantic he would lose her.

"Wait, let me talk to Mom." She bolted from his arms and disappeared into the trailer.

Henny heard women's voices rise and fall, but he couldn't make out what they were saying. He lit a joint and paced nervously, looking toward the road, half expecting to see a fleet of sheriff's cars sent by his father to drag him home. "Damn," he exclaimed, kicking the dirt. "I'm getting paranoid."

Beth and her mother stepped out of the trailer, letting the torn screen door slam behind them.

Cora, her skin lined and rough from years of working in the sun, glared at Henny. "This ain't no way, sneakin' off like thieves. You gotta talk to your father like a man. Let him know up front he cain't treat Beth like no tramp."

"I tried to talk to him; he won't listen." Henny spun away so she wouldn't see tears forming in his eyes.

"He'll have to listen if you stand up to him. Beth's carryin' your kid, you cain't walk away from that." She yanked open the screen door and went inside.

Henny yelled after her, "I don't want to walk away. I want to get married today, before he ruins everything." Perspiration oozed on Henny's forehead.

Beth went to Henny, pulled a tissue from the pocket of her jeans, and wiped his forehead. She put her arm around his waist.

Henny grabbed her and held her so tightly it frightened her. She tried to pull away, but he held her closer and rocked with her.

"It'll be all right, Henny, you'll see. If James Henry don't change his mind, we can go to Georgia later on. We gotta wait till we can be together without him cuttin' you off without a cent.

"I don't give a damn about the money. All I want is you and our baby."

"We can't be happy broke."

"Sure we can. I'll get a job at the mill. We'll get by okay."

"Are you out of your mind? I'm not marrying no millhand."

Henny pushed her aside. "He's right! You do want the money!" He stumbled back to his car. "I thought you wanted me, I thought you loved me. I thought you'd do anything I asked you to." He turned the key and gunned the motor.

"Wait," Beth yelled. She ran after him, wrenched open the car door, threw herself onto the seat beside him, and kissed him hard. "Let's go," she yelled.

James Henry strode out of the office, his long boots pounding on the porch as he sprinted to his car. He drove to the field where Beth's father was working and spotted Cloyd atop a harvester. He motioned and shouted, "Come over here."

The harvester stopped, and Cloyd stepped down. He peeled off his work gloves and walked over. When he spat on the sun-baked soil, tobacco juice spattered James Henry's polished boots. James Henry's lip twitched but he pretended not to notice.

Cloyd lifted his hat and mopped his forehead with a red bandana. "Yeah, Boss?"

James Henry slapped him on the back. "You're a good man, Cloyd, I'm glad to have you working my fields."

Rubbing two fingers along his nose, Cloyd stared quizzically at James Henry.

"But Cloyd, we've got a little problem."

"Oh? What's that, Boss?"

"I guess you know how I feel about Henny seeing your girl."

"Yeah, Boss, you made your feelin's pretty well known."

"It's not that I've got anything against your girl. It's just that I have other plans for my boy. You can understand that."

"Yes, sir, I understand all right." Cloyd scratched his arm slowly, methodically.

"Good. I knew you would. That Henny's a stubborn fool; won't listen to reason. You talk to your girl. Explain how it is. If she thinks so highly of Henny, she won't want to cause him any grief."

Cloyd concentrated on the ground. "They seem to be right fond of each other."

"Henny's young. He doesn't know what he wants. There'll be a lot of women before he's ready to settle down."

"Mebbe so, mebbe so." Cloyd wiped sweat dripping off his nose with his sleeve and looked out across the cane field.

"Got to sow his wild oats." James Henry nudged Cloyd with his elbow. "Know what I mean?"

Cloyd nodded, but didn't return James Henry's smile.

"It's better if we don't let this get too serious. Don't you agree?"

"Well," Cloyd repositioned his cud. "I think it's already got pretty serious. Beth says they're gittin' married. She's knocked up, ya know."

"We can take care of that. We can't let them marry, now can we?"

"I don't see as there's much we can do to stop 'em." Cloyd spit tobacco juice and shifted his cud. "They're of age; don't need our permission. Nothin' we kin do about it."

"There's something that can be done about anything if we put our minds to it."

Cloyd look up warily from under the brim of his sweat-stained straw hat. "Wadda ya got in mind?"

"Well, you wouldn't be able to go on working here on the harvester if they were to get married, now would you?"

"What's that got to do with —?"

Cloyd's voice trailed off as he realized what James Henry had implied.

"No, it wouldn't be right for James Henry the Fourth's father-in-law to be driving a harvester out here with the field hands, now would it?"

Cloyd ground the heel of his boot into the hard earth. "But where would I go? I worked here 'bout twenty-five years. I'm most too old to go anywhere else now. They wouldn't take me on."

"You just see that my boy comes to his senses, and we won't have to worry about that, will we?"

"Guess not." Cloyd's shoulders sagged.

"Of course not. You just talk some sense into your girl. She wouldn't want her father to lose his job, not after all these years, with his pension coming up and all. Maybe even a bonus. You and Cora talk to her. All right?"

Cloyd nodded, eyes downcast.

"All right?"

Cloyd grunted and spat. "Yeah, I'll see what I kin do."

"You see that the problem is eliminated. It will be better all around."

Cloyd opened his mouth to protest, but thought better of it. "Yes, sir," he replied.

"Good. I'm glad we're of like mind."

Cloyd nodded, tight-lipped.

"Well, I don't want to keep you from your work." James Henry slapped Cloyd on the back again and went back to his car, satisfied that he'd solved the problem.

Cloyd pulled on his work gloves and went back to the harvester. "Bastard," he muttered as he mounted the rig. *Wonder what he'd think if he knowed I'm already tryin' to stop 'em from marryin'. I don't want Beth married to no hot-headed weakling that cain't stand up to his promises, a kid what turns to alcohol and drugs to buck him up. What kinda life would Beth have in a family thinks she ain't good enough fer 'em? I'll do all I kin to put an end to it, but not because James Henry threatened me.*

Beth'll be a damn sight better off with Billy Bob Riley. They

growed up together, and he's man enough to stand up for her.
Wants to marry her even when she's got another man's
bastard in her belly. Yeah, I'll see to it that she marries Billy Bob,
all right. He threw the harvester into gear, eager to finish the
day's work so he could go home and talk to Beth and Cora.

James Henry, wanting to speak to Cora, sped along Sugarland
Highway between rows of ripening cane. He would make her
understand the ramifications if she allowed Beth to marry
Henny—she knew he could make her life a living hell if she
didn't go along with him. She had learned that lesson eighteen
years ago.

When he pulled up to the trailer, he saw Cora lumbering
across the lawn toward the hog pen dragging a large bucket,
strands of graying hair blowing across her lined face. She looked
back at James Henry's car, but she didn't stop or acknowledge
him. A small boy clung to her skirt, crying and swiping at his
runny nose with a dirty hand.

Cora glanced down at the boy, then called to an old crone
who sat in a rocker in front of the trailer rubbing panther oil on
arthritic knees. "Snot this kid, will you, Nanny?"

The old woman set the panther oil aside, picked up the hem
of her stained apron, and called, "Come here, boy."

The child ran to her and scrambled up into her lap. Nanny
wiped his nose with the hem of her apron, then settled back and
rocked him gently. He snuggled into her, comforted and content.

James Henry got out of the car and stood beside it. "Cora,"
he called. "Is Henny here?"

Cora glanced at him and moved on toward the hog pen.
"They ain't here. Him 'n' Beth left for Georgia to git married."

"What? Why the hell did you let her go? You know they
can't get married."

Cora proceeded to feed the hogs without responding.

James Henry wheeled around and ran back to the Lincoln.

He roared off in search of a phone to call the sheriff, but decided not to waste time. Instead he headed for the highway to Georgia. He wouldn't trust this to anyone else. He'd go after Henny himself.

"Dumb bastard," he muttered, as his tires hummed, eating up the distance between them. The long drive gave him time to think of his children and the mates they had chosen. He wondered what had happened between Mel and Jason. The marriage had seemed so solid. She sure did love the son of a gun, he thought as he clamped down on the accelerator, increasing his speed.

His lips softened when he thought of Sami and Jeff. *I was wrong about the little Jap. She's a good kid, and no one's ever been loved like she loves Jeff. He's one lucky man.*

When James Henry approached the Georgia border he spotted Henny's low-slung red Jaguar on the highway ahead of him. He pulled alongside and got a moment's satisfaction at the startled expressions on Henny and Beth's faces.

When Henny slowed in confusion, James Henry forced the Jag off the blacktop onto the shoulder.

Beth screamed and grabbed the dashboard to steady herself.

Henny regained his senses, gunned the motor, and maneuvered the Jag back onto the highway ahead of James Henry.

James Henry leaned on the horn and sped after him.

Henny's faster car gained ground, but when an oncoming truck drew even with a car in Henny's lane he slammed on the brakes, narrowly avoiding a crash.

James Henry took the opportunity to force him over, but not without denting both of their fenders.

Henny leaped from his car and ran to James Henry's open window. "What the hell do you think you're doing? You almost got us killed."

"That's just what I'm going to do if you don't turn that car around and get your ass back to Belle Glade."

Henny screamed, threw his arms into the air, and stomped the ground.

"Stop acting crazy, boy, and get in that car — now."

Henny crumpled and crawled back into his car. He turned the Jag around and headed back to Belle Glade, his father's car close behind.

He glanced at Beth, who sat silently, staring ahead. When she didn't respond to his tears or his harangue during the long ride back, he feared she had abandoned all thought of sharing life with him and his controlling father.

After the confrontation Beth refused to see him, so Henny slunk to his room, where he sulked, drank, and drugged. He didn't go to school for weeks, and didn't show up at the field office.

Finally, one afternoon when he needed drug money, he walked into the office as if nothing had happened. He went to his desk, did the pay sheets, entered the tonnage, and faxed the reports to the main office. That accomplished, he approached James Henry and asked for his paycheck.

James Henry stared into Henny's vacant eyes. "How the hell am I going to save you from self-destruction?" He reached to grasp Henny's arm, but he pulled away. "Let me take you to see Doc Johnson, son, he can help you."

Henny shuffled and glanced out the window, shutting off all communication.

Defeated, James Henry said nothing more. He paid Henny and waited to see what his next move would be.

CHAPTER 14

After another dinner without Henny, James Henry turned to Jeff. "Do you know where your brother is tonight?"

Jeff glanced at his mother. When she looked up expectantly he lowered his eyes. "No, Dad, I have no idea. Maybe he's having dinner with friends."

James Henry swallowed a scathing retort and said instead, "Well, at least I can depend on one of my sons. I really appreciate your staying here to help me out."

"Sami agreed we should stay until this business with the environmentalists is resolved."

James Henry scooped the last spoon of custard from the ramekin. "Put extra men in field seventeen tomorrow. I want to get that cane to the mill." He laid the spoon on the plate.

"Right."

When Berlinda started clearing the dessert dishes, Jeff folded his napkin and placed it to the left of his plate. He took Sami's hand, pulling her up with him.

" 'Cuse, please?" Sami bowed respectfully.

"Come," Grace said, rising. "We'll have our coffee on the portico."

"Not tonight, Mama, there's a program on TV that Sami and I want to watch. You and Dad go ahead."

"All right." Grace turned to James Henry expectantly.

"Uh, um, I can't. I have to go see one of the field bosses," he said, avoiding her eyes.

"I understand," Grace said. She picked up her demitasse and carried it out to the portico, where she stood at the rail for a few minutes, enjoying the chameleon colors of the evening sky reflected on the darkened pond. She watched three small brown ducks making their way cautiously around a long-necked white heron that stood knee-deep in the shallow pond.

Grace sighed deeply, turned, and sank into her wicker chair, resignation denting her forehead. A lone gull cruised overhead, beating the cloudless sky with black-tipped wings. Grace sipped demitasse, savoring the bitter taste, the heavy aroma. *I must help Henny*, she thought. *He's so headstrong, so stubborn. He won't accept losing Beth, I know it.*

As the sun melted into a cauldron of burning sky, Grace leaned back into the soft cushions, and continued to muse about Henny. *I should have seen to it that Henny married his Beth. How could I allow him to suffer so terribly?* She shut her eyes and fought her pain of losing Henny's child, her first grandchild.

I should have tried harder to influence James Henry. I should have helped Henny defy him. There was nothing James Henry could have done after they were married. He would have had to accept it. When they had the child, it would all have been resolved. No man, not even James Henry, could resist a grandchild. But she knew she was deceiving herself. For some reason unbeknown to her, James Henry was adamant that Henny would never marry Beth.

A lone owl hooted in the distance; evening breezes wafted the sweet fragrance of nicotiana across the broad portico.

Grace sighed, picked up the cup and saucer, and went into the house.

•   •   •

The next morning Grace waited in the kitchen until Henny came in for breakfast. She sat down at the table beside him, reached for his hand, and held it in hers. "Thank you for returning to school. You know how much it means to me for you to prepare for college."

Henny glanced up at her from beneath heavy lids. "Yeah," he muttered.

Grace, distressed by his shallow complexion, his sunken, empty eyes, his gaunt frame, asked, "Are you all right, Henny?"

"Yeah."

Grace patted his hand and turned to Berlinda, who poured his coffee. "Would you go over to the summer kitchen and start the strawberry jam?"

Berlinda looked from Henny to Grace. "Yes, Ma'am. Y'all want coffee, Miz Grace?"

"No, thank you."

Berlinda set the coffee pot back on the stove and left quickly.

Henny shifted uneasily and withdrew his hand.

"You can't go on like this, son. How can I help?"

Henny shoved scrambled eggs around his plate. "There's nothing you can do, Mama."

"Henny, look at me."

His eyes met hers for a moment, then he looked away.

"You must let me help you. Please let me take you to see Doc Johnson." She put her hand under his chin and lifted his face so their eyes met. "Please see Doc."

"There's nothing Doc can do to help me. Dad's the one who made Beth go away. What can Doc do about that?"

"Away? Where did she go?"

"I don't know." Henny stifled a sob.

Grace took his hand in hers and this time he left it there. "What happened? Tell me." Concern clouded her pale eyes.

Henny's words tumbled over each other as he released his torment, his frustration, his anger. "And now she's gone and I can't find her." He fell into his mother's arms and cried like a wounded animal.

Grace held him, stroked his back, and kissed his neck gently.

"No one will tell me where she is." Henny raised anguished eyes to hers.

"I'll find her, son," Grace said, her jaw rigid.

"How?"

"You just leave it to me. I'll find her."

Henny got up and went to the sink, where he splashed water on his eyes. He tore a paper towel from the roll and dried his face and hands while looking out the window, watching smoke from burning cane swirl across the lawn. He turned and went back to his mother, hugged her, and kissed her on the cheek. "I've got to go or I'll be late for school."

Grace watched him leave, then went to the library and sat down at her desk. She took an address book from the drawer, put on her glasses, looked up a number, and dialed.

"Hello. This is Mrs. Hampton. Is detective Daniel Calhoun in? No? Ask him to call me please. Yes. He has my number; he's worked for me before on a matter concerning my husband. As soon as possible, please."

Grace hung up and sat back. It was only a matter of time until Detective Calhoun would locate Beth.

Days later, when Grace went into the kitchen to give Henny the detective's findings, she found him arguing with Berlinda. Berlinda was trying to put French toast in front of him but he pushed it away. "I don't want it! Just give me coffee," he insisted sullenly.

Berlinda turned to Grace in frustration. "Dis boy won't eat nuthin'. Jes drink all night and lay in bed till noon —"

"Berlinda," Grace interrupted, "please go to the summer kitchen and put the jam away."

"I a'ready done that yester —" She looked from Grace to Henny. "Yes, ma'am."

After Berlinda left, Grace sat down beside Henny and put her arm around his shoulders.

"Did you find her?"

"Yes, I did."

Henny's eyes came alive for the first time in weeks.

"Well — where is she? Is she okay? How did she look?" He searched Grace's face for answers.

"Oh, my poor baby, I don't know how to say this." Tears welled in Grace's eyes and ran down her cheeks.

"What? What is it? Did Dad do something to her?"

"No, she's all right — she's, she's . . . married.

"Married? I'll kill him. I'll kill the bastard. How did Dad make her get married? Who did she marry? What about my baby?"

Grace picked up his hand and stroked it. "It's a terrible thing your father's done. He meant well, but —"

Henny pulled his hand away. "How the hell —?"

"James Henry threatened to fire Cloyd if you two got married. Beth couldn't let that happen. Where would they go? What would they do? Cloyd has worked for your father all his life; he's too old to get another job driving a harvester — a pension."

"That's no excuse. How could she?" Henny crashed around the kitchen, wild with frustration and anger.

Grace winced as Grandma's cookie jar hit the tile floor and smashed. She reached out, trying to calm him. "Beth did what she thought was right, you must believe that. She thought you'd be estranged from your family if you two married." She tried to hold him, but he broke away. "Beth didn't want to cause that. She loves you too much to hurt you."

"Are you crazy? Is she nuts? She married someone else so she wouldn't hurt me? I'm not hearing this. I'm . . . I'm . . . that bastard, he did this to me. I'll kill him, I swear I will." Henny rampaged through the kitchen, knocking over chairs, smashing dishes that he grabbed from the drainer on the sink.

Grace, frightened by his anger, set a chair upright between them and grasped the back. "Please, son, your father thought he was doing what was best for you."

"Best for me? Some other man has the woman I love and my baby, and he thought that would be best for me?"

"Please, son, try to understand. Your fath—"

"How could the bastard do this? To his own son—his grandson?"

"He meant well. He loves you."

"Loves me? He destroys my life because he loves me?"

"He thought it would be best for—"

"For him! That's all he cares about. Everything has to be his way."

Grace set the chair aside and tried to put her arms around Henny, but he tore away.

"And her—how could she do this?"

"She had to think of the baby."

"My baby," Henny shouted. "That's my baby. She has no right—"

"Sit down, son, please. We'll talk calmly about it."

"Where is she?"

"I'm sorry, I can't tell you that. I had to promise her that I wouldn't tell you or she wouldn't see me."

"You have to tell me. I'll go get her. Is she all right?"

"Yes, she's fine."

"Well. Where is she?"

Grace began to crying. "I promised her. I can't tell you."

Henny knelt on the floor in front of her and took her hands in his. "Please, Mama, please tell me where she is."

"I can't, son. I gave my word. It's too late — she's married."

Henny jumped to his feet. "I don't care if she is. I love her. She's carrying my baby." He grabbed Grace's arm and spun her around. When she winced he released her. "Oh, Mama, I'm sorry. I'm so sorry." Henny began to sob. "I'm sorry, I'm sorry, I'm sorry." He pulled her to him and stroked the ugly red welts his fingers had made on the pale flesh of her arm. He turned away and beat the table with his fists. "I'm sorry!" he screamed as he wheeled around and smashed the screen door open. He ran to his car in the driveway, jumped in, and sped away.

Grace watched him leave, then she ran to the library and called Detective Calhoun. "Henny just drove away. Find him and stay with him. He's wild with anger. Don't let him out of your sight until he calms down. Hurry, please!"

She slumped into the chair beside the desk, exhausted from fear, anguish, and frustration. She focused on the gold band on her finger and tried to wrench it from her hand. Her knuckle turned white, then red, as she struggled to be free of it.

CHAPTER 15

Midmorning sun poured through four tall windows in the dining room, warming Grace's back. She looked across to Henny's empty chair. At the slightest sound she straightened and looked expectantly toward the door. He would miss Sunday brunch with his family again.

Berlinda served a strawberry topped waffle to Grace, but when she set Sami's portion in front of her, Sami turned away. Berlinda leaned back and surveyed the girl quizzically. "You sick, Miss Sami? Strawberry waffles your favorite." Then Berlinda brightened, a glow of revelation crossing her face. "You pregnant, ain't you, girl?"

Sami lowered her eyes.

Grace gasped. "Berlinda!" She held a finger to her lips, admonishing her to be silent. "Serve the coffee, please."

Berlinda went to the sideboard chuckling. "Well don't that beat all — a baby in Hampton House after all these years." She lifted the silver coffeepot from the tray and carried it to the table. She served Sami first and patted her shoulder affectionately. "I got some ginger root in the pantry. I'll fix you some tea right now. Take away that queasy feelin'."

Smiling broadly, Berlinda poured coffee all around. "Imagine that, Miss Sami goin' to have a baby. I do declare!" She disappeared into the kitchen to replenish the platter of waffles.

Grace suspected, but she never would have asked.

Jeff reached for Sami's hand, and she glanced up at him, her face ashen.

Grace said, "You may be excused, dear. Why don't you go out and sit on the porch until we finish breakfast?"

Sami scrambled to her feet. "Oh, thank you, Mama Grace, thank you." With a grateful bow she retreated.

Jeff called after her, "I'll be out in a few minutes, honey". He cut into the strawberry-covered waffle. "So much for the formal announcement we had planned. Sami felt shy about it, so we thought we'd wait a few months before mentioning her pregnancy, but we reckoned without sly old Berlinda."

"Good work, son," James Henry said. "We can use another hand around here."

Jeff flinched; his brow tightened.

Grace sipped coffee from a porcelain cup. "If you'd like, I'll take Sami to see Doc Johnson in the morning."

"Thanks, Mama. I'd appreciate that." Jeff devoured the last of the strawberries on his plate.

James Henry yelled toward the kitchen, "Berlinda! Bring more of those waffles, my son is eating for two now." His surprise had been replaced by a smile that stretched to the corners of his face. "My first grandson," he mused.

Grace winced. How could he ignore Henny's child? Was it because he didn't want her lover's grandchild to inherit Hampton Plantation? She quickly dismissed the thought. James Henry seemed to have driven the knowledge of Henny's parentage from his mind. But how was that possible?

James Henry's laughter jolted her from her reverie. "When that baby arrives we'll have the biggest damn celebration we've ever had around here."

Grace tapped the corner of the linen napkin to her lips and got up. "I'll call Melisandra and tell her about the baby. She'll be so happy for you."

"Yeah," Jeff said. "Tell her to buy a godmother dress. The first thing she'll think about is what to wear to the christening."

Grace laughed, went to the library phone, and dialed. When she heard Mel's voice she said, "Guess what? Jeff and Sami are going to have a baby!"

Mel squealed. "Oh, that's fabulous. How wonderful. I'll bet they're excited."

"They want you to be the baby's godmother."

"Egad, what does a godmother wear to a christening?"

Grace smiled. "Jeff said that would be your first concern."

While the women talked, James Henry and Jeff walked out to the portico. James Henry leaned against a column and gazed toward the pond, where cattails swayed in the soft breeze like inverted pendulums. A duck, followed by three ducklings, swam across the still water, leaving a shimmering wake.

Jeff dropped into a wicker chair next to the one in which Sami huddled, and took her hand in his. "Feeling better?"

Sami looked into his eyes beseechingly. "When can we go back to Japan?"

James Henry snapped to attention. "Now hold on. No need for that. We've been having babies here for quite a while. Got it down pretty good by now."

"But we only came for two weeks," Sami said petulantly, "and—"

"I know, I know. It was damn good of you to stay so Jeff could help me out with the environmentalists, but the baby should be born on the plantation like his daddy before him. You can't leave before the little fellow's born."

"The only Japanese baby in all of Florida?" Sami appealed to Jeff for support.

"You're way too late for that," James Henry said. "Couple of dozen Japanese settled here shortly after the turn of the century. Worked a portion of Flagler's Model Land Company over in Boca Raton. Called their section the Yamato Colony. Went all the way from 51st Street in Boca to the Delray Beach border."

Sami brightened. "Yamato is the ancient name for Japan," she said, excitement lighting her dark eyes and enhancing her accent.

"About 1905–1906, I believe it was. A fellow named George Sukeji Morikami tried to start a Japanese agricultural community, but it didn't take. The colony fizzled, but Morikami stayed anyway. He started a produce shipping business. Smart fellow. Invested in real estate and wound up with a thousand acres and well over a million dollars."

"A million dollars?" Sami sat up straight and riveted full attention on James Henry. "He's some rich man!"

"He became an American citizen in the 1960s, then he died about ten years later. But before he died, he deeded most of his land to the state and county. They built the Morikami Museum and Japanese Gardens on 155 acres of his holdings."

Sami jumped to her feet and stood in front of Jeff. "Why did you not tell me? Why didn't you not take me there?"

"Sorry, honey, guess I forgot about the place."

"You will take me?"

"Sure."

"When?"

"Soon."

"Tomorrow?"

"Next Sunday, all right?"

"Yes, we'll go then." She hugged Jeff, then stepped back quickly, glancing self-consciously at James Henry.

He laughed. "Go ahead, snuggle up. You've got the license."

Sami enjoyed an eventful week. Grace took her to see Doc Johnson, who confirmed her pregnancy and found her to be in excellent health. Jeff took her to the Morikami Museum, as promised, and she returned flushed with excitement.

Sami found Grace in the morning room, leafing through a

magazine, her short blonde hair brightened by sun gleaming through tall windows. Sami dropped to the sofa beside her. "Oh, Mama Grace, going to the Morikami Gardens was almost like going home. Katsura Villa is like the Imperial retreat, *Sumi-e* ink paintings, *Ikenobo* flower arrangements, *Origami*—oh, such fun! Jeff promised to take me again in February—if we're still here—for *Oshogatsu*, Japanese New Year. We'll see *odori-zome*, first dance, *hatsuike*, first flower arrangement, first tea ceremony of the year—"

Grace hugged Sami affectionately, grateful to see her happy and content.

"In August, they have *Bon* Festival, All Souls Day, when they welcome back souls of departed. They have drumming by the *Soh Daiko* group, folk dancing, a candlelighting ceremony."

"I remember that. I saw it when our garden club visited the park. It was very beautiful. They called it the 'Candles of Greeting,' I believe."

"Yes, Mama Grace, you're right. Performers from the Kabuki Theater entertain. When it's all over, they float paper lanterns in the pond to guide George Morikami's spirit back. Jeff promised that we'll go to festival in August if we're still here. I can take the baby—show him Japanese customs on boy's day." She giggled behind her hand. "Or maybe girl's day."

Grace made a mental note to be sure that Sami never missed taking the baby to events at the Morikami Museum. He should know his heritage, she thought, as she brushed Sami's dark hair back off her shoulder. "Japan has a rich culture," she remarked tenderly. She laid the magazine aside, thinking that perhaps Sami and Jeff would remain in Belle Glade after all.

CHAPTER 16

When Sami awoke, she reached out to touch Jeff, but he had already left for the field office. She lay in the big, carved-walnut bed, staring up at the twenty-foot dome, thinking of waking in their home in Japan on a *tatami* mat under a low, rice-papered ceiling.

She picked up the small clock on the nightstand and checked the time. Eight o'clock. Before eight o'clock in Japan, her mother would have arranged fresh flowers and placed them in the *tokonoma*. Grace's love of flowers reminded her of her mother, and it was one of the things that endeared Grace to her.

Papa Jim seems to like me more now, she mused, *but Mama Grace still likes me better. I know!* She sat up in bed. *I'll make sushi for Papa Jim. He'll like that.* Sami jumped out of bed, hurried to dress, and ran down to the kitchen.

"Berlinda, Berlinda!" she called, as she burst through the kitchen door.

"Heaven's sake, Miss Sami, what is it?"

"Will you help me prepare sushi for Mr. Jim?"

"Why certainly, chile. I be happy to." Berlinda positioned hands on her hips and scowled. "What's sushi?"

"I'll show you. We need fish. Fresh! Must be fresh."

"What kinda fish?"

"What does Mr. Jim like? Does he like salmon? Perch? Eel? Does he like eel?"

Berlinda's eyes crinkled in concentration and her brow wrinkled as she tried to imagine James Henry eating eel. "I don't rightly know if Mr. Jim eat eel," she said dubiously. "How you fix eel, anyway, you fry it?"

"No! No." Sami's eyes widened with horror. "Sushi raw fish."

"Oh, I don' think Mr. Jim eat no raw fish," Berlinda responded warily.

"He'll like this," Sami said. "Sushi is delicious. Oh, and seaweed. We need seaweed."

"I dunno, I don' think Mr. Jim —"

"And cucumbers. Must be crisp!"

Berlinda shook her head and stroked her cheek as Sami prattled on. By cocktail time, Berlinda had managed to obtain the ingredients, including several varieties of fresh fish suitable for sushi, and Sami had lovingly created an artistic array of delectables.

When James Henry relaxed in his recliner in the library, enjoying his before-dinner cocktail, Sami called for Jeff and Grace to join him. Then she brought in the tray of sushi and presented it proudly to James Henry. "For you, Papa Jim." She bowed respectfully.

"How nice," Grace said, peering over Sami's shoulder.

James Henry, pleased by the beautiful presentation, asked, "What's this?"

"Sushi, Papa Jim. I made it just for you."

Jeff watched, bemused, awaiting his father's reaction.

James Henry selected one of the beautifully sculpted pink rosebuds and put it in his mouth. He began to chew, then grimaced and spit it into a napkin. "What the devil is it? It tastes like raw fish."

"It is raw fish," Sami said uncertainly. "Salmon."

"Raw salmon! You must be kidding." He wiped his mouth with another napkin. "You don't eat that, do you?"

The shine left Sami's eyes.

Jeff reached to select one of the beautifully wrapped slices of pike and placed it in his mouth. "Ummm, delicious. Try another, Dad, it's an acquired taste. Sami has a real touch with sushi."

Sami held the tray out to James Henry.

"Ill be damned if I'll eat fish bait." He stood abruptly, and stalked off toward the dining room.

"He still doesn't like me," Sami said dejectedly, setting the tray on the coffee table.

Jeff popped a pinwheel of cucumber, eel, and seaweed into his mouth. "Of course he likes you; he's just not used to eating raw fish."

Grace reached toward the tray. "Let me try some, Sami. It looks delicious." Grace set a piece of perch on her tongue and chewed tentatively. She tried to disguise her revulsion to the unaccustomed taste. "Oh, my, that is different." She drew her mouth into what she hoped was a smile.

Sami bowed happily, perceiving Grace's comment to be a compliment.

Berlinda saved the day by announcing dinner.

The three went in to join James Henry, who was already seated at the head of the table.

Several days later, when Jeff walked toward the driveway, he saw his mother out by the potting shed planting a giant urn with begonias. Grace wiped the perspiration from her forehead with the back of a gloved hand and waved to him.

"Mom, there you are. What are you doing out here in this heat? Come in the house before you keel over. I want to talk to you about Henny."

"In a minute, I'm almost finished here. We do need to talk about Henny. I'm hoping you will spend time with your brother. I thought maybe Doc Johnson —"

"That's what I want to talk to you about. I tried to get Henny to go to Doc, and when he wouldn't, I arranged for Doc to meet him 'accidentally' in town. Doc tried to talk to him, to get him into treatment, but Henny jumped in his Jag and zoomed off. He wouldn't listen to Doc either."

Grace tamped the pot and laid the trowel on the bench. "Maybe you could speak to him after dinner tonight — if he comes home."

"Every time I try to talk to him, he just starts yelling, 'What do you know? Dad didn't take away the woman you love. You have Sami. You don't know what it's like to lose your wife and your baby.' Before I have a chance to respond, he runs out."

Grace turned away from her work. "I guess seeing you with Sami is an affront. I didn't realize how hard it would be for him to see you two together after he lost Beth. The poor child drinks because he is desperately trying to forget."

"I understand that he took the loss hard, but we've got to get him off drugs and booze before he kills himself. Why doesn't Dad take his car away?"

"He did, but Sheriff Ratch caught Henny trying to steal a car from the parking lot at a bar. There just doesn't seem to be any way to control him. Maybe if you spent more time with him —"

"He won't; he avoids me. Maybe we should take legal action to have him committed for treatment."

"Oh, Jeffrey! The stigma! You know James Henry would never agree to that. No, we must deal with Henny ourselves, but I'm at my wit's end. I can't think what to do."

"We've got to do something, and soon. I'm really worried about that kid."

Grace picked up a potted begonia, turned it over, nudged it

out of the pot, and placed it in the urn. "If you only knew how I worry about that child. I lie awake every night, begging God to show me how to help him." She tapped the pot to settle the soil around the roots. "We'll catch Henny in the morning. Tell your father that you won't be working, but don't tell him why."

"Dad will demand an explanation. You know how he is."

Grace placed the last plant in the urn and stepped back to survey the mass of leaves and blossoms.

Jeff strained to lift the large urn. "Where do you want this?"

"Over there by the door. Sami admired the begonias out by the post, so I thought I'd pot some and put them where she could see them more often."

"That's a nice thought, but you should have had one of the men do the potting."

"Sami is so appreciative of everything I do for her that it makes me want to do more and more. Now that she's pregnant I want everything to be perfect for her."

"I knew you two would hit it off." Jeff carried the pot to the door and set it down. "Here?"

"A little to the right, I think, so we don't trip over it."

Grace took off her gardening gloves, and she and Jeff walked across the lawn to a wrought iron table and chairs shaded by a gnarled pin oak.

When Berlinda came out to shake a rug, Grace called to her. "Bring some iced tea, will you please, Berlinda? It will cool us off."

Jeff added, "And some of your industrial-strength brownies." He turned to Grace and noticed tears in her eyes. He patted her hand and, to divert her from thoughts of Henny, he said, "I'll go see if Sami is up from her nap. She'd enjoy joining us for a snack."

Grace watched Jeff dodge the water sprinklers as he ran across the lawn toward the back door. *He's such a fine young man*, she thought, *if only Henny were more like Jeff.* She rubbed her head, as if massaging away unwanted thoughts, then she called to Berlinda again, "Three glasses, Berlinda, Sami will be joining us."

"Yes, ma'am," Berlinda's voice echoed across the lawn. "I'm a fixin' it."

Grace leaned back in the lawn chair, thinking about Henny and hoping that having his brother home would change his mind-set. But now that Sami was pregnant, it festered his wound to see them together and happily awaiting the birth of their baby. She sighed in resignation, knowing deep in her heart that there was little she could do.

When she thought of Sami and Jeff returning to Japan, the realization of being separated from another grandchild sickened her. She would spend time with Sami, bond with her, so she would want to visit often. Pleased that Jeff had stayed to help his father, she feared that they'd be leaving as soon as the crisis passed. She would miss seeing yet another grandchild develop and grow.

Perhaps Jeff and Sami will decide to stay in Belle Glade, she thought, but then she dismissed the idea as wishful thinking. Their time in Belle Glade would be short. She pulled a white linen handkerchief from the pocket of her smock and patted perspiration from her face.

Jeff returned and dropped into the chair across from Grace. "Sami will be here in a minute."

"I'm going to give a party for you two," Grace said. "You can renew acquaintance with old friends like Ronnie and Pam. They'll love Samiko. It will be nice for her to make some friends of her own age while she's here."

"Great idea, Mama. Does Betsy still live here? Sami would love Betsy."

"Your old girlfriend?" Grace feigned shock.

"She was never a girlfriend, just a good buddy. Sami would

like her for the same reasons I did: great sense of humor, loyal, bright."

Sami came running across the lawn, long black hair shining in the midmorning sun as it swayed across her shoulders. She stopped in front of Grace and bowed slightly. "Mama Grace."

"Come, join us for tea and brownies. Berlinda will bring them out in a moment."

Grace took Sami's hand and guided her to the chair next to hers.

"What are brownies?"

"Probably the best thing in the American culture. Wait until you taste them." Jeff turned to his mother. "Do you have any idea how much cake the Japanese eat?"

"No," Grace said, "I didn't think the Japanese ate sweets."

"Oh, yes! We take little cakes whenever we go to visit. We eat cakes every afternoon. Japanese love sweets." She licked her lips in fond remembrance.

"What did you want to tell us about Mel?" Jeff asked.

"Oh, yes, I got a letter from her this morning. She's having the most marvelous time in Monaco. She and Caroline play tennis every morning, and they're going to the ballet tonight."

"My sister, the princess." Jeff nudged Sami and snickered.

"I wonder if we'll still be here when she gets back. I'd like to hear about her trip."

Jeff scowled. "I hope we're back home by then. I want to get back to my job before they can me. There aren't that many jobs in Japan for an American photojournalist."

The screen door slammed behind Berlinda, and she lumbered across the lawn to the old oak. She set iced tea and brownies on the table, then stepped back and surveyed the three of them disapprovingly. "Don't y'all eat too much. You'll spoil you lunch."

"We'll make brownies our lunch."

"No sir, you won't, Mr. Jeff. I'm makin' heart o' palm and

conch salad for Miss Sami, and I'm servin' it in avocados I picked out back in the grove. Conch come up fresh from Key West this morning."

Jeff beamed at Sami. "You've made another conquest, honey. Berlinda doesn't pull out all the stops for everyone."

Sami giggled shyly. "Thank you, Berlinda."

"You sure is welcome, Miss Sami." Berlinda turned and trudged back toward the house.

Jeff picked up a brownie and held it for Sami to take a bite. "It doesn't get any better than this," he said.

But it would get a lot worse, and very soon.

CHAPTER 17

When James Henry walked into La Vonda's Café a little after eight o'clock, he recoiled from music blaring from the jukebox. He shoved his way to the bar through the early evening crush, and squeezed between two occupied stools.

Chip said, "You're late. We thought you wasn't comin'."

"Had some trouble with the environmentalists. They sure are causing problems."

"What now?" Chip set a cold brew in front of James Henry.

"It's worse than I expected. They're busing kids in from New College in Sarasota to join the protest, and they're parading around with signs. When one of our trucks tries to enter the road to the mill, they lie down in the road and stop it. Television news is milking it for all it's worth. I went out there a while ago to try to cool things down, but the TV crews had the kids worked into a frenzy. They were taking pictures of deputies dragging kids out of the road. I told Otis to call his deputies off until the TV crews leave."

"Yeah, best to let it cool down." Chip pulled a pack of Camels from his shirt pocket and lit one. "Finish your beer, and as soon as the relief bartender gets here we'll start the game. Some of the guys are here — Harley will be over later."

James Henry took a long gulp of the beer and set it aside

before glancing up at the TV over the bar. Sheriff Ratch was throwing a blanket over a body beside the road.

Color drained from James Henry's face. He bellowed, "Turn the TV up, Chip!"

Chip spun around and adjusted the volume, then stepped back to watch.

"— college girl, believed to be from New College in Sarasota." The newscaster continued, "She was found dead near the sugar mill on Route 27. She may have been killed by a truck from the Hampton Sugar Plantation."

"Holy shit! One of the picketers!" James Henry spun away from the bar, knocking his glass over, and ran to the door. Shells scattered across the lot as he zoomed out, speeding toward the accident.

He caught up with an ambulance, siren wailing, and followed it until it pulled up to a group of police cars with red lights flashing. Official vehicles cluttered the scene and TV lights turned night to day.

James Henry leaped from his car and ran to the blanket-shrouded form. He dropped to his knees beside the body, pulled the blanket back, and looked into the face of a young girl. His breath caught in his throat and he swallowed hard. He bowed his head, and remained motionless for several seconds before TV newsmen recognized him and ran over to shove microphones in his face.

"Did your driver kill this girl?"

"Is one of your trucks responsible for this accident?"

"Why are you polluting the Everglades?"

James Henry struggled to his feet and shoved them back. He yelled to the sheriff, "Get these people off me, Otis."

Sheriff Ratch and two deputies ran over and herded the news crew back. A siren screamed as a sheriff's car careened in, braking to a stop where the picketers huddled.

James Henry walked quickly to the driver of his truck, a tall burly man who talked animatedly to a deputy. The driver wiped his ashen face with trembling hands.

"That's all," James Henry said to the official. "No more talking until I get my lawyer out here."

The deputy nodded and walked away, aware that James Henry's word was law in these parts.

The driver turned panic-stricken eyes to James Henry. "I don't know what happened. I never saw her. I didn't hit her — I woulda felt it. First I seen of her was in my rearview mirror. The Mex was screamin' that a girl was hit. I looked in my mirror and I seen her layin' there beside the road. I slammed on my brakes and ran back to where she was, but she was deader 'n roadkill. Oh, Lord, I don't know, I just don't know how it coulda happened." He turned away and rubbed ghost-white hands over wet eyes.

James Henry grabbed the driver's arm and spun him around. "Level with me, Jace, did you hit that girl?"

"No, no, no," the driver wailed.

James Henry studied the weeping man for a moment, then said, "Okay, Jace, but keep your mouth shut. Don't talk to anyone until I get a lawyer."

The driver nodded, brushed tears from quivering cheeks, and reached into his pocket for a cigarette. Fingers shaking, he lit it, and drew in the smoke. He closed his eyes and exhaled slowly, finding a measure of comfort.

James Henry looked over the crowd, then strode to a second of his trucks that was parked off the shoulder behind a police car. The driver slouched behind the wheel, glancing about furtively.

Did you see it, Leon?" James Henry asked.

"Nope. I sure didn't. Didn't see nuthin' a'tall." Leon lifted a worn red peak cap and smoothed sun-streaked hair. "I was takin' this here load to the mill, watchin' out for pickets that was along the road earlier, and I didn't see nobody till I rounded that bend back there. Then I seen them all kneelin' beside the road. I didn't know what the hell was a goin' on."

"Did you see Jace?"

"Yeah. He was off to one side, over there." He pointed a calloused finger toward the opposite shoulder.

"Did you get out of the truck?"

"No, I sure didn't. Thought it might be some kinda trick. I jes set here and watched 'em, see what they was up to. Then this kid, a Mex, he comes runnin' back here sayin' one of our trucks run down a girl. Jace's truck was already parked off to one side there, so I thought maybe he hit her."

"I left orders to hold the trucks tonight. What the hell are you doing out here anyway?"

"Henny said to get the sugar to the mill. Said it was your orders."

James Henry spun away from the truck, breathing hard, and muttering, "Why won't that brat follow orders? Just once, I wish he'd do as he's told. Why the hell would he send these trucks out here tonight?"

Sirens screamed as the ambulance carrying the girl's body pulled away, speeding down Sugarland Highway toward town.

A TV newsman came up behind James Henry, reached around, and stuck a microphone in his face. James Henry reeled around, shoved the mike away, and walked to where Sheriff Ratch questioned an onlooker. He pulled him aside. "What the hell happened here, Otis?"

"Looks like vehicular homicide, but I won't know for sure till I complete the investigation and I get the autopsy report."

"Who is she — the dead girl?"

"Picket. Looks like she mighta been hit by one of your trucks."

"What the hell makes you think that?"

"Your driver says a Mexican kid jumped up on the step on

the passenger side. He looked over at him, and the next thing he knew the kids were all screaming that a girl had been hit. Maybe he hit her when he was lookin' at the Mex."

James Henry bit down hard on the stump of cigar between his teeth and scowled. "What do you intend to do about this, Otis?"

"Have to interview all these kids, autopsy the body, get to the bottom of it. Jace says he didn't hit her, and she was already dead when Leon pulled up, so I don't rightly know that's goin' on. I'll keep you clued in, though." When one of his deputies called to him, he turned and hurried away.

James Henry went back to Jace. "You sure you didn't hit that girl?"

"Honest, Boss, I swear. I'd tell you right off if I did. I couldn't of. I woulda heard somethin' or felt somethin'."

James Henry clasped his sagging shoulder. "All right."

He walked back to a police car and had the deputy get Steve on the phone. When he told him what happened, Steve said, "I'll be right there, Jim."

James Henry handed the phone back to the deputy, and made his way through the crowd to where Sheriff Ratch and the coroner were talking. "What is it? What do you think happened?"

Otis stuck thumbs in his belt, reared back, and said, "He thinks she was hit somewhere else and dumped here to make it look like one of your trucks hit her."

"Can he prove that?"

"Probably."

"Good."

James Henry sat in the Lincoln until Steve pulled up in his blue pickup. Steve jumped out and ran to James Henry. "You okay, Jim?"

"Yeah, I'm okay, but somebody is trying to pull a fast one." He filled Steve in on what Jace, Leon, and Otis told him, then he said, "Go down to the TV station and talk to Vic. Tell him to get the facts from Otis here before he puts a lot of crap out over the air — and tell him to leave our trucks out of it."

"You got it." Steve leaped into his truck and sped off.

The incident got a lot of media coverage. The dead girl's parents came down from New York to try to find out what happened, but the environmentalists had all left town as soon as it was discovered that the body had been moved.

James Henry and Grace met with the parents to offer condolences and try to console them, but it was an awkward meeting. They didn't know what to say to each other, and Grace realized their sincere words sounded hollow.

No one in Belle Glade seemed to know where the girl had been hit or by whom, so there wasn't a lot Sheriff Ratch could do. He came by the office to tell James Henry what little he knew. "Probably a casualty of Route 27," he said. "A hit and run. We get 'em from time to time. Somebody saw a way to use the accident. Thought us rednecks would be too dumb to see through it. It happens."

Sheriff Ratch didn't close the file on the case, but after a few weeks when there were no new clues, the story faded from the news.

It would soon be replaced by a greater tragedy for the Hamptons.

CHAPTER 18

James Henry studied the thermometer outside the window and muttered, "Still dropping. If this keeps up we'll lose half the crop in the outlying fields."

Henny glowered at the rough-hewn cedar walls, scarred floor planking, and ash spattered, small-paned windows of the field office. He threw his pencil on his desk and swung toward James Henry. "You let Mel run all over the friggin' world, but you keep me here in this stinking shanty through the whole cane season. It's not fair!"

James Henry glared at him across the room. "Shut up about it before I decide to throw you off the gravy train."

"You just say the word and I'm outta here."

"You thinking I'd miss you?"

"Oh, you'd miss me all right. You'd be here checking out the pay sheets with the supervisors, instead of over to Vonda's getting laid."

"You shut your filthy mouth. Have a little respect."

Henny sneered. "That's a laugh. Respect for who? For my father who's out whoring or for the whore?"

"Vonda's no whore. We've been friends since we were in high school."

"She's friends with you and every other guy in Belle Glade."

James Henry ground his cigar between clamped teeth and

swung away from the thermometer. A red flush spread up from
the collar of his khaki shirt.

Henny grinned. "You can dish it out, but you can't take it."

Without responding, James Henry grabbed his jacket, and
headed for the door. He jogged to his car, zipping his jacket
against the February chill, and drove to the north field. If he
acted quickly, he might save most of the crop.

Henny watched his father leave before picking up the
phone to dial. "Sledge? It's Henny. You got any? I need it bad.
Yeah, bring it over. He's not here. Hurry up." He slammed the
receiver down and went outside to wait for the drug dealer.

Henny paced up and down in front of the field office, oblivious to the stench of the burning cane and the crazed egrets that
dove into the towering flames. He squinted down the road
between long rows of burning cane, searching for his savior —
his executioner.

A chill crawled up his back and spread to his arms and
legs. He wrapped twitching arms around his shoulders, trying to
still the shaking. Despite the cold, sweat gathered on his forehead. He screamed into the smoke, "Where the hell is the son
of a bitch?" He kicked the cold, dry earth; dust settled on his
sneakers. With shaking fingers he swiped moisture from his
nose.

He strained toward a sound in the distance and watched
expectantly as a long white Cadillac appeared through the
smoke on the horizon. It hurtled toward him, carrying the
contraband he so desperately needed. Henny probed his pockets
for money, and counted out five twenties. He folded them and
crushed them in his trembling hand.

Sledge braked and skidded to a stop beside him.

Henny scurried to the driver's side and thrust the hundred
dollars through the window.

"You in bad shape, brother." Sledge passed the coke to

Henny, threw the car in reverse, and powered off in a cloud of black muck.

Henny mounted the steps to the office two at a time. He hurried to the bathroom, opened the packet with shaking hands, and spread cocaine on a small mirror. He separated it into lines with a razor blade, then pulled a short straw from his pocket and snorted a long line. He tilted his head back and held his nose, experiencing the rush.

At the same time, James Henry arrived at the northern sand field that was usually hit by any drop in temperature. The white tops of the cane confirmed a freeze, but it could have been worse; like the freeze of 1894–1895 that wiped out a hundred million dollars worth of truck farms in a single night. He got out of the Lincoln to take a closer look.

Pleased to see that the freeze hadn't been too severe this time, James Henry mused: If the cutters are careful where they make the cut, they can avoid clogging the processing machines with waste.

When the cane rustled, he looked up to see Steve coming toward him through the stalks. "Oh, hi, Steve. It's not too bad, only the tops are frozen. We'll have time to get it to the mill and process it before it rots. It will yield nearly a ton an acre more than Crystalina and Demarara. Back in the 1930s, this whole field would have been wiped out, but this new strain developed in the '40s can take the cold."

Steve nodded and jammed fists into his pockets. "Bad news, Jim. The union is trying to get the cutters to walk out today."

"Not today!" James Henry cursed and looked over the white-tipped cane. "We'll lose this whole field if we don't get it to the mill right away."

"Yeah." Steve surveyed the damage. "We gotta act fast."

"You get the cutters. Get the best men, the ones they call

Jazzman and Sugar Baby, and get Blinkey, too. You know the
ones. I'll go back to the field office and alert the mill that we
have frozen cane coming in. I'll tell Jeff to get the mechanical
harvesters rolling on the sand acreage."

"Right." Steve turned and ran back through the wilting
cane.

James Henry raced back to the office, aware that the longer
the cane stayed in the field, the less sugar they'd realize.

"Henny," he yelled, as he burst into the office. "Henny!
Where the hell are you?"

Henny, jolted from his drugged reverie, panicked. "Just a
minute, Dad, I'm in the bathroom."

"Again? What the hell's the matter with you, boy? You got
prostate trouble already?"

"No, Dad, I'll be out in a minute." Henny glanced around to
be sure all evidence of his cocaine use was eliminated. Satisfied,
he opened the door and stepped out to face his father.

James Henry, too preoccupied to notice his son's shaking
hands, said, "The union's on us again. Get the field bosses in
here. We've got to negotiate with the cutters. We can't let them
walk out today. We've got to get the frozen cane to the mill.
Well, go on, boy, round up the field bosses and get them in
here."

Glad for an excuse to leave, Henny scooped up his keys and
bolted down the steps to his Jag.

James Henry reached for the phone. "Berlinda? Tell Grace
that Henny and Jeff and I won't be home for dinner. We've got
frozen cane." He broke the connection, waited for the tone, and
dialed again. "Etta? Steve won't be home for dinner tonight, I
need him here." He hung up without waiting for a reply, and
called Jeff at the main office.

"Yes, Dad?"

"Check the sand fields farthest from the lake. That's where
the worst damage will be. Look it over, see what's been hit by

the freeze, then get the mechanical harvesters in there to cut what they can. Send cutters in wherever you see white tops. Show the lead men where to chop the stalk so we don't cart a lot of waste to the mill."

"Okay, Dad, I'll get right on it."

"We'll have to get all of the freeze to the mill within a month to realize any profit for the year. We'll cut night and day until the union shuts us down."

"Right, Dad." Jeff hung up and raced to the field.

Later that night James Henry went out to where the best crew had been assembled in the muck fields. He called to the field boss, "Pull those buses up here and leave the headlights on so the men can see what they're doing. We don't want any injuries. Hurry up! Line those buses up and shine the lights down the row."

James Henry knew that for every three hundred feet of cut cane, they'd have another ton at the mill. "Pile as much as you can on those loaders. Move it!"

The field boss motioned the buses into position, and with the headlights shining down the rows, the cutter's felt more secure in swinging their sharp cutlasses and their speed increased. There was the thump of the initial stroke to the bottom of the cane, then short swishing sounds as the tops were whacked off, and finally, the thud of the stalk being tossed onto the pile along the row.

James Henry, satisfied that he'd done all he could here, jumped in the Lincoln and sped across the field toward the office.

Henny sprang up when he came in. "Finally!" he said. "Can I go now, or do you want to work me twenty-four hours straight?"

"You know the bind I'm in, son. Why can't you help me out just this once?" James Henry's ruggedly handsome face sagged under the stress.

"Why do I have to stay out here with you in this stinking shanty, anyway? Why can't I work in the main office like Jeff?"

James Henry glared at him in shock. "The main office? Why the hell would you want to be cooped up in there?"

"Oh, maybe because the air-conditioning works, or they have a cafeteria, or there are human beings there to talk to."

"Your great-granddaddy built this office with his own two hands. He ran the entire plantation from here. So did my daddy; so am I, and you will, too, one day."

"The hell I will. I'll tear this friggin' shanty down the first chance I get."

"You ungrateful little bastard. You have no respect for yourself or anything or anyone else."

"You want me to respect a shanty? That's a good one." He kicked James Henry's desk.

James Henry drew his breath in sharply and caressed the oak of the old desk. "This was your great-granddaddy's desk, you little snot nose."

Henny sneered. Delighted to have evoked his father's anger, he flopped into the chair behind the desk and slammed the drawers.

James Henry sighed heavily, accepting at last that Henny would never love the cane as he did. It was abhorrent, unthinkable, something he had been unable to comprehend. He was trying to assimilate this when the phone rang.

James Henry picked it up and listened to the voice coming from the main office against the background din of computers, faxes, and copy machines. How could anyone prefer that to being alone out here in the cane?

Wearily he said, "Yes, all right, I'll take care of it." He hung up and looked over at Henny's back, wondering why he wasn't more like Jeff and Mel.

As if he'd heard what was in his father's mind, Henny spun around, seething. "You don't care nuthin' about me! I'm tired of you finding fault, trying to run my life. Everything has to be your way. Well, maybe not. I'll find Beth, I don't care what you say. She'll get a divorce and I'll marry her. I want my baby."

"There is no baby," James Henry said wearily. "Beth didn't have the baby. She got an abortion."

"What?" Henny's eyes glowed wild with hatred. "You're crazy. Beth wants that baby as much as I do. She'd never get an abortion."

"I gave Cora a thousand dollars for the abortion. She talked to her."

"There's nothing Cora could say that would make her get an abortion."

James Henry brought his hand down hard on the desk. "Damn it, boy, I didn't want to have to tell you this." He jammed his cigar into his mouth and chewed on it.

"Tell me what?"

James Henry took a deep breath and cleared his throat. He looked at Henny for a long moment before he said, "I guess there's nothing to do but tell you. I tried every way I knew how to avoid it, but it looks like only the truth will do.

"Seventeen years ago I stopped by Cloyd's one Sunday to see him about spraying the ratoon. He was out pike fishing and Cora was there alone. She was a pretty little thing then — looked like Beth looks now. Well," he paused, then struggled on. "She was drinking a can of Bud and she popped one for me." He hesitated, licked his lips nervously, and continued. "Cora had on little white shorts, her ass hanging out, and, well, you know how it is. One thing led to another, and we, uh, got together. It just happened." He scowled at Henny. "Nine months later Beth was born, so you see now why you can't marry her, why she can't have your baby."

Henny stared at his father, his eyes clouded with hatred and disbelief. "You're a liar! You'd say anything to stop me from marrying Beth."

"No, son, I'm sorry, but it's true. God knows I wish it weren't, but that is the honest to God truth. Cora never said anything, and I never saw her again — that way, just that once. I regretted it, but, well, it just happened. I gave Cloyd steady work all these years, kept him on whether I needed him or not, twelve months a year. Out of guilt, I suppose."

Henny's lips moved, but he was unable to speak.

"I'm sorry, son," James Henry said. "I am. I am truly sorry."

Henny sprang at James Henry. "I'll kill you, you bastard. I'll kill you!" His fists flailed wildly, but James Henry held him at arm's length.

Henny, exhausted, slumped to the floor at James Henry's feet, writhing and sobbing bitterly.

James Henry reached down and stroked his head. "Get up, son," he coaxed softly.

Henny fell over onto the floor and lay there crying, an emaciated, hollow shell.

James Henry stood over him until he could stand it no longer, then he turned and walked out.

A half hour later, back at Hampton House, Berlinda ran down the hall toward the library. "Miz Grace, Miz Grace, come quick! Mr. Henny's tearin' his room apart. You better hurry!"

Grace threw aside the book she was reading, pushed Jade off her lap, and ran down the hall behind Berlinda.

As they neared the east wing, Henny's tortured screams reverberated through the hall. Glass shattered, fabric ripped, and wood splintered.

When they reached Henny's room, Grace ran in the open doorway. "Henny! Henny, stop this. What happened? Why are you doing this?"

He ripped a drapery from the window.

Berlinda cowered in the hall, eyes wide, hands trembling. "You better come outta there, Miz Grace; you come on out. Ain't no tellin' what that boy might do." She backed away down the hall, wringing her hands.

Henny slammed the door closed, and Berlinda's footsteps receded toward the phone in the kitchen.

"Henny, stop!" Grace pleaded. "Tell me what's wrong."

"I'm getting the hell out of here."

"Why, what's —?"

"I won't spend another night under that bastard's roof. He's a dog, an animal."

"What did he do? Tell me."

"I can't."

"You can. You can tell me anything."

Henny looked at her through bloodshot eyes swollen with tears. "Not this. I can't tell you this. I won't hurt you like he hurt me."

"Nothing could hurt me more than seeing you like this — than your leaving. Please, son, don't shut me out. Tell me what happened."

"I can't tell you, Mama, I just can't."

"Please, you must!"

Henny turned away, but she grabbed his arm and spun him around. "Tell me!"

He blurted, "Beth is my sister."

Grace gasped and drew back. "What? What do you mean? You can't be saying —"

"I shouldn't have told you. I'm sorry, Mama, I —"

"He couldn't! Oh, no, he wouldn't. James Henry? No, I —" her voice trailed off uncertainly.

Henny gathered her into his arms. "Oh, Mama, I'm so sorry."

"I'm all right. I am. But you must — you mustn't — oh, son, please!"

Henny broke away and ran to the overturned nightstand. He yanked open a drawer and grabbed a gun.

"Henny! No!" Grace grabbed for the gun, but Henny held it out of reach.

"He deserves killing."

"Wait! Beth is not your sister."

"She is. He told me himself, just now, at the field office."

"I don't care what he told you, Beth is not your sister."

Henny's eyes bore into hers. "Why do you say that? How do you know? Did that bastard lie to me?"

Grace lowered her eyes; her voice trembled. "Beth is not your sister because James Henry is not your father."

"What? Not my father? I don't understand. I —"

"James Henry is not your father, he —"

"Then who is?" Henny threw the gun aside, grabbed her arm, and spun her to face him. "Who is my father? Who?"

"It doesn't matter."

"It sure as hell matters to me. Who is my father? Tell me!" His fingers dug into her arm.

Grace winced, pulled away, and slumped to the bed. "I was in love," she whimpered, almost inaudibly. "I was so much in love — I couldn't help it. Oh, son, I'm sorry. I am so sorry. I made a horrible mistake, and now you are paying for it."

"Who? Who is he? Do I know him?" Henny shook uncontrollably, his eyes blinking, his chin twitching.

"You don't know him. He went away."

"I thought Dad, I mean —"

"James Henry is your dad. He's not your biological father, but he loves you as if you were his son. He wants what's best for you."

"Does he know he's not my father?"

"Yes, but somehow he's managed to block it out. He loves you so much he just won't accept that you're not his biological son."

"He lied to me. Why did he lie to me? Why did he tell me

Beth is my sister if she isn't? The lying bastard, I'll kill him."
Henny grabbed the gun.

"Don't!" Grace struggled with him, crying hysterically. "He
thinks of himself as your father; he thinks of you as his son. It
was my mistake. I'm to blame. Don't blame him, blame me. Oh,
Henny, please don't do this!"

Henny tossed the gun aside, reached out and pulled her to
him. He held her in his arms, consoling her. "Don't cry, Mama.
It's all right, it's all right."

When Grace's sobs subsided, Henny dropped his arms and
walked away. He dragged a suitcase from the closet and threw a
few pieces of clothing into it.

"Don't go, Henny, please. You have to finish high school.
What about college? You start at Florida State next fall."

"I have to go, Mama. I can't stay here now, not with him."

"But where will you go?"

Henny shook his head and threw some socks into the suitcase.

"Please, Henny! Stay for my sake. I need you."

Henny snapped the lock on the suitcase, picked it up, and
walked toward her. "Goodbye, Mama," he muttered.

"Oh, Henny, no! Don't. Please don't go."

Henny brushed a kiss across her cheek and walked out the
door to an uncertain future.

CHAPTER 19

A few days later, after a hearty breakfast of bacon, eggs, and grits, James Henry drove to the field office. He bolted up the steps, yanked the door open, and stopped short when he saw Steve standing by the small-paned window. "Uh-oh. Trouble?"

"Yeah," Steve said. "I thought I'd better let you know; there's talk in Clewiston that the union is planning to pull the men out of the fields today."

"Damn!" James Henry slammed his fist on the door jamb. "I thought we had that all settled. Why the hell can't they leave us alone? We can't afford a strike now. I've got to get that frozen cane to the mill, the workers need their pay."

"Yeah, I know. It's a bummer. Maybe we can negotiate with them. If you want me to, I'll drive over to Clewiston tonight. Get the lay of the land. See if there's anything we can do to stop it."

James Henry nodded. "All right, go see what you can find out — maybe if we jack up the price of a cut row."

"Yeah, maybe, I'll see what I can do. Bye, Jim — Henny."

James Henry glanced at Henny, back at his desk for the first time since he told him that he had fathered Beth.

Henny, badly in need of a fix and desperate for money, didn't answer. Between his drug habit and gambling debts, he was broke and forced to play James Henry's game.

In an attempt to avoid talk of old wounds, James Henry said, "Damn unions still giving us trouble after all these years. Back in '82, three hundred cutters walked out of the fields over at the Atlantic Sugar growers. The owners sent them back to Jamaica the next day. Thought it would teach them a lesson, but it didn't. They pulled the same damn thing in '86 at Okeelanta." James Henry tapped a pen on the desk, waiting for a response from Henny, but he got none. "Damned if they're going to bully me into compliance. Bad enough I had to rebuild the barracks, raise the row price, and put more meat in the rations. What the hell next?"

James Henry swung away from Henny's back, threw papers listing union demands aside, and lit a fresh cigar. He puffed ferociously; clouds of smoke crawled up the plank wall. "You listening to me, boy?"

Henny responded without looking up from the racing form. "Maybe we can get some American blacks from Louisiana or Alabama to replace them."

"Hell, no. Tried that after the walkout in Okeelanta. They all quit after a week or two. Just wasted time and money trying to train them."

"Can't say that I blame them. It's no picnic in those cane fields."

James Henry snorted. "They're in there to work, not to picnic." Finding no common ground for discussion, he said, "Joe was working on the harvester when I left him. Go see if he got it fixed. He worked on it all day yesterday, but when we started it up this morning it spattered juice all over the field. We'll need to keep all of the mechanical harvesters rolling if there's a walkout."

Henny didn't respond, but continued studying the racing form, searching for a long shot that would free him from James Henry's control.

James Henry watched Henny for a few moments, until it

was evident that his son wasn't going to do what was asked of him. Deciding against a confrontation, he turned to leave. "Why the hell can't those union bosses realize that they're pricing the cutters out of reach?" James Henry opened the door. "You come home and have dinner with your mother tonight, you hear? She's worried sick about you." He hurried across the porch, his long boots resounding as he went down the steps to his Lincoln.

When Steve came into the field office the next morning for the pay sheet, James Henry could see that the news wasn't good.

"No dice, huh?"

"Afraid not," Steve said. "They're determined to call a strike. More for show, I'd say. Make an example so the other growers get in line. You're the biggest, so that's where they want to hit. They figure if they get you in line, the other growers will follow." Steve picked up the pay sheets and looked them over.

"Yes, the biggest and the fairest. That doesn't seem to matter to them. They'll hit us for effect, and all the poor devils working for us will suffer. Well, I'm not caving in. Let them pull the men out. If I give in now, they'll be back next year and the year after that with more ridiculous demands. Eventually they'll break the cane industry."

"They're going to make it hard on the workers and their families," Steve said, remembering the lean years they'd had before James Henry gave Vonda and Chip money to buy the café. Real hard times they were, and Steve didn't want to think of the cutters' kids experiencing bleak days like some he had known. "Well, let me know if there's anything I can do."

"Right."

Steve headed for the door thinking, *if anyone can figure how to beat the damn union, James Henry can.*

But it was worse than anticipated. Union reps came down from New York and threatened the cutters, telling them they'd never work the cane fields again if they didn't go along with the strike. They played to TV and newspapers, and television stations carried stories nightly showing pictures of injured cutters, their fingers and toes missing, eyes blinded, faces scarred by bending into cane stubble. They ran shots of the barracks that made them look uninhabitable.

"I wish we had photos of the barracks before the cutters came in," James Henry said. "Then they would see who it is who destroys them. I built them to government specifications. It's up to the workers to keep them clean. Next thing, they'll be demanding maid service."

James Henry stood and paced the worn plank floor. He looked over to Henny. "What the hell are we going to do, son?"

"Damned if I know," Henny sniffled and wiped his nose with his knuckle without looking up from the pay sheets.

"I hate to use mechanical harvesters, especially in the muck. They pull up the plants, spatter the juice, and leave waste on the stalks that foul up the machines at the mill." James Henry picked up the phone, called Washington, and spoke with one of his lobbyists. When he hung up he turned to Henny. "The politicians are all running scared. The unions have too much clout; the senators are afraid to align themselves with the growers."

"What about Senator Rechett? You practically support him and his ditsy wife."

"He was the first to wimp out, the bastard." James Henry picked up the phone, then threw it back in the cradle, out of people to call for help. He cursed and slumped back in his chair, clenching and unclenching his fists.

Henny chuckled. "Looks like you struck out this time, eh, Dad?"

"There was a time when they couldn't get away with this. They came down here when your granddaddy was alive and he told them when to jump and how high. Even President Roosevelt came calling. The power is shifting, son, and not toward the growers."

"Too bad. Maybe now you'll have to pay the cutters a decent wage." Henny's laugh echoed brittle and hollow.

"You watch your mouth, boy. They get paid for what they do. They cut eight tons a day; they stick fifty-six dollars in their poke. Hell, they don't make fifty-six dollars a month in Jamaica. They put in their six hours; they're through for the day. I'm here half the night trying to overcome union demands."

Henny rolled his eyes. He knew how dangerous those back-breaking six hours were. Most of the men sustained injuries from the sharp edge of the cutlass. Some lost eyes, some punctured an eardrum when they bent down and bumped into a cut stalk of cut cane. Others came down with muck sickness. Cutting cane was not work any man would envy.

"It's easy for union men to make these demands," James Henry said. "They don't know beans about the industry. As Henry David Thoreau said, 'Any damn fool can make a rule, and all the fools will follow it.' That won't get the cane to the mill or sugar to America's tables."

He sat in silence for a moment, pondering his dilemma before he stood and stretched. "Well anyway, the environmentalists will soon have us all closed down, then there won't be any cane to cut. We won't need a union to tell us what to pay the workers, because there won't be any work."

Henny glanced up at his father, who seemed to crumple under the weight of his problems.

"Damn," James Henry said. "I feel like Sisyphus pushing a rock up the hill."

"Who?"

"We've overcome hurricanes, drought, cane diseases, and a couple of wars, but if we don't overcome the union and the environmentalists it will mean the end to the sugar cane industry in Florida." A weary James Henry reached for his pith helmet and headed to the fields.

*   *   *

After dinner that evening, he went to see Vonda. She rolled over onto her back and stroked James Henry's cheek. "Satisfied my little cuckoo bird?" she purred.

James Henry looked toward her and grinned. "Why do you call me your little cuckoo bird?"

"Don't you know?"

"No." Thinking it was because of their love play, he wanted to hear it from her.

Vonda turned toward him, propped her head on her hand, and swung long red hair back over her shoulder. "Back in high school, 'bout the same time I got pregnant with Steve, Miss Cramer was teachin' us about birds. 'Bout how the cuckoo bird flies over other bird's nests, checks out the size and shape and color of their eggs, and it lays an egg in their nest that matches the ones already in there. Then off it flies, free as a bird — as a bird —" She laughed at the unintended pun and waved her hand. "Off it flies, free and clear. Leaves somebody else to do the hatchin' and the feedin' and the raisin' of its young. See now why I call you my little cuckoo bird?"

"That's not funny, Vonda."

"Cuckoo — cuckoo —"

"That's enough, damn it. You watch your mouth. Don't you ever call me that again."

Vonda laughed heartily, swung out of bed, wrapped herself in the black satin sheet, and went toward the bathroom. "Cuckoo, cuckoo," she chirped as she showered.

James Henry jumped up, dressed, and left.

When he stepped out into the night, he zipped his jacket against the cold wind blowing across the lake from the northwest. He glanced up at the night sky and thought, *Full February moon. That means a freeze is likely.* He walked across the crushed shell parking lot with shoulders hunched, got in his car, and drove toward Hampton Plantation.

He expected to lose about 10 percent of his crop to frost, but this year the temperature dropped to nearly twenty degrees. The stalks cracked and the la-las, the tender young growth sprouting from the joints, were killed. *Nothing I can do about it,* he thought, *smudge pots don't save the cane.*

CHAPTER 20

After extensive negotiations, the crisis with the union had passed, and James Henry and Jeff enjoyed a leisurely lunch at home with Grace and Sami.

Feeling more comfortable with James Henry now, Sami asked, "Papa Jim, will you take me to the cane field with you someday?"

"Sure thing. How about today?"

"You mean it, Papa Jim? I can go today?"

"Sure. Why not?"

Sami gasped and turned to look at Jeff triumphantly.

James Henry spooned up the last of the mango pudding. "Put on a hat and some bug spray. Hurry up!"

"Oh, thank you, Papa Jim." Sami jumped up and bowed to Grace. "Excuse, please, Mama Grace?"

"Of course, child. You go along." Grace turned to James Henry. "How nice that she has an interest in the cane — but you watch out for her. Remember that she's pregnant."

"Right." James Henry pushed back from the table, his face crinkling with pleasure. "Couldn't get Mel in the cane field if I hid a new Ferrari in there for her, but my daughter-in-law wants to go with me."

"I don't know if this is such a good idea," Jeff said. "Maybe she should wait until after the baby comes."

"Nonsense, I won't let anything happen to her." James Henry stood and walked toward the door, calling over his shoulder, "Come on, young lady."

Sami came running back, clasping a large straw hat to her head. "Is it okay if I wear your hat, Mama Grace?"

"Of course, child," Grace said, sharing in her delight.

"Berlinda sprayed me good. She said I'll get eaten up alive in the cane field."

"We'll try not to let that happen." James Henry led the way out across the portico, with Sami struggling to keep pace with his long strides. She clambered up into the Jeep, James Henry threw it in gear, and they roared off.

They passed several fields of tall, dark green cane that stood motionless in the humid midday air. James Henry pulled to the side of the road and stopped where cutters chopped and stacked cane. He motioned the field boss over.

"That ratoon down in the muck is about a foot high. Spread a hundred and fifty pounds of K20 per acre before it gets any higher. Be sure to rototill it in on the first cultivation."

"Yes, sir, Mr. Jim." The field boss tipped his hat to Sami.

She smiled hesitantly and drew back against the seat.

James Henry pulled back onto the road, and they drove on past endless acres of cane.

"What's ratoon, Papa Jim?"

"Ratoon is the young basal shoot that springs up after the cane has been cut. It replaces the old and renews itself that way."

"Then you never have to replant?"

"Only about once every four or five years."

"Oh." Sami looked out over the fields as the Jeep bounded along. "Look at that big machine!" she said, clutching her hat and turning around to look back.

James Henry glanced in the rearview mirror. "The tractor? That pulls the cane carts up to the loaders."

"Big tires."

"We had quite a time getting the cane out of the fields before we had those heavy crawler tractors, Caterpillar D-6s on rubber tires. We were always getting stuck in the muck; took us half a day to get the cane out of the fields. Then U.S. Sugar came up with the heavy-wheel tractors, and now we can pull four cane carts loaded with about five tons of cane each. They move along at about fifteen to eighteen miles an hour. Powerful machines."

Sami scanned the horizon, marveling at the endless rows of cane. "A lot of sugar cane. Amazing. How you get all this cane to the mill before it shrivels up and dies?"

"Most of the cane is ground within twenty-four hours of being cut. We don't have any stale cane here in Florida. Never more than thirty-six hours from cutting to grinding."

Sami's dark eyes widened in amazement as they bounced along on the taut springs of the Jeep.

"The mills run twenty-four hours a day the whole cane season, November to May."

"Some day would you show me how you get the sugar out of the stalks, Papa Jim?"

"Sure. Different factories use different methods for boiling the sugar." He negotiated a sharp turn and Sami grasped the seat with both hands. "But they all boil three strikes. The end result is the same, though, no matter how they boil — 750,000 tons of sugar a season."

"Seven hundred and fifty thousand tons?" Sami shook her head and released a long breath. "Whew! That makes a lot of Hershey bars."

"Of course, there are also the by-products: molasses, cattle feed, the bagasse goes to two outlets —"

"Bagasse?"

"The waste products. Bagasse is used for furfural manufacture and poultry litter."

"Lot of waste, I bet." She turned her head to look at the leaves on the tall stalks as they whizzed by. "Jeff says you wash sugar first before you process it. Sounds strange. Doesn't the sugar melt and run away with the water?"

"We do wash it, and you're right, we do lose some — about a ton an acre. That's nearly 10 percent of production." James Henry pulled up beside a field boss and got out of the Jeep. "Ready for the burn?"

"Almost. We're wettin' down the edges now." He motioned toward the men on the water truck who were directing a stream of water along the edge of the field.

"Flamethrower here yet?" James Henry asked.

"You're going to light the field with a flamethrower?" Sami asked incredulously, lifting a hand to shade her eyes from the noonday sun as she scanned the field.

"No." James Henry grinned. "That's our nickname for the fellow who lights the field when the cane is ripe for the burn."

The field boss motioned toward a pickup parked nearby, where Flamethrower leaned against a fender, smoking. He drew a long drag, exhaled slowly, snuffed the cigarette on the fender, and tossed it aside. He glanced toward the sun, and seeing that it had passed the meridian, he picked up his fuel pot and walked into the field.

James Henry pointed. "There he is. That's Flamethrower."

Sami nodded, and watched intently while dabbing perspiration from her forehead with a tissue.

"He's the boss of the burn crew. How much sugar we take to the mill, and how much money we take to the bank, depends partly on him. Flamethrower is the best around. We're lucky to have him. He uses that firepot like a magic wand."

"A magic wand?" Sami's nose wrinkled in concentration.

"Yes. He holds it at just the right angle for the mixture of half gas, half diesel, to ignite and drop onto the cane. He can burn sixty acres with just one pot of fuel."

"Why does he mix gas and diesel? Why not just use kerosene?"

"Half diesel, half gas is the right mix to get the job done."

When Flamethrower completed spreading the fuel, he lit the field and it erupted in a roaring burn. Wild hogs ran helter-skelter to escape the flames. Clouds of smoke mingled with the spreading fire, and a stench like that of raw sewage enveloped the Jeep.

Sami pinched her nose and stifled a gag.

"You'll get used to it," James Henry said.

"That smell doesn't make you sick?"

"Nah. I like everything about the cane, even the smell. The cane's in my blood."

Sami shook her head and watched with awe as Flame-thrower sprinted from the burning field.

"He gets a successful burn even if there's intermittent rain or very little wind." James Henry watched with admiration. "The fire never gets away from him like it sometimes does with the other fire starters."

Sami watched as flames thundered toward low hanging clouds, and egrets, crazed by the burn, soared and dipped above the flames on scorched wings.

"Oh, Papa Jim," Sami cried, "Look at those birds! They're going to get killed. Why do they fly into the fire like that?"

"Crazy egrets," James Henry said. "They're hell-bent on destroying themselves. No reason for them to fly in there."

Sami turned away, coughing and choking. "The burn scares me," she said. She inched back toward the Jeep.

"It won't hurt you from this distance." James Henry moved back to stand beside her. He sheltered her with an arm across her slim shoulders, "But you don't want to be in a field while it's being lit. One time a fellow that was inexperienced started a burn that got out of control and burned right over one of our new harvesters."

"Oh, big mistake. It got ruined?" Sami looked up into his face expectantly.

"It didn't exactly ruin it. It still ran, but it didn't look pretty."

Sami giggled, then grew serious again. "Why do you burn the cane, Papa Jim? Can't you cut cane if you don't burn it first?

"Burning saves time and money. Saves hauling all the leaves and tops to the mill. Leaves and tops clog the machinery. Slows the cutters down, too. It's easier for them to cut the day after a good burn. Gets the snakes, wild hogs, and rats out of the field so the cutters don't have to deal with wildlife while they're cutting."

"Doesn't burn hurt sugar?"

"No, we lose a little, but we make more than we lose on a good burn. A really good burn leaves only stalks, and that's where the sugar is. The cutters can walk right through a field that's had a good burn. It's better for machine cutting too."

Sami's eyes began watering from the smoke that surrounded them. "Papa Jim, the smoke makes me sick. Will you take me back to the house now? I'll fix lemonade for you."

"No lemonade for me, Sami. I don't have time, but I'll take you back."

"Oh, thank you, Papa Jim." Sami climbed back in the Jeep and they sped away.

When they reached Hampton House, Sami jumped down from the Jeep, waved good-bye, and walked toward the portico. James Henry watched her disappear into the house as he drove away. Damn fine girl, he thought. Jeff's a lucky man. He threw the Jeep into high gear and headed back to the cane fields.

Sami went to the kitchen where Grace sat at the table discussing tomorrow's menu with Berlinda. Jade jumped down from Grace's lap and ran to welcome Sami.

"Hello, dear," Grace said. "Did you enjoy your trip to the cane fields?"

Sami bent to pet Jade. "I don't like the burn. It smells awful."

"You get all bit up?" Berlinda asked. "I rub some aloe plant on them bites, take out the sting."

Sami shook her head. "No bites." She went to the window and looked through the thick, dark smoke to the distance.

"The burn scares me," she said. "I hope Flamethrower never burns this field next to the house. Why did Papa Jim plant cane so close to house?"

Grace used her fingers to comb her hair back behind her ear. "At first I thought it was greed," she said. "I thought James Henry wanted income from every acre. Now I know better. He just loves the cane so much that he wants to live in the fields. The closer he is to the cane, the happier he is. He wants to be in the cane fields twenty-four hours a day. He'd rather be out in that old shanty he calls the field office than in that beautiful new office complex he built."

"That man be crazy for cane," Berlinda said.

"He does love the cane," Sami said. "He says it's in his blood."

"I do believe it is. Yes, in his blood, in his heart, and in his soul." Grace petted Jade thoughtfully.

"You love the cane too, Mama Grace?"

"I'm just used to it, Sami."

"I wonder if I'll ever get used to it." Sami's eyes glazed with faraway thoughts of Japan.

"You will. After a while it becomes a way of life. It's a very different life for you, but you're adjusting nicely."

Grace walked to her daughter-in-law and laid a reassuring arm across her shoulders. "Are you happy here, Sami?" she asked.

"Oh, yes, I'm happy wherever Jeff is. But," she added wistfully, "I miss my mother."

"Of course you do," Grace said, "especially now that you're expecting a baby. Maybe your mother will come for a visit. Do you think she would?"

"You're so nice to me, Mama Grace. You make me happy here."

Grace hugged her and turned to the window. The two women stood together silently watching the smoke from the burning cane, and the egrets that rose and fell above the leaping flames.

Finally, Grace turned from the window. "Come," she said, "help me plan the meals for Senator and Mrs. Rechett. They'll be coming tomorrow, and we must have all of their favorite dishes. It's very important to James Henry that they enjoy their stay."

"You jes leave it to me," Berlinda said. "When I get through feedin' 'em, they give Mr. Jim anythin' he want."

CHAPTER 21

The next morning, Grace stood at a table in the kitchen placing parrot tulips in an arrangement for the entry hall. She stepped back to squint at the splashes of color before rearranging a few of the red and yellow blossoms. Tulip stems curved gracefully, their fringed petals flaring to reveal black stamens and yellow pistils. Satisfied, Grace lifted the vase and carried it to the foyer, where she placed it on the rich ebony wood of the temple table.

She paused for a moment to appreciate the beauty of the flowers, before rushing to the dining room. She removed a cloth from the buffet and unfurled it over the mahogany table, a billowing cloud of Alencon lace. Quickly she laid place settings of heirloom silver before calling to Berlinda to bring the Haviland china.

She placed a footed silver epergne, heaped with bright orange kumquats and shiny dark green leaves, as a centerpiece. Cut crystal goblets caught the sun, fracturing it into a spectrum of color, spattering rainbows on the ceiling. "Hurry, Berlinda," she called, "Senator and Mrs. Rechett will be here any minute." She stepped back and paused for a moment to check the table.

James Henry rushed past her and took the stairs two at a time to change out of his khaki shirt and jodhpurs. The shower pulsed, and when he appeared at the top of the stairs in silk shirt and sport slacks, Grace called to him, "Hurry, they're here."

James Henry hustled down the steps while buttoning his cuffs. He put his arm around Grace's waist and steered her out onto the portico. "Damn nuisance," he muttered, "but necessary."

Grace shushed him and he bolted down the steps to the senator's limousine.

Senator Rechett, gray-haired and impeccably groomed, stepped out of the car. James Henry grabbed his hand and shook it heartily. "Bob, you old son of a gun, how are you? Good to see you. You look great!"

"I'm fine, James Henry, just fine." He turned to take his wife's hand and assist her from the limousine.

Mrs. Rechett bestowed the practiced smile of a politician's wife on James Henry, and reached to kiss his cheek. "My you do look fit, James Henry," she said, as she turned to wave to Grace who waited on the portico. She smoothed thick brown hair back toward the chignon at the nape of her neck and draped a Chanel jacket over her shoulders.

James Henry took her arm and they mounted the steps of the portico. "I swear," he beamed down at her, "you look younger every time I see you."

She shoved him playfully. "James Henry, you still spilling sugar on the ladies?" When they stepped onto the portico, she reached to hug Grace. "How do you put up with this lady-killer, Grace?"

Grace smiled, shook her head wistfully, and kissed Mrs. Rechett lightly on the cheek. "Did you have a good flight, Mimi?"

"Yes, very smooth." Mrs. Rechett turned to look out over the lawn and gardens, where wanton butterflies pirouetted in the midday sun. She lifted a hand to shade her eyes. "Your gardens are lovely in the spring — all those rose-colored blossoms on the azaleas, and I've never seen so many pink hibiscus. Such huge flowers, they must be doubles."

"They're a special variety our gardener developed. They are

beautiful, aren't they? Come, Berlinda will unpack your things and you can freshen up after you've had a drink."

They walked in across the foyer to the large living room and sat in front of the low Louis XV table, where Berlinda had placed a tray of hors d'oeuvres.

Mrs. Rechett selected a small toasted biscuit, topped it with a bit of grouper marinated in lime and honey, and placed it in her mouth. "Ummm, I see that Berlinda is still with you. No one else could create such delectable nibbles."

"She is indeed, and she has spent all morning preparing a lunch of your favorites." Grace relaxed beside Mimi on the sofa while James Henry mixed martinis at the bar, careful to balance the ingredients just the way the Rechetts preferred them. He passed the martinis around, and after they had visited for a while, Berlinda appeared in the archway to announce lunch. James Henry escorted his guests to the dining room for red snapper en papillote with avocado and Haden melon.

Berlinda knew of Mrs. Rechett's fondness for key lime pie, the kind made with sweetened condensed milk and a baked pie crust, so she had prepared one that morning. When they finished the main course, Berlinda topped the pie with freshly whipped cream and wedges of fresh lime and placed it in front of them. "Ya'll be sure to squeeze plenty of fresh lime juice over that pie," she instructed.

"Yes, Berlinda, I remember." Mrs. Rechett obediently squeezed the lime, took a bite, and rolled her eyes heavenward as the velvety dessert caressed her tongue.

After lunch James Henry and the senator played golf at the club, while Grace and Mimi played bridge in the card room with other growers' wives.

That evening, when they returned to the club for dinner, the maître d' snapped to attention when James Henry approached. He smiled obsequiously. "Mr. Hampton! How nice to see you. Senator, ladies, right this way."

He seated them at the best table overlooking the golf course and the fountains, where pink oleanders, lighted by subtly placed spotlights, swayed gently in the soft evening breeze. The maître d' summoned the wine steward, who took their drink orders while he seated other guests.

Senator Rechett scanned the fare and nodded approvingly. "Nice selection. I see they are featuring corned beef and cabbage for St. Patrick's Day."

"Try the prime rib and lobster," James Henry advised. "They fly the lobsters in from Maine daily, and you know how good our Florida beef is."

"Sounds like a perfect choice." Bob glanced at Mimi, and she nodded assent.

"Grace?" James Henry said.

"I'll have the Chicken Veronique."

James Henry turned his attention to the waiter serving their drinks, then motioned to the maître d', who turned away from the couple he had been greeting to rush to the Hamptons' table. James Henry ordered for everyone, took a sip of his Dewars and water, and turned to Senator Rechett. "Will you be able to stay for the golf tournament on Saturday?"

"I'd love to, but I've got to get back to Washington — big vote coming up on Thursday."

James Henry thought, *Just time to pick up the graft and run.* "Too bad," he said, "a lot of pros are coming in."

After a leisurely meal, they stayed for the St. Patrick's Day entertainment and dancing. It was late when they returned to Hampton House, where they chatted over brandy about their families and the Washington social scene. James Henry suggested that Grace take Mimi out onto the portico to enjoy the night-blooming jasmine.

After they left, James Henry crossed to his desk and took out an envelope that bulged with one hundred dollar bills. He handed it to the senator, who threaded the envelope into his inside jacket pocket. Neither man spoke, but both were aware that the senator had just agreed to vote for sugar subsidies.

Senator Rechett stretched and yawned. "Time to turn in, I guess." He called in the direction of the portico, "Come on, Mimi, time for bed."

James Henry smiled sardonically. Mission accomplished.

After everyone had retired, James Henry slipped out and headed for Vonda's. He had promised her that he would stop by for her St. Patrick's Day party with green beer, and he didn't want to disappoint her.

James Henry pulled in, braked in a spray of crushed shells, and walked across the parking lot. He pushed open the café door, and stepped into cigarette smoke that hung like a blanket of fog over the crowd. Loud voices and raucous laughter almost drowned out music that blared from the jukebox. Vonda danced in front of the colorful blinking lights, aware that all eyes were on her. Her head thrown back, her eyes closed, she moved to the beat of Shania Twain's, "Whose Bed Have Your Boots Been Under?"

The center of attention, James Henry thought. That's the way she likes it.

Couples stood three deep at the bar. James Henry reached between them to take the beer Chip held out to him. Holding it up to the light, he said, "It doesn't look green to me."

"Run outta green beer early." Chip's cheeks sagged gaunt from fatigue. "You'll have to settle for plain old brown pilsner." He tipped his green derby, snapped his green bowtie, and responded to calls for refills.

James Henry turned his attention to Vonda and the men who watched her twist and writhe to the beat. To the delight of the crowd, her kelly green spandex miniskirt worked higher with each gyration. The thin spaghetti straps on her blouse promised to break as her breasts rolled and heaved under the revealing cloth. The men stomped and yelled, inciting Vonda to dance into a frenzy.

When the music stopped, Vonda stood motionless for a moment, as if emerging from a trance. Finally, she opened her eyes, blinked, and sauntered toward the bar. Men jostled each other to position themselves beside her.

She scanned their faces, enjoying the effect she had on them. When her eyes came to rest on James Henry, she exclaimed, "Hey! Where you been? I thought you wasn't comin'."

"I said I'd come, didn't I? Well, here I am. Better late than never." He tossed off the last of the beer. "You didn't save any of that green beer for me."

"Nope, too late." Her bangles clanked as she raised a glass to him and drained it. "Buy me another, mister?" She turned toward the bar and yelled, "Two more over here."

Chip filled two glasses from the tap and slid them down the bar to Jim and Vonda. They picked up the beers, walked to Vonda's booth, and slid in.

Vonda threw her head back and wiped perspiration from her throat with a paper cocktail napkin.

James Henry frowned at her. "Why do you always have to make such a spectacle of yourself?"

"Everybody seemed to like the spectacle." She raised her glass to men watching her from the bar and smiled seductively.

"No need to carry on like that in front of everybody."

Vonda snorted. "Who the hell are you to tell me how to act?" She slurred words; her voice rose in anger. When she grabbed her beer, some splashed in her lap. "Shit," she muttered, as a dark stain spread over the spandex.

Realizing how drunk she was, James Henry tried to smooth things over. "Now Vonda, quiet down. I didn't mean anything by it."

"Quiet down," she shouted. "Ain't that a hog hoot? I don't think so."

Chip pulled himself up onto the bar, swung across it, and hurried to Vonda. "Come on, baby, have a drink with me." He winked at James Henry as he helped her away from the booth. Vonda jerked her arm free and started swaying to the music.

Embarrassed by the unfolding scene, James Henry threw a twenty on the table and strode to the door.

Vonda stumbled to the jukebox and began gyrating wildly, bangles jangling, and red hair reflecting the lone spotlight that she'd had installed for her one-woman shows. Lights from the jukebox flashed red and yellow across perspiring breasts as Shania Twain sang, "Yeah, yeah, I like it that way." The bar crowd cheered wildly as Vonda throbbed to "Any Man of Mine."

The door slammed shut behind James Henry.

Sliding behind the wheel of the green Lincoln he wondered, *Why do I come here?* The tires sprayed crushed shell as he drove away, angry with himself for wanting Vonda, for needing her. *I always thought of her as the town tramp, so what does that make me? I never understood why Chip married her, and here I am drawn to her like a rattler to hot rocks. I guess a man always has a special feeling for his first woman.*

He'd been trying to pull away from Vonda since he'd gotten her pregnant when they were in high school. He had given her money for an abortion, but the next thing he knew, she was blaming Chip, and she soon showed off a cheap diamond ring and announced their engagement.

"What the hell are you thinking?" James Henry asked Chip. "You don't marry a tramp like that."

"I know, I know, but I love her. What can I say?"

Embarrassed, Chip turned away and started whistling.

James Henry barked, "Well, good luck, buddy," and stalked off.

He stayed away from Chip and Vonda for a while after that, but Chip was his best friend and he missed his companionship. When he heard that Vonda had a baby boy that she'd named Steve, he dropped by with a gift, and they resumed their friendship. Vonda and Chip seemed happy together, so James Henry gradually absolved his guilt, coming to think of Vonda as a friend and Chip's wife.

But after Grace gave birth to Henny, everything changed. Doc Johnson warned them that another pregnancy could prove dangerous, maybe even fatal. Grace refused to have her tubes tied, hoping that one day she would be able to have another child, and birth control pills were out of the question because of her medical condition. James Henry didn't like condoms, but he always used protection with Grace, not wanting to endanger her.

Soon Vonda, eager to satisfy her unquenchable desires, had seduced him. He was sure Chip knew, but he didn't appear to mind. He seemed happy to be reunited with his old high school buddy, and the three of them spent more time together as the years passed.

When Steve was old enough to work, Vonda asked James Henry to give him a job, so he started Steve in the cane fields. A smart kid, Steve always volunteered to go the extra mile, and he learned quickly. James Henry couldn't help liking him, and eventually he grew to admire Steve's intelligence, energy, and perhaps most importantly, his love of the cane.

James Henry thought about sending Steve to college, but by then he had become his right-hand man — indispensable.

Maybe someday I'll talk to him, he thought, *explain to him how it all came down.* James Henry yanked the wheel, almost veering off the road as he thought of how close he had come to losing Steve to abortion. He bit down on his cigar and thought, *He looks just like me. Guess everybody in Belle Glade knows he's mine, but I'll be damned if I'll admit it. Not to him, not to Vonda, not to anybody.*

CHAPTER 22

James Henry, relieved to see the last of the senator, turned his thoughts to the union. He picked Steve up at the edge of field #7, before driving to the Clewiston Inn for a meeting with union boss Spencer and his delegation.

Spencer sprawled at the head of the table, jowls obscuring the open neck of his dark blue leisure shirt. He and his men had taken all but two chairs, and those were on one side of the conference table. James Henry smiled knowingly, realizing that a game of one-upmanship had been planned.

He strode to one end of the table where a young man leaned forward on propped elbows. He bumped his arm and motioned to a chair at the side of the table.

The young man glanced uncertainly at Spencer, who nodded, and he moved to the chair that James Henry indicated.

James Henry sat down resolutely, shoulders squared, chin jutting, at what had become the head of the table, leaving no doubt where the power lay.

Steve took the only vacant chair.

After perfunctory greetings, James Henry smacked the table and bellowed, "We're not here to discuss the weather. What's on your mind?"

"You know why we're here," Spencer said. "We need more

money and better living conditions for the cutters. If you don't agree to our terms, we'll pull the men out of the fields."

James Henry reared back, indignant at being threatened. He snorted. "I pay them what they're worth."

"Do you really think thirty-five dollars a cut row is a fair wage for men who work in Florida's heat and humidity? That's a slave wage, and you know it."

"I know no such thing! I didn't bring these men here in chains. They fight for a place on the roster. Ask them; they'll tell you. They'd damn sooner come here and cut cane than lie around Jamaica all winter with empty bellies. These men have families to feed. They want to work."

Spencer leaned back and stared down his bulbous nose at James Henry. "Granted, they want to work, but they should receive a fair wage."

"And who's to decide what's fair? The grower who has to sell the sugar or some guy out of New York that doesn't know a damn thing about the industry?"

Spencer picked up the pack of cigarettes that lay on the table in front of him, tapped one from the pack, and lit it. He exhaled, thick lips forming a circle as smoke escaped. "I know that one in four of the cutters gets injured by a cutlass during every cane season. They lose eyes, fingers, toes, and they get muck itch. I know that they work in fields with wild pigs, snakes, and rats. They leave their families for six months of the year to live in the filthy barracks you provide, and all to make the growers richer."

James Henry leaped to his feet and slammed a fist on the table. "Hold on! How the hell do you think those barracks get filthy? You think I sneak in there when they're in the fields and dirty them up? These men live like they live at home. They wreck the quarters I provide."

Spencer flicked the ash from his cigarette. "Nevertheless, there are some changes that have to be made. Living conditions must be improved. Men can't be expected to live in substandard quarters."

"We're talking about day laborers here, not the president of GM. These men never lived better in their lives."

"I'll give you a list of changes that will have to be made." Spencer picked up his pen and made notes on a small white pad.

"Changes hell! I just rebuilt the barracks to government specifications. They got electricity, running water, good beds, TV. This is a work camp, not some damned resort."

The butt of James Henry's cigar absorbed his wrath as he drew in words he knew he dared not speak. *I should tell the bastard to go to hell so I can get back to work,* he thought, *but if I do, he'll pull the cutters out and the crop will rot in the fields.*

Steve stepped into the void, attempting to ease the tension. "Why don't you lay your demands on the table and we'll negotiate them."

James Henry clamped down on his cigar, reluctant to chastise Steve in the presence of others. *Let Spencer make his demands,* he thought. *I'll not agree to them, by damn I won't.*

Spencer steepled his fingers and tapped his fingertips. "The first order of business has to be the thirty-five dollars a cut row." Spencer regarded James Henry from under heavy brows.

James Henry shouted, "I told you. I can't pay more and still make a profit. Offshore sugar will drive me out of business. We're competing with slave labor in the Dominican Republic. The Dominican government owns those fields — they don't have a union telling them what to pay their cutters."

"We're not here to discuss wages in the Dominican Republic." Spencer said. He continued to make notes.

"We darn well better discuss it. Nearly 10 percent of the sugar on American tables comes from there, and they're buying kids in Haiti for twelve or fourteen dollars a head, some only eight years old. They work those kids from sunup to sundown. How the hell can I compete with that?"

Spencer snuffed his cigarette in the ashtray. "Let's not get sidetracked —"

"Sidetracked, hell. You want me to pay premium wages to my cutters, then compete with grower's that pay twelve cents an hour — and they pay in vouchers that the poor bastards can only spend at the government store."

Spencer studied James Henry, a headstrong maverick who had to be dealt with tactfully. He has a lot of influence with the alliance, and bringing Hampton Plantation into line would make his job a lot easier when he met with the other growers. But, he had a job to do, so he'd better get on with it. "The men have been complaining about the food —"

"Hold on! Wait one damn minute. We cook according to government specifications. They never ate so good in their lives."

"They find the food bland. They'd prefer their native foods."

"Well, la-di-da. Maybe I should hire a gourmet chef. Do you know what the cutters eat in the Dominican Republic? Cane. That's it. They just chew on the stalk, unless they want to work for nine days to buy a pound of rice at the government store."

Spencer shifted on heavy thighs. "About the living conditions —"

"The Dominicans house seven or eight in a one-room shack. No toilet facilities. Hell, they don't even have running water. They drink from a drainage ditch."

Spencer threw his pen on the table and leaned back. "This isn't getting us anywhere. Do you want to negotiate or not?"

"We can't negotiate if you don't face the facts. The Dominicans produce two hundred million pounds of sugar a year; the U.S. imports three hundred thousand pounds of it. We've got to stay competitive. The day I can't turn a profit, this land can all go back to sawgrass. I'll put in a catfish pond like they did on the other side of the lake."

"No one is asking you to work for nothing, but you shouldn't expect the cutters to work for nothing either."

James Henry growled, "I give them what they're worth."

"Maybe we've hit on the problem here. You think you're giving them their wages. These men earn that thirty-five dollars a cut row — the hard way."

"Give, earn, are we talking semantics here or wages?"

Steve cleared his throat, about to speak, but James Henry cut in.

"What about the days they beg off, say they're sick when they're not? We've still got to feed and house them whether they work or not. We're not in the damned baby-sitting business."

"They don't say they're sick unless they are. They're here for the money. They cut when they can."

"What about the days a cutter is in top form and he's cutting faster than the leadsman. You know the leadsman will call him back to slow him down — say he's leaving too much stubble."

The kid next to Steve poured a glass of water and passed the pitcher to Steve, who helped himself. He sipped as the quarrel swirled around him, thinking, *This discussion is going nowhere. James Henry should settle rather than have the men pulled out.* But James Henry wasn't in a conciliatory mood.

Spencer nodded to his second in command, Lawson, indicating that he should take over the discourse. Maybe James Henry wouldn't be as defensive with him.

Lawson, a lean, younger man, cleared his throat and pushed metal-framed glasses up onto the bridge of his nose. "Well, Mr. Hampton, what do you suggest?"

"I suggest you fellows go back to your nice plush offices in New York, and let me get back to the cane business."

Lawson glanced at Spencer, who lowered his head and rolled his pen between puffy fingers.

One of the men at the other end of the table, a kid with pimples and a ponytail, raised his hand tentatively.

Spencer glanced at him warily and said, "Yes."

"Maybe we should take a little break."

"Break, hell," James Henry bellowed. "Say what you got to say and get this over with. I have work to do."

Spencer cleared his throat. "How much more would you be willing to pay per row?"

"Not one damn dime. I just raised the row price a couple of months ago. I can't raise the row price every time you get a bug up your ass. And wages aren't my only expense. What about the fields we're resting? Have to rest a field every five years. That has to be factored in with the four years of production. You ever think about that or didn't you city boys know about resting the rows?" James Henry jammed his cigar back into his mouth and smoke seeped from his nose.

"You don't lose on a field when it's resting," Spencer said without looking up from his notes. "You flood it and plant rice."

James Henry grunted. "See what I mean? You don't know what the hell you're talking about. We don't plant rice to make money. We need two good crops of rice just to pay for the flooding. We plant rice to get rid of the weeds."

Spencer looked up from his notes. "Would you be willing to pay the men when they're sick and can't work up to speed?"

"The ticket writers take care of that with squeezing hours. You think I don't know that they give the cutters credit for extra hours when they get sick and fall behind?"

Losing patience, Spencer said, "A cutter can't refuse to work, but if he's having a slow day the ticket writer can check him out and he loses all the wages he earned before he was checked out. Does that sound fair to you?"

"Hell, we've got to have some leverage to keep them working up to speed. We're not running a day-care center here. They still eat whether they work or not."

Spencer stroked the stubble on his jowls. "We don't seem to be making any progress. If we can't discuss this gainfully, maybe we'd better break."

"Suits me. I'm out of here." James Henry shot up, grabbed his glasses and helmet, and stalked out.

Steve stood, shook hands all around, and said, "Maybe later." He settled his peaked cap on dark hair and followed James Henry outside. "What do you think, Jim? What's the answer?"

"There's no answer," James Henry grumbled. "You know that."

"Maybe we should have stayed — come to an agreement."

"You can't let them bully you, Steve. You've got to play hardball."

"Yeah, but one of these times that ball will come back and smack you in the head."

"Maybe it will — one day, but in the meantime, I'll be hitting home runs."

CHAPTER 23

After a long, hard day in the cane fields, Jazzman and Sugar Baby hurried off the bus and headed for the barracks. When the screen door slammed behind them, they were drawn to a commotion near the center of the room, where men crowded around a cot. A cutter hung from a rafter over their heads, his strong arms falling limp at his sides. A thick rope cut into the flesh of his neck; his tongue hung out of the side of his mouth, purple and swollen.

Voices mingled in a cacophony of fear and apprehension.

"Cut him down."

"No, mon, lift him up."

"Call for de field boss."

Jazzman grabbed Blinkey's arm and spun him around. "What happen, mon?"

"Damn fool kill hisself. Hangin' up there when we come in from de field."

Jazzman studied the dead man's distorted features, eyeballs bulging like large white marbles swirled with red. "Who he be?"

"Gator."

"Gator? I no recognize him. Why he do dot?"

"A woman. Wot else?"

Jazzman wiped perspiration from his face with a calloused hand. "She be his wife?"

"Ya, she run off wid some guy in Jamaica."

Jazzman pondered the situation for a few moments, then picked up his cutlass and elbowed through the men. "Grab him, Blinkey, aroun' de waist."

When Blinkey had a grip on the body, Jazzman swung his cutlass, and Gator dropped into Blinkey's arms, then onto the cot.

The men stood back, talking in hushed tones, fear and revulsion on lean black faces.

Jazzman straightened Gator's legs and folded his arms over his chest. He pushed the swollen tongue back into Gator's mouth, forced it behind clenched teeth, and tried to close his jaw.

Repulsed by the sight, the men began to drift away, no doubt wondering who their wives were enjoying while they labored in the cane fields of Belle Glade .

Jazzman reached into his pocket and pulled out two coins. He closed Gator's eyelids, and placed a coin on each lid. "Get de mon a sheet."

One of the men handed him a ragged, gray sheet that Jazzman pulled up over Gator's face. "Go for de field boss," he ordered.

One of the men sprinted out.

Jazzman strode to his bunk and sank to the hard mattress. "Damn women," he muttered, "do be nothin' but trouble." Soon he had fallen asleep in the eerie stillness of the crowded room.

The cutter who had gone for the field boss awakened him. "He say it not be his worry," he gasped, out of breath from running. "He say grower pay nothing. He say get him out of here; bury him in dat patch behind the barracks."

"Bastard." Jazzman's eyes flashed hatred. "We can't jes throw him in a hole like a dog. He got to be sent home."

"Back to Jamaica? Grower no do dot."

Jazzman slammed his fist on his bunk and looked toward Gator's shrouded body. "Gator got any money saved?"

"No, he got nuthin'. He send it all home to de wife."

Jazzman shrugged. "Den we got to give it up." He reached into his pocket, pulled out a handful of change, threw it in his hat, and handed the hat to Blinkey.

Blinkey put in a few coins and passed it to Warner, who turned away. "I no bring him here. Let de boss man send him back."

Blinkey pushed the hat toward Sugar Baby.

"Who we send him to?" Sugar Baby asked. "His wife sure don want him."

"Who he got?" Jazzman looked from face to face.

Most of the men shrugged, but Lucas stepped forward. "He got a mama, but she be old, sick —"

"We send him to her."

"She got no money to bury him."

"We got no money for to send him back, but we got to do it." Jazzman thought about the red Prince Albert can under his mattress. It held money he had saved to start his reggae band. He looked toward the shrouded body. In that instant, the dreams he held flashed through his mind like pictures on a TV screen. He saw himself fronting his own group, he saw his photo on CD covers, but ultimately he knew what he had to do. He reached under the mattress and drew out the Prince Albert can. Reluctantly, he took it to the hat and threw it in.

Peepers, bullfrogs, and tree toads raised their voices in night song as Jazzman and Sugar Baby walked along Sugarland Highway toward JACK'S. Sugar Baby looked toward Jazzman's silhouette in the moonlight. "You do be sucker, mon, throw all your money in de hat. Why de hell you pay to send Gator back to Jamaica? Boss mon get him out of there when he stink up de place."

Jazzman didn't respond. Consumed by the dream of having his own reggae band, he was composing songs in his head as they walked, hoping that one day they would bring him the fame Beres Hammond now enjoyed. Every time he heard Hammond or Terror Fabulous, he wanted his own band so badly he could feel the vibration of it in his soul.

Sugar Baby's voice rose and fell, but Jazzman didn't hear. He was about to embark on a new path. When he dropped the Prince Albert can into the hat, he began to search for another way. "More than one way to skin a cat," his grandma always said.

They sauntered into JACK'S under the flashing neon sign and pushed through the crowd toward the scarred oak bar.

Mona emerged from the swarm of bodies, grasped Jazzman around the waist, and drew him to her. She ran her hand across his muscular chest and reached up to kiss him. He brushed her lips with his, as he released himself from her grip and followed her to the table Ranilla had staked out for them.

"You're late!" Ranilla shrilled. "You got your nerve."

Sugar Baby laughed and bent to kiss her, but she pushed him away and he fell backward into a chair.

"Watch it, woman. You bruise de merchandise."

Ranilla slapped him. "You owe us. We buy our own beers."

Jazzman motioned the waitress over, crossed his thumb over his palm, and held up four long, calloused fingers. "Four beers."

The waitress nodded, gathered four mugs of beer from those on the tray she balanced on her hand, and thumped them in a cluster on the table.

"Why you so late, baby?" Mona stroked Jazzman's arm and gazed into his smoldering eyes.

Jazzman wagged his head and laid some bills on the waitress's tray. They each picked up one of the beers and took long drinks. Jazzman wiped hard fingers over moist lips.

Mona picked up his hand and delicately licked his fingers.

Jazzman pulled his hand away, laughed shortly, and started tapping the table to the beat of Beres Hammond's "Step Aside," blaring from the jukebox.

Mona leaned closer. "Wanna dance?"

"Not now." Jazzman lost himself in the music resounding from speakers, and tapped the table as he sang along.

Mona picked up her beer and drank from it, without taking her eyes off Jazzman. "What's wrong with you tonight, baby?" she asked above the din of reggae.

Ranilla punched Jazzman's arm. "You got the rag on, honey?"

Sugar Baby's smile disappeared. "Don't you do be talk to Jazzman like dot. I lay one up aside yo' head."

"You do and I cut you good."

Sugar Baby turned to Jazzman. "What's de matter, mon?"

Jazzman shrugged and pulled Mona to her feet. He took her in his arms and maneuvered to the reggae beat.

When they returned to the table, Jazzman nudged Sugar Baby and motioned him aside. "We leave early tonight."

"What do be wrong wid you? Gator got to you?"

"Get the girls." Jazzman turned and strode out of the club.

When Sugar Baby pressed Ranilla to leave, she yanked her arm free and protested loudly. "You just got here."

Mona nudged her. "Come on, let's go." She got up, and went out to join Jazzman, who walked toward Harlem. She hurried to catch up.

"You actin' strange tonight, baby. You in trouble or somethin'? She melted against his side and matched her stride to his.

Ranilla and Sugar Baby fell in behind them, bickering and slapping each other.

When they entered Mona's one-room shack, Jazzman pulled her behind the limp white curtain that divided the room. He unbuckled his belt with unaccustomed urgency. As his pants dropped to the floor, he peeled off his shirt.

When Mona stripped off her dress and reached around to

unhook her bra provocatively, Jazzman didn't watch admiringly as he usually did. Instead he pulled her to him, yanked her bikini pants down, and pushed her onto the metal cot, falling with her.

His lust satisfied, Jazzman rolled off her and lay with his eyes closed, breathing gulps of air.

Mona snuggled into his side and passed her hand over muscles heaving in his chest.

Jazzman pushed her hand away and stood up so abruptly that she fell off the cot.

With panic distorting her voice, she asked, "What happened? What's wrong?"

Jazzman pulled his pants on, grabbed the red polyester shirt, and yanked back the curtain.

A startled Sugar Baby rolled off Ranilla. "What de hell?"

Jazzman yelled, "Come on, mon, we go."

"I'm not finished yet."

"You do be finished if you go wid me." Jazzman strode past them and out to the street.

Ranilla's shrill cries followed him. "What the hell's the matter with you tonight, you shitass?"

Mona ran after Jazzman, calling "Wait! Wait!" She caught up with him and grabbed his arm. "Please, tell me what's wrong."

"Git back in de house, woman, you do be naked." Jazzman pushed her away and glanced up and down the dark street.

"What happened?" Mona tried to keep up with him.

"Nuthin'. Get back in de house." He shoved her hard.

Mona hesitated, then ran back to the house, crying.

Ranilla's shrill curses followed Sugar Baby as he sprinted out, pulling up his pants. When he caught up with Jazzman, he asked, "What be wrong, mon? What—?"

"I do be jump de contract tonight."

"Jump de contract? You can no be serious, you—"

"I leave you now, mon. Catch a ride north."

"North? But, you can no leave jes like dot. Who I do be partner wit?" Sugar Baby's eyes grew wide with confusion and concern.

"You find new partner, mon."

"You tell Mona you leave tonight?"

"I say nothin'. I can't have no damn woman hold me back." Jazzman picked up the pace and Sugar Baby scurried along behind him.

"You can't jump de contract. Dey find you, dey —" Sugar Baby stepped in a hole in the road and stumbled.

"I be far off when dey look for me. I hitch a ride."

"You can no do dot. Nobody pick up a black mon aroun' here. Dey know you jump. Dey haul your black ass to jail. You don wanna land in no jail, not aroun' here, mon."

"I gotta go. You go back." Jazzman broke into a run.

"Dey put de dogs on you, dey catch up wid you!"

"Dey no catch me. I run through de canals. I run all night. De dogs, dey won't git me where I come out."

"Where you go?"

"New York."

"New York?" Sugar Baby stopped short, then sprinted to try to catch up. "What de hell for?"

"Get my band together."

"But you don know nobody in New York."

"I find de brothers. I got to git it started. Can't waste no more time." Headlights flickered over the men as a car sped past.

"You got no money. You throw it all in de hat. You can't split, go north wid no money."

"I don need no money. I work when I get dere."

Sugar baby, breathing hard, fell back. "Okay, you hell bent to go, I go wid you."

"You stay here." Jazzman took one long last look at his friend, then stepped off the road and disappeared into the darkness.

"Wait!" Sugar Baby searched the blackness that had swallowed his friend. Then, his voice low and sad, he muttered, "Good luck, mon, you gonna need it."

Sheriff Ratch combed cane fields, canals, and highways with men and dogs, searching for Jazzman to no avail. James Henry raged, until he was faced with a far more disastrous event.

CHAPTER 24

A few weeks later, flames clawed the night sky as the field next to Hampton House burned. James Henry loomed atop the fire truck like an avenging god, shouting above the roar of the burning cane. "Wet it down! Wet it down! Here. Bring those hoses over here!" Apprehension and panic crackled in his voice as flames crept ever closer to his home.

Cutters and firefighters ran toward the blaze dragging heavy fire hoses, directing streams of water where James Henry pointed, but water had little effect on the inferno.

When Steve sprinted into the out-of-control burn, dragging a gushing fire hose, James Henry yelled, "Back! Get back!" Steve ignored the command and charged the flames, fearless in his zeal to extinguish the fire before it reached the house.

James Henry watched from his perch on the fire truck as Steve stumbled through the heavy smoke, gasping for breath, directing cutters to clear cane from around Hampton House. When frightened cutters bolted, he yelled, "Back! Get back in there and clear that cane, you bastards." He struck one man with a glancing blow that sent him sprawling. Other cutters, now more fearful of Steve than of the inferno, turned and resumed cutting.

Roaring flames drowned the thud of cane knives. When

Steve could no longer be heard, he motioned for the men to load carts with cut cane and move them away from the house.

With that field cleared, Steve directed the men to the next nearest field, but the fire had become formidable — the heat unbearable. The skin on his face blackened and blistered.

Steve motioned the men out of the field and mopped his burned face on his sleeve as he backed away from the flames.

James Henry, finally convinced that the fire might take Hampton House, yelled to Steve, "Go get the women out of the house. Have the men wet the house down — all the water trucks, hurry!"

Steve waved to acknowledge that he had heard and ran toward the house, motioning for the water trucks to follow.

"Hurry, get Grace and Sami out!" James Henry's voice cracked with panic as he shouted after Steve.

"I will! I will!" But Steve's voice was lost in the cacophony.

James Henry yelled, "Jace! Call around — get more water trucks. We're not containing the fire. It's going to take the house."

Jace signaled that he had heard, jumped into his pickup, and headed off to the nearest phone.

Cutters from other farms ran in from all directions to help fight the fire. Field bosses directed them, sometimes putting them in harm's way, in a desperate attempt to contain the blaze.

Rabbits and wild pigs scurried across the firebreak, trying to outdistance the oncoming inferno. Cutters seized the chance to add game to their meager rations, clubbing the animals as they ran across the road.

James Henry moved men and equipment like pawns, seeking a strategy to divert the flames. Using every resource at his command, he fought to change the course of the fire, shifting it away from the house.

•   •   •

Inside Hampton House, Grace and Sami clung to each other, cowering at the kitchen window, watching the fire loom closer. Jade, sensing the women's fear, whimpered in Grace's arms.

Sami sobbed, "Oh, Mama Grace, I'm so scared."

"It's all right, Sami. James Henry will put it out. He won't let it take Hampton House." She hugged the frightened girl, trying to impart a confidence she didn't feel.

"Jeff is out there," Sami said, pointing to the flames. "Maybe he's hurt — maybe killed!" Sami choked on cane ash that caught in her throat and she gasped for air. Tears cascaded down her cheeks. She wiped them away with her fingers, then reached to pull a tissue from the box, without diverting her eyes from the flames.

"Jeff will be all right, Sami. James Henry won't let anything happen to him."

She patted Sami absentmindedly, looking around helplessly. "Why did Berlinda pick this weekend to visit her daughter in Key West? Oh, I wish she were here. She'd know what to do."

The men struggled against the fire, digging firebreaks, setting backfires, and directing water onto the flames.

"The wind's too strong," one of the field bosses yelled. "The fire is getting closer to the house."

James Henry pointed. "Cut another firebreak there."

"It jumps the breaks. We can't stop it." The field boss ducked oncoming flames and bolted from the cane.

Henny climbed up onto the fire truck, his hands shaking, his eyes glazed.

James Henry yelled to him over the noise of the inferno, "Go help Steve get your mother and Sami out of the house."

Henny just stood there transfixed, muttering incoherently.

James Henry cursed and slapped him across the face, trying to rouse him from his drugged stupor, but Henny just stared back at him blankly.

James Henry turned away and searched the smoke, trying to see if Steve had made it to the house.

When Steve crashed through the kitchen door, Grace jumped and screamed in terror, not recognizing his blistered, blackened face.

"It's Steve," he yelled. "Come on, Grace. James Henry said you have to leave."

"No! The fire won't reach the house. James Henry won't let our home burn."

Sami shook Steve's arm frantically. "Jeff — where's Jeff? Is he all right?"

"He's okay. Come on." Steve herded the struggling women toward the garage.

"Wait! The pictures!" Grace spun around in confusion, almost dropping Jade. She clutched Jade tighter, and reached for her children's framed photos, but Steve pulled her along toward the garage.

Sami sobbed hysterically. "Jeff! Jeff!"

"Jeff's all right. He's in town rounding up more water wagons. He's nowhere near the fire. He doesn't even know how bad it is."

Grace tried to pull away from Steve. "My things!" She reached out to her treasures: Grandma's soup tureen, a Haviland vase, and the chest that held her wedding silver.

Steve swept her up under his arm and ran toward the garage, pulling Sami along.

"Where are the car keys?" Steve shouted above the thunder of the flames.

"In the car."

Steve dumped Grace and Jade in the front seat, then pushed Sami into the back. When he slid in, Sami grabbed him with a stranglehold. "Jeff! Please find Jeff. Oh, please, please, take me to Jeff."

Steve broke her hold and threw her back. As he sped off toward Clewiston, he could see that the firebreak wasn't holding.

When James Henry saw them speed by, he yelled to the fire crews to leave the field and save the house.

The wail of sirens mingled with the roar of flames and frenzied shouting, as more equipment arrived from surrounding areas. Crews from other plantations and surrounding towns joined the fight to save Hampton House. Finally, their efforts quelled the conflagration, and by midnight the wind had died down, and James Henry at last felt that the fire was under control.

Steve settled the women into the Clewiston Inn, and on his way back he saw Jeff running along Sugarland Highway toward Hampton House. He pulled over and picked him up.

"Where's Sami? Have you seen Sami and my mother?" Jeff panted. "Are they safe? I had to run all the way into town to find a phone that was working. The lines around the house were all burned. Is Sami okay?"

"Yeah, they're fine. Sami is worried about you. I took her and Grace to Clewiston."

Jeff fell back against the seat, sweating and breathing hard. "Thank God. I was going out of my mind worrying about her. What about the house? Can they save it?"

"I hope so."

When they pulled up next to the fire truck, James Henry jumped down and ran to the car window. "Where are the women?"

"In town. I took them to the hotel. They're scared, but they're all right. Come on, we'll drive to the house and see what's left of it."

As they approached Hampton House, they saw that all of the outbuildings had been burned to the ground. The summer kitchen was reduced to rubble and smoldering ashes. All the jars of strawberry jam that Grace and Berlinda had put up were just shards of broken glass now.

"It doesn't look good," James Henry remarked as they approached the main structure.

Peering through thick black smoke, they made their way between water trucks and fire engines to approach the house.

"It's still standing, Dad," Jeff yelled. "It's okay."

Hampton House had not burned but windows had been broken by the force of water from fire hoses, and water damage was extensive.

The three men surveyed the destruction in silence. Finally James Henry spoke. "It got a corner of Berlinda's kitchen. She'll give me hell for that. It will be a big cleanup job."

"Yeah, Jim," Steve said. "Want me to get on it?"

James Henry nodded. "You do that."

Steve clasped James Henry's shoulder. "Don't worry, Jim. We'll have it back in good shape in short order."

"Right." James Henry drew his lips into a thin line. "I was crazy to plant cane so close to the house. I never planned on burning this field, but still — what was I thinking?"

Jeff patted his shoulder. "No way you could have foreseen this out-of-control burn, Dad,"

Steve tossed the car keys to Jeff. "Here, take my car and go to Sami. Let her see that you're all right. The poor kid's really worried about you."

"Thanks." Jeff caught the keys, ran back to the car, and sped off toward Clewiston.

James Henry and Steve stood silently, surveying the damage. Finally James Henry spoke. "Wonder who the damn fool was that started the burn so close to the house in that high wind."

Steve had seen Henny near the field when he drove Etta and the kids over to visit her mom, but he remained silent.

"You think those union men had anything to do with this?" James Henry asked.

"I doubt it, Jim." Steve quickly changed the subject. "The fire's gone all the way down to the peat. Better keep the land around the house good and wet. It could burn for a year, once it gets into the peat. No telling where it will crop up next."

"Yeah, you're right. Once peat starts to burn it's practically impossible to put it out."

"We'll get it out." Steve studied the structure, wondering where to start the cleanup.

James Henry turned to go. "I'd better get into town. Grace must be in quite a state by now."

"I'll go round up a car for you."

"Thanks." James Henry stood alone in the midst of the crowd that swarmed around him, thinking that he'd lost a lot recently, but the union and the environmentalists would cause him to lose more.

CHAPTER 25

Incoherent with fright and grief, Grace called Mel as soon as she and Sami were in their rooms at the Clewiston Inn. "The field nearest the house is burning out of control," she cried. "Hampton House will burn, I know it will."

"Mama, please don't cry. Take a deep breath. Where are you?"

Between sobs, Grace told Mel where she and Sami were, and what had happened.

Mel asked to speak to Sami. "Try to calm Mama," she instructed. "Call Doc Johnson to come and give her a sedative. I'll leave right now. I'll be there in an hour."

Mel slammed the phone down and rushed to find Gatti, who was snoozing in front of the TV in the library. She shook him awake. "There's a fire at Hampton House. I've got to get to Mama. Come on."

He turned his hands palms-up and shrugged. "I cannot go. I play polo tomorrow. *Mi spiace*—"

Mel yanked on her sandals, snatched up her purse, and ran out before Gatti finished his excuse.

As Mel sped across the sixty miles to Clewiston, thoughts of her life at Hampton House tumbled through her mind. Her youth there was a mosaic of happiness and pain. Things that seemed so trivial in retrospect were of great importance to her as a child. Mama always understood; she had always been there to ease the pain of disappointments and to enhance the joy of triumphs.

Nearing Clewiston, Mel saw the glow of fire in the night sky. A feeling of dread washed over her as she pulled into the parking lot. Smoke and the foul odor of burning cane choked her as she ran to the inn.

When she crashed through the door, the startled desk clerk looked up then smiled obsequiously when he recognized her. "Good evening, Mrs., uh, Princess —"

"What room is my mother in?"

"Room 204. I'm sorry about the fire, I hope —" The elevator door closed behind Mel, blocking out the rest of his sentence.

When Sami answered Mel's knock, Mel brushed a kiss across her cheek and ran to Grace. "Oh, Mama, precious Mama, thank God you're safe."

Grace set Jade aside and clung to Mel.

Mel took one arm from around Grace, reached out to Sami, and held them both in a tight embrace. A loud knock on the door jolted them.

"It's Jeff. Open the door."

Sami ran to the door, flung it open, and leaped into his arms. "Jeff! Jeff! You okay?" When she reached up to wipe smoke stains from his face, he flinched. "You burned!" she cried.

"We all got a little too close to the fire, but we're all right. The fire is under control. Every one is safe — everything is okay." He released Sami, nodded to Mel, and hurried to his mother. "Are you all right, Mama?" He knelt in front of Grace, took her hands in his, and held them tenderly. "Everything is all right, Mama, the house didn't burn."

"It didn't? Really? Oh, thank God. Where is Henny? Where's your daddy?" She looked toward the door.

"Dad's at the house."

"Henny? Is he at the house?"

"He's with Dad," Jeff lied.

Grace searched his eyes. "Are you sure everyone is all right? The house — can we go home now?"

"Not yet, Mama." Jeff restrained her gently. "There's water damage. Windows were broken when they turned fire hoses on the house. It will take a few days to clean it up and dry it out."

Grace slumped back into the chair. "Windows broken, water damage? My things — when can we go home?"

Jeff patted his mother's hand reassuringly. "Soon." He stood and gathered Sami in his arms, held her tightly, and caressed her shoulders in an attempt to comfort her.

Mel said, "I'll take Mama and Sami back to Palm Beach. They'll stay with me until you get things cleaned up."

Sami clung to Jeff, eyes wide with panic at the thought of separation. "No! No! I'll stay with Jeff."

Jeff released her grip on his arm. "It would be better if you went with Mel and Mama. I'll be busy twenty-four hours a day between the cane fields and getting the house repaired. We've got to think about the baby. The house is no place for you and Mama now."

"No!" Sami held him tighter. "We can go back to Japan now."

"We'll talk about it later." He looked to Mel. "Can you stay here with them overnight? Take them to Palm Beach tomorrow?"

"Certainly. We'll get some rest and leave in the morning."

Jeff kissed Sami lightly on the cheek and went to the door. "I've got to get back."

The next morning the family, with the exception of Henny, ate breakfast together at Clewiston Inn and discussed plans for the future.

After breakfast they drove to Hampton House. When Grace and Sami saw the damage, they realized their home was uninhabitable, so they agreed to spend time with Mel in Palm Beach until the house could be repaired.

They gathered water-soaked clothing that could be laundered and worn until they replaced their wardrobes; then they walked to Mel's car.

A sob caught in Grace's throat as she looked back at her home, thinking of Grandma's tapestry chairs, the Aubusson rug, and the window treatments that had been damaged by water. James Henry kept an arm firmly clamped around her waist and assured her that most of her treasures could be salvaged.

"Look after Henny," Grace pleaded as she departed for Palm Beach.

The men began the enormous cleanup, dividing their time between the house and the cane fields.

To distract her mother from thoughts of home and Henny, and Sami from her longing for Jeff, Mel took them shopping on Worth Avenue. Grace found several nice dresses, and Sami discovered a delightful maternity boutique where she replenished her wardrobe. They bought lingerie and shoes at Ferragamo and Louis Jourdan.

Exhausted, they stopped for lunch where they enjoyed prawns en papillote. After a sensational mousse, they felt fortified to visit a posh Worth Avenue salon for a makeover.

They left Jade at Doggie Heaven to be groomed while the staff at Elizabeth Arden gave them facials, pedicures, and styled their hair.

The problems of Belle Glade seemed less traumatic after the distractions of the day, so they dressed in their new clothing and planned an evening out. After taking phone calls from Jeff and James Henry, who assured them that Hampton House would soon be ready for their return, they left to join Gatti for dinner at the Everglades Club.

When they entered the club, Mel stopped short. Grace and Sami followed her gaze to where Gatti hovered over a small blonde seated at the bar. Gatti held her hand in his, about to bring it to his lips, when he noticed Mel.

Gatti dropped the girl's hand. "*Scuse*," he muttered, bowing and backing away from her. He turned and walked toward them.

When the blonde saw Mel, she looked away and busied herself with the short straws in her cocktail glass.

"Melisandra, Mama Grace, Sami, *bona sera*. How beautiful you look. *Que bella*, darling?" His dark eyes avoided Mel's.

Mel knew that the woman was no competition: old money, but not enough of it to satisfy Gatti's expensive tastes: his fast cars, and his stable of polo ponies.

Gatti reached for Mel's hand, but she snatched it away before he could kiss it. Without speaking, she walked toward the dining room, with Gatti following, grasping for her arm. Grace and Sami trailed along in embarrassed silence.

The next morning, the women chatted over breakfast, ignoring events of the previous evening. Mel and Sami played tennis at the club before picking up Grace and going on to Palm Beach Gardens for the croquet matches.

"This isn't like croquet Jeff and I play," Sami remarked, as she watched the players on the largest croquet complex in the Western Hemisphere.

"No," Mel said, "this is far more challenging than the back-yard variety."

"Exciting to watch!" Sami strained to follow the play.

When the women grew bored with croquet, they drove to Royal Poinciana Way for lunch. They sipped iced chamomile tea and enjoyed a salad in the outdoor café while people watching. Mel's friends stopped by the table to greet her mother and

Sami, and the camaraderie distracted the women from the loss in Belle Glade.

After lunch, Grace chose to stay home with Jade when Mel took Sami to see Whitehall, the Palm Beach palace of Henry Morrison Flagler.

"Who is Flagler?" Sami asked.

"The son of an upstate New York minister. One of the founding partners of Standard Oil."

"Standard Oil? Oh, he's rich."

"As Croesus. He built gigantic luxury hotels to lure northerners down here. Almost single-handedly he made the east coast of Florida into the American Riviera."

When Mel pulled into the parking lot, Sami said, "Some house! Those columns make it look like a Greek temple."

"The bastard built this for the filly he married after he divorced his old mare."

"His old mare?" Sami puzzled over Mel's statement as they exited the car and went in to join a guided tour in progress.

The guide intoned, "In 1901 Flagler instructed his architects, John Carrere and Thomas Hastings, to build the finest home they could think of. They constructed a seventy-three-room mansion that the *New York Herald Tribune* praised as '— more wonderful than any palace in Europe, grander and more magnificent than any other private dwelling in the world.' "

"Somebody really lived here?" Sami whispered incredulously.

Mel nodded. "Once upon a time. In the 1930s, I think."

Sami admired the Aubusson tapestries and paintings by Canaletto, Gainsborough, and Romney, but when she reached the music room and saw the largest pipe organ ever installed in a private home, she couldn't contain herself. She shrieked, and lapsing into her native accent she enthused, "Oh, this is fabulous! Beautiful! Wonderful! Did Jeff ever see this?"

"I don't know if he ever came here or not. I doubt it."

"We'll bring him. This he's got to see. It's like a fairy tale.

Oh, Jeff and I would be so happy living in a beautiful place like this. Would you like to live here with Gatti?"

"Might be fun to live here with someone I love," Mel replied wistfully.

"Like Gatti?" Sami's eyes shone with anticipation.

"That bastard?"

Sami drew back; her mouth dropped open. "You don't love Gatti anymore?"

Mel's laugh had a hollow ring. "Anymore? I never did."

Sami stared at her in confusion. "But — you married him."

"Oh, Sami, you are so naïve."

Sami stared at Mel trying to decide if she were teasing. When she realized she wasn't, she looked away to hide her embarrassment.

Mel reached out and took her hand. "There are many reasons for marriage, Sami. Love is just one of them."

"I married Jeff because I love him."

"And he loves you. You're the lucky ones."

"You never loved anyone?"

"Ah, yes, I surely did — and it damn near killed me. I loved Jason so much I thought I couldn't go on living without him, but obviously I did. Come on, we're losing our guide."

That evening Gatti went out with friends, and the three women enjoyed a quiet evening together. When they phoned Jeff, Sami prattled on about the Flagler mansion until Jeff said with a laugh, "Sorry, Honey, I can't buy it for you."

Grace talked to James Henry, and felt better when he told her that he had put three crews on around the clock, and the cleanup was progressing ahead of schedule. When she asked about Henny, James Henry hesitated, and decided not to mention that he hadn't seen or heard from him since the fire. Instead, he reassured her by saying, "He's fine," and changed the subject.

After the call, the women discussed the news from Belle Glade, then Mel said, "Gatti will be playing polo tomorrow. Would you like to see him play?"

Sami brightened. "Oh, yes. I'd like that."

"Perhaps you should be getting more rest, Sami," Grace said, as she stroked Jade's silky fur. "The baby takes so much of your strength."

"I'm fine, Mama Grace, I'd like to see Gatti play polo."

"All right, if you're sure you feel up to it." Grace looked to Mel, concern deepening the crease over her nose. "We've been monopolizing your time, Melisandra. You should be spending more time with Gatti."

Mel scoffed. "Gatti's not missing my company. His life revolves around polo — like Daddy's does around cane." And now, she thought, there's that little blonde. For Gatti a wife is more of an annoyance to be tolerated than a companion.

Mel turned to Sami. "They'll be playing at Wellington tomorrow. Gatti is an excellent player. You'll enjoy seeing his rushes and stop shots."

Grace grimaced, dreading the dust and the sun.

Mel kept them busy, and the weeks passed quickly. Soon they received the news they were anxiously awaiting: Hampton House was ready for their return. Mel drove them back, and for Sami the ride seemed endless.

Jeff waited in the driveway, and when they pulled in, Sami leaped out of the car and ran to his arms. She stretched over her pregnant belly, hungry for his lips, eager for his embrace.

James Henry pushed up from his wicker chair and ran down the portico steps to open the car door for Grace. He took her hand as she got out, and bent to kiss her forehead. He put his arm around her waist as they walked together toward the front door.

"Hello, Mel," he called over his shoulder. "You're going to like what we did to your room. I put in that window seat you've always wanted."

Mel smiled. She'd asked for that when she read *Little Women* over twenty years ago.

Grace glanced around. "Where's Henny?"

Before James Henry could respond, Berlinda rushed out and gathered Grace to her ample breast. "Welcome home, Miz Grace, it's sure good to see you back home."

She looked toward Jeff and Sami. "You, too, Miss Sami. Mr. Jeff, he missed you somethin' terrible."

Jeff gathered Sami closer. "She's right about that."

"Me, too," Sami said, forgetting her Asian reserve and kissing Jeff brazenly.

" 'Lo, Miss Mel," Berlinda called as she steered Grace toward the door.

"I'm so eager to see —" Grace stopped short. Everything had been cleaned and returned to its proper place. Berlinda had even put fresh flowers on the ebony temple table in the foyer. Grace turned to Sami with tears of joy in shining eyes, and said, "Welcome home, Samiko dear."

Sami hugged Jeff tighter and beamed up at him. "Oh, yes, Mama Grace, it's so good to be home."

For a short while life at Hampton House was pleasant and peaceful.

CHAPTER 26

The cutters returned to Jamaica, and the early summer months brought a sense of ennui to Hampton Plantation. As James Henry, Jeff, and a skeleton crew performed the necessary off-season tasks, Sami grew restless and longed to go back to Japan.

"Nonsense!" James Henry blurted. "Suppose the baby comes early? My grandson will be born on Hampton Plantation like his daddy and his granddaddy before him."

Jeff reluctantly agreed to stay, leaving Sami with a gnawing feeling of betrayal. Jeff hadn't taken her back to Japan after a few weeks as he had promised, and now he was agreeing to stay for the birth of their baby.

In an effort to keep Sami occupied and content, Grace and Jeff planned short vacations around the state, and life continued at a leisurely and pleasant pace, despite relentless summer heat and daily thunderstorms.

One morning in June, when James Henry went into the kitchen, he was assailed by the blast of the television. "Turn that damn thing off, Berlinda," he shouted above the din.

"No, sir, Mr. Jim. They got hurricane warnin's up. Storm done took a turn durin' the night, and it's headin' right for us."

"Didn't say much about it in the *Herald* yesterday — just a tropical storm coming across the Caribbean, heading for Texas."

"It done changed its course durin' the night and it picked up force. Full-blown hurricane headin' right for Florida now. Gotta hear when it's a comin' and where it'll hit."

James Henry glanced at the TV screen. The WTV weather forecaster was saying, "— winds increasing in velocity to over 100 miles an hour. The storm will probably come ashore in the Palm Beach area sometime tonight. Looks as if it might be as bad as the legendary storm of 1928."

James Henry had heard stories of the hurricane of '28 from his father. Hundreds killed and injured, water from the Okeechobee flooding all the way up to Tampa, houses leveled and farms destroyed. He gulped his coffee and bolted for the door.

Berlinda ran after him with the plate of fried eggs, sausage, and grits she had been about to serve. "Mister Jim, yo' breakfast! Mr. Jim —"

He called over his shoulder, "No time for that." He clattered down the steps and was gone.

He raced to the field office, slammed open the door, yanked cardboard boxes from the closet, and began boxing files and records.

Steve rushed in. "Say the hurricane's heading our way, Jim."

"I heard. Give me a hand with this. We've got to get these papers over to the main office for safekeeping. Soon as you deliver them over there, get some men over here to batten this place down. Get Yancy over here with his truck. Tell him to take Granddaddy's desk over to the main office. Put it in an inside room on the second floor. First floor will flood if it's as bad as predicted."

"You got it." Steve threw files into boxes and carried them to his pickup. "What about Grace? Anything need to be done at the house?"

"As soon as Jeff comes in, I'll tell him to get men over to the house to board it up. He can take the women to the main office; they'll be safe there. You better take Etta and the boys over there too. We've got some meeting rooms in the center — no windows."

"Mom and Dad always ride out the hurricanes at my place. We're on high ground and it's farther away from the lake; not as much flooding." Steve locked flaps of the last box in place. "That it?"

"Yes, hurry. Store them on the second floor, Dave's office, on the top shelves. When you get that secured, go see if your dad needs help boarding up the café. You or Vonda or Chip need anything, let me know."

"Right."

"Have some men secure the barracks." James Henry flipped on the radio and paused to listen to the weather forecast.

"The storm is traveling in a northwesterly direction. It will probably touch down in the Palm Beach area earlier than expected. The wind velocity is increasing —"

"I better hurry." Steve picked up the last box and was gone.

Steve passed Cleatus, one of the field bosses, on the steps. Cleatus wore his sweat-stained old felt hat pulled down to his beefy nose, so all that was visible was felt hat, nose, and the stubble of a three-day beard. "Big one a comin'," he said as Steve rushed past.

He mounted the last step, pushed open the screen door, and adjusted his cud. "Mornin', boss."

"Take your men over to the main office. Board the windows. Get the pots in off the patio. Take down the awnings and brace whatever limbs need bracing."

"Yes, sir, Boss." Cleatus's work-worn boots scraped the bare floor as he hurried toward the door.

Berlinda knocked on Grace's door. "Miss Grace, y'all better get up. There's a hurricane a comin'."

"Come in, Berlinda. What is it?"

"Hurricane, Miss Grace. Hundred-ten-mile-an-hour winds

now and pickin' up speed. I already move stuff to the top shelves and roll up the rugs. I wrap tissue around all the crystals on the chandeliers — fix 'em with rubber bands. You want I should box up the china?"

Alarmed by Berlinda's tone, Jade sat up in her canopied doggie bed, shifted nervously from foot to foot, and yelped uncertainly.

Grace pulled on a silk wrap and fumbled for her slippers. She rubbed her forehead, trying to clear her thoughts. "Will that be necessary?"

" 'Fraid so. They's predictin' winds over 150 miles an hour — with heavy floodin'."

Grace hurried to the window and opened the drapes. Sun flooded the room. Outside, palm fronds curtsied in the gentle breeze, white egrets strolled elegantly among pink hibiscus, and fish broke the gleaming surface of the pond. She blinked in the bright light and drew the drapes partly closed. "It doesn't look threatening," she mused.

"Now Miss Grace, you live in these parts all your life. You know that sun a shinin' like that don't mean nothin'. Kick up a storm here in Florida 'fore you can grease yo' grits. Forcaster say it's pickin' up speed and headin' right for us." Her voice grew stronger and her eyes widened with alarm.

"What did Mr. Hampton say?"

"Just say he got no time for breakfast. Never even eat his eggs and grits. Just went slammin' out when he hear 'bout it."

"Last night the weatherman said the storm would go ashore in Texas."

" 'Pears forecaster wrong. It be headin' right for us now."

Grace glanced from Berlinda to the window. "I'll get dressed. Where's Henny?"

"Sleepin' as usual, I suppose."

"See that he stays here when he gets up. Tell him to stay home today to help his father."

"No use me tellin' him nuthin' He don't pay me no mind. We better hurry and get that china packed up."

"We'll talk about it at breakfast."

"All right, but we be wastin' precious time." Berlinda stepped out of Grace's room and hurried down the hall toward the kitchen.

Grace flipped on the TV. The national weather channel reported 115-mile-an-hour winds with the storm racing toward Palm Beach. She glanced at her bedside clock and saw that it was too early to call Mel's houseman. *Oh, I do hope he can be relied upon to take proper precautions*, she thought. Melisandra won't hear about the hurricane way over there on the Aegean. She dressed quickly and went to Jeff and Sami's room, Jade following closely at her heels.

When Grace knocked, Sami called, "Come in."

Jeff stepped out of the bathroom, a towel wrapped around his lean waist, dark hair falling in wet ringlets around his face. "Morning, Mama. What got you up so early?"

"Berlinda says a hurricane is picking up speed and heading this way. She thinks we should pack the china. I don't know wh —"

"Hurricane?" Sami's voice quavered. She placed hands on her protruding belly as if to protect the baby.

Jeff switched on the television and listened intently. "Quite a change from last night's predictions; no one thought it would hit here. Sounds as if it's serious. What did Dad say?"

"Berlinda said he ran out without eating breakfast."

"That doesn't sound like Dad. I'll call the field office, see what's up." He picked up the phone and dialed. "Dad? Jeff."

James Henry's voice resounded from the earpiece. "I'm afraid we're in for it, son. I've got everything under control here. You take care of the women and the house. See that Henny stays there. Get some men to board up the windows. Put the patio furniture and the potted plants in the garage. Brace all the tree limbs and cut any that hang over the house. Cut the coconuts or they'll be hitting the house like cannonballs."

Jeff scribbled on a pad beside the phone as he listened intently to James Henry's instructions.

"Fill up the bathtubs. We'll need drinking water if the pumping plant goes out or the water gets contaminated. Be sure you got enough fresh batteries for the radios and flashlights. Get the generators cranking. Get plenty of cold cuts, bread, canned goods, and bottled water. Have some of the men pick the fruit in the grove and bring it in. Be sure the oil stove is working, and have plenty of oil on hand. Get some Sterno. Did I say batteries?"

"Yeah."

"Okay, get on it. Then hurry back and take the women to the office. They'll be safe there in an inside room. I'll come home as soon as I can." The dial tone sounded.

Jeff placed the phone back in the cradle and tore the list from the pad.

"What did he say?" Grace asked, worry setting the crease over her nose.

"Will be okay? Will we be all right?" Sami looked to Jeff for reassurance.

"I don't think it'll touch down before tonight. We'll have time to prepare." He held up the list. "I've got to get dressed and get the crew over here to board up. I'll go to the store and pick up these things."

"What can we do?" Grace asked.

"Tell Henny Dad says he should stay here."

"I will, I will. Oh, I hope he listens."

"You two can clean the tub and fill it. I'll tell Berl —"

Berlinda rushed in through the open door carrying cleaning supplies, and disappeared into the bathroom. "Got to clean the tubs and fill 'em up. Rest of 'em already filled. Hope the drains hold. Mr. Jeff, you go get some canned goods; list on the kitchen table. Get plenty of bottled water, you hear? Get candles, batteries, Sterno."

"I'll get everything we need." Jeff stepped into the walk-in closet to pull on his jeans. He came out, kissed Sami, hugged his mother, and rushed for the door.

"Get Hershey bars," Sami called after him.

Sami and Grace exchanged worried glances.

"We'll be all right," Grace said. "Jeff and James Henry will take care of us. I'm going to Henny's room — I hope he's there. I'll meet you in the morning room."

Jade's silky coat bounced and her short legs pumped like furry pistons as she ran along behind Grace.

Sami dressed and went to the morning room, where bright sunlight filtered through sheer curtains, bathing the furnishings in a rosy glow. A light breeze blew through open windows. She looked out at the abundant blooms of birds-of-paradise, then glanced toward the red and yellow crotons that ringed the old Spanish fountain in the courtyard. She watched a tiny gecko scoot across the sill. It leaped to a shrub under the window, paused, looked back at her, and worked its mouth into what appeared to be a lopsided grin. Sami smiled at it then turned away from the window. "Mama Grace," she called.

"I'm here, in the dining room. I just called Palm Beach. Melisandra's houseman said they've issued warnings there to prepare for a major storm. He's having the place boarded up. I hope Melisandra doesn't hear about the storm and have that worry. There's nothing she can do about it from a yacht on the Aegean." Grace wrung her hands, thinking of destruction and loss of life in previous storms. She looked plaintively at Sami.

Sami put her arm around Grace and hugged her. "Mel's home will be all right."

Grace glanced down the hall. "Henny isn't in his room. Where could he have gone?"

"Maybe he's with Papa Jim."

"I don't know." Grace twisted a linen handkerchief as she paced.

"Henny will probably be back by the time we finish breakfast."

"Oh, I hope so." Grace glanced toward the dining room. "I don't think we'll have to box the china, do you?"

"I don't know. Jeff says hurricanes cause a lot of damage."

Grace touched the soup tureen on the sideboard. "This china belonged to my great-grandmother. Some day it will be yours. Melisandra thinks it's silly to treasure tradition, but you and I think alike, don't we?"

"Oh, yes, Mama Grace, ancestor's possessions great treasures." Sami caressed the fragile, translucent china reverently. "We must take good care of their things."

"We'll pack it right after breakfast. Come."

Seated at the kitchen table, they were startled when a ladder thumped against the house. Workmen called to each other as they went to the roof to cap the chimneys.

By noon, dark, ragged clouds, heavy with rain, swirled overhead. Palm fronds rose and fell on brisk currents of air. The atmosphere squashed into a heavy, foreboding blanket. Winds began to build, and pressure fell so rapidly that the barograph pen ran off the page during a television newscast and it had to be reset.

Grace and Sami packed the china, then huddled together in the library. The rooms darkened as men boarded the windows. Hammering and shouting seemed more ominous as light faded.

Galloping palms, now agitated by forceful winds, slapped the house, unnerving the women. Jade bore into Grace's lap, looking up for assurance, an assurance Grace didn't feel.

They became more apprehensive after all the windows had been covered with plywood. Cowering in the eerie darkness, Grace and Sami were startled by the ringing of the phone.

James Henry called to say Jeff should take them to the main office for safety.

"Jeff hasn't come back; we're worried about him. He's been gone for hours." Grace glanced at Sami, then turned away to hide her concern.

"He probably stopped to give instructions to men in the fields. I'll send someone else to take you to the office."

"No!" Grace cried. "Hampton House has withstood hurricanes for over sixty years. I won't leave my home."

"Stay put, then. I'm on my way."

The hurricane showed no sign of diminishing or changing course as James Henry drove away from the field office. Wind blew steadily toward the west as the car inched along the flooded road. Small metal signs sailed through the air like missiles, and a piece of corrugated roof hit the side of the Lincoln with a sickening thud. Trucks and buses passed, going in the opposite direction, carrying evacuees from outlying areas to churches and the auditorium in town.

As he drove past La Vonda's Café, James Henry saw Chip taping the windows. He swung into the lot and leaped out. Bursting through the door, he shook rain from his helmet and wiped his face. "Steve here? Where's Vonda?"

"Steve's over to your place helping board up. Von went over to stay with Etta and the kids. I'm gonna go over there as soon as I finish taping these windows." Chip ripped a length of tape from the roll and turned back to the window.

"You know if Steve found Henny?"

"Don't know. When's it gonna hit? You hear?"

"About midnight, they think. Why don't you have the TV on?"

"Branch fell on the power line and downed it."

James Henry glanced around the bar. "Haven't you got a battery radio?"

"Batteries went dead and I forgot to get new ones. They say

it might be as bad as the hurricane of '28. Expect it to blow in from West Palm, same as that one did. Belle Glade sure took a hit back then."

Chip finished taping the window, jumped down, and went behind the bar. He drew two beers, set one in front of James Henry, and sipped from the other.

"Thanks." James Henry gulped from the cold brew, then set the remainder on the bar and turned to leave. "I've got to get Grace and Sami to the main office where they'll be safe."

"Better safe than sorry. I gotta stack these chairs, then I'm outta here. Water rose to eight feet in here in the first hour of the '28 storm."

"You better get moving. About two hundred people were killed on the road to Pahokee in '28 — crushed or smothered by debris." James Henry strode toward the door.

"Poor devils," Chip said. "Houses washed off foundations like they was toys. Sure hope it don't get that bad tonight."

"Hope not. If you see Henny, tell him to get his butt over to the main office."

"Yeah, okay. Good luck, Jim."

"You too."

Heavy black clouds blocked the sun, and rain fell in sheets, flooding the road. Palms bent to the ground under the howling wind. A date palm uprooted and blew across the road behind James Henry, making the road impassible for cars that followed. Sweat broke out on James Henry's forehead as he leaned forward, peering through the driving rain, realizing that he might not make it home.

The road had become a river. Stalled cars stood abandoned by the roadside. *Please, God,* he prayed, *let me make it home, and have Henny be there.*

When James Henry pulled up to Hampton House, he hit the garage door opener, but the door didn't respond. He punched it furiously, then threw it aside and shoved against the car door, fighting to open it. A small pause in the gusts allowed him to squeeze out, but when the door slammed shut it caught his hand. He cursed as he was pushed to the ground. The wind and rain caught in his throat, choking him as he struggled to the door on the west side of the house, which had been left open to prevent pressure build-up.

Grace and Sami jumped to their feet when James Henry catapulted through the door. They rushed to see if he was injured, but he pushed them aside.

"Is Henny here?" he gasped, as he struggled to his feet.

Color drained from Grace's face. "No. I was hoping he was with you."

"Where's Jeff?"

"He's not back yet." Sami stifled a sob. "Do you think he's all right?" She searched their faces for reassurance.

James Henry, avoiding her eyes, peered out the door into the driving rain. To distract her, he asked her to get a cigar for him. Obediently, she went to the humidor, but her eyes never left the door.

"You have to go find Henny," Grace pleaded.

"Are you crazy? I can't go out in that." He motioned toward windows that rattled behind plywood. "God looks after crazies and drunks, so I guess He'll take care of Henny, because that kid is both."

Grace gave him a withering glance and turned to Sami, who was straining to see through wind-driven rain outside the open door.

Grace took Sami's hand and stroked it. "Jeff can be counted on to come back safely. Don't worry."

"He should be back now," Sami insisted plaintively, looking from one to the other.

"I think I hear him." James Henry reached the door just as Jeff burst through. He tried to grab him, but Jeff flew across the room and banged against the opposite wall.

Sami screamed and ran to him.

Jeff dropped bags of supplies and tried to regain his breath. "The stores were sold out," he gasped. "I had to run all over town to get this stuff. I was afraid I wasn't going to make it back."

Berlinda came in with towels, gently pushed Sami aside, and said, " 'Bout time you got back." She rubbed Jeff's head briskly with a towel, her annoyance unmistakable. "Next time I'll send your daddy for them supplies."

"We can't make it to the office now," James Henry said. "We'll have to sit it out here."

Ripping pierced the room as wind peeled plywood off a dining room window. Glass shattered. They ran to the dining room to find that a limb had crashed through the window and slid across the dining room table. The driving rain blew glass across the room toward them. The men shielded the woman, rushed them out of the room, and down the hall toward the bedroom.

"Grace's walk-in closet," James Henry yelled above the roar of the wind. "It's on an inside wall and it's as big as her bedroom. We'll ride it out in there."

Grace struggled to free herself from James Henry's protective grasp. "Jade! Get Jade." She looked back over her shoulder, calling for Jade to follow.

James Henry kept his grip on Grace and dragged her along beside him.

Jeff curled an arm around Sami's shoulders, and put his hand in front of her face to protect her from flying glass. Together they ran toward the bedroom.

"Come on, Berlinda," Jeff called.

"Lord have mercy!" Berlinda ran along behind them, her arms full of food, drink, and lanterns. "Lord have mercy on us all."

Sami tugged on Jeff's arm and begged him to go back for

Jade. When they got to the bedroom he settled Sami in the closet, ran back, and found the little dog. The wind had blown her into the fireplace and she wasn't strong enough to fight her way out. Jeff smiled at her, thinking that she looked like a cartoon character flattened against the bricks. He scooped her up and ran toward the bedroom.

James Henry grabbed clothes from the rods in Grace's closet and tossed them out onto the bed to make more room. He pulled pillows and a comforter off the bed and threw them into the closet.

Jeff handed Jade to Grace, then piled an afghan and the vanity stool on the slipper chair, and carried them into the closet.

When everyone had been herded into the closet, James Henry closed the door. Darkness engulfed them, and he wondered if he were sealing them into their tomb.

Berlinda turned on a battery-powered lantern, and the dim light reflected off faces ashen with fear. The radio crackled warnings and bulletins, none of them reassuring.

Jeff held Sami, and Sami curled her arms around her bulging stomach as if to protect the baby from the wind and rain that raged outside.

Grace clung to James Henry's arm, recoiling in fear as debris bombarded the house. Jade snuggled in Grace's lap, shivering in panic.

"Damn, I wish I could have a cigar right now," James Henry said.

"Y'all never mind no cigar, Mr. Jim, you have some of this nice fruit and cheese." Berlinda passed a plate to him.

James Henry put a slice of Brie on a cracker. "Any beer, Berlinda?"

"You can't be havin' no beer in here. Where you gonna piddle?"

"What else do you have?"

"Some nice hot soup for Miss Sami in this here thermos." Berlinda poured soup into the thermos lid. "Here, Miss Sami." After they'd all been fed, Berlinda relaxed against the closet wall, sighed mightily, bowed her head, and began to pray.

The wind grew more intense as the night wore on. James Henry tried to reassure them, but nervous energy permeated the crowded room. Static punctuated intermittent bulletins that crackled from the radio. Winds reached 120 miles an hour.

Something hit the side of the house, rattling everything in it. Grace screamed in terror as tiles ripped from the roof.

Sami trembled and clutched her belly. "What was that?"

Jeff said, "It's okay, things blow around in a hurricane — nothing to worry about." He held her tighter and ran his hand gently, soothingly over her stomach.

Grace wrung her hands and looked to James Henry beseechingly. "Henny is out in this," she sobbed.

"Don't worry. He's probably with the cracker."

"Oh, I hope so. I hope they're safe. You know how he is; he's so reckless."

"He's all right," James Henry said firmly.

"I hope Melisandra's home isn't destroyed. Palm Beach is probably being hit harder than we are. How awful for her to come home to such destruction." Grace's face appeared ghost white in the eerie light of the lantern.

"Her houseman will take care of it. That's what she pays him for."

Tiles rattled overhead as they were ripped from the roof.

Sami gasped and grabbed her stomach, groaning. She clenched her hands and bit her lip.

Jeff sprang to attention. "What is it? What's the matter?"

Grace, James Henry, and Berlinda leaped to help.

Sami sat up slowly. "I'm okay. The pain is gone now."

Jeff shifted uneasily and rubbed the back of her neck.

When plywood sheared from the bedroom window, glass shattered and sprayed the closet door.

James Henry lunged to the door and held it against the onslaught of wind and rain that swirled through he bedroom.

Jeff sprang to his aid, ripping one of the clothes rods from the wall and jamming it between joists to secure the door. Berlinda snatched a towel and wedged it in the narrow opening under the door where wind drove slivers of glass inside.

When Sami groaned again, Jeff dropped to her side and yelled over the wind, "What is it? What happened?"

Berlinda picked up the lantern and held it over Sami, peering into her face. "Take it easy, chile, it will be all right."

Grace wiped perspiration from Sami's face, and asked nervously, "Is it — are you —?"

"Just a sharp pain. It passed now."

"Honey —?" Jeff's question was interrupted by a prolonged moan.

Bathed in perspiration, her breathing uneven, Sami cried, "The baby, it's coming."

With perspiration dripping from the ends of her hair, she reached trembling hands toward Jeff, but Berlinda pushed him aside and took over.

Jeff glanced at the door. "Will it hold, Dad?"

"I hope so, but it's bulging. Jam another rod behind it. We're goners if that door gives way."

Sami's rhythmic moans continued to fill the heavy air.

Jeff dropped to his knees beside her. "What can I do? How can I help? Oh, dear God, please help Sami!"

"Don't you worry none. I've got everything under control." Berlinda unscrewed the lid on a thermos and poured hot raspberry tea in the lid. She said, "Drink this, chile, and that baby slip outta you like a egg outta a hen."

Sami gulped the hot tea.

Berlinda groped in the dim light for the hot brick she had wrapped in a towel and stored in a thermal bag. She laid the warmth against Sami's stomach, and urged, "Breathe, chile, breathe deep, you almost ready."

Grace slid a second pillow under Sami's head and wiped perspiration from her forehead. "It will be all right," she murmured, "we'll take care of you." She looked up helplessly to James Henry, who was working with Jeff to wedge the door.

"Can you handle it, Berlinda?" James Henry yelled above the fury.

"Course I can, Mr. Jim, you knows that."

James Henry bore down on the braces holding the door, and said, "I'll take care of this — you go to Sami."

Jeff dropped to his knees beside his wife and searched her face. "What can I do? Are you all right?"

"I'm all right," Sami answered weakly, grasping his hand.

Berlinda refilled the cup with raspberry tea and urged Sami to drink it. "I give birth to five chillun," she said, "an' I don't remember no pain givin' birth to any one of 'em. Raspberry tea make 'em slide out like puppies."

Sami stifled a scream and dug her nails into Jeff's hand.

"Breathe deeply," Grace urged.

Sami inhaled then exhaled in a rush as pain overtook her.

"Sami, oh, God, Sami!" Jeff's tears splashed on her face.

"I'm okay," she murmured weakly, but her words were drowned in the raging wind.

Furniture skidded across the floor on the other side of the door, glass shards peppered the door like BB pellets, and a torn venetian blind beat a tattoo on the window frame in Grace's room.

Jade crept up and stuck her nose between Berlinda's arms to check on what was happening. Grace snatched her away, tapped her lightly, and scolded her. Jade shook with fear and confusion.

Sami groaned and pushed with all her strength, but the baby didn't come. The labor continued for hours while the storm raged.

Grace bathed Sami's forehead with cool water, and Berlinda stroked her stomach, while coaching her breathing and pushing.

Finally, the baby's head appeared, then the tiny body emerged, and dropped into Berlinda's waiting hands.

"The baby is here!" Berlinda yelled above the din.

"Thank God! Oh, thank you, God." Jeff crumpled with gratitude and relief. He gazed lovingly at the infant in Berlinda's hands as she placed it on Sami's chest."

"Is it a boy?" James Henry yelled.

Berlinda inspected the baby and declared, "It's a boy. A fine healthy boy."

James Henry dropped to Sami's side. "Bless you," he said. "A fine, healthy boy. You all right, Sami?"

"I'm fine. Let me see him." She tried to lift the baby, but her arms lacked strength. Jeff held him up and the happy couple beamed at him.

Berlinda took the baby and held him below the placenta, so gravity would draw the blood out. She placed her fingers on the umbilical cord and felt blood throbbing through.

James Henry took out the pocketknife that he used to cut cane and handed it to Berlinda. "Here, cut the cord with my cane knife."

"Not yet, Mister Jim. Got to wait for it to stop pulsin'. Long as the cord be throbbin', the blood belong to the baby. Got to wait till no blood flow through or Miss Sami hold onto the afterbirth, maybe hemorrhage."

Grace poured hot tea from the thermos over the knife and wiped it clean. She reached for the alcohol that Berlinda had been using, and soaked the blade before she handed it to Berlinda. When the cord became flaccid, Berlinda severed it with James Henry's cane knife.

"You cut his umbilical cord with my cane knife!" James Henry shouted. "Did you see that, son? She cut his cord with my cane knife!"

Jeff nodded and touched the baby tentatively with his fore-finger.

Berlinda held the baby upside down and smacked him sharply on the bottom. For those in the room, the baby's first cry drowned out the roar of the storm. The men cheered, the women cried, and Jade spun and barked in confusion.

Berlinda laid the baby tenderly on Sami's bare breast. His tiny mouth worked, searching for his mother's milk. Berlinda guided him to the nipple and he latched on and began to suck.

Sami gazed on the new life taking nourishment from her breast, then her eyes met Jeff's. Their love overwhelmed the small room.

James Henry shouted, "What a man he will be, coming in on one of the worst hurricanes ever, and having his cord cut with my cane knife. He'll be the salvation of Hampton Planta-tion. You mark my words."

Jeff shook his head sadly, hoping that he and Sami and the baby would be in Japan, far from these cane fields very soon.

"Glory be to God!" Berlinda exclaimed. "He's a fine, healthy boy."

"He's beautiful," Grace said, a catch in her voice as she thought of her other grandchild: Henny and Beth's baby, realiz-ing that their baby would never be a part of her life.

Sami raised her head to count her baby's fingers and toes. She looked at his ears, and touched one gently with the tip of her finger. "Tiny ears. He is perfect." She lay back, content and grateful.

"James Henry the Fifth, born on his own plantation," the proud grandfather proclaimed.

Sami beamed. "James Henry the Fifth. Sounds like king of England."

They all laughed with gratitude and relief as they huddled there together, the terrifying force of the storm momentarily forgotten.

Jeff stroked Sami's forehead tenderly, and looked down at the precious new life in her arms. They bonded in that cramped closet, while 150-mile winds raged outside.

James Henry stood over them, pride and love softening his rugged features. He glanced at Grace and smiled. "Our grandchild."

Grace rose and put her arm around his waist, happier than she'd been in years.

Suddenly, the wind abated, and an eerie stillness permeated the room.

"The eye of the storm," James Henry said, removing the braces from the door and opening it to survey the rubble in Grace's room.

CHAPTER 27

The radio crackled, "Beware of the eye of the storm. It will soon be followed by a repeat of the wind and rain we have just experienced." The forecaster's voice had grown hoarse over the course of the storm. "Beware of the eye of the storm —"

Berlinda rolled her eyes to heaven. "Lord, protect the chile." She picked up Jade's leash and snapped it onto her collar, then tucked her under her arm and said, "Come on, dog, you finally gits to go." Despite James Henry's protests, she sloshed through the water, making her way out of the bedroom over broken glass and debris.

Sami and Grace spent the lull in the storm admiring the baby, while waiting for the eye to pass and the next onslaught to begin.

Jeff and James Henry boarded the bedroom window and provided for securing the closet door.

When winds began to pick up, Berlinda returned carrying Jade, sandwiches, and an armful of fresh linens for Sami. When she dawdled, James Henry growled, "Into the closet now, Berlinda, and stay there."

"But Mr. Jim —"

"Now!"

Muttering under her breath, Berlinda carried Jade into the closet and placed her in Grace's arms, just as a bone-rattling crash signaled the passing of the eye and the return of killer winds.

James Henry slammed the closet door and secured the makeshift brace. "Thank God we've got the bedroom around this closet to protect it or the door would never hold." He reached for one of the sandwiches Berlinda had prepared on the break. "How does it look in the kitchen, Berlinda, much damage?"

Grace grabbed Berlinda's arm. "The dining room — is everything ruined?"

"Mostly it's all right." She patted Grace's hand, reassuring her.

"The chandelier — is it broken? The china —?"

"Good thing you and Miss Sami packed up that china and stored it in the closet."

"It's all right then?"

"Closet door is still closed, so I suppose it be all right. You stop your fussin' now." Her words were drowned by something sliding along the outside of the house.

Grace leaped to Sami's side and spread her arms over her and the baby. "So small and vulnerable," she murmured, cringing when tree roots ripped from the ground and trees catapulted against the house. Coconuts that the men had missed cutting pelted the house; shingles tore from the roof. Would anything be spared?

Sami, now oblivious to the hurricane, gazed lovingly at the baby cradled in her arms. She raised her eyes to Jeff's. "James Henry the Fifth has nice ring to it."

Jeff said, "Lets name him Harry — Harry Cain."

Sami smacked him playfully. "Very funny. We'll call him Jimmy, Little Jimmy."

Little Jimmy and his family rode out the hurricane in the safety of Grace's closet, and when the winds subsided, James Henry and Jeff emerged to reconnoiter before bringing the women out.

During the second stage of the storm, after the plywood ripped from the library and dining room windows, the contents of those rooms sustained extensive wind and water damage.

When the men went outside, they found the exterior of Hampton House battered beyond their expectations. Broken limbs, coconuts, roof tile, and other debris littered a lawn that had been lush and green just the day before. The beautiful hibiscus that Mimi had admired in the spring now lay scattered in disarray.

Since roads were impassable, the family huddled in Hampton House, waiting for their world to return to normal. Little Jimmy provided constant diversion. Grandparents and parents vied with Berlinda for the pleasure of holding and pampering him while his eyes tried to focus on his new world. He cooed and drooled as he experienced sights and sounds for the first time.

Grace waited anxiously for phone lines to be repaired, so she could search for Henny. She wrung her hands and said, for what seemed to her family like the hundredth time, "I wonder where Henny is. I pray he's safe. We must find him."

Then her thoughts turned to Melisandra, so far away. "As soon as the phone lines are repaired, I'll call Palm Beach to see if her home was spared. Oh, I hope it's all right."

Sami patted Grace's hand, trying to reassure her. She, too, was impatient for the phone lines to be repaired so she could call her parents to tell them that their grandson had arrived.

As soon as roads were passable, Doc Johnson came to the house. After examining Sami, he turned to a nervous Berlinda and shook her hand. "Couldn't have done better myself. Mother and baby are doing fine."

Berlinda beamed and made a big fuss over seeing Doc to his car.

James Henry put all his men on the job of restoring Hampton House, and he hired every available outside contractor. A crew of men worked in rain and drizzle for a week to repair the roof. New windows were installed, and the grounds were cleared of debris and replanted.

What should have taken months was completed in record time. Finally, when the house had returned to normal, James Henry turned his energies to planning Little Jimmy's christening party. After many hours in consultation with the staff at the country club, the party plans were finalized and James Henry told Sami to call her parents and invite them to the christening.

Sami beamed at the baby cuddled in her arms. "I'm so excited! My mother and father will love Little Jimmy. He's so cute."

The Hiakawas arrived, and after the obligatory bows to Grace and James Henry, they turned their attention to their grandson, gurgling in his mother's arms. Mrs. Hiakawa's eyes misted, and Little Jimmy's grandfather repeated, "Ah, so," until Sami poked him playfully and said in Japanese, "You're stuck in a groove. How do you like him?"

The two families visited and bonded for a few days before the christening party. Then James Henry called, "Come on, let's go!" Sami hurried to the Lincoln and settled into the back seat with Little Jimmy cuddled securely in her arms.

James Henry helped her mother to the seat beside her and Mr. Hiakawa climbed in front with James Henry. Berlinda and Grace rode with Jeff.

When Sami saw the elegant feast of appetizers displayed magnificently on tablecloths spread with flowers, she exclaimed, "Oh, Mama Grace, look, look, the flowers! White lilies, blue delphiniums, it's so beautiful." She took a deep breath. "The ice sculpture of cherubs riding dolphins is so cute! And look! Alaskan snow crabs, a whole poached salmon, and caviar in a bowl made of ice!" Glancing back over her shoulder at the opulent spread, she allowed herself to be led to the patio where the family would greet the guests.

Florida's summer sun washed the patio, still damp from early morning rain. Little Jimmy gurgled contentedly in the fresh, sweet, air that carried the scent of gardenias blooming in profusion around the patio. A gentle breeze stirred leaves of chinaberry trees, and whispered across the flagstone before being lost in the soft music of strolling musicians.

As the guests arrived, Sami introduced her mother and father and motioned the guests to the bastion Berlinda had established to display Little Jimmy.

Senator and Mrs. Rechett stepped up to James Henry. Mimi kissed him lightly on the cheek.

"Bob, Mimi, good to see you. This is my daughter-in-law, Sami, Jeff's wife." As he passed them on to Sami, he noted the senator's Armani suit, and thought, *I wonder how much of my campaign contribution went toward that?*

Sami watched with pride as Berlinda, decked out in new garb that her seamstress friend perceived to be a nanny outfit, complete with white apron and headpiece, greeted the Rechetts. Berlinda had starched the uniform to attention; it barely moved when she did. The pleats in the apron were honed to a stainless steel edge, and the cap on her freshly hennaed hair held a constant salute.

When Mrs. Rechett bent to touch Jimmy, Berlinda brushed away an imaginary fly, moving her back. "Nice to see you folks down here again so soon," she said with a disarming smile. "Come by the house and I'll bake one of them key lime pies for y'all."

"Thank you, Berlinda. I'd like that." Mrs. Rechett and the senator smiled graciously and strolled on.

As soon as Sami and Jeff could leave the receiving line, they joined Berlinda and Jimmy. Sami, eager to hear all the nice things people were saying about her Little Jimmy, crowded close. "He is adorable," she whispered to Jeff, as a couple who had just admired him walked away.

"He sure is," Jeff replied. "Maybe even cuter than his mother."

Sami punched his arm playfully, giggling behind her hand.

When Mel arrived with Yvonne, Randolph, and Gatti, Sami rushed to greet them. She noted that Mel wore the perfect godmother dress — teal blue linen with a subtle banding of ochre satin at the neckline. She hugged Mel and exclaimed, "Oh, Mel, we're so happy you came all this way for Little Jimmy's christening! Hello, Yvonne, Randolph, Gatti, it's nice that you left the Aegean to come, too." She rushed them to the bastion where they greeted Berlinda and admired Jimmy.

Mel scanned the crowd and leaned toward Jeff. "I don't see Jason here." she whispered. "I asked Mama to invite him, and I'm sure she did, but perhaps he had other plans."

Jeff glanced around. "I don't think he's here. Sorry."

Mel turned to her prince, took his arm and strolled on, introducing him to old friends. She hadn't seen them since she and Jason danced in each other's arms on this same patio at their wedding reception.

Sami turned to Jeff. "Mel is so sad; she still loves Jason. It's heartbreaking." She glanced around the patio. "You think Henny will come? It would make Mama Grace so happy if he came."

"I don't know. For Mama's sake I hope so, but you know Henny — probably drunk or high — sure to cause a scene. It's probably better if he stays away. At least he graduated; there's still hope of his going to Florida State in the fall."

"Oh, I hope he does. It would make Mama Grace so happy." Sami glanced at her son, innocently cooing under Berlinda's watchful eye.

Sami stood by patiently, as politicians and their wives

gushed congratulations to Grace and James Henry and groveled to other growers. Sami remained blissfully unaware that they were using Little Jimmy's christening to fatten their campaign coffers.

Voices rose and fell, couples danced, then separated to join other groups. After an hour, when Grace had ushered guests into the dining room for dinner, Sami asked Berlinda to take Little Jimmy home.

Relieved, Berlinda rushed home to put Jimmy down for a nap before releasing herself from the prison of her starched uniform.

When the family returned home, exhausted but exhilarated, Sami watched James Henry's reaction with amusement as her father bowed to him repeatedly. "Enjoy party so much," her father said. "Friends nice." He bowed several more times.

James Henry lapsed into an aborted bow before nervously extending his hand. "There are some details I have to attend to at the club," he lied. "If you'll excuse me?"

"Ah, yes, certainry." Mr. Hiakawa bowed again, several times.

"Uh, see you later, then."

Mr. Hiakawa continued bowing, as James Henry turned and fled to La Vonda's Café.

CHAPTER 28

After the Hiakawas returned to Japan, Sami pushed Jimmy's carriage to the pond, where still water reflected a fleece of clouds that spun around the late afternoon sun. A roseate spoonbill hovered in knee-deep water, neck outstretched, its spatula-like beak poised to scoop a tidbit from the buffet of marine delicacies.

Sami leaned over Jimmy's carriage and playfully tickled his tummy. He gurgled and cooed, and beat the air with tiny fists.

"*Kirei akanbo*, beautiful infant," Sami whispered. "Your mama loves you so much."

Jimmy's lip curled in a smile and his arms reached for his mother. Sami began to sing a Japanese lullaby. "*Oyasumi nasai*—" She lifted Jimmy from the carriage, cradled him in her arms and talked to him softly in Japanese.

Jimmy reached out, touched her lips, and tried to focus.

Sami held Jimmy up and studied his face. "Are you going to look like me or Daddy? You have a short nose, wide eyes, and a high forehead. You've got Japanese hair," she said, as she tried to smooth the spiky black sprigs into place. "And you're heavy! You're going to be big like your daddy."

When Sami laid Jimmy back in the carriage, he blinked in the strong sunlight, so she laid him on his stomach and lowered the sunshade.

As she turned the carriage around away from the sun, movement caught her eye. She looked up to see a bearded man in tattered clothes watching her. His weathered face distorted into a fiendish leer. Watery yellow eyes shone with desire.

Sami froze. A cold chill ran up her spine.

When the man shoved a tree branch aside and moved toward her, Sami grabbed Jimmy from the carriage and ran back across the lawn toward the house. She crashed through the kitchen door, screaming.

Berlinda jumped up, dropping the peas she had been shelling. She ran to Sami and cradled her in her arms. "What? What's the matter, chile?"

"There's an old man by the pond. He was watching us. I'm afraid he'll hurt Jimmy."

"What did he look like?"

Sami described him and Berlinda nodded knowingly. She released Sami and gathered up the scattered peas. "That jes be old Barney. No need to be 'fraid of him. He's been hangin' around here for years. He's jes a harmless old bum. That screamin' you done bound to scare him into another county. No need to worry 'bout him comin' back any time soon."

Berlinda rinsed the fallen peas, then sat down and went back to stripping the green pods. She tossed a shell aside.

Sami frowned dubiously and walked on through the kitchen to her room, trying to quiet Little Jimmy and reassure him.

When Jeff returned home, Sami met him in the foyer. "When can we go home? You said we came for Mel's wedding. It's time to go home."

"I know, Sami. I didn't expect to get stuck here, but I just can't leave while Dad's working with a skeleton crew. He needs me."

Sami sighed resignedly. "*Wakarimashta*, I understand. I guess you're right."

"We'll leave in the fall when the full crew returns. I'm as eager as you are to get back home." Jeff started for the stairs to shower and dress for dinner.

Sami followed him to their room, "You're not as eager as I am," she muttered.

Jeff kissed the top of her head. "The cane is our livelihood, too. Most of my income comes from here. We couldn't live the way we want to if we had to depend on my salary as a photojournalist."

Sami shrugged. "I don't care. I want to go home."

"Call your mother. That will make you feel better."

Sami glanced at the phone on the nightstand. "I already called. It made me feel worse. I want to go home."

In an effort to distract Sami, Jeff, and Grace thought of ways to keep her occupied. Grace took her to the country club for lunch and introduced her to some young women home from college for the summer. She arranged for Sami to take tennis lessons, and she invited Jeff's friends and their wives for dinner.

One day, when Jeff drove home from the fields, he noticed a small boy sitting by the roadside next to a large cardboard box with KITTENS penciled on the side.

Jeff braked and backed up. "How about a kitten?"

"Sure. You want all of them?" the boy asked eagerly.

"No, just one."

"Which one?" The little salesman picked up one squirming kitty in each hand.

Jeff pointed to a small ball of amber-colored fur. "That one." The boy handed her over.

When Jeff came home carrying the kitten, Sami squealed with delight and reached for it. She kissed the air in Jeff's direction, then held the kitten to her lips and kissed it tenderly.

"Uh-oh, it's started already. The cat is getting my kisses."

Sami giggled and nuzzled the kitten. "Plenty of kisses for you both."

"What are you going to call her?"

Sami held the cat up and studied her intently. "She's as delicate as a plum blossom. That's what I'll call her."

At first Berlinda worried about the old wives' tale that a cat would steal a baby's breath, and Grace worried that Plum would scratch the upholstery. James Henry worried that he'd step on her, and Jade feared that Plum would usurp her place in Grace's heart, but they all worried in vain. Everyone grew to love Plum, and she slept between Jade's paws when they napped.

A few days later, when the scare from Old Barney had subsided, Sami took Plum Blossom and Little Jimmy with her to the pond. Plum watched as Sami fed the koi that Jeff had put in the pond to amuse her.

Sami pushed Jimmy's carriage to the edge of the water, then sat on the grassy bank beside him, enjoying the serenity of the moment. Plum played beside them, crouching like a tigress in the tall grass and chasing butterflies.

A swallow-tailed hawk, with gray black wings and snow-white breast, rose from the cypress stand in the pond to soar gracefully overhead. Ducks glided imperiously, cutting a wedge in the silvery stillness of the pond. A tangle of mangroves appeared to float on murky water, anchored only by a brown fringe of roots that reached into the depths.

Sami broke off a long-stemmed weed and dangled it in front of Plum. Plum leaped and tumbled, striking out at it.

Jimmy gurgled contentedly, tiny feet kicking still air. Sami lay back, closed her eyes, and drank in the fragrance of summer blossoms. The warmth of the sun relaxed and soothed her.

Suddenly a hand gripped her arm. Old Barney stood over her, a grotesque leer distorting his unshaven face.

She screamed and crawled away, struggling to escape.

Barney clamped a hand over her mouth and held her in a viselike grip.

Sami bit into his hand in a desperate attempt to free herself.

Her terrified screams and Jimmy's frightened cries alerted Grace and Berlinda.

When Old Barney saw them running across the lawn toward him, he released Sami and scurried off into the palmettos.

Sami grabbed Jimmy up into her arms and held him tightly.

Grace asked, "What did he do? Did he hurt you? Is Jimmy all right?" She took Jimmy and rocked him gently, trying to quiet his screams.

"I want to go home," Sami wailed.

Berlinda returned from chasing Barney and folded Sami in her arms. "It be all right, girl," she murmured, patting her back. "You be all right now."

Sami pressed into Berlinda's soft breast and clung to her, sobbing uncontrollably. Finally she looked up into Berlinda's eyes and mumbled, "I want to go back to Japan."

Berlinda patted her shoulders. "You'll feel better when Mr. Jeff come home, you'll see." Berlinda rocked her reassuringly. "Come on, we'll go call him." The women moved across the lawn toward the house, Little Jimmy whimpering in Grace's arms.

When James Henry heard what had happened, he called Sheriff Ratch. "That crazy old coot attacked my daughter-in-law. No telling what he would have done if Grace and Berlinda weren't there."

"Jeez," Otis said, "I'll come right over. What do you want me to do about it?"

"Lock the old fool up for a couple of months, then release him in another county, and see that he stays there. I don't want him around my place ever again. You got it?"

"Good as done," Ratch said, reaching for his hat.

With Old Barney securely locked up in the county jail, Sami and Jeff walked to the pond after dinner. Leafy mangrove branches dipped beneath the surface of dark water and gentle breezes carried the scent of divergent species that inhabited the pond and its banks.

They talked about their day's activities and laughed about Jimmy's antics. Jeff skipped flat stones across the shadowy surface of the water as they walked along the path.

When the path disappeared into a tangle of moonvines, Jeff knelt on the shiny pine needles and pulled Sami down beside him. The fragrance of jasmine, an aphrodisiac on the still evening air, enveloped them.

They sat silently, listening as a chorus of southern peepers orchestrated the sunset.

Sami's long shiny hair lifted on the gentle breeze, and Jeff ran his hand over it, smoothing it. She leaned against him, and the warmth of her comforted and aroused him. He leaned down and kissed her upturned face.

Sami lay back on the lustrous carpet of pine needles, an inviting smile on her lips.

Jeff opened the buttons on her blouse and touched her hard breasts, swollen with the milk of life.

Sami pulled his head down until his lips touched hers, then she moved beneath him, eager for his love.

A mockingbird sang in the cherry laurel as darkness deepened over the pond. The moon, a great luminous pearl, floated in a bowl of dark sky.

When they separated, Sami asked, "Will we ever go home?"

"Soon, Sami."

"Why do we have to stay here?"

"Let's not go into that again. Dad needs me. He needs someone he can trust to help him with the problems he has now."

"He trusts Steve." Sami reached out to fireflies that twinkled just beyond her grasp.

"Thank God for Steve. Henny is of no use to him."

"Henny is no use, Mel is not ever here, you're the only one to help. It's not fair."

"I wish things were different. You know I want to go back to Japan as much as you do."

"Not as much as I do or we would go."

"We both want to go. We will, soon. Let's go back to the house and call your mother. It will make you feel better if you talk to her."

"Talk is not good enough. I want to see my mother."

"Invite them to come here. They'd enjoy the trip. You can take them to the Morikami Museum and Flagler house. They'd like that, wouldn't they?"

"I guess so." Sami got up, brushed off pine needles, buttoned her blouse, and started toward the house.

Jeff hurried after her, repeating promises to leave for Japan very soon, unaware that events about to unfold would delay their departure.

CHAPTER 29

Sami called out to Grace as she passed her room, "Good morning, Mama Grace."

Grace glanced in at Jimmy nursing at Sami's breast. He turned sleepy eyes to Grace, and brightened when he recognized her. Grace walked in and stroked Jimmy's head. "Is there any more beautiful picture? I remember holding Jeffrey like that."

Sami smiled, happy, content, filled with love.

"I'll see you downstairs." Grace attempted to flatten Jimmy's dark hair, but it sprang up again, stiff and straight.

The women laughed, and Sami said, "We'll be down in a few minutes, Mama Grace." She snuggled Jimmy to her breast and made sucking sounds to him.

When he had drunk his fill, Sami burped him, diapered him, and washed his baby face. Jimmy cooed and swung little clenched fists as she dressed him.

"Soon *Ojiisan* and *Obasan*, Grandma and Grandpa, will come back to see you again. They love you so much!" Sami poked a finger in Jimmy's fat belly. "Mama's little sumo wrestler."

Jimmy's lips turned up in a sort of smile, as if he understood the humor. He gurgled happily as Sami carried him down the stairs to the living room, where Grace waited with the carriage.

Grace reached out for him, took him in her arms, and

rocked him gently as she kissed his warm head. She settled him in the carriage and pulled up the crocheted throw she had made for him.

They walked out across the portico, and Grace eased the carriage gently down the steps. Jimmy rocked as the carriage swayed, smiling and enjoying the movement.

They strolled across the lawn, and when Sami pointed to the pond, they stopped on the driveway. "Oh, Mama Grace, look."

Grace turned to see a graceful purple gallinule lifting long legs, stepping gingerly from one lily pad to the next to avoid getting its feet wet. The bird, carrying a flower in its beak, stopped in front of its mate and dropped the blossom like tribute before her.

"Oh, how sweet," Sami cooed.

The two women stood together, admiring the tableau, and enjoying a moment of closeness.

Distracted by the roar of Henny's Jaguar, they looked toward the road as the car emerged from a cloud of dust that rose around it.

Grace shook her head and muttered, "He drives too fast."

Unexpectedly, Henny roared into the main drive, instead of pulling into the rear driveway as he usually did, "Look out!" Grace shrieked.

Sami screamed, grabbed the handle of Jimmy's carriage, and jumped back. When her heel caught in the paving she stumbled and fell, losing her grip on the carriage.

Grace watched in horror as it toppled, landing with a dull thud. Little Jimmy's tiny body tumbled out and rolled toward Henny's car. Grace lunged for him, but he was beyond her reach.

Sami clawed the driveway, screaming and scrambling to reach Jimmy.

The wheels of Henny's car rolled over Little Jimmy before the Jag skidded to a stop.

Sami wailed and lurched toward her baby's shattered body,

hysterical, frantic, and disbelieving.

Henny stumbled from the car and stared through coke-glazed eyes at the child's lifeless form, not comprehending the consequences of his actions.

Berlinda bolted from the house. "I called 911. They be comin' right away." When she reached them, Berlinda stopped abruptly and looked down at the torn body of the tiny child. "Oh, no, Mr. Henny! Look what you done now." She fell to her knees beside Grace and Sami, attempting to comfort them.

For a moment Henny stared blankly at the women and the baby's mutilated body. Then an eerie, unearthly, tortured, moan rose from deep in his chest. He spun around, jumped back in the Jag and sped away.

Sami's face dissolved into a mask of despair, her lips slack, misshapen, her eyes wild with the horror of her loss.

She picked up Little Jimmy's crushed, limp body and tried desperately to breathe life back into him. Finally, she gave up and rocked back and forth, screaming hysterically, clutching the broken body to her chest, willing Jimmy back into her womb.

Never again would she and Jimmy play with Plum by the pond, never again would she hear his happy gurgles. She wouldn't see him grow big and strong like his daddy, his spiky black hair would never lie flat. Sucking sounds of Jimmy taking nourishment from her breast reverberated in her head. Never, never, never —

Grace and Berlinda stayed beside her, sharing her grief, trying to alleviate her suffering, while their own pain threatened to choke them. When Sami sagged against Grace, she took Jimmy from Sami's aching arms.

A tiny ear dangled grotesquely from the side of Jimmy's crushed head. Sami touched it tentatively, and with trembling fingers she held it against Jimmy's head, as if trying to reassemble her child.

CHAPTER 30

Grace called the field office, sobbing and hysterical, to tell James Henry of the tragedy. As he listened, his mouth dropped, his cheeks sagged, and his eyes glazed with disbelief. "No. Not Little Jimmy. Oh, God, no!" He crumbled in the chair behind his desk and fought back tears.

As Grace choked out the story, he felt his life ebb. Little Jimmy had filled his heart with hope, with expectation. He pictured the tiny face, the spiky hair, little feet kicking with pleasure when he tickled him. He could feel Jimmy's warm breath when he held him to his chest. "No," he moaned. "Dear God, no! Not the baby."

Then he straightened abruptly and his mouth distorted into a hate-filled, angry line. His eyes glinted the chill of steel. "This time Henny will pay," he vowed. "This time he's going to pay. I'm through running interference for that miserable little bastard."

He dialed Sheriff Ratch. "Henny killed Little Jimmy, Otis. Lock him up and throw away the key."

Otis removed the toothpick wedged between his lips and scratched his receding hairline. "I heard. You sure that's what you want, James Henry?"

"That is what needs to be done. I should have taken action long before it came to this." He slammed the phone back in the cradle. *I lost two today*, he thought, *my grandson and my son.*

James Henry went home to comfort the women while struggling to gain control of his own emotions. He went along with Jeff to the mortuary to make necessary arrangements, and he sent a cablegram to Melisandra. He stood by when Jeff called the Hiakawas, and he spoke to them briefly.

James Henry tried to console Jeff and Sami, but his own grief was so devastating, so all-consuming, that he couldn't find the words. They all jousted with their demons, blaming themselves, trying to understand fate, to somehow justify the death of their beloved Little Jimmy.

James Henry sank into misery so deep that even the cane no longer mattered. His love for Jimmy surpassed any he had ever known. Jimmy was his life, extended. Jimmy was the future of Hampton Plantation. He was the flesh of his flesh, his hope for the cane, and now he was gone, irretrievably gone.

Grace slipped into a zombie-like state. She refused to feel. Life went on around her, but without her. She didn't look at her family, but through them. It was as if acknowledging life would force her to deal with Jimmy's death. She didn't inquire about Henny, and no one mentioned him to her. At the table with her family, she picked at food she didn't eat, then went to her room and closed the door.

A few days later, when James Henry could no longer endure the depths of despair in Hampton House, he went to La Vonda's Café. He sat at the bar talking with Chip when Vonda strolled through the café door, sunlight silhouetting shapely legs under a sheer skirt.

She came directly to James Henry, enfolded him in her arms, and rocked him as one would rock a wounded child. "I'm sorry, Jim, I am, I —"

James Henry shook his head and tried to pull away, not wanting her to speak.

Vonda gripped him tighter, cradling his head to her breast, and rocking him.

The three friends remained silent, sharing a grief that none of them knew how to alleviate.

Steve came in and walked toward them, nodding to his parents. "Mom, Dad." He touched James Henry's shoulder. "Jim," he said softly, "they got Henny. Otis picked him up heading out onto the highway. They're holding him over at the jail, but Otis didn't book him yet. He thought maybe you changed your mind."

"Book him," James Henry said flatly.

"You sure?"

"Book him."

"Wait," Chip said. "Maybe you'd better take a while to think this over."

"Nothing to think over. That doped-up drunk killed a poor helpless baby. Book him."

Steve squeezed James Henry's shoulder before walking slowly to the door. "I'll go see if there's anything I can do for Grace."

Grace lay in her darkened room, her grief sedated by Doc Johnson. When she heard a soft knock on her door, she didn't respond. When someone came in, she forced herself to open her eyes. Startled, she pulled back.

"It's okay, Grace. It's me, Steve."

"Oh Steve, for a minute I thought —" Disoriented, Grace thought it was a young James Henry standing over her with concern and compassion in his eyes. Whatever else La Vonda Wood did, she thought, she raised a fine son. She murmured, "Thank you for coming, Steve."

"What can I do for you, Grace?"

"There isn't anything anyone can do."

"Are you sure? Maybe I could go to the drugstore for something to —"

"No, but thank you for coming."

Steve shuffled helplessly, then turned and walked toward

the door. "I'll go talk to Berlinda. Maybe she needs something from the grocery."

Grace watched as he left the room; the same long strides as James Henry, the same set of the shoulders; she liked Steve in spite of herself.

Grace arose unsteadily, went to the bathroom, splashed cold water on her face, and went to comfort Sami. When she didn't find her in her room, she walked out into the garden.

She tore a red hibiscus blossom from the bush beside the path and contemplated it. *One day*, she thought, *this beautiful flower lives for only one day. A bright, happy flower that brings so much pleasure, yet it is destined to live for only a day.* She crushed the blossom and allowed it to fall from her fingers. She hurried back to her room, where she crumbled under memories of Jimmy's soft little body, his sloppy baby kisses, and bright questioning eyes.

Perhaps Berlinda is right in thinking everything happens for the best. Tragedy is sometimes a blessing in disguise. Who knows what unhappiness Jimmy might have had to endure. Henny was such a happy child, and now he's been thrust into hell.

Unable to bear thoughts of death, Grace turned to thoughts of life — to her other grandchild, Henny's child. *How could we deny him his birthright?* she wondered. *Why did I allow James Henry to alienate us from our grandchild?*

She thought of the enormity of the loss of Henny's child, and she choked on regret. Suddenly it seemed so obvious. She would go to Beth, make amends, and ask for visitation. Yes! She would have Henny's child in her life. She would love him, care for him, provide for him, and share his life. She grabbed her purse and keys, ran to her car, and sped off to talk to Beth.

When Grace pulled up in front of Beth's trailer, she sat for a moment trying to regain a semblance of calm. *I must approach Beth carefully*, she thought. *I can't risk alienating her further.* She breathed deeply, slid out of the car, hurried up the steps, and knocked on the screen door.

She could see Beth slumped in front of a blaring TV, eating ice cream from a dish propped on her belly. Billy Bob sprawled beside her, sipping beer from a can. The sleeping baby lay across his bare, hairy chest.

Grace knocked a second time before Beth glanced toward the door and saw her.

"Mrs. Hampton!" She set the ice cream aside, picked up a soiled diaper that lay on the end table, and tossed it toward the refuse can. It fell short, but Beth made no attempt to retrieve it. She came toward the door, tucking her T-shirt into faded jeans. "What brings you here?"

Grace realized her mistake too late. She should have had a lawyer handle this. But she was here now; there was no turning back. "Hello, Beth, I hope I'm not intruding."

Beth opened the screen door and Grace entered the cramped interior. She nodded to Billy Bob, who glanced away without acknowledging her.

"Turn that thing off," Beth yelled over rock and roll music blaring from the TV. When Billy Bob didn't respond, Beth went to the TV and switched it off. "Well, Mrs. Hampton, what can I do for you?"

"I, uh . . ." Grace tried to look at Beth, but she couldn't take her eyes off the sleeping baby's back. "I . . . you, I thought, uh . . ."

"When I heard that Henny killed Jeff's kid, I wondered how long it would take you to come after this one." Beth tossed her head defiantly.

Grace reeled as if struck. "I . . . oh, Beth, I know we didn't treat you well. I'm sorry — truly, I am. I've come to apologize, to beg your forgiveness. Please, Beth, it would mean so much to me if I could hold the baby, just for a moment. Please."

A cruel smile played on Beth's lips. "You want to hold little

Billy? Sure." She and Billy Bob exchanged knowing glances. She lifted the baby off Billy Bob's chest and turned him to face Grace.

Graced reached for the child, then dropped her arms and fell back. The baby's wide face and flaring nostrils, his black eyes and dark hair, the curl of his lip, made him appear to be a clone of Billy Bob. Even the cleft in the chin was identical to that of his father.

This was not Henny's child! Grace couldn't breathe. She felt suffocated in the small, foul-smelling room. She gasped for breath, turned, and crashed through the screen door. She tried to block out Billy Bob's laughter as she ran to her car, but it followed like a hail of bullets.

"James Henry was right!" She leaped in her car and tore away from the trailer, the words ringing in her head like the deafening clang of a bell. "James Henry was right, James Henry was right." Grace chanted it over and over like a mantra as she sped toward home. "James Henry was right!"

CHAPTER 31

Sami stood at the kitchen window looking toward the sky. Dark smoke from the burn crossed the sun and flames licked low hanging clouds. Egrets dove into the inferno, testing fate.

Sami shivered, feeling that she, too, was descending into the flames of a hell of Henny's making. For one moment she wished him damned, but she quickly recoiled from the thought, ashamed of her emotions. Henny was to Grace what Jimmy was to her. How could she have had such a thought?

She turned to Grace and took her in her arms, bonding in shared grief. She closed her eyes and felt the warmth of Jimmy's tiny body.

Berlinda interrupted. "Y'all come on over here and set down. I made a pot of tea for y'all."

Gratefully, Sami went to the table to sip the hot, comforting brew while she awaited the arrival of her parents.

Berlinda went about the motions of life: three meals a day, laundry, cleaning, but the work no longer gave her the satisfaction it once had. In her heart Jeff was her son, too, and Little Jimmy her grandson. She had rocked both of them in the night, concocted potions for their croup, and mixed elixirs for their ailments. She had loved them with a mother's love, and now one was gone, and the other suffering a hurt she couldn't heal.

When the Hiakawas arrived for Jimmy's funeral, Sami

clung to them and sobbed in their arms, but they were power-less to assuage the grief they shared.

Mr. and Mrs. Hiakawa had lost a grandchild, and now the daughter they knew was irretrievably gone. No longer a girl, a bride, a young mother, Sami emerged from the tragedy a woman. Now veiled eyes held a pain that could never in this lifetime be lifted.

The next day, Melisandra and Gatti arrived from Greece. Mel consoled Sami and Jeff far into the night, and she went to see Henny in jail. She found him high on smuggled cocaine, so she gave up trying to talk to him.

She sat by her mother's bedside, holding her hand, saying things meant to ease her pain. When Grace told her what she had discovered about Beth's baby, Mel was not surprised that James Henry had been right all along; he usually was. She went to the field office and sat with him, trying to help him through the devastation from the loss of his grandson.

Finally, Grace rallied and suppressed her own pain so she could comfort Sami and Jeff. She attempted to make the Hia-kawas feel welcome. She went to see Henny, and realized that both she and Sami had lost sons that awful day.

Henny now shouldered the burden of yet another trans-gression. He sulked in his cell, alternating between the pain of withdrawal and the highs of cocaine smuggled in to him.

Grace begged James Henry to help him, and he finally agreed to talk to Otis about releasing Henny so he could be sent to a drug rehab program.

Otis, expecting James Henry to relent, had made the report out as accidental death. He released Henny to James Henry, who took him to The Willough, a rehabilitation center in Naples, Florida.

With Henny in a facility where his needs would be met, Jeff blamed himself for not helping his brother by getting him into treatment sooner. His mind relived the days before the tragedy, searching for ways it might have been avoided. He blamed himself for not taking Sami back to Japan when she had begged to go. Jeff tried to comfort her, but he was not able to give her what she so desperately needed.

Sami's arms ached to hold Jimmy; her lips longed to touch his warm head. She wanted to feel his tiny demanding mouth on her breast, to suckle and nourish him, and nothing Jeff said or did could satisfy that need. When she couldn't draw sustenance from Jeff, she rebuffed him. She grew silent and remote, and this confused and angered him. Instead of bonding through the tragedy, they grew apart.

One night, after drifting into restless slumber, Jeff awakened with a start. He reached to touch Sami, but she was not beside him. He called softly, and when he got no response, he got up, dressed, and went to look for her.

He went from room to room but he couldn't find her anywhere in the house. He went out to the patio, then to the walks around the house, and finally to the pond, but he didn't find her there either.

Alarmed, he awakened his father. They searched the property for several hours, before James Henry called Sheriff Ratch, who summoned his deputies to join the search. Soon men from town came to walk through the cane with the cutters, directing flashlight beams between the rows.

When night grayed to day and they still hadn't found her, Sheriff Ratch said, "Take me to her bedroom; there should be sompthin' there that will shed some light on this."

James Henry led the way. When they entered the well-ordered room, Ratch took off his hat and scratched his head. "Sure don't look like no crime took place in here." He went to the closet, opened the door, and glanced around. He pointed to an empty space on the shelf. "What usually sets in that space there?"

"I don't know. Why?"

"Never did see no woman's closet without every bit of space

bein' took up, and that there space looks like the right size for a suitcase."

"What are you implying?"

"Mebbe she took off."

"Not Sami, she'd never go away without telling us."

Ratch shrugged and went to the desk. He picked up some papers and looked over the top sheet. "Work sheets?"

"Yeah."

Ratch shuffled through, pulled out a sheet of stationery, and read it. "Here's your answer. She went to Japan."

James Henry grabbed the paper. "Let me see that." He read it and wheeled on Ratch. "Go tell Jeff she's all right, then call off the search. Tell Jeff to come in here."

Ratch raised two fingers in a gesture of salute, said, "Right," and left the room.

James Henry picked up the phone and had the operator connect him with the Hiakawas' home in Japan. Sami's father answered, and after a moment of conversation, James Henry asked to speak to Sami.

"Hello, Papa Jim. I just got here. There wasn't time to call you yet."

"Sami, what would ever possess you to go running off without telling anybody? You had us crazy with worry. We had search parties out looking for you; the cutters are combing the fields; we were just about to call in the FBI when Ratch found your note."

"Oh, Papa Jim. I'm sorry. I never thought — I left a note with the work sheets so Jeff would be sure to see it first thing when he got up."

"He didn't look at the work sheets with you missing. He's out by the pond now. They're getting ready to drain it. We thought you might have gone down there and, uh . . . fallen in."

"Oh, how awful! Poor Jeff! Poor Mama Grace, I hope she's all right."

"She's all right — we all are; we're just worried about you."

"I don't know what to say. I'm so very, very, sorry. I never thought —"

"Why didn't you tell us you were going to Japan?"

"You always say, 'Not now — wait.' I needed to go now. But I'll come back; I'll come right back."

"No, you're there now you might as well stay for a while. You can —"

Jeff burst through the bedroom door. "Is she all right? Are you sure?"

"Here, talk to her yourself." James Henry handed the phone to Jeff and went out to thank the men who had searched for Sami. He called Jace over and said, "Have the bus drivers take the cutters to their assigned fields. Jeff will be out later with work sheets and instructions."

He ran back to the house to join Grace and Berlinda in the kitchen and give them the good news.

Jeff came in and reported, "Sami wants me to be sure you know how sorry she is for the trouble she caused. She thought I'd see the note with the work sheets first thing this morning. I wanted to go over and bring her home, but she thinks a little time apart will help. I sure hope it does; things haven't been right between us for a while now."

Grace touched his hand tentatively. "I'm sure things will work out for you. You will both feel differently after a short separation."

"Yeah," James Henry said. "Let her see what she's missing."

Berlinda mumbled and flipped a stack of pancakes onto a plate for Jeff. "You do what you have to do, Mr. Jeff. Don't you lose Miss Sami. She be one fine woman."

That night Jeff lay in bed watching the sheer window curtain lift on humid air, feeling emptiness like none he had ever known. His arms ached to hold Sami, his loins ached to possess her. Her loss, stacked on the death of Little Jimmy, made living almost unbearable. He choked on his breath and vowed to have her back for their love to flourish as it once had. He closed his eyes in troubled sleep.

Two weeks later, when Sami stepped off the plane Jeff didn't recognize her at first glance. Her hair had been clipped to a short bob and she wore a tailored suit with low-heeled pumps. He rejoiced at having her back, realizing that she was no longer a girl, but a woman. When she flew into his arms and hugged him tightly, he vowed to rekindle a flame that had almost died. He knew that his beloved Sami had returned, and he felt confident that they would never separate again.

CHAPTER 32

With family tragedies suppressed for the moment, and union interference behind him for the summer months, James Henry unwound behind his desk.

Cleatus, one of his best field bosses, entered in the glare from late afternoon sun.

Uneducated, but wise in the ways of the cane, Cleatus and James Henry shared a mutual respect. He was one of the men James Henry kept on through the summer months after the Jamaicans had returned home.

"Hello, Cleatus," James Henry said. "What can I do for you?"

"Well, Boss, it's like this." Cleatus took off his sweat-stained old felt hat and held it in front of him.

"Well, what is it?" James Henry lit a cigar and leaned back in his chair.

"I measured a couple of stools in the next field, Boss. It's eight stalks, three feet high. It'll be forty-ton field."

"Good, we'll come out all right on that one."

"Boss Jim?" Cleatus shifted from foot to foot.

"Yes?"

"Boss, me 'n' Maybelle is gettin' married on Saturday. She wants her a fancy weddin'." An embarrassed flush rose from the collar of Cleatus's worn blue work shirt and spread across sun-burned cheeks that bulged with a cud.

"Well, now. What do you think of that?" James Henry reached to shake Cleatus' hand. "Congratulations."

"Me 'n' Maybelle, we'd like you 'n' the missus to come to the weddin'."

"Why thank you, Cleatus. I'd be most happy to stop by. Mrs. Hampton has been feeling a little poorly, and I don't believe she'll be able to make it, but I'll come by. I surely will. Where are you having it? At the church over in Clewiston?"

"No, sir, boss. We're havin' it right here in Belle Glade, down to Harley's Barbecue Pit 'n' Weddin' Chapel."

"Are you now?"

"Yup. That way we kin have the weddin' 'n' the party right there in the same place. Won't have to go no wheres else a'tall." Cleatus pulled out a crumpled red kerchief and wiped his brow.

"Good idea, Cleatus. Harley's it is. Mighty fine barbecue, best in all of Florida would be my guess. You can get hitched there as well as anywhere. Preacher coming over from Clewiston, is he?"

"No, sir. Harley's goin' to marry us hisself."

"Harley?"

"Yup. He got hisself one o' them mail-order preacher certifications. He's a reverend now, sure as shoot."

"Harley a reverend." James Henry shook his head and chuckled in disbelief. "I didn't know that — and him selling the best bootleg liquor in the county. Maybe that's why his barbecue tastes so good. You get a belly full of that white lightning and anything's going to taste good."

"Mebbe so, Boss, mebbe so. The white lightnin' tastes even better cuz there ain't no revenue sticker on it." Cleatus choked with laughter. "Weddin' gonna start about two o'clock. Maybelle be mighty proud if you stop by, Boss, mighty proud. Thank you, Boss."

"See you Saturday." James Henry made a mental note to stop by Harley's for a few minutes on the way home from his golf game at the club.

"That's right, Boss, Saturday. Two o'clock. Thank you, Boss."

Cleatus backed out of the office. He threw his sweat-stained hat into the air, caught it neatly and mashed it back onto his head, stumbling over his feet as he hurried to catch the bus home. *Maybe Maybelle will realize now how important I am to Boss Jim and the cane business*, he thought as he flagged down the bus.

James Henry didn't mention the wedding to Grace. She never went to the worker's parties, but he knew it promoted good relations, so he made it a practice to stop by for a few minutes when the men invited him.

On Saturday, James Henry stopped in the Remembrance Gift Shoppe in Belle Glade and randomly selected a wedding card. He signed both his and Grace's names, put in a hundred-dollar bill, and sealed the envelope. That done, he headed for Harley's Wedding Chapel and Barbecue Pit.

As he maneuvered between pickup trucks in the parking lot, it occurred to him that he should have come for the ceremony. Seeing Harley as a preacher would have been worth the time.

He walked toward the door to the beat of throbbing country music, and when inside, he pushed through the crowd toward Cleatus and Maybelle.

Cleatus stood by a keg, tugging on the too-short sleeves of a pale blue rented tuxedo. Although the pants had been turned up into a six-inch hem, the legs still fell in folds over Cleatus's shiny new shoes. He wore a matching tie and cummerbund in alternating stripes of blue and hot pink.

"Boss Jim!" Cleatus's face brightened as James Henry approached. He turned triumphantly to Maybelle. "Din' I tell ya Boss Jim would come?"

James Henry shook Cleatus's hand and congratulated him, then turned to Maybelle and wished her happiness.

"How you, Boss Jim?" she yelled above the din of the crowd and the music. She minced, curtsied, and turned completely around so James Henry could adequately appreciate her white polyester wedding gown.

"Do I get to kiss the bride?"

Maybelle, emboldened by the free-flowing beer, flung her arms around James Henry's neck and kissed him on the mouth. It was quite a coup for her to have a grower attend her reception, and a real ego enhancer to have him kiss her.

"Show him your ring," Cleatus urged, nudging her as he turned to James Henry. "I got it at Sears," he boasted. "The best one they had."

James Henry admired the ring, commented on the big turnout, and handed Maybelle the envelope.

"Oh, you din't have to do that, boss," Cleatus said, as Maybelle pulled out the bill, noted the amount, and waved it over her head.

"Look everybody, look whut Boss Jim give me and Cleatus — a hunert dollars." Everyone cheered and applauded, and James Henry turned to go.

Cleatus grabbed his arm. "Have some barbecue, boss." Cleatus pushed a plateful of pungent juicy ribs into James Henry's hand and yelled to the bartender. "A jar of Harley's white lightnin' with a beer chaser for Boss Jim."

Golf had whet James Henry's appetite, and the aroma coming from the ribs proved irresistible. When he looked for a place to sit, he noticed Steve and Etta at a nearby table. He went to join them. "Hello, Steve, Etta. Mind if I sit here?"

Steve moved his chair to make room. "Hey, Jim. Sit down."

James Henry, pleased by a chance to visit with Steve, swung a chair to the table. On more than one occasion James Henry had thought about the love they shared for the cane and their similar views about the operation of the cane fields. He allowed himself to marvel at how much Steve resembled him in both thinking and appearance, and to wish that Steve were his legitimate son.

After a few minutes, Chip came in and joined them.

James Henry looked past him. "Where's Vonda?"

"Von went to George's funeral." Chip pulled up a chair across from James Henry and dropped into it.

"George Taylor's funeral? Why the hell would she go to that junkie's funeral?"

"He died." Chip drew a Camel from the pack in his pocket and lit up.

"He died of AIDS, didn't he?"

"He did."

"Well? Why did she go to his funeral?"

James Henry's voice took on a hard edge as he leaned across the table, trying to hear above loud music and boisterous chatter.

"Von and George was close. Real close."

"What's that supposed to mean?"

"It means you ain't the only one that made regular trips up them stairs."

Steve pulled Etta up and they headed for the dance floor.

James Henry reeled back. "Not George?"

"Yup, she was doin' George too."

"Doing George? You're crazy. A junkie with AIDS? Why would she be doing him?"

"Same reason she was doin' you, I guess. Couldn't get enough of it. No ten men could satisfy Vonda."

"But George?" James Henry stared at Chip incredulously. "She could have caught AIDS."

"Truth be told, Jim, Von did catch AIDS."

James Henry's jaw dropped and he regarded Chip dumbly. "Vonda has AIDS?"

"She does, and that's a fact"

Color drained from James Henry's face. "Vonda has AIDS? Do you? I mean — did you — did she give it to you?"

"Well, I don't rightly know. Mebbe she did and mebbe she didn't. Sometimes it don't show up for months — mebbe years. She mighta' give it to me. Matter of fact, mebbe she give it to you, too."

James Henry's breath escaped as if he'd been punched in the gut. "No!" A flush spread across his features.

Chip gulped from the mug of beer the waitress had just thumped down in front of him and wiped foam from his lips. "Don't matter much, we all gotta go sometime."

James Henry reached across the table and grabbed Chip's shirt. Glasses and bottles smashed to the floor as James Henry dragged Chip across the table. "Don't say that. Do you hear me? Don't say that!"

Revelers at adjoining tables cheered, sure that the obligatory wedding fight had begun.

Steve ran back to the table and loosened James Henry's grip. Chip slid to the floor. "Not here," Steve said, glancing around self-consciously.

James Henry came to his senses and stepped back. He went around the table to help Chip to his feet.

"Damn it," Chip said, "now see what you've done." He wiped blood from a cut on his arm.

James Henry took out his handkerchief and started to mop the cut.

"Watch it," Chip said, "Don't get my blood on you. If I do have AIDS you could get it, too, if you don't have it already."

"Stop saying that! I don't have it. I don't. Oh, hell — no!"

Blaring music drowned out their voices, and the party continued with no one aware of what had caused the row. Since they hadn't heard any of the conversation over the din, they assumed the men were fighting over Vonda's favors. They had wondered for years how Chip and James Henry shared Vonda so openly, yet remained friends.

James Henry wiped his hand across his eyes as if to clear his thinking. "I can't believe that woman did this to us."

"Von didn't do nuthin' to us. We done it to ourselves."

"What the hell is that supposed to mean, we did it to ourselves? That tramp did this to us. It's her fault."

"Oh, is it? And just where the hell were you while all the fuckin' was goin' on?"

"Why in hell would Vonda get it on with George, a drug addict with AIDS?"

"Hey, Von's gonna get it on with anything that moves. I knew that when I married her, and you damn well knew it, too. You don't think I expected marriage to change her, do you? Hell, a man can't pick and choose who he's gonna fall in love with; it just happens. Not that I'm sorry. I wouldn't change Von if I could."

"Are you crazy? The woman probably gave us AIDS. This isn't a case of syphilis. It's not some venereal disease that can be cured with a shot or two. This could kill us."

"We're all gonna die, Jim. Today, tomorrow, what's the difference? We're all gonna die."

"Well, I'm not ready to die."

"They don't wait for you to get ready. When your time comes, you just up and die."

"What Vonda did was unconscionable. It just wasn't right."

"And I suppose it was all right for you to lay down with your best friend's wife."

"You didn't care."

"The hell I didn't! Whatever give you the idea that a man don't care that his best friend is fuckin' his wife?"

"You never said anything."

"What was I gonna say? You come breezin' in there, a wave

and a howdy, and up you go. How do you think a man feels when he watches his best friend goin' up the stairs to his wife?"

"I didn't know it bothered you. We've both been doing Vonda since high school. I never thought about it."

"You'll think about it if you test positive." Chip picked up his cigarette, took a long drag, righted his chair, and sat down.

"Don't say that! Don't even think it."

Chip inspected the cut on his arm, picked up a cocktail napkin, and dabbed it. "You better get tested."

"Where? Where do I get a test?"

"Doc Johnson can give it to you."

"Not Doc Johnson. I know Doc Johnson. What will he think?"

"It don't matter what he thinks. If you got AIDS you won't be around long enough to worry about it."

"Shut up. I've got to think." James Henry's forehead tightened. He stroked his chin with quivering fingers.

"You shudda thought before you went up them stairs."

"I'm getting out of here."

Just as James Henry got up to leave, the door to the club crashed open. Henny stood silhouetted against the bright Florida sun, waving a gun. He pointed it at James Henry. "Turn around and face me, you bastard."

"What the hell?" James Henry stared at his son in disbelief as wedding guests dived for cover. "Why the hell aren't you at The Willough?"

Henny screamed. "I should be marrying Beth today — you should be at my wedding."

A shot exploded from the gun and a bullet grazed James Henry's shoulder.

Henny whimpered, dropped the gun, and ran out.

James Henry clasped his hand over the wound; blood oozed through his fingers.

Tires screeched as Henny tore out of the parking lot.

Cleatus scrambled to his feet and ran to the door. "He's gone," he yelled. He hurried to James Henry. "You all right, Boss?"

"Yes, yes, I'm fine. It's only a game we play. Fake blood."

Steve ran over and grabbed his uninjured arm. "Come on, Jim, I'll get you out of here."

James Henry said, "Get the gun. Get rid of it. None of this happened. You understand?"

"Yeah, Jim, I'll take care of it."

Everyone crowded around James Henry. "It's okay, it's okay." James Henry made his way to the door. "Just a little game Henny and I play." He laughed heartily, and slapped the man nearest him on the back. "I've got to go now — get the little sucker — only a game, just a game." The crowd went back to partying, glad for the excitement.

Maybelle grinned. It would be a while before they forgot her wedding. A grower shot by his own son. Maybe she could go on *Oprah* or *Geraldo* and tell about it. Yeah, she'd call Geraldo.

Steve steered James Henry to the parking lot, got into the driver's seat of the Lincoln, and drove him to Doc Johnson's. They could trust Doc not to report the gunshot wound, and what if he did? James Henry was the law in these parts. His "contributions" insured that.

When Doc dressed the wound, James Henry forced himself to ask about having a test for AIDS, thinking, *this is the most embarrassing thing I ever had to do*. Doc Johnson had treated his football injuries in high school, he had given him and Grace their blood tests when they got married, and he had delivered all of their children. Now, James Henry feared, Doc would pronounce his death sentence as well.

When Doc finished bandaging the wound, James Henry confessed his concern, and Doc gave him a thorough examination. He had his nurse draw blood for the Elisa test.

James Henry watched the blood flow into the vial. Looks

okay, he thought. Then he snorted. *What the hell did I expect it to look like? Green? Purple?* He felt foolish, stupid, embarrassed, terrified.

The nurse put a Band-Aid over the puncture. "I'll call you as soon as we get the results of the test," she said.

James Henry nodded, rolled down his sleeve, buttoned the cuff, and left.

As he drove out of the lot with Steve in the passenger seat, he wondered how he would break the news to Grace. Bad time for this to happen, he thought, with only a skeleton crew in the fields. Then he realized there was no good time for something like this.

James Henry had never thought much about dying. He had always felt indestructible, but today's events had changed that. *Better get my affairs in order*, he thought. *I always expected to pass the cane fields along to my sons like my father did, but it always seemed to be so far in the future.*

Steve interrupted his thoughts. "Drop me off at home, Jim, okay?"

James Henry nodded and continued his reverie. *Maybe Jeff will have another son to take over, my grandson, half Jap, running Hampton Plantation. Well, Jimmy was a damn cute little son of a gun at that. One way or the other, I'll see that the cane survives. I'll dance with the devil if I have to.*

CHAPTER 33

As the summer wore on and the heat intensified, Sami became more restless and eager to return to Japan. Finally, Jeff bought tickets for a flight right after the Fourth of July holiday. When James Henry heard the news, his jaw slackened and his cheek convulsed. He wanted his son to work at his side as he had with his father, and he'd grown to love Sami and couldn't bear to lose her. He tried to dissuade them, but when that failed, he hid his pain and saw as much of them as he could before they left.

On the evening of their departure, James Henry refused to go to the airport, pleading a backache. He said a reluctant goodbye at the house, almost losing his reserve when Sami reached up to kiss him and said a solemn, "*sayonara*." He kissed her tenderly on top of her head, shook Jeff's hand, perhaps a little too hard and too long, and told them to hurry back. He saw them off without recriminations.

When they had gone, he drove to the field office, vaulted up the steps, and threw open the door. "Henny," he yelled. The light was on, but there was no answer to his call. "Henny!" he thundered. "Where the hell are you?"

He went toward the bathroom and turned the knob, but the door didn't open. He rattled the doorknob and pounded on the door, but got no response. He pulled a credit card from his wallet and probed the lock. When it gave way, he pushed the door, but something blocked it. He managed to shove it open far enough to see Henny sprawled on the floor, motionless, eyes fixed and staring, needle and drug paraphernalia beside him.

"Henny!" he yelled. "Henny!"

When Henny didn't respond, James Henry sprinted to the phone and called for an ambulance. He ran back and reached through the opening, shoving Henny's body aside, until he was able to open the door. He knelt beside his son and cradled him in his arms. "Henny, Henny, oh, God, please." He stroked his son's face, white with the pallor of death.

James Henry pumped Henny's chest and gave him mouth-to-mouth, trying to resuscitate him, but there was no response. Finally the ambulance siren wailed in the distance. "Oh, God, please let them get here in time," he pleaded.

The ambulance slid to a stop and the siren faded. White-jacketed attendants sprinted up the steps and burst into the office carrying a stretcher.

"In here!" James Henry yelled.

The paramedics ran to the bathroom, took Henny from his arms, and placed him on the stretcher. When their ministrations got no response, they carried the stretcher to the ambulance, shoved it in, slammed the doors, and sped away, the siren wailing.

James Henry followed close behind in his Lincoln. The drive to the hospital seemed interminable, but they finally came to a halt in front of the emergency room doors. The attendants pulled the stretcher from the ambulance and rushed Henny into the emergency room, with James Henry running along side.

A young doctor walked over, glanced at the lifeless form, then looked solemnly at James Henry. "Please, wait outside," he said.

"No! I'm staying with my son!"

The doctor took Henny's pulse and lifted his eyelid. "I'm sorry," he said. "I'm afraid he's gone."

"Gone? No! No, Henny can't be gone." James Henry threw his arms across his son's chest and held him. "Get another doctor! Call Doc Johnson."

The doctor laid his hand on James Henry's arm. "I'm sorry, there's nothing anyone can do. Stay with your son as long as you like."

The color drained from James Henry's face, and his lips convulsed into a grimace. "No! Oh, God, no. Please, dear God, no!" His tears stained the sheet that covered Henny's emaciated body.

A nurse grasped James Henry's shoulders and tried to lift him away, but James Henry clung fiercely to his son.

Finally, after the nurse cajoled and pleaded with him, James Henry relinquished his grip and took a step back. "Gone," he whispered. "Henny is gone." He felt as if he, too, had died. He turned to the nurse and muttered, "I have to tell his mother."

The nurse patted his arm reassuringly and said, "I'll have someone drive you home."

"No. I'm all right." He made his way out to the Lincoln and drove home slowly, searching for words that would lessen the pain he would inflict on Grace.

Steve had heard the news on his scanner and had rushed to offer comfort and support. He waited in the driveway at Hampton House until James Henry pulled in, then he ran to the car and yanked open the door. "Oh, Jim, I'm sorry. I'm so damn sorry."

James Henry crawled out of the car, a broken man.

"What can I do?"

"Nothing. There's nothing anyone can do. It's too late now. I failed Henny, it's my fault."

"Come on, Jim, it's not your fault. You tried damn hard for that kid. You didn't push that needle in his arm, he did."

"I'm as guilty as if I'd pushed it in myself. I should have stopped him. There had to be a way."

Steve put his arm around James Henry's shoulders and led him toward the house. He asked, "Where's Grace? Does she know?"

James Henry stopped short. "Oh, I forgot. She's at the airport with Jeff and Sami." He glanced at his watch. "Their flight is due to leave soon. I'd better go tell them." He turned to go back to the car.

"You stay here, Jim. I'll go."

James Henry nodded.

"Will you be all right?"

"Yeah, I'm okay. You'd better hurry."

Steve hesitated for a moment. "Go in through the kitchen, Jim. Tell Berlinda." Knowing that Berlinda would look after him, he got in his pickup and sped off toward the airport, dreading the task ahead.

He inquired about the number of the departure gate, then turned and ran toward it. When he approached, he saw Jeff standing with Sami and Grace in the waiting area.

"Steve! Thanks for coming." Jeff turned to Sami. "Look who's here."

"You come to say *sayonara*. That's nice."

Steve shifted uneasily and pulled Jeff aside. "Uh, Jeff — can I talk to you for a minute?"

"Sure, what is it?"

"Jeff . . ." Steve hesitated, trying to find the right words. He glanced around the terminal, rubbed his chin anxiously, and repositioned his cap.

"What is it?" Jeff demanded. "Is something wrong?"

Steve diverted his eyes and blurted, "Henny's dead. Overdose. James Henry just found him."

"Oh, no." Jeff looked toward the women, concern for his mother clouding his eyes. Finally he said, "Poor Henny, that poor, misguided kid." His gaze returned to Grace. "God in heaven, Steve, how can I tell Mama? This will kill her."

"Yeah. It'll be rough. She hasn't had time to get over losing Jimmy."

"I can't tell her here. I'll take her home."

"What about your flight? You'll miss your plane."

"We can't leave now."

"Where are your bags?"

"They're checked through — probably on the plane. It's almost take off time."

"Let me have the claim tickets. I'll see what I can do about getting them. You take Grace home. I'll take care of the bags."

"Yeah, okay, thanks." Jeff approached the women, forehead furrowed, his hands shaking.

"What is it, Jeff?" Grace asked. "What's wrong?"

"What happened?" Sami asked. "Has something happened to Papa Jim?"

Jeff took Grace's arm and grasped Sami's hand. "We need to go back to the house." He strode toward the exit, the women struggling to keep up.

Sami looked back over her shoulder. "We'll miss the plane."

"Something's happened to James Henry," Grace said. "What is it? What's happened?"

"Dad's all right." Jeff walked briskly, steering the women through the crowded terminal.

The speaker just above their heads sounded. "Boarding, gate six, to Atlanta with connecting flights to Tokyo —"

"We'll miss our plane," Sami pleaded, hanging back.

Jeff clenched her arm and pulled her toward the parking lot. When he got the women into the car, he pulled out onto Sugarland Highway.

Grace shook his arm and begged, "Jeff, what's wrong? Tell me. Please tell me."

"It's Henny. Something's happened to Henny."

"Henny? What? Oh, Jeff, what happened?" Grace tightened her grip and tugged on Jeff's arm.

He steered to the shoulder of the highway, stopped, and gathered her in his arms.

She pulled back, staring into his eyes. "What?"

"Henny's gone."

"Gone? Gone where? Where did he go?"

"Oh, Mama, Henny's dead. Dad just found him."

Sami gasped. "Dead?"

Grace stared at Jeff as cars sped by, their headlights flickering eerily on her stricken face.

"Dead." She muttered numbly. "Henny's dead? How? What happened?"

"Dad will tell us about it when we get home, Mama." Jeff held her tightly as she sobbed uncontrollably, and the car rocked in the slipstream of trucks rumbling past.

Sami reached from behind. She and Jeff held Grace between them until her sobbing faded to an anguished whimper, then Jeff pulled back onto the highway.

They finally reached Hampton House, where James Henry waited on the portico. He ran down to the car and helped Grace out. She fell into his arms. He held her and tried to comfort her, but sobs wracked her body. Finally, he picked her up and carried her up the steps and into the den. He endeavored to console her until medication he'd had Doc Johnson order was delivered.

Jeff and Sami stood by helplessly.

When the medication arrived, James Henry spilled two tablets onto his hand and held them out to Grace.

She placed them in her mouth, not asking, not caring what they were. She took the glass of water James Henry held out to her and drank it. Soon the tablets had relaxed her into a state that would allow her to go through the motions of another funeral.

For the next few days, neighbors and friends came and went, bringing casseroles and desserts, saying words meant to comfort.

Grace, only faintly aware of their presence, nodded and per-
functorily thanked them for their concern.

Grace blamed herself for Henny's death. She had gone
against what she knew to be right when she betrayed James
Henry. She had committed a mortal sin when she lay down with
John and conceived Henny, and now she saw losing her beloved
son as punishment for that sin. She believed choosing pleasure
over virtue had cost her a son, and she would live out the rest of
her days in her own private hell, with those thoughts in her
heart.

On the day of the funeral, Berlinda helped Grace into the
plain black dress that hung in the back of her closet, always
freshly cleaned and ready for funerals. Never, ever, did Grace
think she would wear that dress to the funerals of both her son
and her grandson.

Berlinda slid Grace's feet into black pumps and handed her
a small black handbag.

She guided her out to the living room where James Henry
waited. He took Grace's arm, and together they walked out to
the black limousine parked under the portico.

Jeff and Sami, Melisandra and Gatti, and other family and
friends joined the procession.

Grace had sunk into despair so deep she was barely aware of
the service at the church or the burial at the cemetery. She
remained inside herself, clinging to memories of the son she
loved so dearly. A child conceived of love, nurtured in love, and
now buried with all of her love going with him.

James Henry helped her to her feet and put his arm around
her, supporting her as they left the cemetery.

"Our son was a good boy," he said softly. "He took a wrong
turn, but he was a good kid at heart."

Grace leaned into his side, grateful for his support and
words of comfort.

*   *   *

Within a week, Jeff and Sami flew to Japan, and Melisandra and Gatti rejoined Yvonne and Randolph on the Aegean.

Grace and James Henry, left alone to deal with their grief, sat together in the den, night after night, silently trying to cope. Finally, Grace voiced her sorrow. "I failed him," she murmured, as she wiped tears from her cheeks.

James Henry folded the newspaper and laid it aside. "Don't say that. You didn't fail him. Henny wouldn't accept your help."

"Yes, I did. I failed him. We both did. We should have known how to help him."

"We did the best we could. Henny was bent on destruction. He didn't want to be helped." James Henry got up and went over to Grace, pulled her to her feet, and held her in his arms. He felt the rise and fall of her shoulders, and the beat of her heart, as she sobbed silently, painfully.

He choked back his own tears and patted her gently on the back. "There, there, Grace, it will be all right."

The ring of the phone bell startled them back to reality, but they let it ring.

Berlinda finally answered it. "It's fo' you, Mr. Jim," she called. "That union man."

"Hang up, Berlinda."

Berlinda said a few words into the phone before stepping into the room. "Union man say he just call to give his con- condolents. Say he talk to you next year."

James Henry thought, *The way things are going, I wonder if there will be a next year.*

CHAPTER 34

James Henry left the field office and ran to his car, his shoulders hunched against late September rain. He drove to Vonda's and made his way across the flooded parking lot toward the café, attempting to follow the high ground. Shells squished under his boots; rain stung his face.

He stepped into the dark, musty interior and walked toward the bar, brushing rain from his shoulders. "Hi, Chip," he said as he dropped to a stool. Not in the mood for small talk, he was glad to see the place was empty. He shook rain from his pith helmet and laid it on the bar.

"Still raining I see." Chip reached to draw a beer.

"No sign of letting up. How's Vonda today?"

"A little better." Chip always said that, hoping his words would change the truth.

Chip set a beer in front of him, and the two friends drank in silence, grief binding them together like a thorned vine.

Chip studied the smoke rising from his cigarette, and James Henry sipped beer slowly, postponing the time he would go up the stairs to Vonda.

He had worked through his anger with Vonda for not telling him when she found out she was HIV positive, or when she had developed full-blown AIDS, and they talked more now that there was no sexual activity. The realization that he truly loved

Vonda surprised and confused him. He hadn't perceived how much he cared for her, how often he had shared his thoughts with her, and allowed her to comfort him.

Vonda was the one person who understood his feelings about Henny, and he needed her compassion. With Vonda there was no undercurrent of blame; she knew he loved Henny and only wanted to save him from a youthful blunder. Vonda's own weaknesses made her tolerant of weakness in others, and when talking with her, James Henry felt absolution. She had been his sexual playmate and confidante for most of his life, and he realized now how much he would miss her.

Finally, James Henry roused from reminiscing and glanced toward his friend. "Doesn't feel much like fall."

"Nope, hot and humid again today."

"This keeps up we'll have to spray the cane with ripener."

"Yeah, don't look like it'll go below sixty-eight degrees anytime soon."

The silence resumed. James Henry nursed his glass, picking it up and setting it down, printing interlocking rings with the wet bottom. Finally, he drained the glass and set it quietly on the bar. Averting his eyes, he said, "Well, guess I'll go up and pay my respects to Vonda." *If only Vonda were well*, he thought, *she'd make me forget about Henny for a little while.*

He climbed the stairs slowly and hesitated before entering Vonda's room, steeling himself for the encounter. He opened the door slightly and peered in.

"Hi, Sport!" Vonda sat propped up in bed, cosmetics strewn across black satin sheets. She held a mirror and a lipstick in shaking hands. She had used makeup artfully, and in the dim light from the shaded window she almost looked like her old self.

"Come in," she chirped. "Give Vonda a kiss." She patted the bed. "Sit by me."

James Henry sank to the bed beside her and took her hand in his.

Vonda looked into his tortured eyes and saw Henny's ghost lingering there. "Let Vonda make it better," she said softly, stroking his thigh.

He wanted her, needed her, desperately. The longing for her clouded his thoughts. He couldn't see Vonda without an eruption of emotion, but close contact with her made him uncomfortable now. He leaned over from the edge of the bed and lightly kissed her rouged cheek. He yearned to be in her arms, to forget his pain.

Vonda reached for him with eager arms, pulled him to her, and kissed him full on the mouth.

James Henry stiffened, resisting the impulse to wipe her saliva from his lips. So far his HIV tests were negative, and he wanted to keep it that way.

"So," he said, standing up and moving away. "You're looking good today."

"I'm feelin' full of seltzer and salt. Chip heard about a doctor in San Juan — has this mixture o' herbs. He got me some, an' by damn I do believe it's helpin'. Ain't that a hog hoot?"

"Yeah, Von, that's great. Great."

She slid across the satin sheet, and summoning strength, she grabbed James Henry's hand and yanked him down onto the bed. She twined an arm around his neck and pulled him to her.

"You missing Vonda?" She ran her tongue provocatively over her lips.

"I sure do," James Henry replied truthfully.

"Well, I ain't dead yet." She snuggled closer.

The muscles in his groin reacted and he tried to pull away, but she held him with a determined grip.

Vonda attempted to unzip his pants, but he jumped up, almost pulling her off the bed. Still, she refused to release her hold on him.

"Now, Vonda, you know we can't."

"Why not?" Her lip curled in a pout.

"You know why not."

"You can use protection." She appealed to him with hungry eyes.

"I haven't got any with me."

Vonda reached under the pillow and withdrew a condom. "Here, use one of Chip's." She held it out to him.

"You and Chip are still doing it?"

"Hell, yes. You don't think I'd quit while I'm still breathin', do you?" She reached out, grabbed his arm, and caught him off balance.

He toppled onto the bed. Confused, he thought, *maybe it's safe. Chip wouldn't put himself at risk, would he?* He remembered Doc's warning and tried to deaden his desire. "The only safe sex is no sex," Doc had said, but still, with a condom —

"You wouldn't deny a lady, would you?" Vonda caressed his thigh.

James Henry tried to think clearly, but his mind churned. He hadn't had her in so long. He felt himself drowning in a sea of Tabu cologne.

He stood up abruptly and tried to move away, but she held onto his belt, refusing to release him. She slid the zipper on his jodhpurs to the bottom, undid his belt buckle, and his pants dropped to the floor. "Oh, Vonda," he moaned as he gave himself up to her.

Minutes later, he sighed and relaxed onto the black satin sheets, drained but satisfied.

When she rolled away, he saw the condom still clutched in her hand, unopened. He cursed himself for his weakness. *I'm a dead man*, he thought. *The bitch has killed me.*

CHAPTER 35

After another year had passed, James Henry greeted the receptionist in Doc Johnson's office with a bravado he didn't feel.

She said, "Doc's with a patient. He'll see you in a minute. Go to room three. Nurse Rose will draw your blood."

James Henry went in and rolled up the left sleeve of his khaki shirt.

"Hello, Mr. Hampton. How are you feeling?" Rose meant it as a friendly greeting but it brought James Henry to attention. He wondered if she had bad news for him.

Nurse Rose tied the tourniquet around his arm, and James Henry clenched and unclenched his fist, pumping up a vein.

Rose chatted about the weather as she put on rubber gloves, unwrapped a new needle, and inserted it. He winced when she punctured his vein and fought a feeling of light-headedness as she filled three vials with his blood.

James Henry wondered if Rose knew why he came every few weeks for a blood test, then realized that she'd have to know. She had to send the blood to the lab and read the results. James Henry felt violated, ashamed, stupid.

Rose snapped the rubber tourniquet from his arm and put a Band-Aid over the puncture. "That's it, Mr. Hampton. Doc will be in shortly." She picked up the vials, went out, and closed the door.

James Henry rolled his sleeve down. *Why?* he wondered. *Why did I do such a stupid thing? Why did I let it happen?*

Doc opened the door and stepped into the cubicle. "You're looking good, James Henry. How are you feeling?"

"I feel all right, except for a sore throat. I can't seem to shake it."

Doc pulled out a tongue depressor. "Open wide." He held James Henry's tongue down and examined his throat. "When did this start?"

"Last Thursday. I was out in the cane in that downpour, and my throat started burning Thursday night."

"You still seeing Vonda?" Doc asked as he checked James Henry's blood pressure and listened to his heart.

"I have to, Doc. We've been friends since high school. I can't walk away when she's so sick."

"You're not having sex, are you?"

"Not anymore."

"Good. Remember, I warned you. You're betting your life. There's no such thing as safe sex. According to a scientific study, the AIDS virus isn't only in semen; it's usually in the infected person's saliva, their sweat, and their tears as well."

"Yeah, Doc, I hear you." James Henry tried to control the involuntary twitch in his lip.

"There are forty-three sexually transmitted diseases here in Florida," Doc said. "Over forty thousand cases of AIDS and more coming down with it every day. It really would be safer to stay away from Vonda altogether."

James Henry avoided Doc's eyes.

"The latest scientific report concludes, categorically, that infection with the AIDS virus does not require intimate sexual contact or sharing intravenous needles.

"They say that transmission can, and does, occur as a result of person-to-person contact. When blood or other body fluids from a person who is harboring the virus comes in contact with someone else, even if this is a single isolated occurrence, infection can occur. Remember, I warned you. Be very careful." He patted James Henry on the back.

James Henry avoided Doc's eyes. "I heard you couldn't get it from oral sex."

"Actually, oral-genital contact may increase the chance of contracting the virus. If I were you, I'd keep it close to home."

"Right. Thanks, Doc." James Henry got up to go.

Doc said, "Grace should be tested. Why don't you bring her in?"

Panic flashed in James Henry's eyes and distorted his features. "No! That won't be necessary. We use protection. After Henny was born, you said another pregnancy would endanger Grace's life, so I always use a condom. I wouldn't put Grace in danger. I love that woman." He grabbed his helmet and his sunglasses.

"Nevertheless, I'd feel better about it if she were tested." He shook James Henry's hand. "You take care. I'll have Rose call you with your test results when they come in."

James Henry walked out into the summer heat of Belle Glade a chastised man. As he drove slowly back toward the field office, he pondered his chances for a future. When he saw Steve watching for him along the road, he pulled over.

Steve ran up to the car. "You're not going to believe this."

"What now? What happened?"

"That cutter that jumped last year."

"Yeah, what about him?"

"Otis got a lead on him. A supervisor overheard the crew talking about him when they were harvesting rice. Seems he went up to New York and put a reggae band together. Otis checked it out, and I'll be damned if it isn't true. Otis has him located and he's going to come in this afternoon and talk to you about bringing him back."

James Henry snorted. "A band? That's a hot one. Where

would he get money to start a band?" He shook his head in disbelief and chuckled. "Okay, I'll stop by Ratch's office and see what he has to say."

"Right, Jim." Steve stepped back and James Henry rolled up the window and sped off toward town.

When he entered the sheriff's office, Otis glanced up and said into the phone, "I'll call you back." He hung up and motioned for James Henry to sit in front of his desk. "I was goin' to stop by to see you this afternoon. I got some good news for a change."

"Yeah, I just saw Steve and he told me. He says you located that cutter — what was his name?"

"Jazzman. Would you believe he went all the way to New York City? Seems he put together a band up there."

"That doesn't seem likely. What the hell does a cutter know about a band?"

"According to all accounts, he knows enough to make a business out of it. Playin' what they call them 'gigs' all over the East Coast. Got hisself booked into JACK'S for November when the cutters come back. I can go up to New York and get him now or I can save you some money by pickin' him up when he's at JACK'S this fall. Whatever you want me to do."

"Come on, Otis, somebody's snowing you. He couldn't put a band together in so little time.

"That's what the crew is sayin'."

"They say a lot of things. Doesn't mean that they're true."

"Sure sounds like this is one of them times, though."

"Well, if it is true he must be damned good."

"Guess so."

James Henry scratched his chin thoughtfully, then tapped his fingertips. A faraway look glazed his eyes as he thought of what Jazzman had accomplished. He thought of Henny, the advantages heaped upon him, and of his choices.

Ratch interrupted his reverie. "Well, what do you want me to do?"

James Henry scraped his chair back and got up. "Nothing."

"Nothin'? But I thought —"

"Let it ride, Otis. A man that can come out of these cane fields and do what he did isn't getting a free ride. He earned a shot at bettering himself."

"Lettin' a jumper off free and clear? That ain't like you, James Henry."

"I'm not much like myself in any way anymore."

"Wadda ya mean? Why not?"

"I lost a son and a grandson. That's bound to change a man."

Otis looked down at his shoes. "Yeah, I guess. Well, whatever you say, James Henry. I just hope this don't start no trend. Leave this one of 'em off the hook, the others might start gettin' ideas."

"I doubt it. If what you're telling me is true, there's not another in my crew with that ability or that gumption. There's only one man in a million that could pull off what he did."

"Okay, I'll back off if that's what you want. Seems a damn shame, though, got him located and all."

"Be a bigger shame to stand in the way of a man who accomplished all you say he has. See you, Otis." James Henry jogged back to the Lincoln and sped away with a warm glow in his chest. For the first time in recent memory his smile was not forced.

CHAPTER 36

Throughout the long, sultry, summer and into a slightly cooler November, Vonda's desperation mounted. Frantic to find a cure for the virus that devoured her, she sent to mail-order houses for potions, vitamins, and teas advertised to alleviate the symptoms of AIDS.

She even went to Mexico in search of a cure. There she suffered diarrhea, nausea, and vomiting, and she returned more dissipated than when she left. But she hadn't given up hope. Not yet.

Tonight Vonda drove slowly up and down the dark litter-strewn streets of Belle Glade's Harlem section, asking everyone she saw to direct her to the voodoo queen, Black Maggie. Maybe voodoo could save her from AIDS. But the denizens of Harlem weren't about to tell a white woman where Black Maggie could be found.

Finally, Vonda parked in front of JACK'S, elbowed her way through cutters and whores loitering on the sidewalk, and went inside. The laughter, the shouting, the din of reggae, and the overpowering odor of cheap perfume mingled with the aroma of barbecued ribs, almost bullied her into running but she stood her ground.

The sea of black faces melted into one giant wave that swelled and subsided. She gripped the back of a chair for support as she searched the faces, wondering who might direct her to the voodoo queen. A pusher looked at her, smiled, and walked over.

"Pretty white lily, you do be lookin' for me?" He raped her with hungry eyes.

"I'm looking for Black Maggie." She reached into her handbag and took out a twenty-dollar bill. "You know where I can find her?"

The big Black looked from the bill to her face and laughed, revealing a mouthful of large, even white teeth. "You do be in big trouble, eh, lady?"

"Where is she?"

"Cost you fifty."

Without answering, Vonda took another twenty and a ten from her handbag and handed him the three bills.

He grasped the money, caressed it, folded it, and slipped it into his pants pocket.

"T'ree blocks up," he said, pointing a black finger. "Dat way. Pink house on de corner. But Maggie no see you."

Vonda spun around without responding and hurried out.

The crowd in front of JACK'S converged on her. "I got coke, lady, pure."

"I be sweet as honey!" one of the whores called out. The others screamed with laughter.

A cutter grabbed Vonda's arm, but she tore free and quickened her steps. One of the whores ripped the scarf from her neck, jerking her head back sharply. Vonda ran to her car, yanked open the door, and fell in. Tires squealed as she pulled away, making a sharp U-turn. When she looked in the rearview mirror, she saw the whores scuffling over her scarf.

Vonda located the pink house and parked. Moonlight revealed black streaks of cane soot that had washed from the tarpaper roof and escaped the broken drain. Paint peeled around a window that was covered by a torn lace curtain.

Cement steps leading to the door crumbled away from a wobbly, rusted, iron pipe that served as a handrail.

Vonda glanced warily up and down the deserted street before stepping out into the night. *Please, God, let her help me,* she prayed as she went up to the door. She knocked three times before the door opened enough for her to see a large eye peering at her through the opening.

The girl's voice rumbled low and menacing. "What you want?"

"I want to see Black Maggie."

"She not here." The door slammed shut.

Vonda kicked the door in frustration.

The door opened again, but only a crack this time.

"I a'ready tole you, she ain't here."

Vonda reached into her handbag, took out a hundred-dollar bill, and passed it through the crack.

The girl snatched it from her fingers. "You wait here."

The door closed and the lock snapped into place. Vonda glanced up and down the dark street. When she shook with a sudden chill, she kicked the door impatiently.

Heavy footsteps approached. The door swung wide and Black Maggie loomed in the doorway. Her large head sank into huge breasts that rolled and heaved under a stained caftan. Sweat that slid down her cheeks and negotiated her chins was absorbed into the cloth of the caftan, changing the color of the fabric around her neck to a deep blood red.

"What you want? Maggie don see no white women."

"I'm sick. Please, you've got to help me." Vonda's voice caught in her throat.

Black Maggie surveyed her for a few seconds, her huge white eyes bulging like two hard-boiled eggs in a face as round and black as a skillet. The odor of yesterday's sweat mingled with the smell of heated wax from candles burning against unrequited love, haunts, spells, and assorted evils.

"Come in," Maggie grumbled. She turned and walked laboriously across the small room.

When Vonda stepped in, her eyes were drawn to a large crucifix that dominated the room. The eyes of the Black Christ seemed to follow her and penetrate her soul. When a sudden breeze slammed the door shut behind her, she jumped and stumbled against a small table, overturning it. Quickly she righted the table, scooped up the objects that had fallen, and replaced them.

She glanced around the cluttered room. Feathers, bones, pebbles, entrails, the tools of Black Maggie's trade cluttered tables and floor. A bleached human skull leered in the flickering candlelight. The heat was unbearable.

Vonda reached out to a straight-backed chair for support, but it wobbled on shaky legs.

Hog jowls boiled on a stove in the corner. The odor mingled with the scent of incense burning in chipped saucers set around the room.

"Please help me," Vonda pleaded.

"What your sickness be?"

"AIDS," Vonda replied softly.

"AIDS?" Black Maggie clicked her thick tongue and shook her head. "That be big sick, woman. Cost a lot to doctor AIDS."

"Can you help me?"

Maggie's eyes met Vonda's. "Black Maggie can help you, but you needs strong medicine." She shook a fat, black finger in Vonda's face. "You got to do jes what Black Maggie tell you to do."

"I will," Vonda promised, backing away from the wagging finger. "I will, I will."

"Sit down." Maggie pointed to a metal card table draped with a fringed scarf. Vonda look one of the chairs and Maggie fell heavily into the chair across from her. "Gimme your hand," she ordered.

Vonda held out a trembling hand, palm up.

"You be right-handed?" Maggie asked.

"Yes."

Black Maggie lifted a lighted red candle and held it over Vonda's hand for illumination. She studied the lines in the hand for several seconds, then frowned and shook her head dispassionately. "I cain't help you." She folded Vonda's fingers back across her palm and pushed her hand away.

"Please! You must help me." Vonda's plaintive voice reverberated in the small, stuffy room. Incense combined with boiling pork assailed her nostrils, making her nauseous.

Black Maggie sighed heavily, shifted her enormous girth, and asked, "You got money?"

"Yes," Vonda replied weakly.

Black Maggie's eyes bore into hers. She pulled a crumbling cardboard box toward her across the plank floor. She selected some small, bleached bones from the box, dropped them into a black cup, and shook them as she chanted, "Umba, adda, humba, hoon. Umba, adda, humba, hoon." The bones rattled in the cup. "Umba, adda, humba, hoon." Maggie cast the bones across the metal table. They clattered to a stop at the edge of the fringed scarf.

Despite the heat, a chill swept along Vonda's arms. She rubbed them and folded them across her chest.

Black Maggie muttered as she studied the bones, then she rolled her eyes to meet Vonda's. "Be bad," she said. "You be hexed bad. Maggie don't know if she should help you."

"Please!" Vonda beseeched her. "Please help me." Her pale hands trembled and dropped to her lap. "Please help me," she begged.

Black Maggie sat silently, studying Vonda, evaluating. Then she spoke in a low rumble. "You take ten one-hunnert dollar bills, wrap dem in plastic, and bury dem in de belly of a fish jes caught. Jes caught, you understand?"

Vonda nodded eagerly.

"You wrap dat fish in a newspaper tomorrow, a day when de moon be full. You bring dat fish to Black Maggie at midnight tomorrow night. You hear what Black Maggie tell you?"

"Yes. Yes, I understand. I'll bring it. I will. Thank you." Flickering light of the candles reflected off tears of relief that flooded Vonda's sunken eyes.

Black Maggie planted swollen hands on enormous thighs, positioned her felt-slippered feet, and prepared to rise. With labored breath she pulled herself up and shuffled toward the door.

Vonda scrambled to her feet and followed, eager to escape the eerie stillness of the candlelit room.

Black Maggie opened the door a crack and peered up and down the street. Satisfied, she opened the door wide. "You come back like I tell you. Midnight tomorrow. And bring what I say for you to bring."

"I will. I will." Vonda stumbled out into the moonlight and gasped fresh air. She ran to her car and drove like a woman chased by demons. When at last she pulled into the café parking lot and stopped, she slumped over the wheel and let the tears flow.

Chip found her like that when he came out to walk his old coonhound, Fella. He gathered her into his arms and stroked her hair. "What is it, baby? What's wrong?"

Vonda sobbed out her story.

Chip bent down and kissed the top of her head. "I'll get the fish, honey. I'll go to the bank for the money and I'll wrap it in plastic. Don't cry. It will be all right."

The next night, Vonda watched as Maggie drew the plastic-wrapped bills from the belly of the gutted fish. Maggie chanted over the money and blessed it, before shuffling to a battered garbage can filled with dirt. Ceremoniously, she sifted dirt through fat fingers and chanted, before burying the packet of hundred-dollar bills deep in the dirt. "Cemetery dirt," she said as she turned back to Vonda.

Vonda shuddered and looked away.

Black Maggie came back to the table and boned the fish. Then she carried it to the kitchen area where she laid it on a plate that she pulled from a pile of dirty dishes.

Good God, she's going to eat it, Vonda thought.

Maggie returned to her and chanted gibberish while making the sign of the cross on her forehead. "You feel better?" she asked.

"Yes," Vonda replied weakly.

"You come back tomorrow night. Moon be full den. Come twelve midnight. Right at twelve, midnight. You understand?"

"Yes. Yes, I understand."

"Bring a black hen, a live one, and a scarf you wear."

Vonda's hand flew to her throat, remembering the scarf ripped from her neck at JACK'S.

"And twenty hunnert-dollar bills." Maggie studied her reaction.

Vonda nodded stoically.

Satisfied, Maggie swayed toward the door. Vonda jumped up and followed her. When Black Maggie opened the door, Vonda stumbled out into a night shrouded by clouds. She could barely see through her tears as she drove back to the café.

The next day, Vonda asked Chip to get her a live black hen. He gazed at her with compassion, said nothing, and came back an hour later with the chicken.

Vonda watched the clock nervously. As midnight approached, she tied a blue paisley scarf around her throat, stuffed the hen into a pillowcase, tied it with twine, and took the two thousand dollars she'd gotten from the bank. She drove off toward Harlem and the soot-stained pink house.

Once again, eyes peering through a crack in the door responded to her knock, but this time the girl opened the door without asking questions. Silently, she motioned Vonda to follow her to a small inner room where the walls and floor were spattered with dried blood. Vonda shuddered and reached to the doorjamb for support. She wanted to turn and run, but desperation kept her rooted there.

The chicken flapped wildly inside the pillowcase. The girl took it from her, loosened the twine, and let the chicken flop into a wooden cage. It squawked loudly, shook rumpled feathers, and strutted indignantly inside the cage.

Suddenly Black Maggie filled the doorway. She looked from Vonda to the chicken pecking the bars of the cage, then back to Vonda. Her hard eyes bore into Vonda's. "You bring de money?"

Silently, Vonda reached into her handbag, extracted two thousand dollars, and handed it to her.

Black Maggie's brittle, black pupils gleamed like anthracite as her huge hand clamped over the money. She counted it slowly before stuffing it into the pocket of her soiled caftan. "Give me dat scarf."

Vonda pulled the paisley scarf from her neck and handed it to her.

Maggie lumbered to the cage, reached in, seized the chicken by the feet, and pulled it out. It flapped and squawked furiously, but she gathered the wings and held it in a viselike professional grip. She looped the scarf around the chicken's neck, and rolled her eyes back in her head until only the whites showed. Loudly, she invoked spirits and spit incantations. Her huge breasts rolled like bags of water beneath the caftan as she swayed hypnotically

Suddenly, she picked up a narrow-bladed knife and slashed the chicken's throat, beheading it. Blood spurted from the chicken's neck as it careened crazily around the room, spattering blood on walls and floor.

Vonda screamed and leaped back, wildly brushing at blood

that splashed onto her blouse and skirt. Screaming hysterically, she ran toward the door.

"You be gittin' better now," Black Maggie called after her. "You see. You come back. Bring more money. Black Maggie cure dose AIDS."

Vonda dashed to her car and leaned on it for support. Her stomach lurched; a cold sweat washed over her. She lowered her head and gagged, releasing pent-up fear, anger, and frustration into the ditch beside the car.

She swiped a trembling hand across her lips, wrenched the car door open, fell in, and sped away. She never went back, but she held the hope in her heart that Black Maggie's voodoo would cure her.

CHAPTER 37

After another cane season had passed, James Henry picked up the phone in the field office. "Oh, hi, Doc," he said, expecting Doc to tell him that he'd gotten the usual negative result on his Elisa test.

"Hello, Jim," Doc said quietly; he hesitated. "Come by at lunchtime today and we'll have a talk."

"What is it, Doc? What's wrong?" James Henry's voice faltered. He felt his heart pounding against his chest. Why wasn't Doc just giving him the result over the phone as he always had?

"Come in today about twelve and we'll talk on my lunch hour." Doc hung up.

James Henry propped a knee against the desk for support; perspiration formed on his forehead, his hands shook. *He's about to drop the bomb*, he thought. *He's going to tell me I got a positive result. Hell, no, he just wants to talk to me about the poker debt he owes — that's it, the poker debt.* He wiped a hand over trembling lips. But why —? He bolted out to his car and sped to Doc's office; to hell with waiting till noon.

Doc stood down the hall between examination rooms reading a chart when James Henry burst in. He glanced at his watch and started to say something, but James Henry crashed past the receptionist and bore down on him.

"What is it, Doc? What's wrong?"

Doc took off his Ben Franklin glasses, stuck them in the pocket of his white tunic, and motioned James Henry to follow him to his office.

"Well?" James Henry leaned over the desk, his eyes level with Doc's."

"You're early, Jim. I have other patients. I asked you to come on my lunch hour so we'd have time to talk."

"Damn it, Doc, level with me. What the hell is it you want to talk to me about?"

Doc glanced down at the desk, then forced himself to look into James Henry's eyes. "I'm sorry, Jim, the test is positive."

"What? No!" James Henry felt as if he were sliding down a fifty-foot icicle. "It's a mistake. Could it be a mistake?"

"I'm afraid not, Jim. Please sit down and we'll discuss it."

James Henry dropped into the chair in front of the desk. "No! I don't have AIDS." James Henry jumped up, overturning his chair. He thumped the desk and howled, "I don't!"

Doc watched cautiously as James Henry paced the office. He glanced up when Nurse Rose opened the door and looked at him anxiously. "Is everything all right in here?"

Doc nodded.

Rose looked from Doc to James Henry, and closed the door quietly.

James Henry sank to the chair, anger and fear distorting his face. "No," he wailed. "No." He rubbed ashen cheeks with trembling hands and strangled a sob.

Doc got up and came around to him. "I'm sorry, Jim. You tested positive for HIV, but you might never develop full-blown AIDS. There's —"

"No!" James Henry pushed him away. Doc's presence intimidated him. He didn't want to need Doc — he didn't want to need anybody.

Doc patted his shoulder, saddened that there was so little he could do for this man whose life he had been involved with for so many years.

James Henry cursed himself for allowing this to happen. "There's no cure for AIDS, right?"

Doc shook his head slowly, sadly. "There is AZT. You're just HIV positive, you haven't developed full-blown AIDS. There are ways to postpone the worst of it, ways to make you more comfortable. Maybe they'll come up with a cure in time. You know, of course, that Grace will have to be tested."

James Henry's lip twitched spasmodically, but he nodded ascent. *How the hell will I tell Grace? Oh, God, poor Grace. What will she think? What will she say? Who the hell will take care of her after I'm gone?* He got up and bolted out without saying good-bye.

He drove slowly back to Hampton House, went up to his room, dropped his long frame on the bed, and stared at the ceiling. "How the hell will I tell Grace?"

There was a soft knock and the door opened slightly. Grace stuck her head in. "Are you all right?" Her forehead furrowed with concern when she saw his ashen face.

"I'm all right," he replied flatly.

Grace opened the door wider and came to the bed. She felt his forehead. "You're too warm." She sat on the edge of the bed and took his hand in hers. "Can I do anything? Shall I call Doc?"

He didn't answer.

"I'll call Doc." She started to rise.

James Henry reached out, took her hand, and gently pulled her back down. No use postponing it, it's not going to get any easier. "Grace —"

"Yes?"

"Grace, I'd rather be hanged right now than have to tell you this, but —"

"What? What is it?"

James Henry took a deep breath and exhaled slowly. "Grace, I have AIDS."

She drew her breath in sharply and held it for a moment before releasing it in a rush. Her eyes widened and she stared at him in disbelief.

"I'm sorry. Oh, hell, I'm so damn sorry."

"But —"

"Grace, you don't deserve this. I don't know what else to say."

"When? I mean, when — did you find out?"

"Just now. I just came from Doc's."

"What did he say? What can he do? What —?"

"There's nothing to do, Grace. It's a death sentence."

"But —"

"No buts about it. I'm a dead man."

"Are you sure? What did Doc say? Did he say that you're HIV positive, or that you have AIDS? I read —"

"HIV positive, AIDS, what's the difference. It's all over for me."

Dazed, Grace stood and walked toward the window. She turned back to him and started to say something but stopped. She wrung her hands and tears formed in her eyes. She brushed them away.

"I'm sorry," James Henry muttered.

"There has to be something we can do. What should I do?"

"There's nothing anyone can do. I hate to drop this on you out of the blue."

Grace sighed and looked away. "I guess I've been expecting it. When La Vonda Wood —"

His mouth went slack and he turned away from her. It was hard to face her, to face up to his infidelity. "You'll have to be tested."

"Me? I'm all right. It's you I'm concerned about." Grace sat down on the bed beside him, picked up his hand, and brushed the hair off his forehead. "Remember when you found John's poems and letters in my desk?"

He nodded.

"I always respected and admired you for the way you handled that. No accusations, no recriminations. You never mentioned it again after that night. Not once in all these years." Grace drew a linen handkerchief from her skirt pocket and dabbed at the corners of her eyes. "You never changed toward Henny. You never treated me differently." She blew her nose delicately, then pushed the handkerchief back into her skirt pocket. "Now the wheel has come full circle. Now it's my turn. I hope I learned something. I hope I can handle this as well."

James Henry reached out to her, slipped his arm around her shoulders, drew her down, and kissed her gently on the forehead. "Thank you, Grace," he said. "I don't deserve it, but thank you."

CHAPTER 38

Vonda stared into the mirror above the vanity table, searching for the beauty she had lost to AIDS. As new diseases ravaged her and her immune system failed, she found it increasingly difficult to hide her illness under makeup. Vonda's once provocative green eyes sank deeper into her emaciated face, and eye shadow and mascara made them appear hollow — empty. It became increasingly difficult to apply lipstick to dried, cracked lips, and blush seemed only to accentuate the deathly pallor.

Vonda threw a lipstick at the mirror and reached for the glass of water on the vanity. She thirsted for beer and liquor, but Doc Johnson forbade her to take alcohol with her medication. At first she defied him, but alcohol made her so sick she soon realized she would never again be able to have liquor or beer. Vonda tried drinking Coke, Pepsi, and Dr Pepper, but the carbonation made her queasy. She drank only water now — and even that wouldn't stay down.

With her immune system compromised, colds and flu infected her constantly, and even when she managed by sheer force of will to dress and go down to the bar, men moved away from her. That was more painful than the disease. She had always thought men liked her as a person, enjoyed her company, but now that she was no longer available for sexual favors, men shunned her.

In a desperate attempt to overcome the unbearable hurt, she would sidle up to a man only to have him back away. She had to bite cracked lips and clamp vacant eyes to stop the tears. Finally, Vonda stayed upstairs.

Steve stopped to see her every day, and James Henry visited once in a while, but they were the only ones who sought her out. She sat alone in her room with only Mam'selle to comfort her while Chip worked downstairs.

When Chip's workday ended and he came up to her, she clung to him fiercely. She cried herself to sleep in his arms, and he would lie awake, loving her, praying for her, dreading the day he could no longer hold her.

Vonda and Chip grew closer as her illness progressed. Now that other men abandoned her, she realized how much Chip loved her, had always loved her.

It bothered her that she had lied to him about Steve. It gnawed at her conscience until she couldn't stand it anymore. She wanted everything to be right between them before she died.

One night when Chip came up from the bar, she lay in his arms, feeling his heart beating against her. The familiar smell of the Camel cigarettes in his pocket comforted her.

"Chip," she said hesitantly.

"Yeah?"

"There's something I've got to set straight before I get the hell outta here."

"What's that?"

"It's about Steve."

"What about him?"

"Well," it was an effort for her to speak. "I lied to you about Steve. Steve is Jim's kid."

After a moment of silence, Chip said, "I know that, Von."

"Yeah?" She turned and looked into his eyes.

"I always knew it."

"Then why in hell did you marry me?"

"I loved you. I always did, always will. Ain't nohin' gonna change that."

"Well, ain't that a hog hoot?"

"Yeah, a hog hoot."

"Well, I love you, too, you old son of a gun." Vonda fumbled under the pillow for a condom.

Chip took it from her and put it on before taking Vonda in his arms and caressing her wasted body. He took her gently, lovingly, tenderly, considerate of her needs, her desires.

As weak as Vonda was, the sex proved more fulfilling than any she had ever had.

Finally, after all these years, after all the lovers, Vonda experienced sex as it was meant to be: unconditional, pure, complete, caring, and satisfying. At last, it was satisfying.

Vonda felt Chip's strength, Chip experienced her vulnerability, and together they were one whole vibrant being. Chip claimed her as his own that night, his alone, and Vonda finally realized love, true, unconditional love. She would never need or want another man.

That night, as she slept, Vonda passed over to another life. She would wait for Chip there.

When James Henry returned from Vonda's funeral, he slumped behind his granddaddy's desk, dreading what he knew he had to do. Now that Vonda was gone and his own health continued to fail, he realized it was time to make things right with Steve. Having waited for so long only made it harder, but there was no time for further delay.

The next morning James Henry paced the field office, waiting for Steve to come in for the work sheets. He would have to summon the courage to confront him with the truth.

The door swung open and Steve stood framed against the light. "Mornin', Jim, got the sheets?"

James Henry handed over the papers, and Steve shuffled through them.

"Steve," James Henry said tentatively.

"Yeah?"

"There's something I have to talk to you about."

"What's that, Jim?"

"Well," James Henry hesitated.

Steve glanced up from the work sheets. "What?"

James Henry took a deep breath and plunged in. "Well, your mother . . . Vonda . . . and I . . . well, uh, we were friends for a long time."

Steve's brow furrowed. "Right."

"We were friends back in high school."

"Yeah, Jim, I know."

"Well, Steve, it's like this. Your mother and I, well, we sort of got together back then." James Henry's voice trailed off. This was harder than he thought it would be. He valued Steve's friendship and his respect, and he was afraid of losing both. He drew a deep breath, looked directly into Steve's eyes, and blurted, "Steve, I'm your father."

Steve's eyes widened in disbelief. This was a moment he had hoped for all his life, but he never expected it to happen. He squinted to prevent tears from flowing. He walked over to his father and put his hand on his shoulder. "I know, Jim. I've always known."

"Did Vonda tell you?"

"Nah. She didn't have to. I first heard it at school. Beat the shit outta the kid that told me." Steve laughed. "I never said nothin' to Mom and Dad, figured they'd tell me if they wanted me to know. After a while I didn't have to ask. I look too damn much like you."

Their eyes met for a moment before they embraced, father and son.

When they separated, James Henry said, "I want you to stay on here when I'm gone. Take care of the place for Grace."

"Sure, Jim, of course I will."

"I mean as manager, and one of the owners. I should have made things right with you, claimed you as my son years ago, but I took the easy way out — or maybe it was the hard way — who's to say? Anyway, if you'll let me, I'd like to try to make it up to you now."

Steve looked at the man he had so long admired. For so many years he had wanted to bridge this gap, to confront James Henry with the truth. Now here it was, laid out like a gift. Acknowledgment from the man he loved and respected as a father. He loved Chip, sure. Chip was his dad, but this was the moment he had always dreamed of: his biological father claiming him as his own.

"I've talked to Grace and Jeff and Mel. They all agree that this is how it should be. You know the cane like none of them do. It would be best for all of you if you were an equal partner — run the place when I'm gone."

Steve glanced up, overwhelmed, surprise and disbelief in his eyes. He had wanted his father to claim him as his son, but he'd never thought about sharing in his legacy. He had hoped they would keep him on after James Henry was gone, but he felt vulnerable. He often wished he stood in Henny's shoes. He thought of Henny as the lucky one, sitting here in the office next to his father or speeding around in his flashy red Jag. Now he realized he was the lucky one. James Henry had acknowledged him as his son and Henny was dead. He thought, *All this, and I have a wonderful wife and two great sons. I'm the lucky one.*

James Henry roused him from his thoughts. "Well, what do you say?"

"It's quite a bit to digest in one sitting. Of course I'll stay on and help Grace out. I would have anyway."

"I know you would. The cane is in your blood, son."

James Henry held out his hand and Steve shook it awkwardly.

"Well, better get out to the men." Steve walked toward the door. "We've got to get that rice field flooded."

James Henry watched his son jog to his truck, thinking, *He moves just like I did when I was his age.* He dropped into his chair, glad to have the encounter behind him, glad that the truth had finally been acknowledged. *I did the right thing*, he thought — *finally.* He picked up the tonnage sheets and looked through them.

The door opened slightly, Steve stuck his head in and said, "Thanks, Jim," and he was gone.

Through several passing cane seasons, James Henry's immune system weakened. Colds turned to pneumonia. He developed hepatitis, then cancer of the prostate. His T cell count dropped dramatically, and when it fell below 210, Doc Johnson informed him that he now had full-blown AIDS. His desire to live diminished with each illness.

Jeff and Sami returned from Japan to comfort him, and their presence helped him deal with his diminishing spirits. When he talked about going to be with Little Jimmy, Jeff encouraged him to fight the virus, but he turned away, saying, "If I can't be out there in the cane fields, I'm a dead man anyway."

Mel drove over from Palm Beach every Wednesday to sit with him and reassure him, but James Henry appeared weaker each time she visited. She put on a brave face when with him, but her tears flowed in the night.

One day James Henry said, "I've always loved you, Mel, you know that. We've had our differences, but I've always loved you."

"I know, Daddy. I love you, too." Mel wiped his brow with a cool cloth, and watched as he drifted into sleep.

One Wednesday, when she sat with James Henry, Berlinda came to the door and announced, "Phone, Miss Mel, it's for you."

"Who is it?"

"Oh, you want to take this call." Berlinda closed the door discreetly.

Mel got up and went to the phone. "Hello."

"Hello, Mel, it's Jason."

A chill seized her, then she started to perspire. The hand holding the phone shook uncontrollably.

"Mel? Are you there?"

She struggled to keep her voice even. "Yes. Hello, Jason."

"I heard about your father. I'm sorry. I know how hard this must be for you."

"Yes." She wanted to cry, to laugh, to scream. She fought to keep her voice from betraying emotion. "It's nice of you to call."

"Would you object to my coming by the house to see him — and you?"

"No, of course not," Mel replied coolly. *Would I object? I'd give twenty years of my life for five minutes with you.* "But I thought you were in Asia."

"I got back last week. My contract has expired, thank God. I won't leave the States again anytime soon." Jason hesitated. Mel thought she heard a catch in his voice when he said, "I had a lot of time to think about us — about what happened."

"Oh?" She didn't trust herself to say more.

"I hear you married a prince."

"Yes."

"I hope you found happiness." It was more a question than a statement.

Mel didn't answer.

"May I come by in an hour?"

"Of course."

"All right. See you then."

Mel stood transfixed, the phone dangling from her hand. Jason's voice had paralyzed her. *How can I face him? I can't let him see how much I care. I'll leave before he gets here. No, I want to see him. I've prayed for him to come back, and now he has. Oh, God, please don't let me make a fool of myself. But how can I hide my feelings?* She breathed deeply, trying to calm her racing heart. *He's just being polite. He feels obligated to pay his respects to Daddy. Don't take it personally. How can I not take it personally when I love the man with every ounce of my being?* She reached for the arm of the chair to steady herself then she slumped down to the seat. She wept for joy, for sorrow, for what was, for what might have been. She longed to see Jason, but now that she would, she felt only terror.

Berlinda burst through the door. "Just what I expected. You pull yourself together, girl. You gotta get ready to see Mr. Jason. Stop that blubberin' and go fix your face. Take off that dress and let me press it for you. Come on, now. We got to get ready."

Startled, Mel sat up and wiped the tears from her cheeks. She smiled uncertainly, and followed Berlinda to her room. She took off the dress and handed it to her. When Berlinda scurried out, Mel leaned over the dressing table and stared into the mirror. "Please, God," she prayed, "let him still love me."

CHAPTER 39

Gatti leaned against the bar in Palm Beach's trendiest club, his hand shaking as he reached for his Cassis Royale. He took a quick sip from the tall flute, then set it on the bar. He peered through the mist of smoke that roiled in the flashing colored lights, searching for his coke dealer. Although his supply was low, that wasn't the reason for his impatience tonight. Gatti sipped his drink nervously and glanced at his watch, wondering where he was.

"How much you need, man?"

The pusher's voice at his elbow startled Gatti, and when he swung around he knocked his drink over. He dabbed at the spreading puddle with a cocktail napkin, his hands trembling, eyes on the pusher.

"Comin' down hard?" the pusher sneered.

"Uh, *buono sera.* You are late."

"I'm here now, man. How much you want?"

"I must talk weez you."

"Money talks, man. Just lay it in my mitt."

"*Momento.* There ees something else. Come, we go outside."

"What is this shit? You settin' me up or sompthin'?"

"No, no. Ees business proposition. *Prego*, come outside, we talk." Gatti adjusted the knot of his silk tie — his small, dark eyes darting around the room.

"This better be good, man." The pusher slid off the stool and followed Gatti outside.

Gatti glanced up and down the street, then satisfied that they were alone, he turned to the pusher. "I need you to help me weez something."

"What?"

Gatti ran his tongue over dry lips and averted his gaze. "I want someone to be killed. *Capiche?*"

The pusher snorted and looked at him incredulously. "You're nuts, man." He started to walk away.

Gatti grabbed his arm. "Wait! Wait! You no *capiche.*"

"I understand, all right, but killin' people ain't my game. You got the wrong guy."

"You know somebody?"

The pusher stared into Gatti's desperate eyes for a long moment. "You're serious, ain't you, man? Who you want knocked off?"

The neon sign reflected green on Gatti's face. He studied a crack in the sidewalk. His voice wavered when he spoke, almost inaudibly, "My wife."

"Your wife? You been snortin' some bad coke? How the hell do you figure you could get away with that? All that sugar money — hell, they'd never let up on that one. Her daddy owns Belle Glade, the sheriff, the politicians, they'd have your neck in a noose before you knew what the hell hit you. Mine too." He peered into Gatti's distorted face. "Why you want to off her?"

Gatti's thin lips quivered. "She ees going to leave me. She ees seeing her first husband."

"Let her go, man. Take a nice big settlement and get on with your life."

Gatti grabbed his arm. "No, no. You no *capiche.* I get nothing when she goes. Nothing. The prenuptial, it eez —" He spread trembling hands, palms up, desperation pulling his lips into a smear across his face.

The pusher hesitated, thinking, *This guy is serious. One way or the other, that Hampton dame is headed south.* "What you got in mind? When? How?"

Gatti's tongue darted out and swiped dry lips. He leaned forward eagerly. "Soon. Right away. How? Eet does not matter."

The pusher leaned back and studied him. "How much you plan to pay for this little job?"

"You weel do eet?"

The pusher hesitated, contemplating Gatti's face bathed in green light. He said, "Twenty thousand?"

Gatti's lips twitched. His eyes darted up and down the darkened street. He tugged at his tie as if it were a noose, and swallowed hard. "*Sì.* Okay. *Grazie.*"

"I'll see what I can do. Half now, half when the job is done."

Gatti grabbed his arm. "No, I can't. I have nothing now. When ees done I give it to you all."

"Forget it, man. You think I'm nuts? When the bitch is cold you'll stiff me." He started to walk away.

Gatti ran after him, reaching out to him, pleading. "No! No, I swear." Gatti crossed himself. "On my mother's life, I swear."

"I got to get something up front, man."

Gatti's mind raced. He pulled the watch off his arm and held it out to the pusher. "Thees. Take thees, eez a Rolex."

"I don't have to kill nobody for a Rolex. I can get a Rolex for coke anytime."

Gatti slipped the watch back on his wrist and rummaged through his mind. A polo pony — he'd sell one of the ponies Melisandra had bought for him. "You weel geev me a few days?"

"Whatever." The pusher turned to walk away.

Gatti grabbed his arm. "Friday night. I weel have the money Friday night. You do it then."

The pusher shrugged. "It can't go down till I get some bread."

"*Sì.* Okay. Friday night. I weel meet you here."

"Whatever you say, man." The pusher walked into the night.

On Friday, around eight o'clock, Melisandra was startled by the doorbell. She glanced at the clock, thinking Gatti must have forgotten his key. She laid aside the book she was reading and went to open the door. She was surprised to see a strange man and woman standing there. She gathered her robe around her, tied the belt, and pushed dark hair back from her face. "Yes?"

"Are you Mrs., uh, Princess del Gatti?"

"Yes, what is it?"

"I'm Detective Radson." He jerked a thumb toward the woman. "This is Detective Martinez." He held up a wallet with a badge attached. "May we come in?"

"Uh," Mel looked around uncertainly. "What is it? What's happened?"

"If we may step in for a —"

"Is this about my husband? Is he all right?"

"We'd like to talk to you about your husband."

Reluctantly, Mel opened the door wider and allowed them to enter. She motioned toward chairs, but the detectives chose to stand.

"What is this about?" she asked nervously. Scenarios flashed across her mind: a car accident, a drug incident, a heart attack.

Radson cleared his throat, shifted feet, then looked directly at her and said, "Have you and mister, uh, the prince, been having domestic problems recently?"

Mel hesitated. "We . . . why do you ask?"

"I don't know quite how to put this. I guess the best way is to just come out with it." He shifted uneasily. "Your husband tried to hire a man to kill you."

Mel straightened, her eyebrows arched. "My husband — wants to have me killed? But why?"

"He thinks you're seeing your former husband; thinks you may divorce him and —"

Martinez interrupted. "Are you thinking along those lines?"

"I have seen my former husband, yes. My father is dying and he came to see him . . . and me, and well, yes, I have been seeing him. But that's no reason for Gatti to have me murdered."

"Have you provided for the prince in your will?"

Melisandra's eyes darkened. "He wouldn't —"

"I'm afraid so." Detective Radson took a pad from his jacket pocket and referred to it. "Do you know a Denise Whitaker?"

Mel's forehead creased in concentration. "I don't think so."

"A young girl. Her father plays polo with Prince del Gatti." He looked to Mel for recognition.

The blonde, Mel thought. She remembered seeing Gatti with her in the bar, but she hadn't realized the extent of his involvement. She glanced at the detective and nodded distractedly.

"An old Palm Beach family," Martinez said. "The girl is young and attractive. She's interested in the prince, but there's no money there. I guess he's not willing to change his lifestyle." She placed her hand on Mel's arm. "Are you all right? This must be quite a shock to you."

Mel smiled sardonically. *The bastard wants the blonde and the money. He knows he can't break the prenuptial agreement. When he heard that I'm seeing Jason he panicked, afraid of losing his income. The blonde can't support his lifestyle.*

The detectives gave her a moment to digest the news, waiting respectfully for her to respond.

Mel looked from one to the other. "How did you find out about this?"

"The prince approached an undercover cop in a bar. The cop was setting up a drug bust when this came down. He pretended to go for it. It would make our case stronger if you would go along with us."

"How? I won't put myself in danger."

"No, of course not. We'll make you up with some fake blood, photograph you, and show the prince the crime scene photo. When he pays off, we'll have him — case of attempted murder for hire. The undercover man will be wearing a wire, and the payoff will clinch it."

Mel's life with Gatti passed before her eyes. She had heard that's what happens just before death. If Gatti had approached anyone other than a policeman, she would be experiencing the real thing right about now. She shivered. Poor bumbling idiot, he couldn't even do this right. She looked from one detective to the other. "What do you want me to do?"

"We have the police photographer standing by. It will only take a few minutes."

Mel started to rise. "I'll get dressed."

Detective Martinez put a hand on her arm. "No need for that. It was to happen here."

Mel gasped. "Here? Right here in my own home?"

"Yes." Martinez looked away.

"When?"

"Tonight."

"Tonight?"

"Yes."

Mel pulled her robe tight across her chest and up around her throat. "Gatti tried to hire someone to come in here — in my own home — tonight — to kill me?" She shuddered.

Radson said softly, "Martinez will help you get ready."

"All right. What do you want me to do?"

The detectives arranged her for the photos and Mel endured the indignity of the session. Her ivory, satin pajamas were smeared with Hershey's syrup — Detective Martinez said that had the appearance of blood in a photo — and Radson directed her in posing to appear to have been shot.

The session finally over and the detectives gone, Mel sank into a hot bath. She picked up the loofah sponge and scrubbed her skin raw. She washed away the fake blood, imagining it was real. It was hard, even now, to believe that the man she had been living with, sleeping with, wanted her dead. Mel drained the tub then refilled it with fresh water, trying to soak away all thoughts of Gatti.

As soon as Jason heard of Gatti's arrest, he hurried to Mel's side. "It's my fault," he said. "If I had joined AA sooner we would have been together and none of this would have happened. I should have been here taking care of you, not half way around the world. How can you ever forgive me?" He searched her face. "Can you forgive me?"

Mel nodded.

Jason took her in his arms, his eyes glowing with the remembrance of a love shared, cherished, lost, and regained. When he held her, his body hardened with desire and hers softened in response. They kissed hungrily, drawing sustenance from each other, erasing the pain, dissolving hurt, and absolving guilt.

When Mel and Jason lay on her bed, she clung to him with a passion she had almost forgotten. When they made love she was once again alive and whole.

CHAPTER 40

Jeff sat beside James Henry in the library, thinking of the twists of fate that kept him here. Since returning from Japan, he had lost his son, his brother, and now his father was slipping away.

James Henry interrupted his reverie. "I wonder what the future of cane in Florida will be. The industry is dying as surely as I am. If there's no last-minute miracle, we'll both soon be history. We're losing about an inch of soil a year to subsidence; the muck dries up and blows away. If that doesn't kill off the industry, the environmentalists and the union will."

"Let's hope not." Jeff straightened the afghan that covered his father's lap. "Are you warm enough, Dad?"

James Henry nodded. "Steve is right. We have to ante up the penny a pound for the cleanup — try to save the Okee. If we can't figure out a way to stop the chemical runoff from the fields, they'll shut us down and transfer the industry to a Third World country. The overseas growers want the money and the jobs, and they will close their eyes to environmental concerns and working conditions." He slumped, exhausted from speaking.

"Better not talk anymore." Jeff draped his arm around his father's shoulders.

James Henry lifted his head. "But that's not my concern. I can't be responsible for the whole damn world. Hell, I wasn't even responsible for myself." He shook his head in resignation.

"What did Doc Johnson say today? Are you holding your own?"

"Don't worry about me so much." He looked up at Jeff sadly. "If we do the right thing, sugar will still be grown and sold; and we'll all eat our cake. But if we kill off sugar in Florida, we'll forfeit the millions that cane produces. Cane provides jobs for thousands of people — growing, processing, distributing —" His voice weakened and trailed off.

Jeff sprang to his feet. "Are you all right, Dad?" He felt his father's wrist.

James Henry nodded, then continued, his voice raspy, muted. "Some Third World country will accept the cane and what goes with it."

"You're right, Dad. Why don't you rest now?"

"I can't imagine life without cane." James Henry closed his eyes. "Thank God I won't live to see it."

"I think your color is a little better tonight, Dad, I really do."

"My color? A better shade of gray tonight, is it, son?"

Jeff patted his father's shoulder reassuringly. "I think you're looking better, Dad, I really do."

"No use kidding. Six months, a year."

"I can't tell you how sorry I am that this happened."

"I did it to myself — no one to blame but myself. If a man could keep his pants zipped, he would eliminate most of his troubles in life."

Jeff shifted uneasily. The two men sat in silence for a few minutes before Jeff said, "I have some good news for you."

"What is it, son?"

"Sami is pregnant. She wanted me to tell you. She thought it would please you."

James Henry sat up straighter. "Well, well, what do you know? One on the way out; one on the way in. That's the way of life, isn't it?"

"I guess so."

"Does Grace know?"

"No. Sami wanted you to be the first to know."

"She's a thoughtful girl, your Sami. When will your boy arrive?"

Jeff smiled at James Henry's assumption that the baby would be a boy. "In June."

"Call Grace in and we'll tell her. She'll be tickled." James Henry chuckled softly. "My grandson."

"I'll get Sami too."

When Jeff went to summon the women, James Henry struggled to wheel his chair closer to the fireplace. He tucked the afghan around his legs. "Can't seem to get warm anymore," he muttered.

Jeff returned with his mother and Sami. He turned James Henry's wheelchair around to face the women. "You tell Mama," he said.

"Tell me what? What is it?" Grace looked nervously from one to the other, her forehead gathering into a frown.

James Henry smiled up at Sami, took her hand in his, and squeezed it gently.

"Grace, Sami is going to give us another grandchild."

Grace gasped, her eyes widened, and her hands flew up. "Oh, Sami! Jeffrey! What wonderful news! That is the best news you could possibly give us." Grace reached out and gathered Sami and Jeff to her breast, kissed each on the cheek. She hugged them tightly, then released them and bent to kiss James Henry. "Oh, James Henry, isn't that the best news you've ever heard?"

"Yes, Grace, it certainly is." His eyes wandered to the far side of the room as he thought, *Will I still be here when the baby arrives? Probably not. Like the ratoon, we renew life — new shoots to replace the old.*

James Henry grew weaker every day, and life at Hampton Plantation revolved around his needs. Mel stayed at the house full-time now to support him in his final days.

Chip visited James Henry almost every afternoon, and the two friends relived the excitement of their youthful football triumphs and their days of hunting, fishing, and camping in the swamps around the Okeechobee. They shared reminiscences of Vonda and her exploits.

Jeff and Steve kept the plantation running smoothly, carrying out James Henry's whispered orders, and keeping any problems secret from him.

Sami spent her days making James Henry comfortable. She sat beside him, reading to him or just touching him reassuringly when he roused from slumber. Sometimes, when the baby kicked, she would lay his hand on her belly so he could feel his grandchild developing.

The bond between James Henry and Grace strengthened. There was an unspoken dispensation, a forgiveness, each accepting the other's weaknesses, each grateful for their years together.

One day, after the nurse had strapped James Henry into his wheelchair, Grace wheeled his chair out onto the portico and positioned him so he could see the cane field next to the house. She set the brake and started to go back inside.

"Stay out here with me, Grace," he whispered.

"It's too hot out here. The smoke from the burn, the noise—Nurse Betty will be with you."

"You shouldn't mind the burning cane; you've lived with it all of your life. I don't even smell it anymore."

"It's not the smell, and it's not really the heat, either. It's those birds. Why do those egrets fly into the flames like that? I don't want to watch them hurting themselves."

"You play with fire, you're going to get burned. They should know better than to fly in there."

"Why do they endanger their lives? It's so foolish. Why do they do it?"

"Who know why they do it?" It was an effort for him to speak, but he didn't want her to leave. "Why do any of us do the things we do? Maybe we're all egrets flying into the flames."

Grace stood there beside him, the burn reflecting off their faces. It gave James Henry's ashen complexion a false ruddy glow.

Sami came out with medication. "Drink this, Papa Jim. I put raspberry flavor in so it won't taste so bad." She felt his hand. "Are you warm enough?"

James Henry laughed softly. "It must be over a hundred degrees out here, and you want to know if I'm warm enough?"

"Oh, you're too hot? I'll fan you." Sami picked up the napkin she had placed on his chest and fanned him with it.

James Henry smiled. "No need for that, Sami, I'm fine."

"You sure?"

James Henry nodded.

"Okay," she said. "If you want anything, I'll bring it." She bent down and kissed him on the cheek, then turned and went back into the house.

James Henry sat motionless, deep in remembrance. "I love the little Jap," he whispered. The roar of the burn in nearby fields and the wind rattling through the cane near the house drowned out his words.

Grace bent close to his lips in an effort to hear.

"I love her as much as I love my own children." A tear slid down his cheek and dropped onto his withered hand. "I should have been nicer to her when she first came. I should have eaten that damned raw fish."

James Henry tried to wipe away the tears, but he couldn't raise his hand. "I failed Henny too," he whispered. "Soon I'll be with him and I can tell him I didn't mean to. I only wanted what was best for him. I loved that boy; I just didn't understand him. I tried to do what I thought was right, but . . ." Words came slowly, haltingly. "I should have been nicer to you too Grace."

He struggled to form words, tried to reach out to her, but his hand didn't move. His voice trailed away and he slumped in his chair.

Grace's eyes misted and she patted his hand compassionately. "Don't think about it, James Henry. We should all be nicer to each other."

"You were a good wife, Grace," he whispered almost inaudibly, "the best."

His lips moved and Grace bent to hear. "Push me down to the cane," he mumbled.

Grace released the brake and pushed the chair down the ramp to the field that Steve had built.

James Henry closed his eyes and sat motionless for a few minutes. Then his arm slid from the armrest, his head fell forward, and his breathing stopped. James Henry had left the cane field for the last time.

AUTHOR'S NOTE

Although *Egrets to the Flames* is set in the last years of the twentieth century, many concerns for the environment remain unchanged in the new millennium. Smoke still pollutes the air as cane ash swirls over Belle Glade and chemicals seep into groundwater.

In this work of fiction, readers get an intimate glimpse into Florida's sugar cane industry, and the lives of those who live amid the burning cane. Just as egrets dive to their fates in the flames of burning cane, so man chooses the path to his destiny in this saga of love, lust, and greed.